The Honey Queen

Cathy Kelly is a number one bestselling author. She worked as a journalist before becoming a novelist, and has published fourteen bestselling books.

She is also an ambassador for UNICEF in Ireland. She lives in Wicklow with her husband and two sons.

For more information on Cathy and to register for her newsletter, visit her website at www.cathykelly.com, follow her on Twitter @cathykellybooks or find her on Facebook at www.facebook.com/cathykellybooks.

By the same author:

Woman to Woman
She's the One
Never Too Late
Someone Like You
What She Wants
Just Between Us
Best of Friends
Always and Forever
Past Secrets
Lessons in Heartbreak
Once in a Lifetime
Homecoming
The House on Willow Street

Christmas Magic (Short Stories)

The Perfect Holiday (Quick Read)

CATHY KELLY

The Honey Queen

HarperCollins*Publishers*

HarperCollins*Publishers*
77–85 Fulham Palace Road,
Hammersmith, London W6 8JB

www.harpercollins.co.uk

Published by HarperCollins*Publishers* 2013
1

A catalogue record for this book
is available from the British Library

ISBN: 978-0-00-737366-6

This novel is entirely a work of fiction.
The names, characters and incidents portrayed in it are
the work of the author's imagination. Any resemblance to
actual persons, living or dead, events or localities is
entirely coincidental.

Typeset by Palimpsest Book Production Ltd, Falkirk, Stirlingshire

Printed and bound in Great Britain by Clays Ltd, St Ives plc

MIX
Paper from
responsible sources
FSC
www.fsc.org
FSC C007454

FSC™ is a non-profit international organisation established to promote
the responsible management of the world's forests. Products carrying the
FSC label are independently certified to assure consumers that they come
from forests that are managed to meet the social, economic and
ecological needs of present and future generations,
and other controlled sources.

Find out more about HarperCollins and the environment at
www.harpercollins.co.uk/green

For my family, John, Murray and Dylan.
For Mum, Lucy, Francis and all my beloved family, and
for the dear friends who are always there for me.
Thank you.

Part One

The atmosphere of the bees and the hive is determined entirely by the mood and personality of the queen bee. A calm queen will result in a calm, peaceful and productive hive.

The Gentle Beekeeper, Iseult Cloud

Prologue

*L*illie Maguire kept the letter tucked into the inside zipped compartment of her handbag, a battered beige one Sam had bought her in David Jones one Christmas. The handbag was as soft as butter from years of use, and coins would slip down in the places where the lining had split, but she didn't care: it was a part of him.

She had so little left of Sam that she treasured what she did have: his pillow, which still had the faintest scent of his hair, the shirt he'd worn that last day going into hospital, the engagement ring with its tiny opal bought forty years before. And the David Jones bag with the ripped lining. These were her treasures.

The letter was almost a part of the bag now: the edges curled up, the folds worn. She'd read it many times since it arrived a fortnight ago and could probably recite it in her sleep. It was from Seth, the half-brother she hadn't known existed, and the one link to a mother she'd never known.

Please come, I'd love to meet you. We'd love to meet you, Frankie and I. You see, I've been an only child for fifty and then some years, and it's wonderful to hear that I have a sister after all. I never knew you existed, Lillie, and I'm sorry.

I'm sorry too to hear about your husband's death. You must be heartbroken. Tell me if I'm being forward for proffering such advice, but perhaps this is exactly the right time for you to come? Being somewhere new might help?

The one thing I can say for sure after all these years on the planet is that you never know what's around the corner. I lost my job three months ago, and that was completely unexpected!

We'd love to have you with us, really love it. Do come. As I said before: I may be speaking out of turn because I've never suffered the sort of bereavement you have, Lillie, but it might help?

It was such a warm letter. Lillie wondered if Seth's wife, Frankie, had a hand in the writing of it because there was such a welcome contained in it, and yet the wise woman in Lillie thought that Seth was probably still reeling at discovering her very existence.

The sudden appearance of a sixty-four-year-old Australian sister could mean many things to an Irishman called Seth Green on the other side of the world, but most shocking might be the knowledge that his mother, now dead, had kept this huge secret from him all his life.

Women were often better at secrets than men, Lillie had always felt. Better at keeping them and better at understanding *why* people kept them.

They knew how to say 'don't mind me, my dear, I'm fine, just a bit distracted' to an anxious child or a confused husband when they weren't fine *at all*, when their minds were in a frenzy of worry. *What would the doctor say about the breast lump they'd found? Could they afford the mortgage?*

Would their shy son ever make a friend in school?

No, a wise woman could easily make the decision that certain information would only bring pain to her loved ones, so why not keep all the pain to herself? She could handle it on her own, which meant they didn't need to.

Men were different. In Lillie's experience, men liked things out in the open.

So given a bit of time, Seth might feel entirely differently about the whole notion that his mother had borne another child before him when she was very young, and had handed that child to a convent that had in turn handed her to a sister convent in Melbourne. It might just help him, if he were to meet that child.

An open-ended ticket, Lillie decided. That would be the right way to travel to see Seth and Frankie.

Martin, one of Lillie's two grown-up sons, had set the whole thing in motion.

Soon after Sam's death, Martin, who was tall, kind and clever, just like his father, had taken up genealogy and started spending many hours on his computer looking for details of his past. As a university history lecturer, he said he couldn't believe he'd never thought to do this before.

'It's the history of our family, I should have taken this on years ago. What was wrong with me?' he asked, running hands through shaggy dark hair that made Lillie's fingers itch to get the scissors to it, the way she used to when he was a kid.

The thought of him as a child, of *her* life when he and his brother were children, made her breath catch.

When Martin and Evan were children, she'd had her darling Sam. Now he was gone. He'd died six months ago, gone to who-knew-where, and she was just as heartbroken as if it had happened yesterday.

No matter that Lillie told everyone that she was coping – her sons; her daughters-in-law, Daphne and Bethany; the girls in the book club; her best friends Doris and Viletta; her pals in the Vinnies shop where she put in a few volunteer hours a week – she wasn't coping. Not at all.

On the outside, she could smile and say she was fine, really. But inside was different: the entire world had a Sam-shaped hole in it and she wasn't sure she could bear to live with it any more.

In this new world the sky was a different blue: harsher somehow. The sun's heat, once glorious, had a cruel quality to it. And the garden they'd both loved felt empty without the two hives Sam had kept for forty years: there was no gentle hum of bees lazily roaming through the flowers. In the early stages of his illness, Sam had given his hives to his best friend in the local beekeeping association.

'I think they're too much for you to handle, sweetheart,' he'd told her as he watched, with sad eyes, while Shep carefully got the two traditional-style hives with their little pagoda roofs ready for transportation.

'Shep could come in and open them every eight or nine days,' Lillie had protested. 'He does it when we're on holiday, he could do it now.'

'I think I'm worn out looking after them,' Sam said. Lillie knew he was lying, but she said nothing. Deep down, Sam knew he wasn't coming out of hospital, but he'd never tell her that. He'd always protected her and he was still doing it.

Now, *afterwards*, there were plenty of jars of honey in the pantry, but Lillie, who used to love a glossy smear of golden honey on wholegrain toast, couldn't bring herself to open a new one.

Nothing tasted the same. The flat whites she loved from the little shop near the library tasted so strange that she'd asked the girl behind the counter if they were using a different coffee.

'No, it's the same. Fairtrade Java. Do you want me to make another one? No sweat.'

Lillie shook her head. Of course the coffee wasn't different. *She* was different.

It must have been his father's death that prompted Martin's interest in the family tree.

Martin's wife, Daphne, groaned good-humouredly to her mother-in-law about Martin's passionate new interest. 'Between Martin being permanently attached to the PC on genealogy sites,' she said, 'and Dyanne glued to hers on chat rooms, *saying* she's only talking to school friends, when she's supposed to be doing schoolwork, I should add, I could walk out and neither of them would notice.' A cheerful and kind midwife, Daphne now appeared to have a second full-time job – keeping an eye on Dyanne, their fourteen-year-old daughter, who had recently discovered her power over the opposite sex and was keen to test it out.

'There's not much of my side of the family to research,' Lillie said ruefully. At her age, she'd decided she was long past the pain of the concept that her birth mother had given her away as a baby. She'd always known that she was adopted, and at fifteen it had been achingly painful. At sixty-four it was merely a part of her past. 'Adoption was different in those days, Daphne. I don't think they put half of it down on paper. From the little bits I know, he won't find anything from my side.'

Daphne smiled.

'That won't stop Martin. You know what he's like: when he gets into something, he's obsessed. The number one topic of conversation at dinner every night is either Martin's latest haul of illegible records or how every kid in Dyanne's class is going to a concert apart from her and it's not fair that we don't trust her, after all she's *nearly* fifteen. We are a pair of fossils, she says. By the way, any chance you'd come to dinner on Friday?'

Lillie always said she was lucky to have such wonderful daughters-in-law.

'It's not luck,' Daphne and Bethany would insist.

'It's because you're the way you are. You never interfere,' Bethany once told her.

7

'But you know how to help when it's needed,' added Daphne.

Both of them knew girlfriends with mothers-in-law who needed to be locked up in high-security premises, if only there was a loophole in the legal system allowing for this. A special hard labour camp might be set up for those who continually brought meals over to their married sons' homes *'so they could eat proper food instead of takeout'*.

Within weeks, Daphne had been proved right about her husband's tenacity. Martin must have had termite blood somewhere in his genealogy because he'd burrowed into every crevice until he found out that Lillie had been given up for adoption in a Dublin convent by one Jennifer McCabe; father unknown.

Evan and Martin Maguire had conferred about this information, and then Martin had burrowed even deeper in the records to discover that Jennifer McCabe had subsequently married a Daniel Green, and from this union there was a son, Seth, now in his fifties.

Teaming up, just like they used to when they were kids, two years apart in age, Martin and Evan arrived at their mother's home waving pieces of paper and airplane schedules.

They had her brother's address and every detail they'd been able to glean about him from the Internet. Seth Green was an architect; he'd designed a school which had won an award, they told her delightedly.

'What?' Lillie stared at her sons, united in their happiness over this information.

'We've found your brother!' said Evan. 'We haven't contacted him yet, but we will if you say we can. He's your family – *our* family. We'll talk to him and then you can fly to see him. We'll pay. Doris could go with you . . .' Evan, cheerleader in the expedition, took after her with his strawberry blond hair and freckled Celtic skin. He had his father's wonderful kindness too – it shone from his eyes. 'Mum, the last six months or so have been so terrible for you. Maybe doing something new would help you recover from Dad's death – not that you would ever recover,' he added hastily. 'But, you know . . .'

Both he and Martin looked at her expectantly, hoping and praying this plan would help. She could see it in their faces and she loved them for it, but it was all too much, too fast.

She might be able to smile at people from the safety of her Melbourne home, but away? In a foreign country with people she didn't know and a brother who might hate the sight of her? As for Doris, she was so scared of flying there wasn't a snowball's hope in hell of getting her on a plane.

'Let me get the iced tea out of the freezer and then we'll talk,' Lillie told her sons and left the room as fast as she could.

In her and Sam's clapboard Victorian house with its pretty curlicued verandah and lush garden, the kitchen had been very much Lillie's room. It wasn't that Sam hadn't cooked – his barbecue equipment had been treated as lovingly as a set of a carpenter's tools, washed and put away carefully on the grill shelf after each use. But barbecuing was outdoor work.

The kitchen, with its verdant fern wallpaper, pots of Lillie's beloved orchids on all surfaces, and the big old cream stove they'd had for thirty years, was her domain. She stood in it now and briefly wondered where the small tray was, where the tea glasses were. Shaken by the news that she had a brother, Lillie was suddenly overwhelmed by a wave of loneliness. She and Sam had often talked of travelling to Ireland.

'We could kiss the Blarney Stone and see if the Wicklow and Kerry Mountains are as beautiful as they say,' Sam said.

'As if you need to kiss any Blarney Stone,' she'd teased back.

He'd known that she didn't want to search for her birth family. That had been the dream of a younger woman.

I know it's out of love, but why do people keep coming up with things to make me feel better, Sam? she asked now, looking up.

She didn't know where he was or if he heard her, but talking to him helped. She just wished he'd answer in some way.

Grief was a journey; she'd read that somewhere. A person didn't get over it, they moved through it. One of the worst parts was not knowing where she was on the journey or if she was on it at all yet. The pain was still so bad. Perhaps she was still only at the entrance to the grief journey, buying her ticket, looking out at an endless plain in front of her where people were to be seen shuffling along in parallel lines, time slowed to a snail's pace.

'Mum—' called Martin.

'Hold your horses,' she called back, finding the cheerful mother voice she'd always been able to summon. Her sons had their own lives and families. Mothers cared for their sons, they didn't expect the sons to have to care for them.

She carried the tray of iced teas into the living room.

'Show all the documents to me,' she said, sitting between them on the big old couch with the plaid pattern. 'A brother!'

Seth Green had immediately responded to Martin's email. Martin printed out the reply and read it to her, but Lillie didn't like this email business. She was a letter or a phone call person. How could you tell what sort of person was writing to you on a computer when you had no voice to listen to or no signature to consider? Seth was apparently happy to hear about her and that was just fine, but nonetheless she felt stubborn. Seth and Frankie could visit her if they wanted to. She was busy, she told her sons.

Then, a fortnight ago, Seth had sent a letter via Martin, the letter that nestled in her handbag and called to her so that she read and reread it many times a day.

Her adopted mother, Charlotte, the only mother she'd ever

known, had often talked about Lillie's background and all she knew of it. She'd told her how in 1940s Ireland illegitimate children and their mothers were so badly treated that most women were forced to give their babies away in tragic circumstances. A nun called Sister Bernard had been travelling to Melbourne to join the Blessed Mary Convent in Beaumaris and she'd taken baby Lillie with her for adoption. Mother Joseph, who was in charge of the convent, knew how much Charlotte and Bill wanted a baby after all the miscarriages, and so baby Lillie had come into their lives.

As Martin proudly handed over the letter to his mother, Lillie knew that he hadn't considered the possibility that she might not want to see her birth family. She'd thought it wouldn't bother her, but at that exact moment, she discovered that there was still a tiny place inside her that ached with the pain of rejection.

For two weeks she'd been carrying the letter in her handbag. This morning, just as she was about to drive to the park for a walk with Doris and Viletta, something had made Lillie open her handbag and take out the now worn letter one more time.

Her mother had often told her the Irish had a way with words and it was true. The letter was proof of that. Such warmth and such pure honesty all wrapped up together. And all from someone she had never met. Crazy though it seemed, it was as if this person thousands of miles away could see into her heart and understand the hopelessness inside. Lillie wondered again if it was partly written by Seth's wife. Because whoever had written the letter had gotten through to her in a way that nobody else had since Sam's death.

Please come . . . I may be speaking out of turn because I've never suffered the sort of bereavement you have, Lillie, but it might help?

11

She stood in the hall, lost in thought. Outside, the sun was blazing down. It hadn't been the best summer but now that autumn had arrived, the heat was blistering. Nearly forty-two degrees on the beach the day before, according to the radio. Even as a child, Lillie had never been a beach bunny. Not for her the shorts, skimpy vests and thongs that her friends ran about in.

'It's your creamy Celtic skin,' Charlotte would say lovingly, covering the young Lillie with white zinc sun cream.

Years later, as a married woman, Lillie had pretended irritation with Sam that he, despite also being of Celtic descent, was blessed with jet-black hair and skin that tanned mahogany.

'You're only pretending you've got Irish blood,' she'd tease. 'You came from Sicily, no question.'

Not a freckle had ever dusted his strong, handsome face and the only time his tan faded was as he lay wasting away in the hospital bed. His skin turned a dull sepia colour, as if dying leached everything from a person.

'I'm sorry, love. I don't want to leave you and the kids, the grandkids . . .'

Those had been almost the last words he'd spoken to her and she treasured the memory.

Lillie had struggled to find words to comfort him. Then it had come to her, a gift to the dying, the only thing she could give him: 'We all love you so much, Sam, but it's the right time to go, it's safe for you to go. We don't want you to suffer any more.'

Saying it and meaning it were two entirely different things. In her breaking heart, Lillie didn't want Sam to die. She could now understand people who kept loved ones alive for years even when they were in a vegetative state from which there was no return. The parting was so final.

But people sometimes needed to be told to go. One of the hospice nurses had explained that to her. Strong people like

Sam, who had fiercely protected their families all their lives, found it hard to leave.

'They worry there's nobody there to take care of you all,' the nurse had said. 'You need to tell him it's OK to go.'

And Lillie had.

When Sam had been dying, the hours seemed to fly past because she knew they were his last.

Since then, time had slowed to a snail's pace . . .

Now, standing in the hall, she rubbed her eyes furiously as more tears arrived. She was so tired of crying.

Her cell phone pinged on the hall table with a text message.

Are you coming walking today? I did my stretches and will seize up if we don't start soon. I am leaning over our park bench and will be stuck like this. Doris xx

Lillie smiled as she put her hat on and grabbed a pair of sunnies from the table at the door. Doris could always cheer her up.

As soon as she rounded the corner at the community centre at the Moysey Walk, she saw Viletta and Doris gossiping happily as they half-heartedly did stretches ahead of their walk – five miles today.

It was a beautiful trail to walk. The girls had been walking along the beach, local parks and now, along the Moysey Walk for nigh on twenty years, long before everyone and their granny began extolling the virtues of walking. Today, autumn leaves were beginning to fall from the trees, and to their left, lay the glittering sea below. 'Hi, girls,' Lillie said, glad that her sunnies were hiding her eyes.

Hearing the faint catch in Lillie's voice, Doris looked at her shrewdly. 'You've just missed a gang of young rugby guys jogging,' she announced, keeping her tone upbeat. 'Viletta told them they had great muscle definition and they all went red.'

13

Viletta laughed. 'I could be a cougar,' she said with a put-on sniff. 'They're the hot thing in Hollywood – young blokes wanting older women.'

'Older *rich* women, honey,' said Doris, and Lillie joined in the laughter this time.

They walked two or three times a week, fitting it in between their chores and pursuits. Viletta, the oldest of the trio at sixty-nine, was a yoga buff and nobody seeing her in her walking sweats and simple T-shirt would imagine she was a grandmother of five. Her hair, she liked to joke, was the giveaway – pure white and falling poker straight down her back; she kept it tied in a knot for the walk. Doris, tall with salt-and-pepper hair and a tendency to roundness, regularly complained she wasn't as fit as Viletta, who set the pace.

'You get toned blokes in yoga classes and I get knee injections in the surgery,' Doris would say in mock outrage. And Viletta would smile at the notion. She hadn't looked at a man since her husband had died more than fifteen years before, for all her talk of cougars.

Lillie liked to amuse herself considering how the three of them must appear to strangers on their rambles: Viletta would appear to be the trainer, a lean, tanned woman urging her two more curvy friends on.

Though she didn't have Viletta's toned muscles, she didn't look like a woman in her mid-sixties. That was most likely down to the hair, she reckoned: even a few greys in her thick strawberry blonde curls couldn't diminish its warmth. Her Irish inheritance coming through. In the mirror she saw her face had become thinner since Sam's death and underneath her iris-blue eyes were faint violet shadows. She hadn't used make-up to hide them: vanity seemed so futile in the wake of her loss.

They were halfway into the walk and had settled into their regular rhythm when Doris managed to get herself beside

Lillie, a few paces behind Viletta, who was storming ahead as usual.

'You look a bit down, Lillie,' she said conversationally. 'Everything OK?'

Doris had known Lillie long enough to realize the effort required to maintain a smile on her face, a smile that would disintegrate the moment somebody put on their *Poor dear, lost her husband* voice or showed pity. Which was why Doris talked to her friend the way she'd always talked to her, in the same warm, vibrant tones.

'I've been thinking about my brother in Ireland . . .' began Lillie.

Beside her, she could sense Doris relax.

'I'm going to Ireland to visit him and to find out about my birth mother,' she said. There, it was done: she'd decided.

When Doris grabbed her and hugged her tightly, Lillie was so surprised she almost lost her balance.

'I'm so glad!' shrieked Doris, never one for volume control. 'It's exactly what you need. Oh, honey, I'm so glad!'

Lillie relaxed into her friend's embrace. It felt lovely to be held. There were fewer people to do that these days. Her sons weren't huggers, not the way Sam had been. Her hugs now came from her grandchildren. From Martin's daughter, Dyanne, and from Shane, Evan's seven-year-old, who held her tight and told her she was the best nanny in the world.

'If I'd known you wanted to be rid of me that much, I'd have gone ages ago,' she teased Doris when they separated.

'Witch!' said Doris, wiping her eyes. 'I'm happy for you, Lillie. There's no secret recipe for getting through what you're getting through, but doing something different might add another ingredient to the pot, so to speak.'

Lillie nodded. 'I've been thinking it over and over. Sam and I had talked about visiting Ireland, but I don't think I'd ever have done it by myself at my age. But now Martin's so excited about finding Seth and Dyanne's desperately hoping the Irish relatives are rich so she can stay with them when she goes off on her big trip.'

Both women smiled. Dyanne was the same age as Doris's grandson, Lloyd. Many amused conversations were had about their grandchildren, who were both going through an 'I want to be famous' phase, when they weren't too preoccupied with 'Can I have an advance on my pocket money?'

'Are you stopping for a rest?' Viletta called back to them.

'No,' yelled Doris, and they started walking again. 'It's going to be tough, Lillie, you realize that? You'll be alone on a very emotional trip.'

Lillie nodded. She could rely on Doris for utter honesty.

'I'm going to be fine,' she said, and gave her friend a smile.

For the first time since Sam died, Doris caught a glimpse of peace in her friend's iris-blue eyes.

'Sam will be with me,' Lillie added, touching one hand to her chest above her heart. Then her lips quirked in a smile like the Lillie of old. 'I'm ordering him to come!'

Chapter One

Frankie Green woke bathed in cold sweat. The bedroom was dark and she felt so disorientated that for a moment she almost didn't know where she was.

Her phone lay on her bedside table and she fumbled for it, pressing the button so that the screen lit up. With light, she managed to find her glasses and look at the time.

Two fifteen.

Oh hell, she thought. She had a hectic day ahead, she hadn't been able to get to sleep for ages and now she was awake again.

Beside her, Seth was a long mound under the duvet, sleeping soundly, which was infinitely annoying. *He* didn't have to get up in the morning.

Which wasn't his fault, she reminded herself, as she did so often these days as a sort of guilty afterthought. He hadn't joyfully decided to retire and let her continue working, he'd been made redundant three months ago and hated it. Yet, it *felt* like his fault that he could sleep late while she – now the major earner – had to haul herself out of bed come rain or shine.

Pushing back the duvet, she went into the horrible, poky bathroom she swore she would never get used to, shivering as the cool night air hit her soaked cotton pyjamas.

In the bathroom's cold light, a tired, white-faced woman stared back at her from the mirror: dark hair plastered to her skull, face sheeny with damp, nightclothes sticking like a second skin.

She looked as if she'd been running through a rainforest for days. She looked – Frankie realized the correct word with misery – old.

Somehow, while she'd been busy trying to raise two children, run the Human Resources department of Dutton Insurance and be a wife to Seth Green, age had crept up on her. She'd been so busy working, doing school runs and making vast meals to freeze, checking homework diaries and worrying about exam results, mopping up teenage tears and making rare date nights with her husband, that the blur of her thirties had morphed into her forties and suddenly, here she was, forty-nine. Calcium, collagen, oestrogen – *everything* was leaching out of her. Soon all that would remain would be a dried-out husk and if she stood still long enough, she'd be stuffed in a museum as an example of tinder-dry womankind. Even her marriage felt dried out and empty. That was the worst thing and she couldn't bear to think about it.

Is this all normal? she silently asked the mirror-image Frankie. If it was, nobody talked about it. Not her sister, not her friends. If only her mother was a bit normal, she might have asked her, but there was nothing normal about Madeleine. Her mother, pushing eighty and still fond of causing havoc, managed to be old in years without being old in any other way. Madeleine to most people, but plain old Mad to her two daughters, had never bothered with creams or unguents. In her forties, she'd lain in the back garden toasting herself under layers of coconut sun oil, happiest when she was nut brown. When hot pants were the 'in' clothes for teenagers, Madeleine had worn them herself, not caring that other mothers wore normal summer skirts and cardigans. If she passed a building site and somebody whistled, Madeleine would blow the builders a delighted kiss, while her teenage daughters, Frankie and Gabriella, would exchange horrified glances.

Why couldn't Mother be more like other mothers?

As Frankie grew up, she began to appreciate her mother's unconventional spirit but even so, she wondered at the secret of her parents' long marriage. Eventually, Frankie decided that it worked because Dad was a placid person who managed by saying 'that's fine, dear,' to whatever Madeleine wanted to do.

They still lived in a cottage in the fishing village of Kinsale, and when Madeleine went through her phase of 'forgetting' her costume when she went for her morning dip, Dad greeted people's outraged comments by saying 'Isn't she a great woman for the swimming, all the same.'

Madeleine's marriage guidance advice, if she offered it, would be to get married to a calm man in the first place, and then ignore him happily thereafter. Dad never seemed to get sad or tired. He was just Dad, content with his paper and the crossword, able to keep his spirits up no matter what happened, happy to let his wife be exactly who she wanted to be.

Beauty-wise, the sun had taken a cruel revenge on Frankie's mother and now her face was more wrinkled than a very old crab apple. But in true Madeleine fashion, she didn't mind in the slightest. She continued to wear bright-red lipstick and dye her grey hair a glossy dark brown and had no problem facing herself in the mirror.

Frankie's mother was one of the happy people who liked what they saw when they spied their own reflection.

At Sunday lunches in Frankie and Seth's house, Madeleine would happily discuss the way her hair was still silky and obedient, and say: 'Frankie, I was thinking of getting a more angular bob in the hairdressers. Lionel says I've got the bones for it.'

Lionel was Madeleine's hairdresser and, as far as Frankie was concerned, he clearly liked living on the edge, sending his older clientele out with styles their daughters wouldn't dream of risking.

But maybe Lionel and his clients were right, Frankie thought gloomily. They didn't worry about wrinkles – what was the point?

Frankie had been careful with the sun. She used serums and suncream. She read articles in magazines about the latest products, she never ventured out with anything less than a factor 25 moisturizer. And look at her now. She might write to all those serum and suncream people and tell them they should be fined for filling people's heads with insane dreams. In the cold light of the basement bathroom, with bluish shadows under her dark eyes and a spiderweb of lines around them, she could have passed for eighty herself.

Maybe it was time *she* started visiting Lionel – the sort of deranged, angular haircut that Lady Gaga would balk at might be the very thing. At least it would take people's eyes away from her face.

Turning from the mirror, she stripped off the damp pyjamas and balled them up into the laundry basket. She dried off her hair and body, then, still using her phone for light because she didn't want to wake Seth, found fresh nightclothes.

By the bed, she had lavender oil and she rubbed a bit on her wrists and temples. Nobody looked good when they woke in the middle of the night, she told herself, but at least she could smell good.

She was tired, that was all. But instead of going back to sleep, her mind began to race the way it so often did. The previous day at Dutton Insurance unfurled like a film reel, and she thought of all the things she ought to have done. Next, the following day's meetings and potential problems began to roll out. The company employed nearly a thousand people, so as human resources director there was always something for Frankie to worry about.

Tomorrow – or rather *today* – she had to conduct five

interviews for the position of deputy marketing director. Then there was a particularly tricky case of sexual harassment involving a woman in the motor insurance department and her boss. The claims department was in uproar over holiday policy, and the intervention of one of Frankie's HR team had only succeeded in making matters worse, so that needed sorting out. And on top of that, one of the department heads wanted to take her to lunch to 'pick her brains' about something.

'Lunch!' she'd vented to Seth the previous evening as they sat at the kitchen table after dinner. Seth had cooked a very nice Thai curry and Frankie had eaten so much she'd had to open the button on her jeans. 'I don't have time for lunch! I'm supposed to run a team that isn't actually big enough for the size of the company, recruit fabulous staff at high speed when required, *and* be free for lunch whenever some other executive wants to *chat*!'

'You used to enjoy having lunches with the other executives,' Seth said innocently.

'That was when I had *time* for lunch. These days I barely have time to snatch a sandwich at my desk,' she hissed. Did he understand anything?

'There's no need to snap,' he said, with a hint of a snap in his own voice.

And of course, Frankie felt sorry for taking it out on him. But at the same time, she *was* angry. It seemed that she spent her life tiptoeing around male egos, both in the office and at home. Trying to allay other people's worries when she was overwhelmed with her own. Sometimes Frankie felt it like an actual weight on her shoulders: worries about staff redundancies, about how pale and withdrawn Seth was, about how they were ever going to find the money to sort out the house.

The house. That was their biggest worry of all.

A dream Edwardian red-brick house with a large garden, Sorrento House has many unusual features the piece in the newspaper had purred. It had leapt out at them from the property supplement because Seth and Frankie had been talking about moving for years. They'd started married life in a narrow end-of-terrace house from the turn of the nineteenth century. When Emer and Alexei came along, they remodelled the place so that the front retained the period features, while the back was modern with a glass extension that Seth had designed, giving them a light-filled kitchen-cum-family room.

Much as they had loved that house, it was small. For years Frankie and Seth had talked about buying a big old house they could do up.

'When Emer and Alexei are older,' Frankie would say, during the mad junior school years when long division sums, homework and careful nurturing of delicate young souls took up every hour she wasn't in the office.

'When they're settled, not an exam year,' Seth would say when Emer and Alexei were teenagers, caught up in another phase of life where careful nurturing was required.

Then the previous July twenty-two-year-old Emer had finished college and decided to spend a year travelling the world. Inspired by his sister's example, Alexei, just eighteen, had set off on a gap year with three school friends.

Looking back, Frankie could see that the whole moving house thing had come about as a coping mechanism for empty-nest syndrome.

She hadn't wanted to stop being busy for long enough to think about her children leaving.

'What if we moved house while you were away?' she'd asked them. It had been June, and the four of them were sitting around the table in the light-filled kitchen, making the most of the last few weeks before her beloved children departed on their travels.

'Go for it!' said Emer.

Emer was the wild child of the family. She might have

inherited her paternal grandmother's strawberry blonde hair and bright blue eyes, but her eagerness for fun and adventure owed more to Grandmother Madeleine, Frankie thought ruefully. Still, four years at college, finishing with a masters in business studies, appeared to have calmed her down. At least, Frankie hoped it had.

'It's your turn to do things now, Mum,' said Alexei gently. Her darling, thoughtful boy; she felt like leaping up from the table to give him a hug. Four years younger than his sister, he was gentler and quieter. There had been no baby after Emer and finally Frankie and Seth had turned to adoption. Since the small Russian boy with the blond hair, fine bones and a lonely look in his misty grey eyes had come into her life, Frankie had never ceased wanting to protect him.

The idea of Alexei travelling the world made her heart physically hurt. She'd thought taking care of small children had been hard, but nothing could be harder than watching those same children grow up and leave the nest.

'It's just a wild thought,' said Seth, ever sensible. 'We'd probably be insane to move. The economy's so bad.'

'The property market's not great,' Frankie agreed. 'We should have done it years ago; we missed the boat.'

And then, alone in their family home with what seemed like the actual *family* part gone, they read about Sorrento House and went to see it.

What had made them fall for the place? Frankie remembered that first visit. It had been September – always the start of the year for Frankie, with its associations of back-to-school. The leaves on the trees were almost golden in the autumn light, and the beech tree with its bronzed leaves drooping outside the old stone pillars had given the house at the end of Maple Avenue a sort of faded glamour.

It brought to mind the endless leaves she'd gathered with the children for school projects, days spent trying to do leaf rubbings into copybooks, and the fun of decorating the house for Halloween, as Alexei and Emer eagerly discussed what costumes they'd wear that year.

If only they were here to see this, she thought sadly. But then she brightened up at the prospect of what a welcome home it would make, to arrive at this lovely house.

There was no doubt that the house was unusual. The porch and front door stood at a right angle to the façade, almost hidden behind great swathes of rhododendron that overran a garden at least three times the size of their old one.

The property agent was a man with a finely tuned sense of when not to speak, so he kept his thoughts to himself about the amount of work that needed doing. He'd learned the hard way not to say anything along the lines of 'it needs updating' because such words could prove fatal where potential buyers were concerned. Some people loved a challenge and were dying to get their hands on an industrial sander. Others thought you needed a hard hat and a guide to navigate the hardware shop.

So Seth and Frankie wandered around Sorrento House by themselves, seeing only the possibilities. The name itself called to them. Sorrento was where they'd gone on honeymoon.

The house, two storeys above a dark basement flat, had not been a single residence for years. The upstairs bedsits were miserably decorated in wallpapers at least thirty years old. On the ground floor, two of the bigger rooms, which Seth and Frankie could imagine transformed into gracious living rooms overlooking the garden, were divided in half with cheap plasterboard.

'You'd think a person would be ashamed to put anyone in these rackety spaces,' Frankie said in disgust, not even wanting to touch the filthy curtains half hanging on the windows.

Seth put an arm round her waist and steered her to face the long-neglected garden at the back.

'Look,' he said. 'Then close your eyes and imagine how it will all appear when we're finished with it. A gorgeous kitchen, a bit like at home, but extended out into that long garden. Don't you love those copper beeches and the apple trees? And see that maple in the far left corner? It's changing colour – in a week or so it'll be a glorious crimson.'

Frankie sighed. 'If I close my eyes, I'll realize we're mad to even consider buying the place. We'll have to get it checked for damp, then rip off all that wallpaper, tear up those hideous nylon carpets, paint every inch inside and out, and . . . oh heck, the windows—' She looked down in alarm. 'Do you reckon this frame is rotten? Are the windows on borrowed time?'

'I've been checking with my penknife while you were upstairs just now,' he said. 'The windows are actually fine. So's the roof, as far as I can tell. Otherwise, we really would be mad to buy it. It would still be a lot of work interior-wise, and of course the extension would take time, but I can see how it will all come together. We just need to sit down and work out the numbers. Think, it will be our dream home, love. Sorrento House. That sounds a bit grand. We could change the name. Sorrento Villa is nicer, more homely, don't you think?'

The words 'dream home' combined with the vision of glorious Italian coast magically mingled in Frankie's mind. She'd been brought up in Kinsale, a jewel of a town perched beside the sea, and her sister, Gabrielle, had chosen to live in the seaside town of Cobh, about half an hour from Cork.

Another plus was the location: Redstone. It was a part of the city that had gone from fashionable in the nineteenth century, to down at heel in the twentieth, but was now growing in popularity again thanks to the regeneration of the area.

Seth had a development map which showed that their house faced others that backed on to the allotments behind rows of one-time council houses, the St Brigid's estate. 'Part of the waste ground beside the allotments is being turned into parkland,' he explained, 'which adds value to the neighbourhood.'

After seeing the house, they went for a coffee at the

25

crossroads, which was the centre of Redstone. The place sealed the deal for both of them.

'It's perfect,' said Frankie wistfully, admiring the sycamores growing at the roadside.

'Very nineteen thirties,' mused Seth as they walked along hand-in-hand, deciding which place to go into. 'Look at those façades.' He pointed to one block decorated with period signage.

They admired the clothes boutique, the delicatessen with windows full of cheeses and all manner of exotic meats, they walked past a pretty pink-and-brown beauty salon, and finally settled in a coffee shop where they ate the best raspberry-and-almond muffins they'd ever tasted.

'We can do it,' Seth said, enthusiastically outlining his plans.

He was sure, from experience, that planning permission wouldn't be a problem. He would design the new parts of the house, a builder he'd worked with would agree a reasonable price for the work, and Seth could manage the build himself. With two decent salaries coming in, they should be able to find the money.

'Can you cope with living in the basement while we do up the rest?' Seth asked her the day before the sale closed. They were walking through the property again, imagining grand neo-classical fireplaces from the salvage yard instead of the bricked-up fireplaces and the hazardous two-bar electric fires that the previous owner had installed everywhere.

'I can cope with anything,' Frankie had said excitedly, eyeing up the kitchen and imagining how marvellous it would look when the extension was built and the whole room had been turned into an open-plan kitchen/breakfast room. She'd got an idea for a conservatory, too. She could just see a couple of huge planters filled with exotic ferns beside the imaginary doors. And the garden. Gardening had never really been her thing, but here there was so much possibility. Or there would be, once the jungle of weeds and wild brambles had been torn away.

I can cope with anything. Famous last words for sure.

A month after they'd moved into the basement flat of the newly named Sorrento Villa, Seth was made redundant by the big architectural practice where he'd worked for fifteen years. The company was in dire financial straits, the senior partner explained: they had no option but to downsize.

Shocked, Frankie recalled that same senior partner – Seth's friend since college – at the previous year's Christmas dinner, where much had been made of the company's resilience in the shaky economic climate. A glass of red wine in his hand, the man had toasted each member of staff. Frankie had clapped loudest of all when he'd said 'Seth Green, the man we all aspire to be,' then raising his glass, 'quietly professional, dedicated and loyal.'

Loyalty hadn't gone both ways it seemed. Seth wasn't a full partner, but on a high wage, so his name was at the top of the redundancy list.

If she was shocked, then Seth had been devastated.

'I've failed you,' was all he could say. Despite his years of hard work for the company he'd only been given the statutory legal pay-off. There was no vat of cash to help fund the work on Sorrento Villa. They had savings but it would be madness to plough them into such a project. 'How will we manage financially?' Seth asked in despair. 'With the new house . . .'

'We'll manage,' said Frankie, magically switching on the same positive tone that had worked so well during the children's teenage years. 'We'll manage somehow.'

But inside, her stomach was churning with fear. How could they survive on only one salary? If only they'd stayed in their modest old house instead of thinking they were the sort of people who should own a detached Victorian red-brick villa on a half-acre site in Redstone. Christmas had been just over a month off, both children were staying away – Emer in Australia, Alexei in Japan – and she and Seth had to face a dark and depressing festive season on their own. Three months later, they were still far from managing.

Coping with *anything* had turned out to mean a husband who sloped around in sweatpants and could barely summon up the energy to walk to the crossroads for a daily newspaper. He'd lost his zest for life when he'd lost his job. All the great plans for the house now lay untouched under a mound of bills at one end of the kitchen table.

Redundancy had settled over their house like a heavy grey storm cloud.

Frankie, who had been responsible for setting up counselling sessions for Dutton employees following a series of redundancies at the company, now saw the problem from the other side of the table. Her husband was in despair.

Work doesn't define women in the way it defines men, she remembered telling her team in the HR department at the time. *Men find it hard to cope with being out of work.*

Platitudes delivered straight from the most basic HR psychology books.

Those words were certainly mocking her now as she lay beside this shadow of the man who had been her husband, waiting for sleep to claim her. Sleep didn't come.

It was the Sleep Theorem, she told herself. The number of hours you lost sleepless in bed was always in reverse proportion to the amount of work you had to do the following day. Eventually, she drifted into an uneasy doze filled with nightmares involving Emer and Alexei in danger, when she couldn't run fast enough to save them. And darling Seth, once her mainstay in life, was watching all and seemed paralysed into indecision.

At six the alarm went off. She woke exhausted and decided that, at that precise moment, the word for the day was *shattered*. While Seth carried on sleeping, she showered, dressed and had some muesli for breakfast before heading into work.

As she pulled into the underground car park of Dutton Insurance at seven twenty-five on that clear but cold February morning, Frankie felt a low drag of anxiety in the depths of her belly. Steeling herself for the day ahead, she grabbed her briefcase, got out of the car and strode towards the lifts.

The doors closed behind her with a satisfying swish. The inevitable muzak drifted into her head. She hated that music. The lifts from the car park were workmanlike and industrial. Important visitors to Dutton Insurance parked in a designated section of the car park and made their entrance through much more glamorous lifts. She pushed the button for the lobby, the lift shuddered and brought her up. She used to make it her business to run up the stairs at least once every day but these days she was too tired.

'Morning, Mrs Green,' said the fresh-faced security guard as she slid her recognition card into the slot on the barrier.

'Morning, Lucas,' said Frankie cheerily, suppressing the thought that he looked even younger than Alexei, standing there in his uniform as if ready to defend Dutton Insurance from invaders. The policemen were looking younger too. Was she finally at that age at which all the old clichés start becoming true? She headed across the Italian marble floor to the gleaming brass-fronted lifts that were the public face of the business.

These lifts were mirrored on the inside and Frankie could see herself from every angle.

As a girl, she had grown up confident in herself, confident in her tall, athletic body and never embarrassed about budding breasts or menstruation. In fact her only worry had been that her mother might run around brandishing a packet of tampons and screaming *You're a woman now!* at the top of her voice when Frankie had finally had her first period.

Frankie had never dieted like the girls in her class at school, hadn't denied herself food, had loved her body for the things it could do, the sports it could play. She was captain of the netball team and a fabulous long distance runner with those long, lean legs. In her teenage bedroom, she'd had a small haul of medals and trophies from track and field events.

For most of her life, her body had done whatever she asked

of it and it never occurred to her to worry about curves here and there, or fine lines around her eyes.

Until now.

As she stood on her own in the lift, harsh lights accentuating every flaw, it struck her that the woman in the charcoal skirt-suit, the subtle pearl earrings, and the long, dark hair tied up neatly into a knot, looked old.

Frankie closed her eyes and waited for the lift to arrive at her floor, then marched out without another glance at herself. In her office, she switched on her computer and keyed in her password.

The instant messaging icon flashed that a message was waiting. It was from Anita, Frankie's closest friend within the company, a mother of two who was second in command in the legal department. She clicked on it.

You in yet? Have gossip – not nice gossip.

Where are you? typed Frankie.

About to go to canteen. Need coffee. War when I left the house. Julie knows it's my early day but she still hadn't turned up when I was leaving, Clarice was on the kitchen floor screaming, Peaches was throwing baby porridge around and Ivan was glaring at me, as if it was my fault. I only got out by the skin of my teeth.

You should fire her if she's late again. I told you about giving her written warnings.

It would be simpler to fire Ivan. Husbands are easier to come by than good nannies. See you in five?

Frankie grinned and set off for the canteen, walking at speed through the vast open-plan beige kingdom that was Dutton Insurance. She certainly didn't believe that a husband was easier to come by than a nanny. Besides, Ivan was actually a sweetie. Francesca knew it was useless to point out yet again that Julie was invariably late, barely listened to half of what Anita said and was paid as much as the head of the UN Peacekeeping Force. Last time she had said this, Anita's voice had veered

30

into near hysteria as she protested that Julie was the one person in the world capable of managing her two children: 'She's been with us since Clarice was a baby and she's the only person Peaches will settle with. Even Ivan's mother can't make Peaches go to sleep – and she had eight kids.'

'Blimey, eight kids,' said Frankie. She'd have loved more children herself, but not *that* many.

Anita was in the empty canteen pushing a tiny dark-red pellet into the trendy Nespresso machine that the Chief Financial Officer had installed on all the floors of the company two years before, when they'd achieved record profits, despite the state of the economy.

In ten minutes, the canteen – which served the executive floor – would be buzzing with people in early for the monthly status meeting, attended by representatives from all the divisions. It was a largely for-show meeting because all the real business was done behind locked doors, but the CEO was keen on making everybody feel a part of the team.

'Have you heard anything?' Anita said, as she waited for Frankie to get her coffee.

'Heard what?' Frankie said slowly, again feeling that low drag in the pit of her stomach.

It was obvious from Anita's face that, whatever she'd heard, it wasn't good news.

'Heard that we're in trouble, that there's a takeover on the cards.'

'Oh.' Frankie reached for the nearest chair and sat into it. 'Where did you hear it?'

'Oh, the usual labyrinthine methods whereby gossip gets around. Someone in the executive dining room was overheard by one of the chefs who told his girlfriend on the third floor. I heard about it last night, haven't been able to sleep. I mean, if we're taken over by another company, loads of us are going to lose our jobs. What'll I do? The mortgage is huge and we can only just manage it with both our salaries.'

She looked so distraught that Frankie, who had spent her working life mentoring colleagues, ignored her own shock and pain to comfort Anita.

'Now listen here,' she said, 'it's just a rumour. Companies thrive on that sort of stuff. Besides, whatever happens you can get through it. *We* can get through it. We're made of stronger stuff. We've gone through childbirth! You had a ten-pound baby, Anita. There's nothing you cannot cope with.'

The comment had the desired effect. Anita gave a snort of laughter.

'Yeah, I guess,' she said, shaking her head ruefully.

Baby Peaches had been a positive Goliath, taking after her tall, broad father rather than her petite five-foot-two mother.

'I know there's no medal for childbirth, but there should be,' Frankie went on. 'A ten-pound baby – you should get gold for that. No, platinum.'

They talked a while longer and then Frankie looked at her watch.

'Time to move,' she said, finishing her coffee. '*Once more unto the breach* and all that.'

She hurried back to her office, rumours of a takeover now adding to the turmoil in her mind. Stay focused, she told herself. Panicking never got anyone anywhere.

With the office still empty she decided to grab the chance for a speedy morning email to Emer and Alexei.

Beautiful Emer, currently in Sydney but thinking of moving to the US for a few months, was waitressing by day and putting years of piano lessons to good use by playing in the restaurant of a boutique hotel by night.

It's incredible here, Mum, you've got to come out before I leave, she'd emailed only last week. I love it. The sun, the people, you'd love it. too.

If Frankie, who had read many CVs in her time, had to come up with one word to sum up her daughter, that word would be *light*: the shining light that flowed out of her like the sun. Emer was vivid and sparkling and prone to mischief. Frankie had been the same as a child.

'How come you always know, Mum?' Emer would demand crossly when Frankie would take one look at her child's eyes shining naughtily in her tiny little face. 'You *always* know what I'm doing – have you got X-ray vision?'

'Yes,' Frankie would say gravely, suppressing the urge to laugh. 'All mothers have it. As soon as the baby is born, *kapow!* – we are given the gift. I can see through ceilings. So I know you have been upstairs doing something *verrry naughty*.' She'd drag out the syllables in pretend menace.

Emer was a kind person too, but in Sydney she was far removed from the pain in Sorrento Villa and it was out of the question to let on that there was a problem. That would only have her rushing home to help Frankie cope.

So when Emer telephoned and asked: 'Dad sounds down on the phone, is he all right?' Frankie made herself smile into the receiver and slipped into her cheery, buoyant tone.

'No, love, he's just relaxing, taking time off from being a wage slave.'

'Has he started work on the house yet?' Emer said.

In the background, Frankie could hear happy voices and could almost sense the sunniness of Emer's new world. Wishing some of that sunniness would beam out of the phone and light up the gloom in her world, she upped the cheeriness a notch:

'Not yet. We're still discussing things. You know your dad, he wants it to be perfect. Now, tell me all about you, darling. What's the weather like? It's chilly here, I can tell you . . .'

It was a struggle to come up with snippets of cheerful news from home, so her emails followed the same tactic of swiftly shifting the focus from life in Redstone to the latest goings on in Sydney and Japan. It was a little trickier in Alexei's case, because he was hugely intuitive and much more liable to pick

33

up on things. While Emer took after Frankie, drawing on a tough nugget of strength buried deep inside of her, managing to stay positive no matter what, Alexei was a worrier.

She pictured him now, with his wide Slavic cheekbones, grey eyes and the shock of blond hair, so different from everyone in the family. He might not have been born from her body, but he was very much the child of her heart. It had been a wrench, letting him go off on a gap year before college. The thought of her daughter travelling alone actually troubled her far less than the thought of her son venturing out into the world with three other boys for company. Emer had street smarts in abundance while Alexei was softer, much more vulnerable than his feisty sister, who'd signed up for a self-defence course months before she left.

'Got to be able to look after myself, Mum,' she'd said, showing off some of her techniques.

Alexei took after Seth: he was gentle, thoughtful and prone to staring into the distance when working out a problem, his mind drifting off to some higher plane just the way Seth's did.

Seth. All her thoughts came back to Seth. If a person was supposed to get better at things over time, why didn't that dictum hold true when it came to marriage? Perhaps, she thought, closing her personal email and opening up her business mailbox where fifty new messages had arrived overnight, a visit from Seth's long-lost half-sister might succeed in lifting his spirits.

He'd been so thrilled when he got the email from Melbourne. Thrilled, with a tiny and utterly-to-be-expected element of shock.

'I have a sister,' he'd said in wonderment as Frankie leaned over his shoulder to read the email. As she carried on reading he'd sat staring at the email as if it was a thing of fantasy that might vanish at any moment. 'I'd always wanted someone else when I was growing up, a brother or a sister. And I had one all along . . .'

34

Frankie hugged him, aware even then that she could support Seth over this, yet the words that would help him with the grinding pain of his redundancy escaped her. Her career as a human resources executive was built on a mastery of effective interpersonal skills, arbitration, mediation, appraisals, setting goals and accomplishing them . . . but when it came to Seth, instinct told her that there was nothing she could do for him. If he was going to crawl out of this misery, he would have to do it by himself. Without her help. And Frankie, who wanted to solve everyone's problems, hated herself for that.

Chapter Two

Peggy Barry had spent a long time searching for the perfect place: a town far enough away from home for her to flourish – and yet near enough for Peggy to drive to her mother if she was needed. Her mother was the reason she hadn't left the country altogether, but nobody, including Mrs Barry, had to know that. Peggy wanted to remain in Ireland in case one day her mother would accept the truth and phone her daughter. Until then, she travelled, searching.

Since she'd left home at the age of eighteen, an astonishing nine years ago, Peggy had lived in all of Ireland's cities and many of its towns and still hadn't found the perfect place.

She had almost resigned herself to the likelihood that it didn't exist, that there was no town or village or suburb where she could feel as if she belonged.

'What are you looking for exactly?' the owner of the last bar she'd worked in had asked her.

Peggy had liked TJ, even though he wasn't her type. Mind you, in the past year, nobody had been her type. Men and dreams of a future didn't appear to work well together. Guys mistakenly thought that tall, leggy brunettes working in bars wanted quick flings and couldn't possibly be serious about saving money for their own business or about waiting for the right guy to settle down with.

The bar – lucrative, loud, boasting a vibrant Galway crowd – had been quiet once the last stragglers had been sent home. TJ was cashing up and Peggy was cleaning. Her shift ended in half an hour and she yearned for the peace of her small flat two storeys above the dry cleaner's, where there was no noise, nobody gazing drunkenly at her over the counter and telling her they were in love with her, and could they have two pints, a whiskey chaser and a couple of rum cocktails, please?

'Sanctuary,' said Peggy absent-mindedly in reply to TJ's question as she went from table to table with her black plastic bag, bucket, spray and cloth. She'd already gathered up the ashtrays from the beer garden and put them to soak in a basin. The glass-washing machines were on, the empty beer bottles collected. The floor, sticky with alcohol and dirt, was somebody else's problem in the morning.

'Saying "sanctuary" makes you sound like a nun,' remarked TJ.

'OK, peace, then,' Peggy said in exasperation.

'If you want peace, you need one of those villages in the middle of nowhere,' TJ said, reaching for another piece of nicotine gum. 'Sort of place where you get one pub, ten houses and a lot of old farmers standing at their gates staring at you when you drive by.'

'That's not at all what I want.' Peggy moved on to the next table. Somebody's door key was stuck there in a glue of crisps and the sticky residue of spilt alcohol. Peggy scrubbed it free and went back to the bar, where she put it in the lost property tin. 'TJ, you can't run a business in a village in the middle of nowhere and I want my own business. I told you already. A knitting and craft shop.'

'I know, you told me: knitting,' TJ repeated, shaking his head. 'You just don't look the knitting type.'

Peggy laughed. She seldom told people about her plans for fear they'd laugh at her fierce determination and tell her she was mad, and why didn't she blow her savings on a trip to Key West/Ibiza/Amsterdam with them? But whenever she did mention her life plan, it was astonishing how often people told her that she didn't look 'the knitting type'.

What *was* the knitting type? A woman with her hair in a bun held up with knitting needles, wearing a long, multi-coloured knitted coat that trailed along behind her on the floor?

'I want to run my own business, TJ,' she said, 'and knitting's what I'm good at, what I love. I've been knitting since I was small: my mother used to knit Aran for the tourist shops years ago. She taught me everything. I know there's a market for shops like that. That's what I'm looking for – somewhere to start off.'

'You told me, but I'm not sure I believe you.' TJ's eyes narrowed. 'What exactly are you running away from, babe? You should stay here. You're happy, we appreciate you.'

What got a woman like Peggy trailing all over the place looking for peace? A man, he'd bet tonight's takings on it. When women moved all the time the way Peggy did, a man was usually behind it all.

Women like Peggy, tall and rangy with those steady dark eyes half-obscured by curls of conker-brown fringe and a hint of vulnerability that she did her best to hide, were always running from men. Not that she couldn't be tough when she was dealing with angry drunks pulling at her clothes and making suggestions. But she was soft inside, despite the outer tough-chick exterior and the black leather biker jacket and boots. Too soft. He wondered what had happened to her.

'I'm not running,' Peggy said, straightening up from the final table and facing him squarely. 'I'm looking. There's a difference. I'll know when I find it.'

'Yeah.' He waved one hand wearily. The soft women who'd been hurt by men all said that.

'It's not what you think,' Peggy insisted. 'I'm looking for a different kind of life.'

But as she walked home that night, hand wrapped around a personal alarm in one pocket of her leather jacket, she admitted to herself that TJ was sort of right – only she would never tell him that. He thought she was running away from a man, and in a way she was. Except it wasn't the ex-lover TJ undoubtedly imagined. She was running away from something very different.

On a beautiful February day, shortly after leaving the bar in Galway, an Internet property trawl led Peggy to Redstone, a suburb of Cork that somehow retained a sense of being a town.

On the computer screen, the premises near Redstone Junction had it all: a pretty, Art Deco façade, a big catchment area and lots of other shops and cafés nearby to bring in passing trade.

Now, as she drove her rattling old Volkswagen Beetle slowly through the crossroads, she felt a sense of peace envelop her. This might, just *might*, be the place she'd been looking for.

It helped that it was such a lovely day, the low-angled winter sun burnishing everything with warm light, but she sensed that she'd have liked the place even if it had been bucketing down with rain. There were trees planted on the footpaths, stately sycamores and elegant beeches with a few acid-green buds emerging, giving a sense of the country town Redstone had been before it merged with the city. The façade of one entire block was still dedicated to Morton's Grain Storage, pale brick with classic 1930s lettering chiselled into the brickwork itself, although the grain storage was long gone and the ground floor had been converted to a row of shops that included a pharmacy, a chi-chi delicatessen-cum-café and a clothes shop. Peggy parked the car and walked back through the little junction, loving the black wrought-iron street lights with their curlicues where the lamps hung. It was impossible to tell whether they'd been installed a hundred and fifty years ago or were a more recent addition.

She loved the trees and the flowers planted diligently around them, probably by a team of local people involved in the Tidy Towns competition, she thought. They'd obviously chosen a host of bulbs, for now buttery yellow early crocuses and pale narcissi were sweetly blooming in wooden troughs at the base of each tree along both arms of the crossroads.

Nobody had ripped up the flowers or stubbed cigarettes out in the earth. The people here obviously admired how they brightened up the street.

Even before she'd looked over the premises for rent – a former off-licence, which had unaccountably gone out of business – she'd felt a kind of peace in Redstone.

The vacant property was a double-fronted shop with two large rooms out the back and a flat upstairs, should she wish to rent that too, the estate agent added hopefully.

The downstairs would need only cosmetic work, but the upstairs needed a wrecking ball, Peggy thought privately. The fittings were old and hazardous. Besides, living over the shop was a mistake, she knew that after working as a waitress in a Dublin bistro and living upstairs.

'Downstairs is enough for me,' Peggy said. 'I don't have a deathwish.'

The agent sighed. 'Ah well, plenty of people are looking for bijou doer-uppers,' he said over-confidently.

'As long as the floor's safe and they don't come crashing down to my place when they're using the sander,' Peggy replied. 'The landlord's responsible.'

The agent laughed.

Peggy eyeballed him. What was it about a woman in tight jeans and leather jacket that made people think you were both ignorant of the law and a pushover?

'I mean it,' she said.

The deal to rent the shop was signed five days later.

She found a small cottage for rent at the end of St Brigid's Avenue, on a 1950s estate of former council houses, about a mile away from the shop. The house wasn't overly beautiful with its genuine fifties decor, but it was all she could afford.

Peggy celebrated her new life with a quarter-bottle of champagne and a takeaway pizza in front of the cheap television-cum-DVD player she'd bought years ago. She slotted *Sleepless in Seattle*, her favourite film of all time, into the player, sipped her champagne and toasted herself.

'To Peggy's Busy Bee Knitting and Stitching Shop,' she said, happily raising her glass before biting into the pizza. She'd achieved her dream and her life would be different from now on. The past was just that: the past. Then she settled down to watch Meg Ryan and Tom Hanks nearly but not quite miss each other, and she cried, as she always did.

The process of renovating the shop had to be accomplished as quickly as possible so she could begin trading. Peggy knew exactly what she wanted and loved the hard work of rolling up her sleeves and getting into it – discussing the finish of the shelving with Gunther, the carpenter and shopfitter, and working with a sign-maker to get precisely the signage she had in mind.

'You certainly know what you want,' the sign designer said. 'So many people dither for ages over different styles.'

Peggy had smiled at her. 'I've been planning this for a long, long time,' she said.

But in spite of all the activity over paint, wood finishes and what shape to have on the cast-iron sign that hung at a right angle to the door, what Peggy hadn't expected was to fall quite so much in love with Redstone itself.

She loved the small-town feel of it all, though it was nicer than any of the many towns she'd lived in through her life.

She loved the way people greeted each other cheerily.

'How's the leg, Mick?' one man had yelled at another at the crossroads one morning as Peggy made her way to the shop.

'Ah, you know,' replied a tall elderly man with a stick and a small dog bouncing at the end of a lead. 'Not up to line dancing yet, but some day. Did you ever get that thing sorted out?'

'No,' said the first man solemnly, adjusting his briefcase so he was holding it under the other arm. 'It's the timing, isn't it? Still, I might yet!'

The lights changed and the man with the dog limped off in the direction of the small shopping centre tucked snugly away behind Main Street.

What was the *thing*, Peggy wanted to know. Why wasn't it sorted yet? She had to control herself not to run and *ask* Briefcase Man, who was crossing the road and heading off in the opposite direction.

What was this madness that possessed her? Wanting to know about people? It was unlike her. She'd spent her entire life avoiding getting to know anyone. That way, they didn't want to know you. Peggy was the girl who'd live in a town for a year, blending into the background as far as possible, remaining on the fringes of everyone's lives. She'd spent too long as a solitary child to learn the gift of easy friendship as an adult. After a while, when she'd had enough, she would simply pack up her belongings and drive away. She had never allowed herself to put down roots. But for some reason here in Redstone she had an urge to belong, and belonging meant meeting people.

Because she was nice and early, there was plenty of parking outside the shop. She felt her spirits lift as they did every time her old blue Beetle shuddered to a halt at the kerb and she looked up to see the old-fashioned swing sign that read *Peggy's Busy Bee Knitting and Stitching Shop*.

Nobody looking at this modest establishment with its fresh

lavender paintwork and unfinished inside could imagine the sheer joy it already brought to its owner. It was still something of a miracle to Peggy. The miracle had involved years of hard work, hard saving and loneliness as she'd gone from job to job, getting experience in wool shops when she could, doing accountancy courses at night so she'd know how to run her own business, and working in bars or restaurants when she could get nothing else.

Now, she felt that all the sacrifices had been worth it. She, Peggy Barry, who had never been on any school's most-likely-to-succeed list, had finally found exactly what she'd wanted all her life: a business doing what she loved best and financial independence. She was her own boss and she would never answer again to any man.

The money from her grandmother's will – a grandmother she'd never even met – had been a godsend. The day the cheque arrived she had banked it in a high-interest account and then left it there, watching it grow year by year. Without that, she wouldn't have been able to open her own shop.

Surveying her empire as she got out of the car, Peggy ran through the sums in her head. It would take only one or two more days at the most for Gunther, the carpenter, and Paolo, his apprentice, to finish. She'd considered several quotes before giving the job to Gunther. His had not been the cheapest, but he'd been the most professional of the carpenters she'd talked to, and he hadn't given her a flirty grin, the way the young guy with the lowest price had.

As soon as the woodwork was finished, Peggy mused, she would clean all the dust from the shop and start painting the walls the same lavender as the outside—

'How'rya, Peggy,' yelled Sue from the bakery across the road as Peggy put her key in the shop door.

'Hello, Sue!' she called back.

Sue and her husband, Zeke, were always in at five in the morning. By the time Peggy arrived at half past seven, they were already halfway through their day's work, baking organic breads and muffins to be delivered to shops and office canteens around the city.

Peggy enjoyed talking to them about the difficulties of setting up your own shop. And they'd been so helpful.

'Advertise in the *Oaklands News*, don't bother with the *Redstone People*. They charge twice as much and will mess up your advertisement every time,' Sue advised. 'Our ad for "hand-crafted cakes" turned into "dead-crafted cakes". There wasn't exactly a rush for them after that.'

'What's your web presence like?' said Zeke.

'A bit basic, but I'm working on it.'

'Good. In the meantime, stick up your cards everywhere,' he added, admiring the lavender-coloured notecards Peggy had commissioned with the shop's name and pen-and-ink illustrations of wool and fabrics along with the shop's address and fledgling website. 'Be shameless. Ask everyone who has a noticeboard if you can put one up. Introduce yourself everywhere, even if you're shy.'

Peggy had blushed to the roots of her dark hair. She'd spent a few days casting glances over at the bakery before Sue had marched across the road with a tray of muffins and said, 'Welcome to Redstone. I thought I'd give you a week of staring at us like Homeland Security before I'd make a move. We don't bite. Well, I might bite the odd time, but I only do it to Zeke and he's used to me because we're married.'

She had made it seem the easiest thing in the world to walk across the road and make friends but Peggy's usual ability to put up a pleasant front seemed to have deserted her. It hadn't ever been real, that was the problem. Years of moving from town to town had obviously taken its toll. The older you got, Peggy figured, the harder it was to put on a brave face.

That evening, Gunther had suggested that Peggy join him

and Paolo for a Friday-night drink in the Starlight Lounge. Peggy, worn out cleaning the back room which was full of junk and damp, had said yes straight away.

She was hungry, too tired to cook, and after a week of Gunther and Paolo, she was very fond of them and thought it might be nice not to eat on her own for once.

The Starlight Lounge was a quirky establishment about a quarter of a mile from the shop. The name and the decor didn't quite match. The façade resembled a working men's pub where women were only allowed in to clean up, while the inside turned out to be a confused combination of Olde Oirish Pub and fifties Americana, complete with mini jukeboxes in the booths.

'My friend owns it,' said Gunther when he saw Peggy looking round with amusement. 'It's a mess, I know. He was experimenting with styles . . .'

She admired the line of tiny disco balls on the ceiling behind the bar.

'Crazy.' Gunther shrugged. 'He has no money now to do anything, but the bar food is good.'

Peggy chose a semi-circular booth with a round Formica-topped table. On the wall behind a picture of Elvis hung beside a watercolour print of a forlorn Irish mountain. Gunther's friend had clearly been trying to appeal to a very diverse audience, but it worked. Despite the mad decor, it was welcoming.

Gunther grabbed menus and studied his with total concentration while a languid bargirl lit the red lamp on the table. Paolo stood at the bar gabbling in Italian to some friends.

Glorious aromas drifted from the kitchens and Peggy realized she hadn't eaten anything but an apple since breakfast.

'What's good?' she asked Gunther.

'The fish and chips,' he said.

Peggy's mouth watered. 'Sounds good to me.'

By eight o'clock, Peggy had eaten cod coated in feather-light batter, and was considering a dessert, while a stream of Gunther and Paolo's friends had come and gone after joining them for a drink.

Gunther was in no rush: his wife was at her mother's with the children and Paolo was meeting his girlfriend in town at ten. The jukeboxes, disco balls and the house speciality cocktail, Starlight Surprise, were working their magic, and a few people were dancing close to the bar. Paolo was talking to a tall, athletic guy who'd arrived at the table. He couldn't take his eyes off Peggy.

'David Byrne,' he said, leaning in to shake her hand.

'Peggy Barry,' she said, smiling.

He was good looking, but not really her type. Despite fighting it, she'd always been drawn to bad boys and David Byrne was clean-cut and good looking, the sort of guy who'd been captain of the football team, head boy and undoubtedly Pupil Most Likely to Succeed. He probably helped old ladies across the road, which wasn't a bad thing – *she* helped old ladies across the road. But for some reason, those sorts of guys never lit her pilot light.

Closer, she could see how handsome he was, with dark hair, blue eyes and a stylish suit – even though he'd taken the jacket off and loosened his tie. Despite the clean-cut handsomeness, there was something indefinably interesting about him that Peggy, who'd spent years watching people from the sidelines, couldn't pin down.

And then, when Paolo slipped out of the seat to take a phone call, David slipped in. She found herself sitting next to him. He kept staring at her as though he'd been searching for something all his life and she was it.

Utterly disconcerted, Peggy stared back. His eyes weren't blue, as she'd first thought, but a green-tinged azure, and around the black of the pupil were striations of amber like shards of sunlight. She couldn't look away. His gaze wasn't predatory or sleazy. It said: Finally, I've found you.

'Paolo says you just moved into Redstone,' David said, smiling.

His voice was deep, gentle. And kind. How could you tell that from a voice? You couldn't, but still, he had a kindness about him that drew her in. Jolting herself back to reality, she said: 'Yes, I'm new to the neighbourhood. I've taken over the old off-licence – now, *how* could a place that sells drink go out of business!'

Oh heck, she thought, now I sound like a deranged boozer who needs alcohol 24/7. And to prove it, I have two cocktail glasses in front of me!

She tried to surreptitiously shove the empty cocktail glass behind the ketchup and sugar containers.

What was *wrong* with her? Her stomach was swooping as if she was on board a ship in a force-ten gale.

'That off-licence was a bit of a dive,' David said. 'Back when I was a teenager, it was the hot spot for under-age drinking. My father warned me and my brothers to stay out of it or there would be hell to pay – which isn't really much like my Dad.' He grinned. 'What sort of business are you setting up?'

'A knitting and craft shop,' said Peggy, back on familiar ground. She waited for him to say she didn't look like a knitting type of girl.

'My mother knits. She says it's meditation,' he said instead.

'Yes!' agreed Peggy, astonished. 'That's exactly what it is – nobody else ever gets that unless they are a knitter.'

'I can see it on my mother's face when she knits,' he admitted. 'So, it's just you on your own in Redstone, not your . . . family.'

'No, just me,' said Peggy, eyes glittering now.

This gorgeous man *was* interested in her. She wasn't imagining it.

'No husband, then?'

47

'No husband,' agreed Peggy, loving this courtship – because that's what it felt like.

'No harem of men relying on you . . .?' His eyes were glittering too now, looking directly into hers, making Peggy feel as if they were alone, and he was saying something wildly sexy to her, even though he wasn't and they were in a busy bar. It was that low, rumbling voice and the way he looked at her. As if he *knew* her already.

'No male harem,' she whispered.

He had evening stubble on his jaw, she noticed, as he loosened his tie some more and undid the top button of his shirt. Why was that so erotic?

'Good. Could I persuade you to go on a date with me, then?' he asked. 'Since we've cleared up the harem situation.'

'You don't have any harem situation yourself?' she asked, even though she knew he didn't. Exactly how, Peggy couldn't have said, but she was sure that this man had no other women in the background.

He shook his head. 'No, nobody for a long time. I thought it was because I was busy with work, but it turns out I must have been waiting.' He smiled at her.

'That was a bit—' Peggy had been about to say *corny*, but she didn't. Because he'd meant it. *Waiting for her.*

'—sorry, I nearly said "corny", but it's not corny and you're not corny, it's lovely,' she said instead, and then thought how ridiculous *that* sounded. She took a gulp of her cocktail to hide her embarrassment but then realized she hadn't wanted to look like Drinker of the Year, so pushed the glass away.

'What work do you do?' she asked, then added: 'I mean, people always tell me that I don't look like a woman who knits, but you didn't, so I don't want to guess wrong about you . . .' She had to stop this babbling.

'I run an engineering company,' he said, 'which is not boasting about being a captain of industry. I'm an engineer

48

and I've set up on my own recently. Every cent of my money is being ploughed into the company, hence the reason I live with my two brothers instead of in a magnificent penthouse, where I could invite you back for a glass of vintage wine and impress you with my riches.'

'I wouldn't be impressed by that,' said Peggy truthfully.

David smiled at her, azure eyes meeting her dark ones.

'I didn't think you would be.' He put his head to one side and looked at her. 'I understand why people say you don't look like a person who knits,' he said.

'Why?' she demanded.

'You're more like a faerie from the forest,' he said, 'a creature from a fable or from the old Celtic myths we used to learn in school. It's the trailing hair the colour of wet bark and those big eyes watching me, and the sense that you might disappear at any moment . . .'

He leaned forward and gently brushed back a coil of hair that had fallen over one of her eyes.

Peggy had absolutely no memory of ever blushing in her whole life but she could feel it now: redness rising up her cheeks. He'd got one thing right: she did disappear whenever she wanted to. But not this time. For now, she was perfectly happy where she was.

Peggy Barry, tired of being alone but almost resigned to it because she knew from experience that alone was the only way to go, somehow crumbled. When David said he'd been waiting for her, his words had the ring of truth in them – and suddenly she realized that was because it felt as if she'd been waiting just for him.

'Would you come to dinner with me tomorrow night?' he asked.

Peggy nodded first, then said yes in a voice that sounded too faint to be hers.

'I'd love to.'

* * *

49

Peggy felt jittery and wildly excited all the next day. She couldn't concentrate on the task of cleaning the filthy back room and kept stopping and staring dreamily into space, returning to earth to find her bucket of soapy water stone-cold.

She found herself thinking of *Sleepless in Seattle* and how love could hit you in the weirdest way, like Annie, who knew she could never marry Walter, hearing Sam on the radio and knowing, just *knowing*, she had to meet him.

Peggy had seen it hundreds of times: when she had the flu, when she wanted cheering up, when she was happy, when she was so sad she thought her heart might break. And she'd loved it. But she didn't think something like that could actually happen . . .

At lunch, she went to buy a sandwich from Sue, and stood in the queue gazing at the bread behind the counter until Sue had to say 'Peggy' loudly to wake her from her reverie. She'd never felt this before about a date, ever, and she wished she had someone to share her feelings with.

If only she could phone her mother and tell her she felt as if she'd found 'the One'. Mum knew all about *Sleepless in Seattle*. They'd watched it together. But she couldn't call. Just couldn't.

By seven that evening, she'd had a long shower to wash the shop dirt from her skin, had washed and dried her mane of hair until it fell in waves around her shoulders, and had rubbed handfuls of almond body cream luxuriantly into her skin. All this preparation felt right. She wasn't ordinary Peggy getting ready for a dinner – she was the woman David Byrne stared at as though she was a goddess.

She was Annie waiting for Sam.

When David rang the bell at five to seven, she rushed to open the door.

'I'm sorry I'm early,' he began, his gaze locked on hers.

'I've been ready since half six,' said Peggy in reply. There would be no games here. This was too serious, too wonderful.

'You look beautiful,' he said, eyes travelling over the old-fashioned teal chiffon blouse tucked into skinny jeans that made her long legs look longer than ever. She'd worn kitten heels because David was taller than her. Few men were. Walking beside him to his car, she felt like the faerie he'd talked about, fragile and beautiful. She didn't know what it was to feel beautiful. There had been no compliments in her young life and so there was no foundation on which to build even a hint of belief in her own beauty. But with David's eyes upon her and his hand holding hers, she felt as beautiful and desirable as any movie star.

He took her to a small French restaurant a few miles away where the atmosphere of those Parisian bistros she'd seen in films had been perfectly recreated. With its red-checked table-cloths, low lighting and candles dripping wax everywhere, it was the perfect venue for an intimate dinner and she wanted to clap her hands with glee when she saw it.

'It got a bad review in the papers for being a cliché,' David said as they ignored the menu and stared at each other over the candles on their table. 'But the food is delicious and the staff are great. So what's wrong with candles and red tablecloths?'

'I love it,' said Peggy happily. 'Let's eat all the clichés tonight!'

'And hold hands across the table,' he added, reaching forward to take her hand.

'Yes,' she said, folding her fingers into his.

The bistro staff came from a variety of countries around the world and could speak a lexicon of languages, but all of them could recognize diners wrapped in romance and oblivious to everyone else. So Gruyere-topped French onion soup, crusty bread, boeuf bourguignon and good red wine were delivered to the table silently, leaving the couple to eat and talk uninterrupted.

Peggy felt as if they were encased in a magical bubble which nothing could break: this evening was simply perfect in every way.

David wanted to know all about her – unlike so many of the men she'd met over the years, who were too caught up in determining their own wants and needs. He asked what films *she* liked to see, what food *she* liked to eat. He'd cook her dinner at his place, he told her as they drank their wine: all he needed was to get his brothers out of the house.

Then, when talk inevitably moved onto their backgrounds and he asked about her childhood, she gently batted him away: 'Let's forget everything except now,' she said. 'Tonight is all that matters.'

As she said it, she knew this wasn't merely a ruse to stop him asking about her past. Suddenly, her life before him had ceased to matter. Whereas normally, it coloured everything. But this wonderful night with this wonderful man had changed all that.

'Sorry, I didn't mean to sound like Interpol – I want to know all about you, Peggy,' he said, and she smiled across the table at him, lean and rangy in a casual grey shirt.

'Why are you calling the shop Peggy's Busy Bee Knitting and Stitching Shop? There's nobody less bee-like than you. You're so calm and serene. You don't buzz around.'

'I don't have a very good answer, I'm afraid,' she said, finally giving up on the boeuf, knowing that she would feel full for a week. 'My mother does wonderful embroidery and for a while she embroidered napkins for a gift shop. The lady who ran it, Carola, said my mother was the most artistic person she knew and told Mum to embroider whatever she wanted. Mum chose bees. They were beautiful. Each napkin was different because she said no matter how hard you tried, each embroidered bee ended up different, same as people.'

Peggy's bubble of happiness quivered and she felt the familiar emotions welling up in her. Thinking about her mother always made her want to cry. Sitting here with this good, kind man, she wanted to tell him everything because he ought to know. But of course, she couldn't.

'Dessert,' announced David, as if he could read her face and wanted to spare her thinking about whatever was clearly hurting her. 'I don't think it's very French, but they make a wonderful cheesecake here.'

And the sadness passed. Peggy pushed it all out of her mind. She'd been alone for so long and she deserved this, didn't she?

During that glorious week, they went out three times. The second date was to the cinema; on the way there, David walked on the outside of the pavement, he automatically paid for the cinema tickets, and stood back to let her enter the line of seats so she could pick the one she wanted.

He was gentlemanly, she decided, as the film began. Such a weird, old-fashioned word, but it suited him.

And there was no denying that she was intensely physically attracted to him. From the moment she'd spotted him walking towards her in the wine bar where they'd arranged to meet before the movie, broad-shouldered and handsome in a sweater and jeans, she'd found herself imagining that body close to hers. In the darkness of the cinema she experienced pure pleasure when David put an arm around her shoulders and whispered into her ear: 'Are you enjoying the film?'

'Yes,' she said, although in truth she had hardly paid any attention to it. She'd been too preoccupied thinking about him, sitting beside her.

As the week went on, the real world forced its way into her head and reminded her that happy endings were for movies. She tried to dismiss the voice inside her head, telling her this, that it was better to stay away from people like David. The Davids of this world expected a girl to be normal, with an ordinary background and a loving family behind them. He wouldn't know what to make of Peggy's past. The voice said it was time to back off, to stop him from getting too close. The business ought to be her focus. She had no time for men. Even the nice ones couldn't be trusted.

Persistent as the voice was, it was just possible to ignore it. Because David Byrne was trying so hard to prove that he could be trusted and because Peggy wanted the dream to stay alive for a little while longer.

He loved her beautiful shop when she showed it to him and said he and his brothers would give a hand with the painting. Due to lack of funds, Peggy had been planning to do it all herself.

'No, it's fine,' she said, instinctively, aching inside at how hurt he looked.

In moments of clarity, she wondered how the hell had *she* attracted this gorgeous, decent man? His family sounded wonderful. The townhouse where he lived with his two brothers was only half a mile away from the home where they'd grown up in St Brigid's Terrace, just round the corner from Peggy's cottage. He and his two brothers often went home to Mum for Sunday lunch, he told her. On odd occasions – well, once a week, actually, he said ruefully – their mum turned up at the bachelor house to tut about the state of the place and do his brothers' washing.

'I keep telling her not to, but she insists on doing it.'

'You do yours?' she asked, thinking how utterly lovely this all sounded.

'As I keep telling Brian and Steve, if they're old enough to vote, they're old enough to know how to work the washing machine,' David said.

He mentioned, too, that he had a sister, Meredith.

'She lives in a pretty swanky apartment in Dublin,' he said, 'and runs an art gallery with someone else. None of us get to see her much.'

'Oh.' The words slipped out: 'Do you not get on with her?' Meredith seemed to be the one flaw in the Byrne family.

'No, I get on with her fine,' he said thoughtfully. 'She's changed, that's all. I think she got caught up caring about the wrong sort of stuff. Money, labels – you know, that type of thing. I miss her, actually, but she's moved on from us.'

Peggy detected a flash of something in his eyes: not rancour but sadness.

Though their own children had all flown the nest, his parents still had a teenager in the house: David's cousin Freya. His face lit up when he talked about her.

'Crazy like a fox,' he said. 'Knows everything. Fifteen going on thirty-seven. Myself and the lads keep an eye on her, because there's no knowing what she might get up to next.'

'Why does she live with your mum and dad?' Peggy asked, not wanting to sound too much like a grand inquisitor but utterly fascinated all the same. Hearing about the family was like basking in the glow of their loving normality. Besides, asking questions was a great way of distracting people from asking about her, and the more she knew David, the more she didn't want him to know her truth.

'My dad's youngest brother, Will, died in a car crash and his wife, my Aunt Gemma, had a nervous breakdown. I don't know what the psychiatrists called it but that's what happened,' David said sadly. 'She never recovered from his death. Not that anyone would recover from that,' he added, 'but after-wards, she literally ceased to function. She'd always been an anxious person but she simply went to pieces. Freya was their only child and after a while, when it became apparent that Gemma wasn't functioning, Mum stepped in and said Freya couldn't live like that any more. Gemma would forget to buy food, forget to cook dinner, forget to get Freya from school, that sort of thing. So Freya's with Mum now and it's brilliant. She keeps Mum young, Mum says. We all get a great kick out of her. Gemma's doing much better now, too. She can't work, though, but she sees Freya all the time, things are good there.'

Peggy loved hearing about his family. Apart from poor Aunt Gemma, they sounded nice and normal: the sort of family she'd love to have been a part of. That's when she knew the fantasy was over and that she had to listen to the voice telling her she should end it. Normal wasn't for her. She'd screw up normal. She was probably a lot more like Aunt Gemma than anyone else in David's grounded family. Not that she was likely to forget to buy food or cook – Peggy was incredibly organized and seldom forgot anything – but she was far from normal.

'Now you know all about me,' he said. 'Tell me about you, about your family.'

Peggy had a well-rehearsed story about a small family who lived in a bungalow in a town in the centre of the country: a gentle mother who loved needlework and knitting, and a father who was a mechanic. He'd come from a farming background, while her mother had been born in Dublin's city centre.

'No brothers or sisters, I'm afraid,' she said. 'I'd have loved to be part of a big family like yours. I'm jealous. I was such a tomboy when I was younger, climbing trees with the boys, having fights!'

Normally, people lapped up this story and laughed at the notion of Peggy getting into fights. It was a perfect distraction and nobody had ever questioned the truth of it. Until now.

David's brow furrowed.

She looked at the face she wanted to touch, so she knew each contour and felt a yearning gap inside. It had to end and soon.

'I can't see you having fights,' he said finally. 'You're too gentle. You're joking, surely?'

Peggy summoned up a smile in the middle of her misery. 'No, I was a tomboy, honestly.'

'Apart from the knitting and sewing, then,' David said, still looking as if he didn't believe her.

'Oh, yes, apart from that,' Peggy agreed.

He was too clever, too able to see inside her, she thought. How had he got inside her head so quickly?

In bed that night, unable to sleep, she practised different ways of telling him it was over: 'I'm too young, David, too young for the picket fence and the two-point-five children.'

Even in her head, the mental David had an answer to that argument: 'How do you have two-point-five children? I've always wondered.'

She'd never left anyone properly before. She'd had dates and boyfriends over the years, but nothing serious, nothing that couldn't be undone by packing up and moving on. She had no experience of how to handle this.

Two days later, she was so preoccupied trying to come up with a way to end it that she somehow found herself agreeing to go back to his house for dinner on their third date.

'The lads are out for the evening – I almost had to bribe them. They want to see this woman I can't stop talking about,' he told her on the phone.

Peggy beamed at the thought of David talking about her.

'And I cleaned the house and told them that, if they messed it up, I would destroy Brian's electric guitar and put Steve's precious football jersey, the one signed by the Irish team, into the wash.'

They both laughed.

'You'd never do that,' Peggy teased.

'What, you don't think I can be cruel and dangerous?' he said, laughing.

'No,' she said quietly.

How easy it would be to let herself fall further in love with this man and spend a lifetime with him. It seemed there would be no arguing, no fights, none of that constant tension in the house. But what if he changed? That's what men did, and you had to know how to deal with that. Peggy already knew that she couldn't. She was better off on her own.

'What happened there?' he asked, picking up on the change in her voice. 'You sounded so sad. Tell me, please.'

'No,' she said. 'Sorry, I can't.'

'There's a lot about you, Peggy Barry, that I don't understand. Yet,' he added.

'Gosh no, I'm very boring,' she said lightly. It was her standard response and she'd used it during their first dinner, but she knew he wanted to know more now and that her made-up family background wouldn't keep him satisfied for long.

'Hey, Ms Knitting Shop Owner and future entrepreneur of the year,' he said, 'I don't think you're boring for one moment, but if that's the story we're running with right now, then being allegedly boring hasn't turned out too bad for you.'

'Yeah, sure,' she said. 'I'm trading the Beetle in next week for a Ferrari.'

'Red or yellow?' he asked.

'Do they only make them in those colours?' Peggy demanded. 'Red is so obvious. If a guy gets a red Ferrari, he has to have pouffed-up hair, an open shirt, a medallion and a supermodel beside him.'

'At least I've got the supermodel sorted!' he joked.

On the night of their dinner date, David offered to pick Peggy up from her house but she suddenly decided that she might need to get away under her own steam.

'No need for you to come out,' she said brightly. 'Give me directions and I'll get there myself.'

'It's complicated if you don't know the area – I'll drive to the shop and you can follow me in your own car,' he said.

She pulled up behind him as he parked the car outside one of a row of attractive townhouses. He came round and opened the car door for her then led her through a tiny front garden, and unlocked the door . . .

'It's not such a bad place really, for three men living alone,' he said, as he showed her inside.

The house was very obviously a bachelor establishment. There was a big leather couch in the living room, the inevitable enormous television and fabulous stereo system, and a coffee table littered with papers and sports magazines.

'Steve,' he growled, moving swiftly to the coffee table and tidying the papers into a neat pile. 'This was spotless this morning. He's a menace.'

She couldn't have imagined any of the other men she'd dated hastily organizing it all the way David did, sorting out the cushions on the couch.

'Steve sits here eating breakfast and when he's finished, he just goes off leaving all the papers left scattered around. I think he imagines we've a maid. That's the only explanation.'

'Is he an older brother or younger?' said Peggy, looking at the family photographs crowded on the mantelpiece.

'Youngest,' David said, showing her a picture of a smiling young man holding a football. 'I'm the second eldest after Meredith, then Brian, then Steve. Brian's the one who's getting married. He's spending a lot of time in his girlfriend Liz's flat so he doesn't contribute as much as he once did to the mess, but he doesn't tidy up any of it, either.'

'It must be nice, coming from a big family,' Peggy said idly, examining the photos. There were several big family groups. Three tall young men standing with an equally tall father and a shorter woman who was obviously David's mother, big smiling face and fluffy white blonde hair clustered around her face. Beside them was a thin, dark-haired teenager wearing Doc Martens, ripped tights and a mini skirt, with a huge grin on her face. There was another young woman in some of the pictures.

She was always a little apart, a tall woman in her early thirties with long blonde hair and elegant, expensive clothes. In each one she was standing apart from the rest of the group.

More photos decorated the shelves loaded with CDs and video games. There was a Christmas shot, everyone except the tall blonde woman in Christmas hats at a table; and what appeared to be a family holiday snap, taken on a beach with everyone very wet because it was pelting with rain, but with genuine smiles for the camera. They all seemed so happy, so at ease with each other.

There was something almost voyeuristic about looking at these photos, Peggy felt: this was proper family life. She felt a void inside her.

'Big families are great fun,' David said. 'It's a support system, a team who are always there for you.'

She noticed that he didn't say any of the stuff she'd half-expected him to say, like: 'Big families drive you mad.' No, he loved it, *relished* being part of it.

'Is that your mum and dad?' she said, pointing to the older couple all dressed up, smiles on their faces but still a bit stiff and formal in front of the camera, as if they weren't entirely at ease with posing.

'Yes, that's their twenty-fifth wedding anniversary. We sent them to Crete. Mum hates flying, had to go to the doctor to get something to calm her down for the flight. Dad said she was funny because she took one tablet and fell asleep. He practically had to carry her off the plane.'

'They look lovely,' Peggy said wistfully.

'They are.' There was real warmth in his voice. 'You'll have to come and meet them. You could come for lunch next Sunday, if that's not all going too fast? Mum would love that. Freya would love it too – I'm warning you, she'll interrogate you. She's a junior Miss Marple. Nothing escapes her.'

Peggy smiled at the vision of the teenager with the lumpy shoes as a Miss Marple.

'Maybe I could come and meet *your* parents sometime?' David said. 'They need to know that their daughter isn't dating a madman. I promise I won't shame you dreadfully,' he added, grinning.

'Maybe,' Peggy said, after an uncomfortable pause.

Ignoring this, David took her hand. 'Come on, I'll bring you into the kitchen.'

He led her into a kitchen painted blue and white, with jolly blue and white sprigged curtains over the sink and old stained-pine cupboards.

'Mum and Freya did the decor,' David said. 'We keep thinking we're going to change it. Steve wants to get one of those modern kitchens, shiny red cabinets and stainless steel splashbacks, but with Brian leaving to get married it's difficult making decisions.'

'It's a bit old fashioned, but it's nice,' said Peggy.

The kitchen in her flat was nowhere near as pretty as this. It was full of odd freestanding bits of furniture. She was scared to look underneath in case there might be dead bodies or live mice. This sweet traditional kitchen was rather adorable and certainly sparkling clean.

'We've got wine, tea, coffee, juice?' said David. 'What would you like before I start on dinner?'

'Tea would be lovely,' she said.

He boiled the kettle and Peggy leaned against a cabinet, watching him as he moved around the kitchen. He was so much taller than her, she thought absently, that she'd have to look up if he kissed her.

'Excuse me,' he said coming close, opening a cupboard right beside her. 'Mind your head.' He touched her gently as if to make sure the cupboard door wouldn't hurt her. And then the cupboard was quite forgotten. Their eyes met, and in an instant his mouth was on hers and it was so tender and sweet that, for a crazy moment, she felt she was a flower opening in the sun.

Then Peggy wasn't thinking any more. Their kisses grew hotter, suffused with passion and want. She buried her hands

61

in his hair, pulling him to her. His hands slid down to her waist, fitting her comfortably against him.

After a few minutes, David's long fingers began to undo the buttons of her cotton blouse. Peggy leaned back, letting him touch her, wanting him to.

But then he paused, took a step away from her, leaving her staring up at him, lost.

'I'm sorry. Is this too fast?' he asked. 'It has to be right, Peggy. I don't want to rush you. You're too special, do you understand?'

Peggy had looked up at those azure eyes, darker now with desire.

He wanted it to be right for her. He wanted her to be happy, not rushed. How beautiful that was.

She reached for his hands and pulled them back to her blouse.

'It's right,' she said softly. She laid her palms on either side of his face and drew his mouth to hers.

Peggy woke in David's bed, wrapped in his arms, the duvet tangled around them. Outside it was still dark. She didn't know what time it was, but she felt no panic at being somewhere different – only a sense of rightness at being beside him, a feeling she could honestly say she'd never felt before.

He was sleeping deeply and as her eyes adjusted to the darkness she could make out his profile against the pale colour of his sheets. She had been to bed with other men, but she realized now that with them it had just been sex. Sometimes wonderful sex, she knew, but it had been purely mechanical. Bodies merging in mutual need, and when the lust was slaked, both parties had been happy to go their own way.

But this . . .

Peggy closed her eyes again and snuggled against David's warm body. In sleep, he shifted so that he was wrapped more closely around her and she relaxed into the sensation. They hadn't had sex, they'd made love. There had been lust *and* tenderness, true closeness, and now that she'd experienced it, Peggy knew the difference. If she stayed with David, she could have this. She could come home and lie in his arms at night: loved and sated. She could tell him about her day and he'd touch her face gently, and be glad or sad for her, depending on the circumstances. He would be her support in all things and Peggy, who'd had no experience of such a thing in her entire life, began to cry silently at the thought of what had to be done.

She hadn't told him about her background, for all that he'd asked her. She hadn't told anyone.

He'd asked her to lunch with his parents, but there was no way Peggy could go, she knew that. She should never have slept with David. She should never have gone out with him. Right at the beginning, she'd known that he was different from all the other men she'd been with. He was a good man. And she was . . .

Well, she wasn't able for that sort of relationship. He *would* want two-point-five kids and the white picket fence, and Peggy couldn't do that. She didn't know *how*. She would mess it all up because you did what you'd grown up with, right?

Silently, she slid out of the bed and picked up her discarded clothes. She dressed in the bathroom, then tiptoed quietly downstairs. David's wallet and keys were on the coffee table. She'd leave a note there, better to do that than go back upstairs with it and risk him being awake. She found a scrap of paper and a pen, and wrote:

David, I'm sorry but I can't go out with you any more. You are a lovely guy and you deserve to be happy. Just not with me. It would be easier for us both if you don't contact me. Please don't come to the shop.
No hard feelings,
Peggy

She slipped the note into his wallet, so he'd find it easily, then left. It was the right thing to do.

Her priority should be the shop, she told herself as she drove home in the yellow glow of the streetlights. She had no time for someone like David. There could be no place in her life for him. She knew that and it was easier to end things now, before it went horribly wrong, which it would. It was bound to. So why was she crying?

Chapter Three

Sitting at the scarred wooden desk in front of the small window of her eyrie on St Brigid's Terrace, Freya Bryne was smiling. She was reading an email from a sweet foreign gentleman – from Nairobi this time – who had a few million dollars to invest in her country and wanted her to assist him.

He was a prince, and due to problems in his country, and the fact that his father, the king, was under threat, he couldn't invest it himself. But she could help . . .

She really did have the worst spam filter on the planet, Freya decided. No matter what she did, genuine emails ended up in her junk box and funny ones from people pretending to be investors or proclaiming that she'd won a lottery and all that was needed were her bank details and passport number, were forever popping into her inbox. She started to type a reply:

> OMG, I can't believe I'm writing to a real prince!!!! Mom is going to be, like, aced out! You have no idea how good a time this would be for us to have friends in new places – and a prince! Wow, as we say in Headache Drive. Mom hasn't had a proper holiday since that incident with the

airline company. She needed two seats and we thought that had been made plain from the start but no, she only got one and that sweet guy beside her – well, the feeling did come back into his arms a day later but it was very stressful for all concerned. Now, obviously, we have to visit before we work on this million-dollar deal – again, what LUCK! Mom has maxed out her credit card trying to buy the scratch card with the £25 million ticket and she needs a holiday. If you can get a hold of the royal plane, that would be perfect. Just remember: NO SUGAR ON BOARD. She might get her hands on some and . . . well, the less said about that time in the chocolate shop the better. We settled out of court, which was good for all concerned. But she is very partial to that South African creamy drink. Four bottles ought to cover it. We can stay in a nice hotel if you have recommendations, but from a financial point of view, do you have spare rooms in the palace? And any brothers? Mom is worried about marrying again but I read her tarot cards for her online today and by an AMAZING COINCIDENCE, it said she'd meet someone new . . .

'Freya, lovie, it's nearly eight,' yelled her aunt Opal from downstairs. 'I have scrambled eggs on . . .'

Opal's voice trailed off. She was always trying to stuff Freya with protein in the mornings, while Freya was more of a coffee and a sliver of toast kind of person.

Poor Opal didn't understand. Apparently, at breakfast every morning the three boys had wolfed down food as if they hadn't eaten for a week and now she felt that this was the correct way to feed Freya.

Desperate as she was not to hurt her aunt's feelings, the thought of an egg in the morning turned Freya's stomach.

She finished her email with a quick:

Reply soonest. We'll start packing. Mom does tend to overpack but I am assuming this won't be a problem on the royal plane, right? Hugs,

Cathleen Ni Houlihan

Freya grinned as she clicked *send*.

If only she could fly through the Internet like her email and perch on the computer of the man receiving it, to see his astonished face as he read it.

Just outside her window, she could see the blossom on the apple tree in the postage-stamp garden below. Behind the fence her uncle Ned had painted pale green the summer before, the council had started turning a scrap of deserted land into a proper park. The adjacent allotments would stay the way they were, despite the plans for the park, which was wonderful. Uncle Ned would have died if he couldn't go to his allotment every day. She could see some of the plain but sturdy sheds from the window and the neatly planted allotments themselves. Ned grew tomatoes, strawberries, potatoes and all manner of salad greens on his. In the distance Freya could make out the spires and towers of the city, but it seemed a long way away, giving the sense that Redstone was out in the country instead of being part of town.

All in all, Freya felt that the view from the third-floor bedroom of the narrow house more than made up for the tininess of the room.

'You're sure it's not too small?' Aunt Opal had said anxiously four years ago when Freya had come to live with them. 'Meredith wouldn't have this room – she said it was a spiders' paradise up here in the attic. Mind you, Steve was happy enough in here.'

'I love it,' Freya had replied. She wasn't in the slightest bit scared of spiders for she had spent years taking them gently out of the bath for her mother and releasing them back into the wild. Now the bedroom had a DIY bookcase on one wall, and Freya's own artwork on another. She'd painted the old wardrobe so it looked like part of Opal and Ned's colourful garden down below, although Opal didn't have any enquiring and abnormally large caterpillars on her flowers, or indeed, a Venus fly trap with a shy smile.

Freya checked her watch. Eight o'clock. Time to grab some toast and leave for school.

She clicked off her inbox, unplugged her phone and picked up her schoolbag. This rucksack contained her life, although it hardly looked the part: a greying canvas thing inherited from her cousin David, she'd decorated it with butterflies interspersed with gothic, dangerous-looking faerie creatures, all painstakingly coloured in – often in lessons – with felt-tip pens. She skimmed down the narrow stairs, light on her feet, racing past the second floor where her cousins' old bedrooms were. Opal and Ned's bedroom was the biggest, but it was still small compared to Freya's old home. Not that she cared. Twenty-one St Brigid's Terrace might be cramped and shabby, but the difference was that in this home she felt loved. Beloved. Something she hadn't felt for a long time with Mum.

Opal was standing at the cooker in the kitchen that she, Ned and Freya had painted Florida sunshine yellow last Christmas.

'Too bright?' Opal had said doubtfully in the paint shop, as the three of them had looked at the colour chart.

Freya hated to see even the faintest hint of worry in her darling Opal's face.

'No such thing!' she reassured her with a hug. 'Yellow makes people happy, you know.'

And Opal, who would have done anything to make Freya happy, was satisfied.

The tiles on the kitchen splashback were a riot of citrus fruits far too fat to be normal and Opal herself had run up a pair of yellow gingham curtains on her old sewing machine.

'Freya, love, good morning,' said Opal now, her face creasing up in a smile as her niece flew into the kitchen. A small, plump woman with a cloud of silvery, highlighted hair, Opal had one of those faces that made everyone want to smile back at her. It didn't matter that, as she neared sixty, her face was wreathed in wrinkles or that she didn't walk as fast as she used to because of her arthritis. She was still the same Opal.

Freya had long since decided that her aunt was one of life's golden people: someone from whom goodness shone like light from a storm lantern on a dark night. Someone who brought the best out in everyone.

'Morning, Opal,' Freya said and bent over to give her aunt a kiss on the cheek.

Freya wasn't tall herself but Opal was really tiny.

Foxglove the cat, a black-and-white scrap that Freya had rescued near the allotments two years ago, sat on the radiator licking her paws. Freya gave her a quick stroke, which Foxglove ignored as usual.

Almost instantly Opal began to fret about Freya's breakfast. It was a routine that the two of them played out every morning.

'Look, pet, it's after eight and you have to get going. You haven't had a bite to eat or a drink of water, nothing. Honestly, I can't let you out the door like this. You know they say that young people have to have a proper breakfast in them before they can study. Now I was doing eggs for your Uncle Ned and I can easily pop in a bit of toast and give you some . . .'

Opal went back to the cooker where she was stirring an ancient saucepan with a wooden spoon. Opal's scrambled eggs were better than anyone else's, fluffy clouds glistening with butter. But Freya had neither the time nor the appetite this morning.

'Sorry, Opal,' she said, popping a piece of toast out of the toaster, grabbing a knife from the drawer and spreading a hint of butter on it. She took a few bites and set it down on

69

the table without a plate while she filled her water bottle from the tap, then reached into the fridge and snagged the lunchbox she'd packed the night before, stuffing it into her duffel bag. Finally she picked up the toast again. 'Have to go, Opal, can't be late.'

Opal sighed the way she did pretty much every morning.

'Pet, I don't feel I'm doing my job if you're not eating properly,' she began. 'Your four cousins never left the house without their breakfast – and that includes Meredith and I have to say she was fussy about her food. But the boys . . .'

Freya gave her aunt a quick hug to stem the tide of how Steve, David and Brian could vacuum up meals at Olympian speeds.

'Have to go, Aunt Opal. I know, the boys ate everything you put in front of them and still do. Don't worry, I won't starve. I made lunch last night. I've got to race in.'

'Don't forget to brush your hair, pet,' Opal called after her niece.

As she swung out of the kitchen, Freya caught a quick glance of herself in the old mirror in the narrow hall. Dark eyes and the same long slim nose as her mother. Wild dark hair that reached to her shoulders and probably would have hung halfway down her back if it had ever gone straight in its life. She ran her fingers through it quickly. Brushing only made it worse. The top button of her shirt was open and the knot of her tie was too low. Someone in school would give out to her about it, but she'd deal with that when she got there. Freya didn't worry too much about being given out to. There were certain people in life who felt their day was lacking something if they hadn't remonstrated with at least four people. The vice-principal, Mr McArthur, who hovered perpetually just inside the main door of the school, was one of them. Freya was used to it now. She didn't mind. Words didn't really matter. Actions were what counted. And people like Opal.

'See you this evening, Opal. This is my late day at school, don't forget,' she roared as she shut the door behind her.

The house was bang in the middle of a terrace of tall, skinny red-brick homes and to make up for the postage-stamp-sized patch of garden at the back, there was quite a sliver of front garden.

Opal had worked her magic there too. Pink was her favourite colour.

'I've loved pink ever since I was a girl,' Opal admitted bashfully to Freya when she'd moved in.

It had been summer then and despite how shell-shocked Freya had felt after the six months that had followed her father's death, she'd noticed that her aunt's garden was a riot of every shade of pink. From the palest roses tinged with sun-blush to outrageous gladioli with their vivid crimson flowers. There was no grass, only a scatter of gravel amongst which grew a selection of herbs and alpines. There were a few varieties of sedum here and there, busily colonizing entire areas, creeping towards the roses like marauding drunks at a party. The rose bushes were Opal's pride and joy. This early in the year there were only tiny green shoots on the stems. During the winter months the colour in the garden came from the many varieties of shrubs that Opal and Ned had collected over the years. There were laurels, glamorous plants with dark green glossy leaves and heathers with golden fronds. When the boys had lived at home, Opal told her, they'd been heavily involved in the garden. Freya was pretty sure this wasn't because they loved gardening but because they loved their mum. When she said, 'Will someone go out and take the weeds from between the gravel,' the boys would groan good-naturedly and do it. Now of course they lived two streets away in a three-bedroom rented townhouse that couldn't hope to contain all their mess. Opal would go over once a week and get them to tidy it up and Freya kept trying to persuade her that this was a terrible mistake.

71

'Aunt Opal,' she would say (Freya only called Opal *Aunt* when she was remonstrating with her), 'Aunt Opal, you are not doing the boys any favours. They need to learn to organize themselves. How else will they develop into clever wonderful men who will make marvellous husbands?'

'Well, Brian's going to make a marvellous husband already,' Opal would insist. Brian was getting married at Easter to Elizabeth, a primary school teacher. 'And you know what Steve's like, God love him. He's hopeless with the washing machine.' Given that Steve was a computer programmer, Freya felt this was a particularly feeble excuse.

David was the most dutiful when it came to tidying up. The sensible, soft-hearted and handsome one who had inherited the best qualities of both his parents, David knew how to use the vacuum cleaner, knew that the same dishcloth could not be used for three weeks running and understood that toilets occasionally needed to have bleach poured down them. Freya couldn't help smiling when she thought of David. Her best friend, Kaz, had a long-range crush on David because he reminded her of the guy who played the lead in *Australia*, and would go puce whenever David said hello to her.

'He is *so* like Hugh Jackman, I wish he'd notice me,' Kaz would wail.

'You are many years too young for him, that's why he doesn't notice you,' Freya would explain. 'It would be like a first year fancying you.'

'Eurgh,' Kaz said. 'Point taken.'

With a last fond glance back at the house with its shining turquoise front door, Freya swung out the gate. Ned had put his foot down when it came to painting the exterior woodwork. 'I had to,' he'd told Freya. 'I mean, the whole place would be pink if I'd let her. Imagine the lads . . .' His voice had trailed off into a shudder at the thought of his three big strong sons coming home to a pink palace. 'At least turquoise can be sort of manly.'

72

Thanks to Opal, Freya knew everyone on the street. On one side was Molly, who liked to drop in every day on the hunt for sugar, a drop of milk, or the newspaper, because there was a nice article she'd heard about and wanted to read. Aunt Opal always said that if a day went past when Molly didn't drop in for something, the world wouldn't feel right.

On the other side was shy, sixty-something Luke, a widower who had vowed he would never remarry after his beloved wife had died.

'Not that it stops some of the ladies on the road from dropping in with cakes and pies and things,' Opal would say. 'Poor Luke, he really does want to be on his own.'

'Why don't all the women realize that?' asked Freya.

'Some women think it's unnatural for a man to live by himself,' Opal said sagely. 'They're waiting for him to see he needs someone else. He's such a dear, they're all determined to be the one.'

Next to the beleaguered Luke's house lived the Hiltons, a young couple who had managed to produce four small children in three years. Their garden – unlike Luke's, which was tended by his lady admirers – was a disaster zone of overturned trikes, weeds taller than the children and a dead tree in a pot outside the front door where Annie Hilton had desperately tried to inject some beauty into the front of the house only to forget to water the damn thing. Freya had babysat the children a couple of times and she could understand why the tree was dead. Watering a tree had to come very far down Annie Hilton's list of daily chores.

The terrace curved as it got towards the main road and Freya looked in, as she always did, at the house where Meredith's one-time best friend Grainne lived. Meredith was the only one of the cousins Freya didn't see regularly. In fact, Meredith was something of a mystery to her. And Freya didn't care for mysteries.

Meredith was the eldest; she'd moved away from Redstone

as soon as she left school, and hardly ever returned. Oh, she'd show up for a big event like Uncle Ned's sixtieth birthday party, but Freya couldn't quite get a handle on Meredith. She seemed to have distanced herself from her family and Freya, who adored Opal and Ned and her three cousins, simply couldn't understand it. Why would anyone blessed with such a wonderful family turn their back on it?

And the Byrnes weren't the only people that Meredith had turned her back on. Since her divorce, Grainne was back living at home with her parents, along with Teagan, her sweet four-year-old daughter. Freya always said hello to Grainne and Teagan if she bumped into them on her way home from school. Although she was thirty-something, the same age as Meredith, Grainne looked about seventeen. She was always smiling as she walked down the road holding the back of Teagan's pink bike as the child wobbled along on her stabilizers.

'Any news of Meredith?' she might ask occasionally, and Freya would fill her in on the latest details.

'The gallery's going very well, apparently. It's the Alexander *Byrne* Gallery now – there was a big write-up in the paper about it.'

Freya didn't let on that Opal had proudly cut out the clipping from the paper and put it in the scrapbook she kept about Meredith. Nor did she say that Meredith hadn't rung to tell her mother of this great event, which implied that she was now a full partner in the business. No, Opal and Ned and the boys had had to read about it in the paper. 'She was asking after you,' Freya would lie. And every time she said it she'd wondered why, because what was the point of lying about it?

Meredith never asked about anyone. Her phone calls were brief, as if she only rang home out of a sense of duty. On the rare occasions she visited, she never asked about anyone in Redstone. It was as if, in leaving home, she'd somehow distanced herself from the place totally – and that included her old school friends. Still, it was worth the lie, Freya decided, just to see the smile on Grainne's face.

'Send her my love back, will you, and tell her we must meet up next time she's in town. Explain I don't get out to cool events like her gallery openings,' Grainne would add. 'Not with this little bunny here—' And with that she'd grin down at Teagan, who'd dimple back at her.

Freya wondered yet again what had happened to Meredith to make her walk away. Although her cousin was perfectly friendly on the rare occasions they met, it was obvious that something had changed her. One day Freya was going to figure out what it was.

Freya's ten-minute trip to school took her past the crossroads, and if she had the money for a takeaway coffee she'd stop at the Internet café, where cool-looking guys sometimes hung out. Freya noticed everything. She liked Bobbi's beauty and hair salon, too. Bobbi was Opal's best friend, going back years. Outwardly, she was the complete opposite of Freya's aunt, in that she looked as tough as old boots, but under the patina of foundation, platinum hair and the killer glare was a woman with a heart of gold.

Deciding that she was too late for coffee today, Freya crossed over at the lights, walking past the new lavender-painted shop where the old off-licence had been.

The new shop was as different from Maguire's Fine Liquors as it was possible to get. Maguire's used to look as though it had been dipped in a combination of nicotine and scotch, and the smell of both swirled around it. The lavender of the new place looked fresh and beautiful; Freya imagined that when the shop finally opened for business it would smell of a combination of fragrant French roses and wild lavender. A cast-iron sign with swirly writing hung at ninety degrees to the shop over the glass door and the name was painted in the same writing above the large front window: *Peggy's Busy Bee Knitting and Stitching Shop*.

Freya peered in and saw a young woman in workman's overalls up a ladder, diligently painting the ceiling. Decorating was clearly not her profession because her rich brown ponytail was splattered with white paint.

As if she sensed someone watching her, the woman turned, saw Freya, and smiled at her.

Freya smiled back and toyed with the idea of going in and chatting, but she'd be late. She lengthened her stride, ran her fingers along the peeling bark of the oldest sycamore, and turned down the alleyway that was her shortcut to school. Out of the alleyway and across the road, she joined the heaving throng moving slowly towards the school building, blending in immediately: just one more small, dark-haired fifteen-year-old girl in clumpy shoes and an ill-fitting school uniform.

Chapter Four

The wedding invitation felt as if it was burning a hole in Opal Byrne's handbag. It was the gold envelope that was part of the problem. Gold envelopes, rather. The sight of so many of them on the mat that morning had given her quite a shock, and she'd hastily gathered them up without a word to either Ned or Freya. There were the usual bills (brown envelopes), fliers (white envelopes), something tax-related (a brown, evil-looking envelope) for Brian and there, in the middle, like a bit of false fairy glitter come to St Brigid's Terrace, the five gold envelopes.

Noel and Miranda Flanagan invited Opal and Edward Byrne to the wedding of their beloved daughter, Elizabeth, to Brian Byrne in the Church of the Holy Redeemer, Blackfields, Co Cork, and afterwards to a dinner in the Rathlin Golf and Country Club.

Opal's mind had gone blank then. There was one for her and Ned – why hadn't they called him Ned? Nobody called him Edward – except for his mother and she was dead, God rest her, and had never so much as set eyes on Liz's parents. Another one for Freya and guest, although that was asking for trouble because Freya would do her best to find the least country-club-looking one of her friends and pitch up with him just for pure devilment. Freya had a hate/hate thing going on with Liz's mother, and the wedding would be the perfect opportunity to up the ante.

And there was one each for David, Steve and Meredith plus guests, which Opal felt was for some reason an insult to Meredith and the boys, but she couldn't quite put her finger on why yet.

Meredith had a flat – sorry, apartment – in the city with panoramic views, curtains that closed if you pushed a button and a sports car that had no room for groceries in the boot, not that Meredith was likely to venture into a supermarket. Miranda could have asked Brian for the address and posted the invitation to Meredith's apartment but she hadn't. She knew David and Steve's address because it was the same as Brian's. But no, she'd sent them all to St Brigid's Terrace, which was the same as saying 'You're all from the wrong side of town, no matter how posh Meredith's address is these days.'

That was it. That was the insult. Opal fumed quietly as she walked towards the shops.

Redstone was a suburb that had only recently been deemed 'up and coming' after years of being considered 'the wrong side of town'. Opal had been raised half a mile from here and recalled how everyone had looked down on Redstone in those days. It was the place where men with 'bad backs' avoided earning a living and instead spent working hours listening to the radio in the bookies. The houses were lined up in terraces and women stood chatting over the fence as they hung the washing out.

That was how it was between her and Molly next door. As soon as she saw Opal out at the line with her laundry basket, Molly would come out with a cup of tea for her and they would talk.

Now that Ned had taken early retirement from the bus depot, he might come out to do a bit of pottering in the garden and Molly would make him tea, too.

Not everyone was as lucky with their neighbours, Opal knew.

St Brigid's Terrace had changed a lot over the years. During the boom, property prices had gone up wildly on the terrace and in Redstone in general. Several new housing estates had been built on the fields beside the old lightbulb factory, which had been turned into an apartment complex with electric gates. And the crossroads in the centre of Redstone no longer boasted four pubs, two chippers and a bookie's. Instead, there was her friend Bobbi's beauty salon, a delicatessen, the bakery, a mini-market that sold expensive ready-meals, two cafés, a bank, a boutique that sold outrageously priced clothes, and the wool and craft supplies shop that was due to open soon. Opal was thrilled about that because she loved knitting.

Opal's mother wouldn't have recognized the place. She wouldn't have recognized Opal either, now that she had highlights in her hair every few months.

Freya had made her do that.

'Aunt Opal, I can see bits of grey. It's not a good look,' Freya had said kindly the year before.

It was funny, Opal thought, that after raising three sons and one daughter, it was the niece she'd taken into her home who was lighting her life up now that she was within striking distance of sixty.

Freya brought her home the first daffodils of February; it wouldn't have occurred to the boys to do such a thing. Freya was the one who noticed when Opal's ankles were swollen on Sundays and made whoever was over for Sunday lunch pitch in and help out so their mother could sit down.

Meredith would have noticed too, Opal thought loyally, but she was always too busy to drop in to see them at weekends. The boys were different. They liked a good feed on a Sunday. She invited Meredith to these lunches but Meredith rarely came. When she did, she barely ate. She was so slim that Opal worried her daughter wasn't eating properly.

Opal was quite sure that cooking wasn't Meredith's strong point. She'd refused to do Home Economics in school. Even back then, her mind had been set on loftier things. Whenever she thought about Meredith, Opal felt a sense of failure. They didn't have mother-and-daughter days out the way some of her friends did. Meredith had never suggested they go away for a weekend to one of those spa places, though she knew Meredith liked those stone treatments and suchlike. Opal had never been herself and, to be honest, she wouldn't have cared for it. But she'd have gone if Meredith asked her. Except Meredith didn't ask.

Opal grinned as she thought of her niece. Freya was a different kettle of fish altogether. She probably knew how to do all sorts of mud baths at home herself. There was nothing Freya didn't know. Opal thought of herself at fifteen and what a naive, bewildered young thing she'd been. And look at Freya, clever as anything and kind with it. Lord, she'd better not show the wedding invitations to Freya. Freya would instantly understand the insulting code behind Miranda's addressing of the envelopes. She'd probably phone Miranda and say something. Above all else, Opal hated people *saying* things.

By now, she was nearing the crossroads. She walked past the bus stop with a nod and a brief 'hello' to the two old fellas sitting there, Seanie and Ronnie. They were always sitting there. Freya joked that they never actually got a bus anywhere. They just liked to watch the workings of the village carry on around them, smoking Woodbines and commenting on life, the universe and everything.

'Grand day, isn't it, Opal?' said Ronnie. 'Aren't we blessed with the fine weather?'

'We are indeed,' agreed Opal.

'And isn't it a lovely day to be sitting here taking it all in?' said Seanie happily, with an expansive wave of his hand as though sitting on a seat at a bus stop at the side of the road in a small suburb outside Cork was on a par with sitting on a private jet and flying off somewhere fabulous for the day. The height of excitement and all a person could ask for. Freya thought the two of them were wonderful and quite often she squashed in between them for a chat.

Opal suspected she took the odd Woodbine too and smoked it, although she'd yet to catch her at it. That was the thing with Freya: you never caught her doing anything bad. Perhaps she'd trained the men to grab the cigarette out of her hand as soon as any of her family came into view. Opal had tried sniffing Freya's clothes for the telltale smell, but Ned smoked five cigarettes a day, and even though he did it outside the back door, that confused matters. Besides, once Freya set her mind to do something, she just did it.

Opal passed the bakery and waved to Sue in the window, whom she could see arranging a big batch of bread on the shelves. Opal loved the bread in the shop, especially all of the different fancy ones with olives and rosemary in them. There hadn't been anything like that when she was a kid. But it was expensive. She walked on by and went into the dry cleaner's. Moyra was sitting there as usual, head in a book. She looked up with a smile when Opal came to the counter to hand over her things – a bag that included a pair of good navy trousers belonging to Brian. She'd had to smuggle them out of the house without Freya seeing, because there'd have been war if Freya spotted the contents of the bag.

'Aunt Opal, what are you doing, taking Brian's things to the dry cleaner's?' Freya would have demanded. 'He's well able to do it himself. And if he can't for some mad reason, there's always Liz. Doesn't she have hands, legs and a car? What's wrong with her?' Freya liked Liz, though she didn't think it was right the way she let Miranda get away with being rude to Brian's family. Since the organization of the wedding had begun to gather pace, it was getting harder for Freya to hide her dislike of Brian's future mother-in-law.

Opal had also brought a couple of ties belonging to Ned and a jacket that Steve had somehow managed to get curry sauce on. Lord knows, that was never going to come out, but Moyra said she'd do her best.

After the dry cleaner's, Opal got the paper and some milk in the corner store. Then she crossed the road to the gleaming peony pink and chocolate façade of Bobbi's Beauty Salon. She hadn't planned to drop in, but she wanted to share her upset over the gold envelopes with someone who'd put it all in perspective. If anyone could do that, it was Bobbi.

She and Bobbi had been friends since they were four-year-olds in pigtails, shocked by the harsh world of junior infants – or 'low babies' as they used to call it in those days. Fifty-five years had flown by since then. Bobbi had built up her empire to the beautiful salon she now ran with her daughter, Shari.

'It's not an empire, Opal,' Bobbi would say fondly and yet proudly whenever Opal used the term.

''Course it's an empire,' Opal would respond on the rare occasions when she went in to have something done. 'Look at it, it's beautiful.'

And it was. Lovingly decorated by Shari's husband, the salon was a haven of loveliness.

Bobbi's husband Richard hadn't turned out to be as solid as Opal's Ned. He'd run off with one of the junior stylists many years ago. But Bobbi hadn't flinched, she'd held her head high. A small woman, like Opal, there was steel behind the platinum curls that framed her face.

'He's not getting a ha'penny out of this business,' Bobbi had insisted – and he hadn't.

Richard still turned up from time to time, normally to borrow money, and occasionally, Bobbi lent him some.

'He *is* Shari's father, after all,' was all she'd say.

Today, Bobbi was at the front desk with her glasses on, scanning the appointment book when Opal walked in.

82

'Hello!' said Bobbi, looking up delightedly. Then, with a canny look at her friend's face, she added: 'What's up?'

Bobbi could read Opal's face like a map.

'Well . . .' began Opal.

'Come through.' Bobbi abandoned the appointment book. 'Let's have tea. You can tell me what's happening in private. Caroline,' she called to a stylist, 'take over the desk.'

The back room was decorated in the same pretty pink brocade wallpaper as the rest of the salon. Bobbi had seen the inside of too many places where the staffroom looked as if the owner didn't care about where the workers had to sit for their breaks.

'Let's make it pretty,' she'd said. 'I want the staff to see how important they are to the business.'

Three years previously, when the salon had last been redecorated, the staffroom had undergone a complete transformation too. There was a big couch in one corner. One of the young beauty therapists was sitting there now, muttering on the phone in a language Opal didn't understand.

'Right, pet, how are you?' Bobbi went straight to the kettle while Opal put down her handbag and sank into one of the chairs at the table. 'Didn't think I'd see you today. What's happened?'

Opal found the gold envelopes in her handbag and handed them over.

'This is what's wrong,' she said. 'I don't know, I just have a bad feeling about the wedding. Not about Liz – she's a lovely girl, no question of that – but the wedding itself . . .' Opal sighed. 'I'm not sure I'm able for it. Miranda's making it into such a production that you'd swear nobody ever got married before. We had "hold-the-date" cards in December, then there was weeks of discussion about bridesmaids. According to Brian, Miranda flew herself and Liz to London for their dresses – I haven't even looked for one, and the wedding's just round the corner. Now this. Gold envelopes that cost a fortune.'

Bobbi placed a cup of steaming tea in front of her friend and passed her the milk and sugar. 'We're down to custard creams,' she said, handing over the packet of biscuits. 'The chocolate ones have all run out. There was a bit of a crisis early on this morning.'

She looked in the direction of the distressed girl on the phone.

'Boyfriend trouble.'

Bobbi always knew what was going on in her staff's lives. She lowered her voice so the girl on the phone in the corner couldn't hear. 'Poor Magda, she's been going out with this dreadful, dreadful lout who treats her like muck. She gave him the boot yesterday and this morning she's in floods of tears because he turned up outside the flat last night roaring drunk and yelling, "Take me back, I promise I'll change."'

'Oh no,' said Opal, feeling the girl's pain as if it were her own.

All her life, people had told Opal to stop being so sensitive to everyone else's problems. Freya was the only one who said: 'Opal, stay exactly as you are – it's what makes you so special.'

'Here I am complaining about a silly wedding and that poor thing's miles away from home—'

'Now, Opal, there's nothing you can do for Magda. I had a pot of tea with her. I opened the chocolate biscuits and I told her what her mother would tell her if she was here instead of in the Czech Republic: that man will bring her nothing but trouble. But despite all of that, she's on the phone to him now. Going back to him. You can only tell a girl so much. I don't know why the loveliest girls always find the worst men, but they do. Anyway, between the jigs and the reels, the chocolate biscuits went. The custard creams aren't bad, though.'

Bobbi sat down with her own tea, took a bite of biscuit then set it aside to examine the gold envelopes. 'Oh hello,' she said, examining the copperplate writing on the front.

'These must have cost a bob or two. Clearly they're not skimping on anything.'

'They have the money,' Opal said.

'Just because you have the money doesn't mean you have to let everyone *know* you have the money.' Bobbi's tone was scathing.

She looked at the third envelope and got it in an instant. 'Even Meredith's one is addressed to your house,' she said. She kept flicking. 'And David's and Steve's. That was a low blow.'

'I thought so too,' said Opal. 'It's as if—'

'—as if she's saying, *You lot are common, low-class muck and all of you come from the wrong end of the city.* I get it,' said Bobbi grimly.

'I shouldn't let it upset me so much,' Opal went on, 'but it did. I thought I'd come down and tell you and you'd make me feel better. Because I'm so angry and it's wrong to be like that. If you're angry, you put anger out into the universe . . .'

Bobbi reached out and held her friend's hand. 'Pet, I'd say the Dalai Lama would feel the urge to slap Miranda's smug face if he spent any time with her, so stop feeling guilty about it. Concentrate on how wonderful it is that Brian's getting married. Once he's done it, they'll all be marrying. Think of how often you worry about the three of them and why they haven't settled down.'

Bobbi deliberately didn't mention Meredith here. If there was any sign of Meredith settling down, they knew nothing about it and Bobbi was aware just how hurt Opal was to be cut so efficiently out of her daughter's life.

She went on: 'Liz is a wonderful girl and she and Brian adore each other. But you have to face up to the fact that her mother is a complete cow – there's no point in beating around the bush here. Nothing ever pleased that woman in her life and you can bet she won't be happy till she's upset someone about this wedding. Let's just decide here and now that it won't be you or Ned, right?'

Opal nodded.

'We'll get your dress sorted and make you look a million dollars. I'll be looking a million dollars too. We'll show Madam Miranda that we might not have been born with silver spoons in our mouths but we know how to enjoy a day out.'

'Yes,' said Opal, 'that's what we'll do. It'll be a great day, and then life will go back to normal.'

'Not quite normal,' Bobbi pointed out. 'She is going to be your fellow granny, remember that. As soon as Brian and Liz start having children, the granny wars will be under way, you versus her. And, let's face it, the girl's mother gets the most time with the grandchildren.'

Opal's sweet face fell again.

'I shouldn't have said that,' Bobbi muttered. 'It'll be fine. Do you think Meredith will come to the wedding?' she asked, desperate to change the subject.

'Heavens, I don't know. I was talking to her a couple of weeks ago and she sounded very busy, you know, going to art fairs and things like that.'

'Hmmm,' said Bobbi meaningfully. 'With all the travel she does, you'd think she'd make it down this way once in a while.'

'I know,' said Opal. 'But she's a successful woman, she's got her own life.'

It was a well-worn subject and Bobbi had learned to leave it be or risk upsetting Opal.

'Anyway,' she went on, 'when are we going shopping for your dress? We'll have a brilliant day, you and I. I'm really looking forward to it.'

'Me too,' said Opal.

Of course, Meredith wouldn't be joining them on the big adventure to buy Opal a suitable mother-of-the-groom dress. That hurt, but Opal didn't let on. She wouldn't hear a word said against Meredith.

'I tell you what,' said Bobbi, who could tell all this as plainly as if it were written on Opal's face, 'we've a spare appointment this morning. Will we give your hair a wash and blow-dry? Cheer you up? Always works with me,' she said, patting her own curls, brightened with a lustrous dose of platinum once a month. 'On me, naturally.'

Usually Opal said no to these offers, but today she thought how good it would feel to lean back and have somebody gently massage shampoo into her hair, letting all her cares and worries drift down the sink with the suds. 'All right,' she said. 'Thank you, I'd love that.'

'Great,' said Bobbi. 'Let's get you started. You're not to worry about the wedding.' Behind her back, Bobbi crossed her fingers. 'It'll all be fine. At least Brian and Liz are right for each other.'

They glanced at the red-eyed girl sitting on the sofa, still talking earnestly on the phone.

Chapter Five

When she got to Singapore, Lillie emailed Doris. She tried phoning first and left a message on her friend's cell phone because Doris didn't pick up. Lillie had felt terribly lonely on the flight from Melbourne to Singapore and now she was there with three hours to hang around, she felt like a lost soul walking around the airport. She kept seeing couples everywhere, people the same age as her and Sam enjoying themselves. The plane had been full of them, laughing happy people flying all over the world together and she was there alone feeling herself growing smaller and tighter like a little gnarled nut.

And so she found a seat and typed out an email:

Hi Doris

I'm glad we had those silver surfer lessons at the library, at least I can use this thing. You're only about my fifth email ever. Just thought I'd drop you a line . . . that sounds wrong, doesn't it? That's what we used to say with letters. I decided to say hello because I'm in Singapore airport on my own. It's very lonely and I'm sorry I'm here. I'm sorry I came, sorry, sorry, sorry. I know Martin and Evan mean well and everything but I'd be better staying at home. Travelling alone is a very sad thing. Sorry to be dropping all this on your head, Doris, but you did say I could.

    Love,

    Lillie

The second part of the flight wasn't as bad, partly because she was so exhausted trying to get comfortable in the upright seat that she actually fell asleep for a while.

The boys had wanted to upgrade her to business class.

'Mum, you're sixty-four, you need to stretch your legs out. You could get DVT,' said Evan, but Lillie wouldn't hear of it.

'No,' she said, 'it's a ridiculous amount of money. I'll go the way we—' She stopped herself. 'I'll go the way your father and I always went: economy.'

She'd have liked one of those business-class beds now, but at least she was on the outside of a row, so she could get up and walk around the plane between her intermittent periods of dozing. It had grown quieter, more peaceful, once the food had been served, the lights had been dimmed and people began to fall asleep. The stewards and stewardesses were finally sitting down, taking their break. With most of the plane quiet, she didn't feel quite so alone as she stood outside the bathroom waiting her turn, stretching her legs and wriggling her ankles the way the video they showed had told her to do.

Inside her head, Lillie found herself talking to Sam again.

I hope this is a good idea, Sam, she told him. *You've got to look after me. Please, my love, I need you. I wish that you were a presence beside me. I wish I was a psychic so I could feel that you're there instead of this nothingness: that's what scares me. You'd have told me to do this. You'd have told me to go and see Seth and Frankie, meet the family. You'd have loved it, you'd have come too and it would have been so different. The fun we'd have had. We might have stayed over in Singapore for a couple of nights in a posh hotel, done the tour. I don't want to upset you. You wanted me to be OK and I said I would be. I told you to go. But it's so hard without you . . .*

The toilet door clicked open in front of her and somebody stumbled out. Lillie didn't really want to go to the loo but she locked herself in anyway, put the lid of the toilet down and sat, just to be here on her own and cry. Was she mad, coming on this trip?

She coped at home because she was among the familiar things, among familiar people, but so many thousands of miles away from home, how could she not feel lost?

Worst of all, that niggling thought that she'd been deftly shoving to the back of her mind kept wriggling its way to the fore: what if she felt bitterness when she met Seth? What if all she could think of was that their mother hadn't given *him* up for adoption?

Lillie had never been a bitter person, but then, she'd had her beloved Sam. While he was alive, she'd had so much love in her life, that she was able to give love and kindness to other people.

'You're an earth mother,' Sam told her once, 'always finding lost souls to help and pulling them close.'

'Do I drive you mad with my schemes to help people?' she asked thoughtfully. Sam had never said anything like that before and she felt a hint of worry that he was tired of her endless good works. A colleague in the charity shop had once given her advice on balancing healing other people with taking care of her family: '*Lillie, you're one of life's givers. Mind that you don't neglect your own family. Much as they'll admire you for being a good person and helping others, they still want to know that they come first. They'd rather have you home making dinner than out saving the world.*'

Lillie had tried always to bear that in mind, but when Sam told her she was an earth mother she wasn't sure whether this was a good or a bad thing in his eyes. So she'd asked him.

'No, chicken,' he said, smiling. 'I love you for it. You can't stop yourself: that's what you do. Why should I change you?'

In the cramped plane toilet, she dried her tears and hoped she was still the earth mother her husband had loved. She'd hate it if his death had changed that and she no longer had anything left to give.

Seth Green drove to the airport with so many thoughts and feelings crowding each other that he had to force himself to concentrate on the road ahead.

The whole business of finding out he had a sister had reawakened the huge sorrow at the loss of his wonderful, kind mother.

He'd always adored her. Even when other boys muttered in school about how their mothers drove them mad, and were always wittering on about wearing coats in cold weather and having a decent breakfast, Seth had never had a bad word to say about Jennifer. She was gentle and endlessly calm. He could picture her now with her strawberry-blonde hair framing that round, smiling face and those beautiful flower-blue eyes.

It was hard to believe that this loving woman had given up her first child and then carried that huge secret locked inside her the rest of her life. Of course, she'd given birth to Lillie a long time ago, a time when the past wasn't just another country, it was more in the line of another planet altogether. A planet where women did not give birth to children outside marriage and keep them. Such babies were symbols of shame to be bundled off as quickly as possible, regardless of the mother's feelings in the matter.

91

He'd often wondered how the young Jennifer McCabe had summoned up the courage to marry Daniel Green – a Jew, though admittedly non-religious, when her family were Catholic. That, too, must have been scandalous at the time. Perhaps in light of the 'sins' she'd committed according to the tenets of her own unforgiving Church and society, Jennifer had simply resolved to defy convention and marry the man she loved, irrespective of religion.

Seth pulled up at a set of traffic lights and checked the clock on the dashboard. He still had plenty of time.

The secrecy of it all was what had shocked him the most. He couldn't imagine his mother as a scared teenager because the woman he'd known had always been so strong. She'd dealt with many things through the years, even taking in his father's elderly aunt Ruth, a woman who'd never recovered from her years in a concentration camp. Ruth had somehow survived but a huge part of her spirit had been crushed. When she'd become old and frail, it had been Seth's mother who'd taken such care of her, understanding the nightmares and the fear that never left. Jennifer was the one who'd go in to comfort Ruth in the middle of the night, changing her night-gown, being gentle and kind, sitting with her until Ruth drifted into sleep.

His mother had also been a very honest, straight person: 'Be truthful, Seth,' she would tell him. 'Whatever it is you've done, always tell the truth.'

Yet she hadn't told him the truth – or rather, she'd avoided telling him the whole truth – about herself.

When the email arrived from Lillie's son, carefully worded, trying to find out information about his mother, Seth had been astonished. Frankie, of course, had been thrilled, fascinated and full of enthusiasm. It was the way his wife was.

'You've a long-lost half sister!' she'd said delightedly. 'How wonderful! Do you suppose your father knew? I doubt there was any way of knowing where the baby went or if there were any records linking her to your mother. It's an amazing thing to happen now though, isn't it, finding out?'

'I suppose so,' he said, although, as with so many things involving his wife, it was taking a little longer for the information to sink into his head than into hers.

Frankie responded to everything so readily, her quicksilver brain processing facts at high speed. His no longer seemed to work so fast – something that he suspected irritated her these days. Seth felt that these days, his very existence irritated his wife.

He knew their marriage was going through a bad stage – something that they'd never encountered before – but he felt too broken to attempt to fix it. All he could do was to let things take their course and hope that he and Frankie would come through it all.

And then the email had come with news of Lillie's existence.

Frankie had been so . . . well, Frankie-like about it.

'Lillie must come to stay. I know this place isn't great for guests, but we can fix up a room for her somewhere,' she'd said firmly.

It was only when Frankie began searching for the phone book, saying, 'What's the dialling code for Melbourne? We must ring this Martin now, and then get Lillie's number and phone her,' that Seth found his voice and said *Stop.*

He had a sister – 'half' didn't matter: she was his sister – and she'd been out there in the world all along when he thought he was an only child. He *thought* he was pleased, although it was all still being processed in his head, but he wanted to do things slowly, all the same. He needed time to get used to the idea.

'Her son emailed. He might get a shock if we just ring,' he said to Frankie. 'Plus, there's the time difference. We can't ring now. Let's email back.'

'Well, she obviously wants to get in touch or she wouldn't have agreed to her son doing this. It's only natural that she should want to meet you, that must be the whole point of it, that's what people do,' said Frankie eagerly. 'Who better to tell her about your mother? She's sure to have lots of questions. And aren't you curious to see her – find out what she's like, what she looks like? I can't wait to tell Emer and Alexei. They're going to be so excited – just think, a whole new branch of the family they never knew existed. I'll send them an email right away.'

'We should probably take it slowly,' Seth counselled. He worked out the dates. 'Lillie's sixty-four, ten years older than me.'

Frankie frowned slightly. He'd noticed that she didn't like hearing how old he was. She'd suddenly become touchy about anything to do with age. When her driving licence had come up for renewal the previous month she'd been tight-lipped as she filled in the form, attaching an admittedly not very flattering photo of herself.

'Bloody photo machines,' she'd said, staring at it crossly. 'Makes me look as if I'm about ninety and sitting on a stool of nails.'

'You're a mere sprite of forty-nine,' Seth had said, trying to cheer her up. 'Talking of which, we should organize something for your fiftieth next—'

'No!' Her shout startled them both. Recovering, she said lamely: 'Sorry. I just meant that we don't have the money, that's all. It's a lovely thought and all, darling. But no.'

So Seth added age to the list of things he and Frankie didn't discuss any more.

Age, the house, the state of the garden, and how it was no use him even trying to get a job, because who would want to employ him? *That* in particular drove her insane. She refused to accept that losing his job had transformed him from a man with a career to a man with nothing.

94

It was so enormous, so emasculating. Frankie simply didn't understand. The discovery of Lillie's existence was all the more wonderful, because at last they had something they could talk about.

When Lillie's son responded to their email by saying that his mother didn't do emails, and that a letter would be the best way to talk to her, Frankie had flung her hands up in despair.

'A letter,' she groaned. 'Nobody writes letters any more.'

'Lillie probably does,' said Seth, smiling. He wondered whether his sister's handwriting would resemble the curling, light hand of their mother, as though an angel had danced across the page. And then he realized that, without his mother to teach her, Lillie probably wouldn't write like that. Wasn't handwriting a product of environment?

'We'll ask her to stay,' Frankie went on. 'He doesn't mention whether other members of the family would be interested, but we should invite them too. We'll have them all,' said Frankie, as if this was the most obvious thing in the world.

'Let's start with Lillie,' Seth said firmly.

His wife had always been generous and enthusiastic. Frankie's glass wasn't just half-full, it was brimming – and she wanted to share it with everyone. It was what made her so good with people and so good at her job. Nobody could resist an HR boss like Frankie.

It didn't make her so easy to live with when you didn't have a job, though.

He knew she couldn't help contrasting his handling of the situation with the way she'd behave if her job was suddenly snatched out from under her. Frankie would go at it like a whirling dervish, turning everything upside down, tossing aside any obstacles that planted themselves in her path.

Her enthusiasm for Lillie's visit had swept aside Seth's

reservations. But now that the time had arrived, they were starting to creep back into his mind. After all, this wasn't a long-lost relative returning after a time away. This woman had never known her birth father and mother. She had been cast out of her homeland and sent to the other side of the world for adoption. What was she going to make of Seth, the child her mother had kept close?

Seth drove slowly into the airport car park, took the ticket from the machine and circled the floors of the multi-storey until he found a parking spot. He did everything slowly now. It was as if life itself had wound down. During the day, he watched TV and there'd been a programme on redundancy and its effect on people. He had all the worst symptoms and then some. With nothing being built because of the recession, nobody had any use for an architect, especially a fifty-four-year-old one. Even if a job did appear on the horizon, he was far too old and too qualified to start somewhere new and was, therefore, unemployable.

Slipping the parking ticket into the pocket of his navy corduroys, he walked towards arrivals. He was early enough to get a coffee and a paper, to sit and wait. Lillie's son had emailed him a photograph so he would know what she looked like. It had been taken at a family gathering. Two strong Celtic-looking men – his nephews, he realized with a jolt – were standing beside their parents. Lillie appeared to be as tall as Jennifer had been and with similar colouring; she was standing beside a man who must have once been tall but looked to have shrunken, turned in on himself. He was smiling though.

Dad's only been dead six months, Martin had said in his email. We think this is wonderful for Mum – finding you and going to stay with you. It's really generous of you. Obviously, it's been painful for everyone since Dad died, but particularly for Mum. They were married over forty years. I hope it all works out. Just email or phone if there's any problem or if Mum gets upset. We'll fly her home in an instant. I know you said she can stay indefinitely, and thank you for that. Mum wants to recompense you both for her visit.

Don't worry, Seth had replied, we'll take care of her, I promise. She can stay as long as she likes and I won't hear of her paying anything. She's family.

He hoped they'd be able to fulfil the promise of taking care of Lillie. Now that she was nearly here, he hoped he'd be able to love her. But it would be strange.

He'd read his paper from cover to cover and the coffee cup had been dispatched into a litter bin by the time people started trailing through the arrivals gate. Seth scanned the faces, wondering if he'd recognize her from the picture. He had made a sign with *Lillie Maguire* written on it, just in case, but he felt self-conscious standing there holding it. When he saw her, approaching slowly as if walking was hard for her, he knew her instantly. This woman pushing the trolley with two mismatched suitcases could only be his sister. She wasn't as tall as he'd thought, but he was struck at once by the resemblance to his mother. It hadn't been so noticeable in the picture but now, seeing her in the flesh, freckled from the Australian sun and wearing a bright coral top, it was as if he was looking at Jennifer. She, too, had worn her hair tied up in a bun with bits trailing around her face. Lillie's eyes were the same as his mother's. Even her mouth was the same, soft and curving in a sweet expression.

At that moment, a huge surge of emotion shot through Seth. It was almost as if his mother had come back to life, as if some part of her had been preserved in this woman. He had a sister.

He moved towards her, trying to smile but wondering whether he might start to cry, overwhelmed by the feeling that another chance had been given to him; another chance to be with his mother through Lillie.

For a moment, Lillie kept pushing her trolley. Once the plane had landed and it sank in that she was really here and it was time to meet her brother, her nerves had got the better of her.

Sam, help me, she begged silently. *I don't want to feel bitter. I had such amazing parents. It's not as if I ever lost out by being adopted. Nobody could have loved me more than they did. I don't know what it was like for my birth mother all those years ago. Just help me remember that.*

Seeing her name on a piece of card, and then looking at the dark-eyed man nervously holding it, she came to a complete halt. This was a meeting for which there were no rules, she had no framework, nothing in her wealth of experience to draw on. This was the great unknown. It could turn out to be fantastic . . . or it could go horribly wrong.

No, a voice inside her said. Her own voice. It would not go wrong. As he stepped hesitantly towards her, she gazed at him, eyes wide as if she might cry.

'Lillie,' Seth said. 'Welcome home.'

Lillie held on to Seth's hand for quite a while after they left the airport. It was lucky the car was an automatic, she thought, with a little hiccup between tears. She wasn't sure why she was crying. Tears of joy? Just pure emotion leaking out of her, grief over Sam combined with trepidation at meeting her brother, an actual brother after all these years. She felt as if something had reached into her very soul and squeezed it in a tight embrace. From the look of him, Seth was equally choked.

'I meant to show you all the sights of Cork,' he said as they drove along, 'but I'm not able to find the words. I think we should just go home. You need to sleep, anyway, after that trip. Three flights. You must be shatterered.'

She nodded. 'I can't talk much either – and that's a miracle, if you listen to my sons on the matter,' she said. 'Here, take your hand back, dry your eyes.'

'You sound just like my . . .' Seth paused. Out of the corner of her eye, Lillie could see him grin. '*Our* mother,' he corrected. 'Yes, you do sound like her. It's uncanny. Even though the accent is different.'

For a moment, neither of them spoke, the huge chasm of Lillie's adoption gaping between them.

It was Lillie who broke the silence.

'I was very worried on the plane journey,' she said slowly. 'I thought you might resent me because I was a secret. You told Martin that you never knew of my existence. It must have come as a huge shock. And I was terrified that I'd feel bitter when I saw you – which is stupid, because I couldn't have had a better childhood. But . . .'

Words failed her again. She looked out of the window, curious to see the part of Ireland where she had been born. On the approach to the airport on the final flight from London, she'd had an aisle seat and hadn't been able to see much.

Now, she could see that the airport was built on a hill and as they drove away, Cork city and county were spread out before her. 'I don't feel that now,' she went on truthfully. 'I feel as if this is something special, something that most people don't get to experience. So let's go slowly and try to appreci- ate it.'

Beside her, Seth nodded.

At first, they drove in companionable silence, Seth occa- sionally pointing out places, the way he did on family trips to the pretty seaside village of Cobh, where Frankie's sister lived.

'My wife's parents live on the other side of the city, in Kinsale – it's a resort town, very picturesque, and full of gourmet fish restaurants,' he said. 'They're all dying to meet you, Frankie's family. Her mother's a real live wire. I think she has some plan to take you to Dublin on the train and show you everything there too. I said I was going to take you to Beara, where our mother was from, and then Madeleine, who comes from Dublin, said you can't possibly visit Ireland without going there. Not just yet, though,' he added, in case Lillie felt overwhelmed.

Lillie thought about it. She had an open ticket and she could go home when she wanted to. In another week, she might be up for a trip to Dublin. This wasn't like home; Ireland was a small country where you could easily drive from one side to the other in half a day.

'I think I'd enjoy that,' she said. 'And Beara. I definitely want to see where she – Jennifer – came from. I want to know what she was like, what your childhood was like, everything.'

It was so easy to say it now, and yet she'd been so full of angst beforehand. This slender man with the sad dark eyes was clearly far more worried about her feelings than she was. He was going out of his way not to talk as if Jennifer McCabe had been his mother first and foremost. He wanted to share her.

'Don't worry, I'll tell you everything,' he said, and then paused as if he had something important to say, something he'd rehearsed. 'I was a bit nervous that you'd be angry because she gave you away, that maybe you'd resent me for having had her as a mother when you didn't . . . '

Lillie was sure it was one of the hardest things he'd ever said.

'No,' she said, shifting in the front seat so she was facing him. 'I'm not angry. Those were different times, I understand that. My mum and dad in Australia explained it to me. I know things weren't the way they are now.'

They were driving through the streets of Cork now, and Lillie looked around with interest.

100

'I'd love to take you all over the country,' Seth said, sounding a bit more relaxed. 'We've got mountains, castles, fairy forts – but no leprechauns, I'm afraid.'

'Oh darn it,' joked Lillie. 'And there was me thinking I'd go home with a little green-clad creature and a pot of gold.'

The tension was broken. Suddenly they were talking so fast they were practically gabbling. Lillie was telling him about her two sons and her grandchildren – his great nephew and niece. About Sam, the final days. How he'd have wanted her to go to Ireland. 'People always say that when someone dies, don't they?' she said. '"This is what he would have wanted" . . . Truth is, no matter how well you know a person you can't really tell what they'd have wanted. All I can say is, I know Sam is in my heart, always.' She touched her chest. Turning to him, she added self-consciously, 'You must think I'm crazy. All these years and suddenly you've found yourself with a crazy sister!'

'I don't think you're crazy at all,' Seth said softly, and he took a hand off the steering wheel, laid it on hers and squeezed tightly. 'I'm just so glad you're here.'

They talked and talked. Soon they were driving through streets where houses clustered close together and trees lined the roadside. Seth told her about his family, about Emer and Alexei, the smartest, most wonderful kids that two parents ever had. He talked about Frankie, the love of his life, the most wonderful woman in the world.

As he said this, he was conscious that while true, his words were also misleading. Frankie remained the love of his life, but things had been so tough recently. How could he say any of that to a woman so obviously in pain after the death of her own husband?

'You're going to love her,' he said, determinedly cheerful. 'Everyone loves Frankie. You'd love the kids too, but they're both away until July at least. Alexei is adopted, by the way.' He shot a sideways glance at Lillie.

'You've an adopted son?' she said, delighted.

'Yeah,' Seth nodded, beaming. 'Full circle, eh? We tried so hard after Emer, then in the end Frankie didn't think she'd ever get pregnant again and we decided to adopt instead.'

'I can't wait to meet them all,' Lillie said. 'My new family.'

They'd reached Redstone now. Lillie was delighted by the pretty crossroads and Main Street, with its huge sycamores leaning over the road.

'The trees are one of the things that drew us to this area,' Seth told her. 'You don't get many trees growing in cities and towns in Ireland. Unlike Melbourne – I've looked it up on the Internet,' he said. 'I spent a lot of time looking, trying to imagine what your life would be like, but you never can work out what other people's lives in other places are really like, can you?'

'Probably not,' said Lillie, then as they stopped at the traffic lights by a pretty coffee shop, a craft boutique, and a beauty salon with the name Bobbi spelt out in regal lettering, she asked: 'Have you always lived here?'

'No. And that's where it all goes a bit downhill,' Seth admitted. 'We saw an ad for the house, came to see it in September and fell in love. We moved in a month later, full of ideas about how we were going to do it up, but work was keeping me busy at the time. I was planning to manage the job myself, see to it that we'd get everything done at cost. And then a month later, in November, I was made redundant. Retrenched, I think you call it. No chance of finding another job with the economy the way it is.' He shook his head. 'So now we've got this beautiful, rather wrecked house and we can't afford to do it up. I'm here all the time but I don't have the expertise. A lick of paint here and there isn't going to fix it up.'

Seth wondered why he was spilling his guts to Lillie. But now that he'd started, he couldn't stop.

102

'Every day, I plan to start on the garden but I look out and all I see is a wilderness – and not a nice sort of wilderness, if you know what I mean. It's overwhelming,' he said with a sigh. It was strange, finding he could tell Lillie things he couldn't tell his wife.

'I could help you with the garden,' Lillie volunteered. 'I love gardens. I'm at my happiest surrounded by my roses.'

'You wouldn't be surrounded by roses in our garden,' Seth said as they drove through the traffic lights and took a right turn along a pretty terrace called Lavender Road. After a few moments of weaving through the side streets he announced, 'This is it: Maple Avenue. Ours stands out because it's the one that looks as if it's been recently vacated by squatters.'

'Don't be silly,' said Lillie, looking with interest at the once handsome red-brick façade. 'I can see exactly why you fell in love with it.' She sensed the distress behind her brother's humorous comments and saw he needed to be comforted.

She thought how Sam would have hated to be out of work. How it would have affected him as a man and she could see instantly that Seth was the same. It was there, written all over his face. Seth Green was not a man who could hide things, she thought fondly, and she liked him all the more for it. Sam had been the same. Every emotion had been written across that broad, tanned face.

He'd spoken the truth about the house. Lillie could see that, in its day, it must have been a beautiful grand residence. It was built in old red brick – not the brash modern kind that hurt the eyes but the dusty, old type that called to mind pretty Victorian houses with roses clambering all over the porch. Clearly some type of plant had grown around the front porch here, but all that remained of it were dead branches and rapacious ivy. Still, there was no doubt in her mind that the house, and even the disaster area that constituted the garden, *could* be restored to its former glory but it would take lots of money or huge amounts of time. And yet, the house was lovely despite the lack of care: like an old, grand lady who'd once been beautiful and could be again, if only care was lavished on her.

Seth didn't take Lillie up the steps to the front door; instead they descended a perilous, moss-covered staircase to a basement door which required a shove to open it. It led into a large basement flat that had been painted creamy white in an effort to banish the darkness. Frankie and Seth had obviously done their best with it, she thought as she looked around: everything had been repainted, and the walls were hung with colourful paintings and photos of the family.

Happy faces smiled out of the photos: a girl with laughing blue eyes and a cascade of streaky strawberry-blonde hair standing beside a lanky blond boy with a shy smile. Emer and Alexei, Seth told her. His wife was a stunning woman, almost as tall as Seth – and he was only an inch or so shy of six foot. Everything about Frankie, from the mass of curling dark hair to the glowing eyes and high cheekbones, seemed to radiate energy and vitality.

'I'll give you the full tour later,' Seth said over his shoulder as he set her bags down beside the door on to the hallway and led the way into a big, low-ceilinged kitchen. It obviously doubled as their living room, because one end boasted two red couches and armchairs covered in floral throws set around a small wood-burning stove. 'I'm sure you're dying for a sit down. I'll make you a cup of tea and then you can go and lie down for a nap if you like,' he went on.

'I don't feel tired for some reason,' Lillie said, wandering around, looking at everything. The house retained many of its original features, like the stately French doors that opened into the garden. She went across to them, saying: 'Do you mind if I go outside?'

'By all means. You must treat the place as your home,

do exactly as you please,' said Seth, busily filling the kettle.

Lillie turned the key and stepped into the garden, a long rectangle of untamed vegetation. At the end, she could just make out a stone wall with an arched gate built into it, probably the entrance to what had once been a peaceful retreat for the lady of the house a long time ago. There was no garden path, just rampant weeds, nettles and fierce brambles filling every inch as far as she could see, though some marvellous trees could be seen rising from the chaos.

Lillie breathed in the scent of earth that was at the same time familiar and yet different from the smell of her own garden at home. She could see why a non-gardener would be disheartened every time they looked out at this wilderness.

To her, the garden at least was fixable. Perhaps if she were to help Seth make a start on the garden it would give him a sense of purpose, restore his pride a little.

While they drank their tea, Seth showed her more photos.

'Your family are beautiful,' Lillie said, squeezing his hand tightly. 'I wish Alexei and Emer were here so I could meet them.'

'You will,' said Seth confidently. 'If not this time then next. If Emer's still in Australia when you go home, she'll go to see you. I think she'd have raced to Melbourne as soon as we told her about you, except that I wanted to meet you first. They'll be back in July. Hopefully,' he added. 'I think Frankie's scared they'll be having so much fun that they'll stay away for another couple of months.'

They spent the rest of the afternoon poring over family albums from when Seth was a boy, and he watched his new sister trace the contours of their mother's face in the old black-and-white photographs.

'You look just like her,' he said, 'maybe taller.'

'I can't imagine what it must have been like for her then,' Lillie said wistfully. 'I was never angry with her for giving me up because my parents, my adopted parents, they explained it to me. They talked about how there were plenty of Australian girls, too, who were shamed when they had babies without a husband. Can you imagine it – being made to feel like nothing because you'd brought new life into the world?'

'What makes me sad is that I didn't find out about you until now,' Seth said. 'That I didn't get to know Sam and that you didn't get to know our mother and that' – she could see the tears in his eyes – 'she kept this secret. How can you know somebody so long and they keep something of such great importance from you?'

Lillie laid a hand on his arm to comfort him. Despite her fears that she'd be consumed with bitterness towards him, she found herself instinctively reaching out to comfort him. The last thing she'd expected was to feel this sense of kinship with a complete stranger.

'People keep secrets. And the longer a thing's been kept secret, the harder it becomes to bring it out into the open. But the longer you live – and this is something I know all about, being older than you, my darling – the more you realize that the secrets aren't important. It's the love that's important. She loved you. She loved me enough to give me away because she thought that was the right thing at the time. That's all that matters.'

Seth studied his sister with her Celtic skin and its scattering of freckles. She had many wrinkles on her lovely face.

'Signs of a lifetime,' she said ruefully, realizing what he was looking at. 'Plus too much time spent in the sun,' she added. 'They're the lines of my life. I've got two best friends I go walking with and we joke about how we feel twenty-five until our knees start hurting. To me, the lines are proof of all I've learned. Viletta, now, she hates her wrinkles. She must spend a fortune on Retinoid or Retinal or whatever you call it.'

Seth looked blank.

'It's a cream that smoothes wrinkles,' Lillie explained. 'But I don't want mine gone. They're part of the package.'

Seth felt a wave of love for this new sister. The resemblance to his mother wasn't just skin deep, she had that same serenity about her, the same ability to make you feel better about yourself just being in her company. Maybe, just maybe, she would be able to work some of her magic on Frankie and cheer her up on the subject of age.

'How did you get to be so wise?' he asked fondly.

Unlike many Irish people, who couldn't take a compliment on pain of death, Lillie didn't bat it away. She took the statement as her due. 'We're all given gifts,' she said, 'and that was one of mine.'

Frankie sat at her desk scanning her emails and trying very hard to be mindful. Mindfulness was a wonderful concept – holding on to the now, appreciating the current moment. Everyone was at it; half the office were sitting at their desks, smiling, determined to be in the present moment. Once the office had been full of people doing spinning classes, racing back from lunch, puce in the face and bursting with hyper energy. Then the yoga fad had taken hold: Iyengar, Bikram, Flow, whatever, and suddenly the most unlikely people began standing up at the end of meetings giving a small bow, hands in prayer pose, and murmuring 'Namaste'.

These days, Mindfulness was all the rage.

Living in the now, enjoying the present, taking deep breaths and sending bright bursts of love out to random people who cut them up in traffic.

'Mindfulness is so good for you, you know,' said Lauren from Frankie's office who had embraced Mindfulness with the zeal of person captured by the nuns years ago and told they had a vocation. 'We all spend far too much time thinking about the future.'

Frankie half wished she had time to be mindful but who'd hold the fort if *someone* wasn't thinking about tomorrow?

'That's all very well for you,' Frankie told her, 'but I don't have the luxury of dwelling in the moment. My job is about the future – working out what will give people a sense of purpose, a stake in the company. Working out who we hire and where to put them so they can fulfil their potential. It's the future that pays my mortgage,' she said, knowing her voice was rising. 'What's wrong with the future?'

The look of alarm on Lauren's face stopped her in her tracks. Embarrassed, Frankie hurried back to her office. Since when had she turned into this grumpy cow who went off on a rant at the slightest thing? She found herself muttering under her breath, constantly in a state of extreme irritation. And then she'd get all hot and bothered, literally, her core body temperature rising until she could feel the flush rising from her chest up through her neck. Thankfully her face didn't go all red, which was something, but she'd taken to wearing silk scarves to hide the telltale redness on her throat.

Nothing hid the sweat, though. The expensive Dior foundation she relied on to hide the wrinkles and give her a subtle glow was no match for the beads of perspiration that would suddenly erupt on her forehead and start running down her face. Her choice of outfit each morning was now determined by whether it would conceal her sweaty armpits or highlight the problem. There was nothing more mortifying than having to clamp her armpits down, pray she was wearing enough perfume to hide the sweaty smell and discreetly mop her face with a tissue when nobody was looking.

It was ridiculous. She couldn't be going through the menopause. She wasn't old enough, surely. Or perhaps she was. Clearly something was playing havoc with her hormones.

She bashed away at her keyboard, pounding out a reply

to an email. Responding to emails when you were irritable was probably not a good idea. She carried on regardless. Rita in the claims department had it coming. Rita reckoned she was undervalued in claims. According to Rita, she'd been undervalued in every department she'd been in so far. Frankie was of the opinion that Rita was the kind of person who would feel undervalued no matter where she was or who she was working for. Rita would probably feel undervalued if she was made president of the EU. And given that she couldn't even process an insurance claim satisfactorily, the presidency might just be a tad beyond her abilities . . . Aaaarghh! There she was – at it again. This damned irritation!

She deleted the *Dear Rita, I am afraid there will never be any job in this company where you will feel happy because you are determined* not *to be happy* . . . And started again.

Frankie had done a bit of Googling on the subject of the menopause, and Dr Google's verdict had been far from encouraging.

First, there were endless contradictory pages on drugs – go natural/don't go natural. Black cohosh will make you feel ten years younger/black cohosh will make your ears fall off.

It was probably easier to teach yourself to remove somebody's appendix with a fish knife and a soup ladle than it was to work out what worked best for menopausal symptoms.

What's more, the blasted thing had squillions of symptoms. Frankie felt as if she had every last one of them. It was a bit like looking at the 'possible side effects' bit on leaflets for tablets.

Frankie always found that if she read these, eventually, she'd convince herself that she had every single one of them. So these days, unless the doctor said something specifically about a certain drug, Frankie had trained herself not to look at the symptoms. The nocebo effect it was called. But with this bloody menopause thing, she was coming to the conclusion that she had them all. Irritability, grumpiness, hot flushes, headaches, feeling tearful at the oddest moment and, she had to admit it, absolutely no interest in sex.

Dealing with this was not quite as difficult as it might have been. As a human resources boss, Frankie knew all the theoretical downsides of people losing their jobs and for men in particular, lack of libido was a common problem. For the first month after Seth had been made redundant, it had affected him terribly. It made it worse that his bosses had chosen the month before Christmas to do the deed, and with the children both away, it fell to her alone to try and comfort him. She'd hoped that making love would succeed where words had failed, but after a few minutes' hugging, Seth would kiss her on the forehead – a definite *Thanks, but no thanks* signal if ever there was one – say goodnight and roll over.

Frankie had felt rebuffed, as if the comfort she was offering wasn't good enough. As if *she* wasn't good enough. And now . . . now it suited her not to have to think about sex.

The sad thing was that they'd always been so wonderful in bed. Seth's love-making had been so tender and passionate, she'd never doubted he felt the same way about her as she did about him.

Lately, they'd turned into one of those couples whose idea of bedroom bliss was twin beds and a stair lift. No, she thought grimly, twin *rooms*, so they could say goodnight on the landing, shuffle through adjoining doors and climb into bed with a cup of cocoa and a crossword to keep them occupied till they fell asleep.

Frankie didn't want to be that sort of person – ever. She certainly didn't want to be that sort of person now.

Mindfulness . . . yes, she thought. Mindfulness, that's it:

think of the now. Think calm thoughts. But she couldn't. Feeling irritable always gave her a headache and she had the mother of all headaches hammering in her skull.

Was it high blood pressure? Heightened blood pressure was one of the things she'd read on one of the peri-menopause sites. Oh heck, something new to worry about. Maybe she should go to the doctor, talk it over.

That was it, she'd go to the doctor.

She picked up the phone and dialled. If she begged, she might get an appointment tonight. And then she remembered: Lillie. This would be her first night in their house. Damn! She'd make the appointment for later in the week.

Seth had felt apprehensive about introducing his wife to his new sister.

That evening, when Frankie swept in with a shopping bag full of goodies and a bouquet for their guest, it was immediately clear that she had taken to Lillie in a big way. Seth had never doubted that she would. That was the thing about Frankie: she was always so full of warmth towards other people, why should Lillie be any different? No, his apprehension had another cause.

Though he knew it was entirely childish of him, he wanted his long-lost sister to be *his*, like a child in the playground who didn't want anyone else to play with their special friend. He'd been afraid that Frankie would burst in with all her energy and vitality and Lillie would cease to notice him.

But it didn't happen that way.

'Lillie, it's wonderful to meet you,' said Frankie, embracing her. 'You look the image of Seth's mother. Has he told you that already?'

'Yes,' said Lillie, surprised at how moved she was to hear this again.

'We've spent the afternoon going through the photo albums,' Seth said pointedly.

111

'Lillie, you must be exhausted after that flight. Seth, she needs to sleep,' Frankie went on, taking over.

'She said she was fine,' Seth replied tightly.

Observing the exchange between husband and wife, Lillie immediately picked up on the undertones. This had all the hallmarks of a marriage in trouble. Not on the edge of the precipice, yet, but definitely heading in that direction.

Briefly, she considered grabbing her suitcases and checking into a hotel. She didn't need to be in the middle of this. But then something changed her mind. Even though they'd been strangers until today, Seth was still her blood. She'd spent a lifetime wondering about her birth family. And now that she was here, she wasn't about to turn her back on them.

'Do you know,' she announced, breaking the uncomfortable silence that had fallen, 'I think it's time we had more of that famous Irish tea. And then maybe we can have a look at your albums again. I brought mine, too, so we could look at those. I think you'll find that Martin, my eldest, has a look of our mother about him. It's funny, isn't it, the way, even where there isn't an obvious physical resemblance, one person will have some indefinable something about them that puts you in mind of someone else?'

She beamed at her brother and sister-in-law, willing them to smile with her, willing them to let go of whatever tension was there.

'I suppose so,' said Frankie.

'Possibly,' said Seth.

'And I want to hear all about when you were young, Seth,' said Lillie, turning back to him. 'Now that I've found you, I want to know everything. I bet you've some great stories too, Frankie,' she added.

This time, both Frankie and Seth smiled.

'I've some tales all right,' Frankie agreed, wryly. 'I'll go and I'll make the tea and then we can look at the albums together.

I know you've seen some of them but it'll be fun because I haven't looked at those for years, have I?' she said to Seth.

Lillie could see the flicker of warmth in her brother's eyes. Perhaps she'd been imagining the tension. She was tired, after all, and Frankie and Seth must be under such pressure, what with the loss of his income and the worry over whether to spend his redundancy on doing up the house or wait and see. No wonder they were tense.

Part Two

Honey has been used for healing since at least 2000 BC and its use has been recorded in texts from Egypt, China, Greece and Ancient Rome. The Egyptians used it most widely, for everything from wound care to asthma. In these ancient cultures, bees were revered and honey itself was treated as a great enhancement to the joy of life.

The Gentle Beekeeper, Iseult Cloud

Chapter Six

On her second morning in Seth and Frankie's house, Lillie woke in the spare bedroom to sun streaming in through the badly fitting curtains. The bed was fabulous. Big, soft with cool beautiful smooth white sheets and a plump duvet that nestled around her body. Even though Seth said it was remarkably warm for this time of year by Irish standards, it was still cold for Lillie, more accustomed to the beautiful heat of Melbourne.

The previous evening, Seth had served dinner in the garden. Lillie had been somewhat dubious about sitting outdoors on an Irish March evening, but he'd been so enthusiastic she couldn't refuse.

'The weather's going to be nice today, so we can have dinner outside,' he'd announced. 'I realize it's a bit of a jungle, but we have the patio table and chairs from our last house, and I can drag the patio heater out so you won't freeze.'

She and Seth had taken a stroll around the garden together beforehand. Everyone here called their back yard a garden, even if it was nothing more than a desolate space clogged with weeds – and Frankie and Seth's home fell squarely into the latter category. There were weeds Lillie didn't recognize and vicious nettles. She'd stung her legs and Seth had instantly found a big fat ugly-looking leaf which he'd pronounced to be a dock leaf and rubbed the sap gently into the stinging bumps on her legs.

It was such a tender gesture and she'd had a sudden vision of them if they'd grown up together with him as a protective brother helping her along the way. Of course such a thing couldn't have happened. She was ten years older than Seth. By the time he'd been old enough to know what a dock leaf was, she'd have been a teenager, looking out for *him*. Nevertheless she felt a tinge of sorrow for the relationship they'd missed out on.

Though she'd only been here a short while, already she felt at home. Lying in her comfortable bed, she felt a sense of calm, almost as if her beloved Sam was by her side. She could almost feel his big hand resting affectionately on her shoulder the way he used to stand when they went on tours years ago and the guide would list out details of the various places they'd been, Ephesus in Turkey, the oracle at Delphi. How bizarre that in this far-away country of her birth, where everything should be alien, the sense of enormous heart-shattering grief over Sam's death had somehow abated. She didn't know why, and couldn't put her finger on it, but that was how she felt.

And Lillie, who normally wanted to get to the bottom of every feeling and understand it fully, decided it was safer to just let it be. She would enjoy the comfort and the peace without questioning lest she disturb it somehow.

As she lay in the soft bed wriggling her toes and stretching luxuriously, she took in her surroundings. Aside from the bed, the spare room was dreadful. In truth, the whole house was dreadful, apart from the bits of the basement they'd repainted.

Seth was clearly mortally embarrassed at the state the place was in.

'It's a mess, I know,' he said. 'I suppose you're wondering why I haven't been doing it up during the months I've been out of work, but DIY's not my strong suit. I thought about having a go at ripping down the walls between the bedsits on the first floor, because they're only wood, but chances are I'd end up doing more harm than good if I tackled it. I can't get my head into stripping wallpaper or sanding the floors in the other rooms either,' he said. 'But at the same time I feel as if I should be doing something because Frankie's out earning the money. Only for some reason I can't make myself start. I just feel so useless.'

She'd looked at the tears welling in his eyes and her heart had melted the way it used to with her sons. It was always easier for an outsider to see the truth and Lillie could plainly see that her brother was trapped in an emotional quagmire. The things he could have clung to in order to haul himself out of the morass had been snatched away from him. His job, the sense of manhood that came from providing for his family – gone. And he couldn't cling to his wife either. Frankie, bless her, dear Frankie with her energy and her vitality and her 'can do' spirit, didn't appear to see Seth's pain despite loving him with all her heart. She was also obviously losing patience with his inability to extricate himself. Lillie hadn't been imagining the tension between the two of them that first night: with each day, she saw new signs that it was there, away under the surface.

It was as plain as the aquiline nose on Frankie's face that she couldn't understand why, when he'd spent the last four months hanging around the house with nothing else to do all day, she still came home to find the place in the same sorry state. She'd never come out and say it, but Seth knew what was going through her mind: *Since it's down to me to pay all the bills now, thanks to your redundancy, how about you do your bit? Get on and fix this disaster of a house instead of moaning about needing contractors to come in and do the work.*

I know I've failed you, was Seth's unspoken response.

119

Watching all this silent messaging going on around her was painful.

What do you think, Sam? Lillie said. *Seems to me there's a bit of a mission here.* She grinned, recalling the way Sam would smile to himself whenever she got it into her head to try and sort out other people's problems. He'd tease her, telling the boys dinner might be late tonight because their mother was on one of her missions, but he was always behind her all the way. *I reckon these two need my help, and I haven't felt needed in a while. You'll help me, won't you, darling?*

Lillie felt again that sense of peace filling her heart. It was answer enough.

She got up, showered and dressed, all the while making plans. There was so much to be done. Fixing the house and garden would be a breeze compared to mending Seth and Frankie's marriage. If something wasn't done soon, they could end up drifting so far apart that nothing would be able to bring them back together. She'd seen it happen before. If she could help in any way, she would. Not interfere, Heavens no, nothing worse than interfering relatives.

At that thought, she laughed out loud: *This is my brother and sister-in-law – I am a relative.* Well, all the more reason for her to help them.

And her first move would be to help Seth regain his lost vitality.

Seth had promised to drive Lillie down to the centre of Redstone that morning, but the dishwasher had broken and he needed to stay in for the repair man.

'If you remind me of the way, I can walk,' said Lillie. 'It'll do me good to stretch my legs.'

It was a cool morning, but the sun was out and Lillie enjoyed looking at the houses, admiring the flowers coming into bud in people's gardens. She paused to say hello to a woman of her own vintage who was walking a small fluffy black dog with a tartan bow in its hair.

'I'm so glad the winter's behind us,' said the woman, happy to stop for a moment. 'I love the spring. It's not easy to make yourself go for a walk when it's cold and wet all the time. Poor Noodles hates the rain.'

Noodles was busily sniffing around Lillie's comfortable trainers.

'What a sweet dog,' commented Lillie, bending down to stroke her. 'What breed is she?'

'A bitza,' said the woman proudly. 'A little bit of everything. Tell me now, your accent – you're not from around here. Australian?'

It was a conversation Lillie quickly became used to having. She'd decided to go into a few of the shops in Redstone to familiarize herself with the place so that she'd feel part of it all. She'd also offered to cook dinner that evening and was looking forward to seeing what ingredients she might pick up. It didn't take long to discover that there was no dropping into places anonymously in Redstone.

The girl in the bakery introduced herself as Sue. She was thrilled to discover that Lillie was from Melbourne. 'We were there once ourselves, on a gap year. Feels like a million years ago,' she said, 'doesn't it, Zeke?'

'Indeed it does,' said her husband, poking his head through the hatch between the shop and the kitchen.

Sue didn't know Frankie even though Lillie described her in some detail, but she'd seen Seth around.

'Quiet man, tall with sad dark eyes?'

'That's the one,' Lillie agreed. 'What does he buy when he comes in here?'

'A bit of French stick,' said Sue. 'I've tried to tempt him with our spelt bread and some of the wheaten loaves or the cakes, but he's not interested.'

'Spelt bread, let's try that,' said Lillie firmly. 'Is that

baklava?' She pointed to a tray of tiny cubes of nuts, honey and filo pastry.

'Yes,' said Sue.

'Fabulous,' said Lillie, thinking of both dessert and the restorative qualities of honey, something Sam had instilled into her over the years he'd kept hives. 'Let's have twelve.'

'Planning a feast?' said Zeke, coming through into the shop.

'A feast! What a wonderful idea,' Lillie said. 'It could be a feast to say thank you for having me stay with them.'

In the delicatessen, she bought salad greens, olives, feta cheese and some tapas from two friendly men who moved around behind the counter serving different people with all the grace of a couple long married.

They introduced themselves as Paul and Mark, and told her they longed to go to Australia but now that they had the deli, they couldn't just up and leave it.

'It's our baby,' Paul explained, and Lillie watched him smile over at Mark lovingly.

Lillie beamed back at them. Their good cheer was quite infectious.

Next she popped into the beautician's to get a brochure so she could book a relaxing treatment for Frankie as a thank you. The salon was called Bobbi's and when she discerned that the lady at the desk was the Bobbi in question, Lillie went over to introduce herself.

'What do you think would be the best relaxation treatment for a woman who has no time to herself and dearly needs a treat?' Lillie asked.

'What age would this lady be?' said Bobbi, tapping her chin thoughtfully with a pen.

'Mid-forties,' said Lillie diplomatically.

'Does she have facials or anything? Does she look after herself, is what I mean. Because if she's used to facials, I'd recommend one, but if she's not, perhaps a massage and a mani-pedi?'

Lillie regarded Bobbi. 'To be honest, I have no idea if she does any of the above. All I know is that she's wildly busy and pretty stressed right now. How about I give her a voucher that will cover either – could you set her up with someone who is qualified to do whichever treatment she chooses on the day?'

'I understand loud and clear. That's no problem,' said Bobbi and smiled. 'Now, where did you say you were from?'

They do things differently here, Lillie emailed to Doris a week after she'd arrived in Redstone. She was using Seth's computer and was delighted that she was able to get into her email account so easily. Those lessons in the library back home had really paid off.

And it's as if they speak a different language. When they say 'I'm grand', it means 'I'm OK'. Mad doesn't mean mad in the sense we use, either. Seth keeps telling me that Frankie's mother is a bit mad, but that doesn't mean she's medicated – although Seth laughed and said she should be. He means she's a bit eccentric, I think. Either way, I'm going to find out soon because Frankie's family are coming over at the weekend for dinner.

The other night, Seth asked Frankie where she'd put the yoke for doing potatoes. Turns out he meant the peeler and 'yoke' means anything you can't remember the name of. If you're 'gas', you're funny, not inflammable.

Even something as simple as ordering coffee gets complicated – flat whites aren't so common here. They're more into lattes and cappuccinos, although the woman behind me in the queue said 'far from lattes we were reared'. I had to ask Frankie for a translation when I got home. She said it's a common refrain, something people say to remind themselves that there was a time when the country didn't have baristas and cafés, and that they

123

shouldn't get above themselves, which is considered a terrible sin in Ireland.

I told Frankie that it's far from lattes that *I* was reared and she roared with laughter and said I'm getting the hang of it all.

Seth took me to see his childhood home yesterday. I had to steel myself beforehand, to be honest. I was afraid I'd break down and cry, and we both know I've done enough crying these past months. But I didn't . . .

Seth had been all chat as he drove a winding route around Cork up into the south side. The houses there were a lot like the ones in Redstone, so far as Lillie could judge, but he was brimming with excitement and she didn't want to shatter his enthusiasm.

They were going to look at the place where her birth mother had lived after giving Lillie away. They'd see the streets she walked to the shops, the school where Seth went as a child . . . Lillie was afraid this might be the point when the bitterness would finally take hold and she'd start to feel angry at this woman who'd been able to give her away.

Please don't let me feel that way, she prayed as they drove along, Seth pointing out landmarks along the way.

'That's St Murtagh's,' he said, slowing as they passed a small red-brick school. 'It's still going after all these years. Mother kept me back a year and I didn't start till I was five, which was unusual at the time. I had a bad chest as a child and she used to make me eat lots of eggs to build me up.'

Please, prayed Lillie, *I don't want to feel bitter. It was a different time and who knows what it was like then. She did the best she could for me.*

'That was the corner shop,' said Seth, when they reached a small crossroads. 'It's a mini-market now – same thing, I suppose. Now this,' he slowed to walking pace to let her see

124

the name plate on the wall of a house, 'was our road. Lismore Road. We were halfway along, number twenty-three.'

It was a short road and the houses were small single-storey, red-brick ones. The front yards were minuscule, a few square feet at most.

Lillie held her breath.

'The parking's always mad here,' Seth went on, then he glanced at Lillie and saw her white face. 'Sorry,' he said. 'Nerves, makes me chatter.'

He put a hand on her knee comfortingly.

'Will I drive by, or do you want to park and walk up to it?'

'Park,' said Lillie, finding her voice. 'Martin and Evan want photos.'

'I have the camera,' Seth said, pulling in.

Together, hand in hand, they walked to number twenty-three. It looked the same as all the other houses on the street: small and pretty.

'The bedrooms were at the front,' Seth said quietly. 'My parents had the one to the left of the door and mine was to the right.'

They looked at the tiny yard, which had been paved over. A gardener must live there now, Lillie thought, because there were several planters beside the black door, and healthy shrubs spilled out over the edges.

'We had one bathroom, a small kitchen and the living room ran the width of the house,' Seth went on. 'When my father's aunt came to live with us, the one I told you about who'd been in a camp, Dad got an extension built to make a room for her. There wasn't much room in the place, but we were happy.'

Lillie held on to her brother's hand and took in the old house where a woman she'd never known had raised a son, nursed a haunted old lady, and apparently lived a happy life, leaving the trauma of her youth behind her. Sixty-four years

125

ago, when religious men held the moral compass in their hands, when pregnancy out of wedlock was considered a heinous sin, she had given birth to a baby girl and placed her in the hands of the Church.

She pictured the woman from the photos, living in this house with her husband and son, and then she tried to imagine what it must have been like, knowing that somewhere far away her daughter was being brought up by strangers.

Jennifer wouldn't have had the comfort of knowing that Lillie had found the best possible home and was being raised with huge love by Charlotte and Dan. How she must have worried, Lillie thought with sadness. She knew that *she* would have been torn apart with worry over her beloved child if she'd ever had a baby adopted years before. How hard it all must have been for Jennifer.

The wise woman inside Lillie felt no bitterness or anger looking at this small home. Jennifer had done the best she could and had carried that burden for the rest of her life.

Lillie hoped fervently that Seth's father had known about it all; at least then, Jennifer would have had someone in whom to confide those doubts and fears.

'Are you all right?' asked Seth, anxious because Lillie was standing white-faced, staring fixedly at the house.

Perhaps it had been too much for her, he thought. She'd lost her husband so recently and now, coming here to the place where their mother had lived – well, it would be overwhelming.

Lillie turned to him and smiled. Some of the colour returned to her cheeks.

'I'm fine,' she said. 'I'm glad we came. I needed to see it and I sort of understand it now. Being here makes it more real. I can imagine life then, I can imagine the fear she must have felt, and the courage it took to give me away.'

'I thought you were going to faint,' said Seth, relieved.

'No,' said his sister. 'But I'm ready to go home for a cup of tea.'

'Right,' he said. 'I'll take a quick photo. Do you want to be in it?'

Lillie paused, then shook her head. 'Better if I take the photo,' she said. 'Then you can be in it. I was only here in our mother's heart. That's the way it should stay.'

Seth is going to attach the photo of the house for me, Doris. Martin and Evan will be thrilled to see it, too. They think I can do a high-speed trip through the past and send all the photos instantly. But I want to take my time. Seth and I are feeling our way, you see, and going back to those times is very emotional.

I can understand why my mother did what she did. In her place and in those times, I'd have done the same. What choice was there? We still can't find out who my birth father was. Seth and I have looked through all his mother's papers and there's nothing from that time. She wasn't a letter writer and didn't keep a diary. I guess we'll never know.

On a lighter note, complete strangers still talk to me all the time – it's clearly not just a Melbourne thing. I already know more people in Redstone than Seth does. I've gone to the shops a few times on my own and when Seth came with me today, he was astonished at the number of locals saying 'Hello, Lillie, how's the jet lag?'

I've found two great new pals, Seanie and Ronnie. The pair of them spend all day sitting at the bus stop every day. I don't think they travel anywhere. They just sit there, admire whoever's passing and chat in between smokes. They remind me of some of the old guys on the books at the Vinnies – or the St Vincent de Paul society, as they call it here.

Seth said he'd never noticed the two guys before. Seth isn't a noticer, not the way you and I would notice things.

There's a sweet bakery here that you'd just adore. Heavens,

I have to watch out. All those kilos I lost from our five-mile walks, I'll put them all right back on again. I've started to go in there with Seth to buy fresh bread, maybe a cake, and then we grab a coffee to go. The couple that run the place are trying for a baby. Poor Sue's had four goes at IVF with no success.

Yes, people are still telling me things. When I told Seth on the walk home that I'd had this lovely but quite personal chat with Sue (I didn't want to tell him exactly *what* she'd said. She didn't say it was a secret but I felt she wouldn't want people who came into the shop to look at her and know her business) he looked at me in amazement. 'But why would she reveal such personal details to someone she barely knows?'

'I have that sort of face,' I told him. 'It happens to me everywhere. If a day goes by when I don't hear at least one secret, I start to worry.'

I'm not sure he knows what to make of me, but he's glad I'm here and that's enough for the moment.

Seth and I have drawn up a list of things that I want to do while I'm here. Like visiting my mother's grave and seeing her relatives in Kerry, even though Seth says there's not many of them left.

And we're going to clear out the garden. Yes, it's really a job for the combined forces of Martin, Evan and at least five other huge blokes, but right now there's just me and Seth. I'll try and get my hands on some young fellow who needs a bit of work for a few dollars. Seth is too shell-shocked to think about it himself.

I'm working on getting him interested in beekeeping. I know, don't say it: he's not Sam and there's no point making him take up Sam's hobbies. But bees are so calming. Taking care of them is the closest thing to meditation you can get, Sam used to say. Let's see if they can work their magic on my brother.

You'd love Frankie, his wife. She's the type of person who could run the country, given half a chance. With so much on their plate already, you'd think she'd be giving me the evil eye

128

and saying 'When are you going home?' but instead she's gone out of her way to make me feel welcome.

In fact, she and Seth have been pleading with me to stay for a few more weeks at least. I think it suits them to have another person around the place. I want to pay for my stay but they keep saying they're insulted by the very idea. So I'm doing a lot of cooking, and Frankie's very grateful. She works so hard and she seems so tired.

Plus, they're going through that dreaded *second phase*. I remember how hard it was for me and Sam when the boys left home. We were at each other's throats for a whole year! I feel guilty about it now; it's as if we wasted that precious time, hating every moment we spent together. I have to keep reminding myself of that talking to I got from Viletta at the time. She sat me down and told me it was just a case of marriage and life entering into the second phase, where you're past the young love and the running around with the kids bit, and it's back to being a couple again. Only this time you're older and, not beating around the bush here, grumpier (typical Viletta!). Plus, you're teetering on the edge of being menopausal – which doesn't help when you need to patch things up and move on to the next stage.

That's where Frankie and Seth are right now, with the added pressure of money problems and a house that's falling apart around them.

I can't give Seth the lecture Viletta gave me because he's not up to hearing about how you have to work at marriage, and I don't spend enough time with Frankie to get on to the subject – but I will. And no, I won't be interfering! I can hear you say it across the world, Doris! I'm just going to explain how it was for me and Sam. It's always easier when you know it's not just you, that everyone goes through it.

OK, that's enough of the deep stuff. Even though it's spring here, it's still incredibly cold. I miss our long walks by the sea but we'll have plenty of time for that once I'm home. In the meantime, I'm happy. Sam's with me. I can really feel his presence here. The bees were his idea – yes, I know you think I'm crazy, Doris. I'm not, I promise. The other morning when I was in Redstone I went into an antique shop, hoping to find a gift for Seth and Frankie (they refuse to let me contribute towards my upkeep, so I have to make do with buying groceries and cooking meals). The guy in the shop was putting something in a display case: a golden locket with a bumble bee on it. As soon as I saw it, I knew it was a message from Sam.

Bees, he was telling me, clear as if he was standing next to me. *Get Seth into beekeeping.*

Then I went into the organic vegetable shop and they had all these jars of local honey with the beekeeper's number on the label. So I rang him. He said he'd be delighted to give Seth a few pointers, tell him a good course to go on – he'd even donate a couple of hives. Turns out he's getting a bit old and is finding ten hives a bit too much to cope with. I offered to buy his hives, but he said, 'Absolutely not. No money is to pass hands. They will be a gift: that way, the bees will be happy.' I never heard that one before, even in all the years Sam was beekeeping.

So, I'm happy. I've people to take care of and that always makes me happy, doesn't it?

Now, tell me all your news. Is Lloyd still keen on my Dyanne? I've emailed her. You'd have thought I'd piloted a space shuttle around Mars; she wrote back: *Gran, you're on email!* So I told her I'm a silver surfer. She's sent me a couple of emails since, but they're all about school and home – no mention of boys. Guess she thinks I'd be shocked. Kids today, they think we don't know what it is to fall in love! We could tell her some stuff, couldn't we, Doris?

Chapter Seven

Frankie's doctor, Felix, was a calm, gentle man her own age who'd seen her through one pregnancy and the early years of Alexei's adoption when he'd seemed to pick up every bug going.

'I'm too young for this menopause thing,' she said to Felix with irritation after what felt like a month in the waiting room one evening after work.

'Actually, menopause is – as I've no doubt you've read – precisely a year after your last period,' Felix informed her calmly. 'And you're still having periods.'

'Well peri-menopause or whatever,' said Frankie grumpily. She didn't want to be having this conversation, it was inherently depressing.

'Let's do the blood test to check your hormones, and a thyroid test. We should probably take your blood pressure as well. Then we'll know what we're dealing with and we can discuss the options.'

'Let's discuss the options now,' Frankie said miserably. 'I'm not in the mood to wait. It could be stress, you know. I am stressed.'

'Why?' said Felix.

Frankie felt irritated with him for being so reasonable.

'The basics,' she snapped. 'Money, worrying about the future, the whole nine yards. Seth's lost his job and that puts a certain pressure on me to pay the bills. The house is a pressure too.'

'The house?' he said.

'The Money Pit. We moved into this old house and we were going to do so much to it and now we don't have the money. It's like living in hell. We're in the basement and the rest of the place is a disaster zone of horrible bedsits. I lie in bed at night thinking about the state of the place over me: damp, with smelly, rotten carpets and awful old walls that haven't been stripped in donkey's years.'

'Right, financial pressure, that's a huge issue. And Seth losing his job, yes, I can see that would make you stressed,' said Felix, still being Mr Calm.

Suppressing the urge to bash him with her handbag and say 'No shit, Sherlock,' Frankie replied: 'So I mightn't be peri-menopausal at all? I might just be normally stressed.'

She liked that idea a whole lot more than the menopause one. Stress was a far better prospect than a one-way trip on the Old Woman Express.

'The blood tests will tell us,' Felix said. 'But there are lots of ways of coping with stress.'

'You're going to suggest Mindfulness, aren't you?' said Frankie beadily.

Felix laughed. 'No,' he said. 'Actually I was going to suggest finding a hobby, something that would help you relax.'

'I don't have time for hobbies,' Frankie said. 'I haven't bothered with hobbies since . . . I can't remember when. I've always been too busy looking after the children or working. Hobbies? Who has hobbies?'

'Lots of people do. Painting, gardening—'

She interrupted him. 'You should see the state of our garden! It needs a mechanical digger then a fleet of experts to plant things before you could even think about any actual gardening a normal person could do.'

'Doing up the house could be a relaxing hobby?' Felix suggested, unperturbed.

Frankie started to laugh and felt the rage and resentment flood away. 'Felix, you are funny. I'm just being a bad-tempered old cow. I'm sorry, this is all you need when you've got a waiting room full of really sick people.'

'People don't just come to the doctor when they're straightforward sick,' Felix reminded her. 'And being peri-menopausal is something you need to deal with. Hormone imbalance is no fun, so we'll find out what the results say and I'll ring you, OK? And think about that hobby thing,' he added as she got up to go.

'Yes, Felix. By the way, how many hobbies do you have?' Frankie stood at the door, grinning.

'Touché,' Felix said, smiling. 'But give it some thought anyway. It would be good for Seth too, having something to occupy him. You know the effects of not working on the male psyche.'

'Oh yes,' she said grimly. 'I could write a book about it. Thanks, Felix. Bye.'

Seth. If only he did have something to occupy him. He could have done some voluntary work, maybe offered himself as a mentor for young architects – but all the young architects had left the country. There was no one left to mentor. So instead he'd given up on life and now she had to deal with the fallout.

At least he'd picked up a bit since Lillie had come. But she wouldn't be staying for ever, and then what would they do?

Frankie decided she'd best warn Lillie about her mother well ahead of dinner.

'Madeleine is very energetic,' she said on Saturday afternoon as they sat beside the French windows with pale spring light beaming in on them. Energetic was a good word, Frankie decided. Her mother had been on the phone several times since Lillie had arrived, dying to be invited over.

'Seth says Lillie's the image of his mother,' Madeleine had said excitedly. 'Jennifer was a fine-looking woman. I think we'll get on like a house on fire. I told Seth I want to drive her to Dublin for a few days' sightseeing and that kind of thing. Bring her to a show. It'd be great.'

'Seth told me your mother's very lively,' Lillie replied. 'I'm looking forward to meeting your parents, they sound wonderful. Your sister Gabrielle and her husband are coming too?'

Lillie was being polite, Frankie thought.

'They are,' she agreed. 'Look, what I'm trying to say is that Mum's great but she has all these plans for you and I don't want you bamboozled into going on a mad trip with her. She's talking about taking you to see the Book of Kells and Glendalough and—'

'That sounds wonderful.'

'But you were talking about visiting your mother's child-hood home on the Beara Peninsula,' Frankie reminded her. 'I don't want you tired out.'

She couldn't tell Lillie what was really worrying her. Having Lillie about the house had cheered Seth up no end, but if Madeleine got hold of her, that would be that. Lillie would be dragged off to Kinsale and they'd never see her again.

Frankie's parents, Madeleine and Seamus, were first to arrive, along with their dog, Mr Chow, a Pekingese who left trails of fur after him wherever he waddled.

'Mother.' Frankie went to hug her but Madeleine had already shot past her into the flat like a heat-seeking missile locked on target.

'She's dying to see Lillie,' said Seamus apologetically, giving his daughter a hug. 'She's been like a cat on a hot tin roof all week waiting for this.'

'How are you, Dad?' asked Frankie, feeling strangely emotional in the embrace of her father.

'I'm grand,' he said. 'Here.' He produced a canvas supermarket bag. 'A bottle of wine and some crab cakes. I have them in an insulated bag to keep them cool, so give me that back, love.'

Frankie knew that this little something extra would have been her father's idea. Madeleine only brought wine to dinner parties.

They went on through to the kitchen-cum-living-room, where Madeleine was happily perched beside Lillie on the sofa, talking at ninety miles an hour.

'Melbourne sounds wonderful. We never did get that far on our travels, did we, Seamus? And talking of travelling, Seth tells me you haven't strayed much out of Redstone since you came.'

'We went to my old home,' Seth piped up.

He was in the kitchen part of the room, shaking up the salad dressing Lillie had made. He loved the Thai-infused concoctions she'd been introducing him to. For years, he and Frankie had been using salad dressings out of bottles, but now he was whisking them up himself or watching Lillie do her magic with lemongrass and ginger or honey and mustard.

'Have you taken her out of the city yet to show her County Cork?' demanded Madeleine. She turned back to Lillie: 'I'd be delighted to show you around – there's so much to see.'

Lillie could see where Frankie got her energy from. Her mother was a human dynamo, racing along at full tilt. But having noticed the way Frankie and Seth both tensed up at Madeleine's suggestion, she shook her head and said, 'That's very kind of you, but I'm taking things at a slow pace for the moment. Seth's running the show and looking after me.'

Beside her, Frankie smiled.

'Right,' said the irrepressible Madeleine. 'We'll talk about it again. Now,' she cast an eye at her son-in-law, 'have you opened that bottle of wine yet?'

Freya Byrne basked in the early March sunshine, swinging her legs as she sat on the wall behind the school. She waited while Kaz took three puffs on the cigarette then reached over to take it from her.

'Wish they still sold them to us in the off-licence,' said Kaz.

'Fags are bad for you,' said Freya, inhaling deeply. She could get by without cigarettes if truth be told, which was just as well because she couldn't really afford them.

She'd negotiated two precious cigarettes that morning in exchange for doing one of the sixth year's art homework.

'It's supposed to be a still life,' said the girl, Mona, who couldn't draw for toffee but had chosen art because she'd been dating an arty sort of guy at the start of fifth year, when she'd had to choose her subjects.

Freya thought it was a good thing Mona hadn't been dating a physics dude.

Mona's interpretation of a bottle and two bananas looked like something an absinthe-addicted painter might have done in full hallucination mode: two yellow sausages and the Eiffel tower.

'Bananas are difficult,' Freya muttered, taking the sketchbook and the conte crayon from Mona and beginning to sketch in the lines. 'Never arrange them facing you: it's too hard to get the sense of perspective.'

Mona watched Freya. 'Yeah,' she said. The finer points of perspective were lost on her. When Freya was done, she proffered three cigarettes.

'Two's fine,' said Freya, feeling guilty for accepting anything from Mona, who really was so guileless that it felt like taking sweets from a first year.

'You should have got three,' said Kaz, taking the cigarette

back and inhaling one last time before lighting the precious second cigarette from the dregs of the last.

Kaz had fewer scruples than Freya. She lived with four older sisters, all of whom teased her unmercifully. The five of them had a bartering system for cigarettes, make-up, money and clothes that would rival that of the New York Stock Exchange. At least Kaz had sisters. Freya had felt very lonely before she moved in with Opal and Ned.

'What's wrong?' Kaz asked, seeing Freya's glum expression.

'It's my weekend with my mother.'

Freya didn't have to say more. She and Kaz had been friends ever since they both turned twelve and had started secondary school together. That was the same year Freya had finally left her mother's care.

Leaving primary school for the big school meant a putting away of childish things for most of the first-year students, but it had signalled a return to a proper childhood for Freya. Aunt Opal cooked dinners, washed Freya's clothes and fussed over her lovingly. Her own mother hadn't done these things for a long time. Freya sometimes wondered if her mother had ever done them, or if Dad had done it all? She couldn't remember. It was strange how that part of her childhood felt as if it all happened a long, long time ago. Everything had changed when her father had died. She should have remembered better – she'd been nine, after all, but so much of the past was a haze. While certain things stood out the rest seemed to just recede into the distance.

That evening as she walked home from school, Freya tried to recall that line from Shakespeare about the unwilling schoolboy creeping like a snail. How did it go? She was woolly about lots of the stuff she'd learned. Huge tracts of school work had been gobbled up by her brain, but she doubted she'd ever be able to pull them out for an exam.

In her case, she was creeping *away* from school, sluggish

137

and unwilling because it was her weekend with Gemma. Back when Dad was alive, life had been wonderful. Nobody had parents like hers. So in love, so much fun. So open to everything.

Sure, Mum was often nervous, but Dad had the knack of soothing her. He was a lot younger than Uncle Ned; in fact you'd hardly know they were brothers. Dad was a lot more outgoing, with a wide circle of friends who came from all walks of life. He'd do impulsive things like bringing home some busker off the street to have dinner with them, offering him a bed for the night. And if Mum had fussed – because even in those days she did fuss – Dad would calm her down.

'It'll be all right, Gemma,' he'd say. 'We've got so much, let's just give a little bit.'

'But what if he robs us in the night or something?'

'He won't,' Dad would say firmly.

Freya could picture him saying it, those beautiful clear grey eyes full of wisdom and kindness for the human race. She wished her own eyes were like her dad's, but she took after her mother in looks. Skinny, long crazy dark hair, dark eyes. Even in those wonderful days when there had been so much joy in life, Freya had known that it was her dad she wanted to take after. She loved when they were alone in the car going somewhere and he talked to her, teaching her all that he knew about the world: about goodness and decency and how to look beyond the outer trappings of a person to see what was hiding inside.

He was impetuous but at the same time steady. The boom of thunder, a bit of the roof falling in, an enormous tax bill, next-door's dog coming in and chasing the three cats around and around until the whole place was destroyed: he'd respond to it all with the same calm equanimity. 'It'll be fine,' Dad would say. 'Nobody died, did they?'

And then *he'd* died. A car accident. He'd been killed instantly, people kept telling her, as if that should be a comfort to her. But at the age of nine, all that mattered was that he was dead.

'You'll get through it. You're a clever, strong girl and you have to be there for your mum,' one of her mother's friends had told her. Someone who hadn't understood that parents actually had responsibility for their children, Freya thought with pure rage.

What about me? Who is going to be there for me? Freya had wanted to screech back at this stupid woman.

With her father gone, Freya realized he'd been telling the truth about all the 'catastrophes' her mother would get so agitated about. They hadn't been catastrophes at all. The house could be sorted out after next-door's dog had run through it, something could be done about the tax bill and the roof. Everything was fixable but death.

And it turned out that her mother wasn't fixable either. Daniel Byrne had been her anchor to the world. Without him she had begun to drift away, like a helium balloon spiralling beyond reach, carried off on the slightest breeze.

Once a month Freya went to her mother's for a weekend. It was a duty.

Kaz could never understand why she didn't wriggle out of it. 'Why do you go if it drives you so mad? After a weekend with her you come in and you're all stressed, you're not normal. You're wired.'

Freya had given up trying to explain. Kaz didn't get it when she said that she felt guilty for abandoning her mother for the calmness of Aunt Opal and Uncle Ned's house. One weekend a month felt like a small sacrifice for what she had with her aunt and uncle. Life was wonderful now. Not as wonderful as it would have been if her father was still alive, but at least she was loved, happy and secure.

As for her mother – depending on Gemma's state of mind, the house on Waldron Avenue was either super tidy in an obsessive compulsive way or else looked as if a travelling circus had recently vacated the premises and a rapscallion army of monkeys had run amok. Freya never knew quite what to expect when she rounded the corner by the overgrown hedge and turned up the drive. It wasn't the most beautiful of bungalows, but her father had done his best to prettify it. He'd erected a verandah around it in an effort to lend a faint air of Southern charm, like the houses in Georgia – a place he and Gemma had visited before they had Freya.

'I'd love peach trees,' Dad would say wistfully, 'but it's too cool to grow them here.'

Instead, he'd planted damask and bourbon roses, and honeysuckle. Once carefully pruned by her father, these days the plants just ran riot. Now, as she walked up the short drive to where her mother's car was parked askew, Freya noticed that some frenzied cutting back of the climbing plants had been going on. The handkerchief of a lawn had been cut too, but in a haphazard fashion, with all the cut grass left on the weed-filled lawn to rot. Unusually, the edges were trimmed neatly. Freya knew her mother was as likely to have trimmed the verges with scissors as the proper clippers. 'I can't find things,' Gemma would say. 'I don't know where your dad put anything.'

'They're in the shed with all the other gardening tools,' Freya would say calmly. She'd found that saying things calmly was the only way to go. There was no point recriminating or touching on difficult subjects, and certainly no point in arguing. Her mother operated best if she was allowed to make wild statements unchallenged.

Two big sea-green planters sat outside the front door, each spilling over with recently-planted garden centre shrubs and flowers. Freya wondered where the money for those had come from. Her mother's income did not leave room for such frivolities. The front door had been painted too, with another coat of bright white paint, but her mother wouldn't have done any of the sanding down and priming stuff that Dad always did, which explained why the flaky navy blue it had been before was visible underneath. Freya took a deep breath, stuck her key in the lock and went in.

'Hey, Mum, it's Freya, I'm home,' she called into the echoing hallway.

'Hello, darling. I'd forgotten you were coming, but how lovely to see you.' Gemma appeared from the kitchen wearing one of her husband's old shirts, which was splattered with paint. Her hair was tied up into a crazy bun, also paint spattered, and in one hand she held a paint roller.

It was difficult to judge dispassionately how one's own mother looked but Freya had once overheard her cousin Steve say that Aunt Gemma was sexy for an older woman. Freya thought he was probably right.

Her mother was small and slim with dark hair, like Freya's, but her eyes glittered in a dangerous way that men might find alluring, and she favoured silky T-shirts worn over skinny jeans and quite often went out bra-less.

Today, the skimpy look had given precedence to keeping her clothes clean, although the shirt was open to her breastbone and Freya was pretty sure there was nothing beneath it. 'I'm decorating. The place hasn't been painted for ages and I can't afford to have anyone in, so I'm doing it myself.' Gemma's face shone with delight. Her eyes sparkled. 'Come on, you can help. I thought purple for the kitchen. I fell in love with that very expensive paint with all the interesting names, only I can't afford that, *obviously*,' Gemma said with the grimace she invariably used when discussing financial matters. 'So I mixed my own. You can get the shop to do it, but what's the fun in that? So I got this dark purple – two pots, actually – and a smaller pot of pink. It's nice, don't you think? There's a warmth to it.'

Freya wished, as she so often did, that she was not quite so analytical. Nobody else would make the mental leap from her mother spending too much (plants for outside, tubs of purple paint) to reach the conclusion that Aunt Opal would have to find extra money from somewhere to buy food for Gemma.

Uncle Ned never really knew what went on.

'It upsets him to see your mother this way,' Opal had explained once when Freya caught her purchasing a full week's shopping for Gemma, who'd splurged all her own money on hair extensions 'to cheer myself up'. 'Ned cares about your mum and wishes there were something he could do to help.'

'Nobody can help,' Freya said flatly, and had been rewarded with the warmth of Opal's worn hand creeping into hers.

'We'll help her,' Opal had whispered. 'But we won't upset your uncle Ned by telling him, OK?'

That night, Freya had sat in her cosy eyrie at 21 St Brigid's Terrace and stared out at the glowing amber lights of the houses around them, wishing that she didn't have a mother who needed to be helped.

Now, with a whole weekend to be spent with her mother and no light at the end of the tunnel until Sunday night when she'd return to Opal and Ned's, Freya had the same thought. If only her mother was different. Sometimes she wished Opal were her mother, but then she felt guilty for that. It wasn't her mother's fault. Some people weren't as strong as others. The real world was just too hard for them and they preferred the world of their own creation where they could believe anything they wanted.

'Are you going to keep painting for much longer this evening, Mum?' Freya asked in the calm voice she used with her mother. The faintest hint of disapproval could send Gemma over the edge at speed.

'What time is it?' Gemma looked down at the wrist bearing her husband's old watch, with the brown leather strap that was too big for her, no matter that she fastened it on the tightest hole.

'Half five,' Freya said.

School ended at three on Fridays but she hadn't been able to face her mother that early and had gone instead to the café near her mother's house, where she'd made a hot chocolate and a bun last as long as she could. Only the darkening of the March evening had sent her out into the cold.

'Time to stop painting,' said Gemma cheerfully. 'I haven't anything in for dinner, Freya. I forgot you were coming. We could get a pizza?'

'And a DVD, perhaps,' suggested Freya. If they had something to watch as they ate their takeaway pizza, then they wouldn't need to talk and Freya wouldn't have to listen to her mother discussing how life would have been different if Daniel was still alive. It wasn't as if Freya didn't wish her father hadn't died – of course she did, but she knew he was gone and that she had to cope with it. Only her mother seemed incapable of grasping that.

In the car on the way to the pizza place, they stopped to get a DVD.

'You look and see if there's anything good,' said Gemma, handing Freya her store membership card but no money. She headed towards a nearby off-licence. 'I'll just grab a couple of bottles of wine. Coke or Seven-Up for you?'

'Seven-Up,' said Freya numbly.

In the DVD shop, she took the money Opal had given her that morning from her pocket.

'Just in case you need it,' Opal had said.

Freya felt her eyes sting with tears and wished she were with Opal and Ned now. Her mother was going to nibble pizza and drink glass after glass of wine all evening.

If Gemma was the adult, how come it always felt the other way round?

That Friday evening, in her pretty kitchen, Opal busied herself cooking dinner, feeling miserable. The house seemed empty without Freya. Freya always had stories from school. Yesterday she'd told Opal and Ned how Miss Lawrence, who taught French, had clearly been in a foul humour and had given them a test.

'There should be a law against teachers setting tests just because they're in a bad mood,' Freya said. 'You know, a conflict of interest law or something. If I ever run for government, I think I'll put it in my election manifesto. It would be the same for people in charge of companies, like David. But I can't see David making people suffer just because he's in a bad mood.'

'He is in a bit of a bad mood right now,' Ned had said, surprising them both.

Ned was not normally the sort of person who noticed moods. He was a great man for cheering people up but not because he sensed that people needed cheering up. Ned just liked to see people laughing.

'Is he?' said Opal, astonished. 'I hadn't noticed.'

'I reckon it's girlfriend trouble,' Ned went on, clearly pleased that he'd spotted something his wife hadn't.

'What girlfriend? I didn't know he was going out with anyone,' Freya said, feeling put out because she liked to have her finger on the pulse.

'I don't know who she is or was, but it's off now,' said Ned. 'I heard him saying something to Brian on Sunday. Brian was trying to set him up on a date with Liz's bridesmaid, Chloe, but David didn't want to know. He said he didn't want to date anyone ever again – those were his exact words. Then Brian said there was no pleasing some people, and they left the kitchen.'

'Why didn't you tell us before, love?' asked Opal, worried now. 'Poor David. And he didn't say a thing.'

Her sons might be grown men, but to her they would always be her children. When they hurt, she hurt.

'I forgot about it till now,' Ned said, looking sheepish.

144

'Don't worry about it,' he added hastily. 'You've enough on your plate, what with the wedding.'

'The wedding! Dear Lord,' said Opal. 'I keep forgetting to phone Miranda to thank her for the blessed invitations. I sent off replies, but I should have rung to say how lovely they were. She's bound to be mad, you know.'

'Why?' asked Freya, who'd opened hers and was already plotting to bring Kaz. Kaz loved weddings and one of her sisters had a leather dress that would look fabulous, apparently, and shock Miranda nicely. 'Just because she's devoting her life to this wedding, you don't have to phone and congratulate her on every little thing, Opal.'

'I know I shouldn't, Freya, but she'll be expecting me to tell her how wonderful they are, I know she will,' Opal said, sighing.

Almost two weeks had passed since the blasted gold envelopes had landed on her mat. She'd forwarded Meredith's and heard nothing back. Opal guessed that Miranda would expect messages of praise as well as the reply card, and had been meaning to phone but she'd put it off. She just didn't have the heart for being talked down to. Any contact with Miranda was guaranteed to leave her feeling miserable. The whole wedding hung over her in a way she knew it shouldn't.

It was like this weekend, Opal thought now as she cut up some carrots for her and Ned: all a bit empty without Freya.

Only that morning, she'd talked to Molly next door about her wedding nerves and Molly, who had only boys but who'd heard all sorts of horror stories about 'mother-of' competitiveness at weddings, kept telling Opal not to give in without a fight.

'Just because they've the money to have a big wedding at a posh venue doesn't make them better people, does it?' Molly had said, poking round in Opal's cupboards to find more sugar because the bowl was empty.

She knew where everything was in the kitchen as well as Opal did.

'I can't believe you haven't got your dress yet, Opal. You're cutting it fine, you know. It's less than four weeks to Easter. What if you can't find anything in the shops and have to get it made? Then you'll be in trouble. If you'd take my advice, you should go all out and go to some of the expensive shops, Opal, love. Let Madam Miranda see that we know how to do things in style.'

Opal began to fret. She knew she'd left it terribly late to get her dress for the wedding but she felt so overwhelmed by Miranda. Opal was beginning to think that she might as well wear something old, because either way, Miranda would be rude about it. Brian, bless him, wouldn't notice what anyone but Liz wore, so he wouldn't mind.

'I'm wearing my blue suit,' added Molly, who was, of course, going to the wedding as part of the Byrne family contingent, along with Bobbi and her daughter, Shari.

'The one you wore to Gilda's fiftieth?' asked Opal. 'That really suits you.'

'I was thinking of getting a fake-tan spray,' said Molly, who had never tried it before but was determined that Brian's side of the wedding party would not be outshone. 'You should too. That would be one in the eye for Miranda.'

Opal wished Freya was here now so they could talk about the prospect of Molly getting fake tanned and whether Opal was being old-fashioned saying she didn't want to try it. Some women came away looking gently bronzed, but she'd seen others who looked as if they'd been rolled in peanut butter.

Freya would have made her feel she wasn't an old fuddy-duddy for wanting to stick to her own skin colour.

The house was so lonely without her.

But at least, Opal consoled herself, she and Bobbi had a nice treat lined up. The new knitting shop was having a grand opening tomorrow at half five. She'd thought it was a bit late in the day for an opening, but Bobbi had pointed out it was the perfect time because there'd be plenty of people around and the other shop owners would be able to drop in to support the venture before closing up themselves. Opal planned to treat herself to some wool because she hadn't knitted anything in ages.

'Peggy's a sweetheart,' Bobbi told her when she phoned to say she'd accepted on both of their behalves. 'There's a bit of a mystery there—'

'And you're determined to get to the bottom of it,' said Opal, laughing. 'You and Freya are like peas in a pod: both mad to know what's going on all the time.'

'It's good to stay informed and on top of things,' Bobbi said.

Opal didn't feel particularly informed or on top of things this evening. Freya was gone to her mother's and who knew what she'd be fed when she was there. Gemma's notion of cooking was either a basin of couscous and bean sprouts if she was in a save-the-earth mood or McDonald's if she was in a lazy frame of mind.

David was miserable over a girl and he hadn't told her, which made it all the worse. What sort of girl could turn down someone as kind and thoughtful as David? Opal thought indignantly. She must be a complete fool if she'd thrown over David. And the matter of phoning Miranda still hung over her. Had Meredith replied to her invitation? Come to think of it, she hadn't heard from Meredith for some time, another source of sorrow. Opal had become very good at pretending she was fine with Meredith's glamorous new life in Dublin but real friends, like Bobbi and Molly, knew how much Meredith's absence and rare contact hurt her mother.

The gravy done, Opal put two plates in the oven to heat and sank onto a kitchen chair to wait for Ned's return. Everything felt so skewed lately. She wished she could wave a wand and make things right.

Chapter Eight

On Saturday, the morning of the grand opening, Peggy woke suddenly and sat up in bed, feeling the heat of a bad dream suffusing her whole body. She'd been having the strangest dreams for the past week. Not ones about having finally opened her shop, the culmination of years of hopes and dreams. Nor about the strange and yet sadly familiar conversation with her mother on the phone two days before.

'I wish you would come and see it, Mum. You'd like the shop. It would be your sort of dream: shelves piled with wool, these amazing bamboo needles, all sorts of clever accessories for marking your stitches and storing your bits and pieces . . . gorgeous stuff.'

'I can't,' Kathleen Barry had whispered. 'I just can't. You know what he'll be like about it.'

He was Tommy Barry, Peggy's father. She hadn't wanted him to come to the opening, wouldn't have dreamed of asking him, and she knew it was expecting too much of her mother to come to Cork by herself. Even assuming he'd let her.

'Sorry, Peggy. I'll call you later. You know how it is . . .'

The phone had gone dead abruptly. Which was nothing new. But familiarity didn't lessen the pain for Peggy as she stood there, tears rolling down her face. She'd so wanted her mother to share in her moment in the sun, but that type of thing was for other families, normal families.

As she cried, Peggy realized that time, distance and even months of counselling hadn't helped as much as she'd hoped.

Replacing the receiver, she sank into the brown tweedy armchair which was the piece of furniture she hated most in the house, and for the next half an hour she just let the tears flow.

Climbing out of the abyss of the past was one, glorious thing: but the realization that not everybody might want to make the climb with you, was another.

Kathleen Barry was going to maintain the façade that her life was going well. This piece of artifice had enabled her to cope with her life. Peggy should have been used to it by now.

But it wasn't the pain of that realization that had made its way into Peggy's dreams, disturbing her equilibrium.

Last night, she'd dreamt the same dream she'd had every night since she crept out of David's bed. In the dream, they were living in a small cottage – her own cottage, but prettier, all done up. She could see David standing in the doorway, waiting to welcome her home, but she couldn't get past the gate. Each time she opened the gate, the ground would open up, tipping her into a gaping chasm. Her arms weren't strong enough to climb out. David was on the other side of the crack and couldn't help but he kept calling her name all the time.

When she woke, she felt exhausted. Even awake, the dream haunted her. It had to mean something, but she was too afraid to think what. Had she made a huge mistake in leaving him? The thought was almost more than she could bear.

It had been two weeks since she'd crept out of his bed in the middle of the night and run away, leaving him that note. It made her sick to the stomach when she recalled how he'd turned up at the shop the next morning, holding the note in his hand.

He looked angry, which was terrible in itself because she'd thought he wasn't the sort of person who could look angry. Yet he was: his eyes were dark with emotion and his face was flushed. Instinctively, Peggy had taken a step backwards. Anger frightened her so much. It made her click into her chameleon state of mind when she would do anything to blend into her surroundings in an effort to avoid being the subject of the anger.

That was why she'd learned to knit and sew in the first place. She could be in the house and yet out of the line of fire. Nobody looked at the silent child knitting in the corner.

Gunther and Paolo had finished their carpentry and gone, but Peggy had hired a sparky shop assistant called Fiona – Fifi for short. When David arrived on that terrible Saturday morning, Fifi was in the kitchen making tea.

'How could you run off and leave me a note like this?' David demanded.

Today, in this angry state, he seemed so big and tall, and she felt the old instinctive fear take over.

'I can't believe you'd be this cruel, Peggy,' he added, brandishing the note. 'We weren't a seven-day fling, we were special, we had something special. What was wrong? Why did you run out on me?'

Her rational mind told her he was a good, decent man who had every right to be angry, but the irrational part of her, nurtured over her lifetime, made her scared.

'Fifi!' she screamed.

Fifi's head appeared in the doorway.

'Something wrong?' she said.

'Yes, t-t-there is,' stammered Peggy.

David had calmed down but was looking at her strangely.

'You're scared, aren't you?' he asked in astonishment. 'Peggy, I'm angry but I would never hurt you,' he said, as gently as he possibly could. 'I came to say I'm crazy about you, really crazy in love with you to be honest, and I've never

150

said that to another woman, not ever. It was love at first sight for me but I . . .'

He took a step towards her, but she flinched and moved away. When she went into the fear zone, she couldn't come out of it: she felt frozen in fear, in emotional lockdown. Nothing could break through.

'Peggy. Stop looking at me like that. You look as if I'm going to hit you or something. I swear I would never do that, never.'

She could see the bewilderment in his eyes and suddenly he looked like her David again: not threatening at all.

But still, he was a man. She knew what men were like, how their mood could change in a flash, how the hail-fellow-well-met air would suddenly vanish into tyranny. And women with pasts like hers inevitably chose men who'd give them a similar future.

With Fifi behind her, she could tell him to go. It was the only thing to do. Love at first sight and crazy love weren't for someone like her. The past had marked her too much to ever fit into that simple mould.

'Please go,' she'd said. 'Now.'

'You heard her, David,' said Fifi.

With one sad look at Peggy, he left.

'Do you want to tell me what that was about?' Fifi asked, and Peggy shook her head. 'I grew up not too far from where he lives,' Fifi added. 'He's always seemed a decent guy – but I've been proved wrong about that sort of thing before. Did he hurt you or upset you? If so, we have to do something about it. No guy should get away with that.'

Again, Peggy shook her head. Some guys did get away with it, for entire lifetimes, and nobody ever called the police because nobody ever saw it. The only people who did were the people who lived with them, and if they'd said anything about it, nobody would have believed them anyway.

151

Sure he's a lovely man. A real family man. I won't hear a word said against him.

When she'd been small, she'd learned that people didn't want to believe in tyranny unless they saw it with their own eyes, and how could they when the tyrant in question was so skilled at fooling people? Street angel/house devil didn't go any way to explaining the truth behind the façade. When nobody saw, nobody helped.

'No,' she whispered, trying to calm herself. 'He's a good guy but . . .' She didn't know how to explain. It would sound so strange to Fifi. 'I slept with him and then I realized it was a mistake,' she said. 'He was nothing but kind to me. It's my problem, Fifi, not his. That's all I can say.'

Fifi stared at Peggy, questions in her eyes, but thankfully she didn't ask them.

'Fair enough. If you want to talk, I'm here. Now, tea?'

'Hell yes,' said Peggy.

They hadn't mentioned it since, but sometimes Peggy caught Fifi looking at her, trying to figure out what to make of her.

That evening, David had phoned her mobile. When Peggy didn't pick up the call, he left a message:

I don't know what was going on this morning, Peggy. I know I frightened you and I don't know how, because that wasn't my intention. I like you. A lot. I felt something special with you. I'm sorry if it was one-sided but I didn't think it was at the time. Good luck with your life. Bye.

Peggy listened to the message with a combination of misery and relief. If only she hadn't gone out to the Starlight Lounge that night, if only she hadn't met David. How could he ever understand? Nobody could, not unless they'd gone through it. The way she had.

* * *

152

Life had never been fair to Tommy Barry – or at least, that was his firm belief. He hadn't been given the family farm in Carlow, even though he was the eldest son. That honour had gone to his younger brother, Petey. Tommy had interrupted the reading of the will by flinging back his chair and shouting at his mother when the solicitor read it out.

'I'm the oldest, he's only a boy, what does he know about running a hundred acres of fine land?' Tommy raged, his anger directed towards his mother.

The solicitor, the older Mr Burke, had seen many a fight on the reading of a will and he had been warned by Mrs Barry that voices might be raised at this one. So he had his secretary, Miss Reagan, waiting at the door to phone the police if things got too heated. He was surprised to see Tommy Barry in such a temper because Mr Burke had always thought Tommy was a charming young man, very friendly to all he met. But still, money and the leaving of it did strange things to people.

Constance Barry, for all her obvious pain now that her husband was dead, had kept remarkably calm, Mr Burke thought in admiration.

Constance herself had known this would come. Tommy had expected everything to go his way from the time he was a child. To her abiding sorrow, and unlike her other three children, he had never understood about hard work or kindness, for all that he was outwardly so charming. That was the worst of it, Constance thought: Tommy's ability to fool people with his act. That her own son should turn out that way was heartbreaking.

He'd left the farm years ago. Farming wasn't for him, he'd said haughtily. Even though she'd written to him, he hadn't turned up when his poor father was ill and Petey could have done with help milking the cows. But he'd responded when he heard his father was dead, sure enough. He'd made sure he was home for the funeral and the reading of the will, dragging his poor young wife with him and that sweet baby who went rigid every time her father held her. Babies had great wisdom, Constance thought sadly, knowing she might never see little Peggy again once Tommy had stormed out in temper, which he would.

She only wished there was something she could do for poor Kathleen and little Peggy, but what?

'You haven't worked on this farm since you were sixteen and got a job in town,' she told him now, her voice calm and clear. 'Your father wanted you to go to agricultural college, but you said no, you preferred to be making your way—'

'Only till I got the farm,' said Tommy furiously.

'Once you told your father you weren't interested in the farm, there was no question of you taking it over,' Constance went on. 'Pete has worked so hard.'

Tommy looked angry enough to hit her, though she'd never known him to be violent. Looking at his pale, anxious wife, Constance hoped that this was still the case. Kathleen seemed to have grown thinner and more fragile in the two years since Tommy had married her.

'I'll fight you in the courts,' Tommy hissed at them all. Then he grabbed Kathleen by the arm. 'Come on! Don't stand there looking up at me like an idiot, we need to get out of here. I won't have them laughing at me,' he cried, half-dragging her from the room.

Constance watched with great sadness. What had she done wrong to bring up such a son? He'd always been different but should she have done something about him when he was a child, worked out how to make him like his siblings who were all easygoing? Tommy had always had a darkness about him, yet people didn't seem to notice it: instead, they saw the great charm, the attractive face. Those things must have lured in the fragile Kathleen but why would she stay with such anger?

Constance sighed at the thought of the life ahead of Kathleen

154

and little Peggy. Kathleen might have chosen to marry the sort of man she was used to and their baby would grow up knowing nothing better, an unbroken cycle. If only there was something Constance could do to help in some way.

Peggy learned from an early age that her father wasn't like the fathers of other children. He didn't sweep her up in a great hug when he got home from the garage the way Letty's dad did, and he never smiled at her mother in that romantic way Sarah's father smiled when Sarah's mother handed him a cup of tea and a biscuit.

What was oddest for the young Peggy was that her father was so charming in public, smiling at her and her mother, making people like him – and then the moment he was alone with his family again, it was as if he'd flicked a switch, turning off the public display of charm. Then, he'd be bitter and controlling again, demanding his dinner. If he was in a bad mood, even the sight of Peggy would make him angry. When she was little and hadn't yet learned how life was, she might cry, at which point Tommy would shout at her to get out of his sight or he'd show her the back of his hand and really give her something to cry about . . .

She didn't understand it at all.

'Your father hasn't had what was rightfully his, so he gets a bit upset,' Kathleen would whisper by way of explanation whenever Tommy flew into one of his rages, a state of affairs that could be brought on by all sorts of circumstances from someone annoying him at work or putting his money on the wrong horse at the bookies.

Theirs was not a home where people were invited in on a regular basis, but on the few occasions they did have visitors, the charming Tommy held sway: praising his daughter for her cleverness at school and prophesying great things for her in the future.

In public he'd even be complimentary about her mother.

'Isn't this a great apple pie?' he'd say as everyone sat down to eat while Kathleen hovered nervously. 'My wife has a light hand with the pastry, that's for sure.'

When they were alone, no such nice words ever passed his lips. He communicated through the medium of spite, telling his wife that her outfit was ridiculous on her, or telling Peggy that he'd been disappointed in her school exam results. Nothing was ever positive, no compliments ever passed his lips.

He was forever changing jobs, so they moved many times when Peggy was young. She got used to always being the strange child in the schoolroom. She knew how to blend subtly into the background so that no teacher ever asked what was going on or why. That was the easy way to do it.

As Peggy got older, the family settled in the ugly bungalow outside Portlaoise, but Peggy remained a mystery to most of the kids in her class. She wasn't allowed to go to anyone's home because she could never invite anyone back to hers. At least her father wasn't a drinker, she thought as she got older. If he had been, she and her mother would be dead. His rage plus alcohol would have made for a lethal combination.

She learned how to sit quietly in a room so as not to be noticed while her mother made embroidered napkins for Carola Landseer's craft shop in the summer and handknitted sweaters in the autumn. Peggy learned how to knit and sew too and she'd sit, fingers clicking, creating something beautiful and soft to bring in a bit of extra money for Kathleen. Early on, Peggy discovered a safe place inside her head that she could retreat to, dreaming of a time when she and her mother could leave Portlaoise and set up a knitting and craft shop of their own.

She'd paint it the lavender of the Farmer's Kitchen, a quaint establishment where her mother worked several days a week, serving tea to elegant ladies like Carola Landseer and her friends. Carola's husband was a Presbyterian minister, a decent man who was always fighting for the rights for the under-privileged, even though he and his wife lived in a large home on the outskirts of town. Carola began to take a special interest in the shy woman who served her tea and who made such beautiful things for her shop.

Peggy suspected that Mrs Landseer had long since guessed that something was amiss in the Barry household. If Mrs Landseer caught sight of Peggy making her way home from school, she would call her over. It was subtly done, but there was a running theme to her questions.

'And your mother, is she doing well?' Mrs Landseer might say. 'She seemed a little strained the other day. Is everything all right at home?'

How Peggy longed to tell her the truth. But her mother would have been mortified to discover that someone she admired was privy to their business. There was a danger that if Carola heard what went on in the Barry household, she'd confront Tommy. And then Peggy and her mother would pay the price.

All through her teenage years, Peggy imagined her mother and herself living in peace somewhere far away from her father. They'd be happy, just the two of them, never needing anyone but each other, with no overpowering presence colouring every day with fear and darkness. Carola became closer to Kathleen, talking to her and telling her she was a victim of abuse.

'He doesn't have to hit you to abuse you,' Carola explained once, when she visited the house at a time when Tommy wasn't home. Peggy stood outside the door and listened, praying with all her heart that her mother would pay atten-tion to Carola, even if she didn't pay attention to Peggy.

'Look at you, Kathleen, you're skin and bone from fear. Nobody has to live like that. You must leave him. I will be here for you.'

When she was eighteen, Peggy told her mother she was

leaving. She wanted to earn money so the knitting shop could become a reality for them both instead of just a dream.

She had to wait till she was twenty-one for the money left to her by Grandmother Constance, a woman she'd never met. The will had stated that the money should be held in trust for Peggy until she came of age, a fact which enraged her father, who ranted that the money should by rights have been his. He was furious that 'the old bitch' had kept his inheritance from him.

'Come with me, Mum, you don't have to stay with him,' begged Peggy at the time. 'Nobody should live this way, being shouted at like you're a dog. Even a dog shouldn't be treated the way he treats us. It will never get better, never. And without me, he'll grind you into the ground even further.'

'I can't leave,' Kathleen said, grey eyes huge in her thin face.

Peggy guessed her mother weighed about six and a half stone now, whittled down to skeletal thinness by a life of anxiety and psychological abuse.

'Why can't you leave?' Peggy had said in despair. 'He doesn't love you, we both know that. He doesn't love me, either. He uses you as a mental punchbag. Nobody else I know lives like that.'

Kathleen flinched at this and Peggy hated being so blunt. She could tell from the look in those frightened grey eyes how much these words must hurt, but she had to do it, it was her only hope of saving Kathleen.

'Do you think Claire Delaney across the road lets Mike talk to her like that?' Peggy went on. 'Of course not. He wouldn't dare. Or Miriam from the café? Does her husband treat her like dirt? No, he doesn't. Dad's not normal, he's full of rage and bitterness. Please come with me.'

'I can't. Please don't ask me,' her mother had said. 'And don't let your father hear you say such things. He'll go mad, you know. He'll go mad when he hears you're leaving. He needs me, you know he does. And what would I do out there? What can I do? I'm too old for anything, too stupid.'

'That's *his* voice talking,' Peggy said furiously. '*He* tells you you're stupid and old, but you're not! You've worked in the Farmer's Kitchen for the last six years, you spent years sewing and knitting to make the money to feed and clothe us when he wouldn't give you any housekeeping. You're so clever, you can do loads of things. That bastard has made you feel as if you're hopeless, useless.'

'Don't call your father that,' said Kathleen. 'I can't go, I can't.' She was crying now and shaking.

Peggy had known she was defeated. Years of Tommy telling Kathleen she was useless had made her believe it with her heart and soul. Peggy often wondered what sort of screwed-up family her mother had come from for her to be so cowed into believing that she deserved Tommy Barry as a husband. Her mother's background was even more of a mystery to her than her father's. But it had certainly included an abusive male figure – Peggy was sure of that. Which was why she was going to stay single. Women were drawn to the familiar, no matter how damaging. But not Peggy, no way.

'You should stay and go to college,' her father raged when he heard she was leaving home. 'You'll never amount to anything without exams.'

He didn't have exams. His education had come to an end at the age of sixteen, which had been his family's fault, he said. He had plans for Peggy. Plans to show everyone around the town that his family were bright and smart and his girl would make fools out of them all because she was clever, good at studying. And she'd still live at home, under his thumb.

Instead, here she was, up and leaving. No sign of college or university, just heading off into the bright blue yonder without so much as a by your leave.

'Say something, Kathleen, will you?' he'd growled at her

mother. This was a turn-up for the books. He never normally asked her mother's advice on anything.

'Peggy, you know your father is right. It's harder and harder to get a job, and the more education and letters after your name, the easier . . .' Her mother's voice had trailed off.

Peggy wondered if her mother had finished a sentence for years now.

As if she knew there was no point finishing a sentence because her father didn't listen to them anyway.

'You're absolutely right,' Peggy told him. 'I'm sure I'll be back.' This was, she'd discovered, one of the best ways to treat her father. Agree with him on all things, and then do exactly what you wanted to do anyway. This particular method infuriated him beyond all other things but somehow he didn't lash out at her the way he did with her mother. It was as if he knew that Peggy wasn't that much like her mother and wouldn't have taken it.

'Yes, you'll be back,' he'd said ominously as she'd stood at the door.

By this time both she and her mother were crying. Peggy's giant rucksack was standing by the door, packed and fit to burst.

'Of course, I'll be back lots of times,' she had said.

'And there's lots of scoundrels out there,' her father hissed, as if the world was a heaving, seething mass of evil people just waiting to pounce.

'You're right, Dad, I'll be careful,' said Peggy seriously, thinking that the most dangerous person in the world could so easily be the person who had fathered you.

But there would be no point in saying that, not when her mother was still there, living with him. She'd be the one who'd suffer. For her mother's sake, Peggy had gone through the motions, hugging her father, telling him she'd miss him. She'd even steeled herself, found something deep inside and said, 'If I need advice, of course, I'll phone you, Dad.' He'd liked that; it appealed to his vanity. She'd only done it for her mother's sake, but it had still hurt her to do it because it was so fake. Peggy was determined never to be fake again. She would find a life for herself and it would never involve any man.

Marriage and children were a total mistake for someone like her. A recipe for disaster. She knew that. It was in the genes. Everything was genetic. Parenting skills certainly were, as was picking the right man. Peggy would be no good at all at that, so she would avoid it. It was the best way, she told herself.

After the confrontation in the shop and that one phone message, David stopped phoning. But Peggy couldn't stop dreaming about him every night.

On the day of the opening, she got up early, showered, dressed and left without breakfast. She'd go straight to the shop, open up and make a coffee there. It was impossible to think sad thoughts in her lovely shop.

As always, she felt pure joy when the first customers of the day arrived. They would wander around her shop with the lavender baskets she'd bought, flinging things in with wild abandon. She'd knitted so many items over the years and kept them, and with the shop she was finally able to put them to good use. Hanging up beside the wools were scarves and shawls, intricate cardigans in Fair Isle, beautiful Aran sweaters. For every type of wool she had knit up a little piece so people could see how the wool knitted up. There was a section of the shop dedicated to 'just beginning', and people who wanted to get involved with knitting but knew absolutely nothing about it, loved that part. Peggy's shop didn't make them feel like idiots in a world of nimble-fingered knitters.

Years ago, when the shop had been no more than a longed-for dream, she'd read about someone with a similar business who'd offered knitting and sewing evening classes to grow

161

her customer base. Peggy had decided that she would do the same and now she was eager to get the classes off the ground as soon as possible.

If only she could tear her mind away from . . .

'This stuff,' said a woman, holding up a skein of beautiful Peruvian hand-dyed wool. 'What size needles do I need with it?'

The woman's question dragged Peggy back to the here and now. This was what she had to do. Build up this shop, make a good living for herself, make herself successful and strong and get enough money behind her. Then she wouldn't have to live like a caged animal under anyone's power ever again.

Chapter Nine

O n Saturday afternoon, from the mezzanine balcony,
Meredith Byrne watched the woman walking into the
Alexander Byrne Gallery. Age: who knew? Good cosmetic
surgery, that was for sure, if she was older than forty-five.
Flat ballet pumps: genuine Chanel, not knock-offs. Grey
coat that could only be cashmere even though it looked
like something a person who'd never actually seen a coat
might construct. That was cutting-edge fashion for you.
Faded skinny jeans and the expensive sort of blonde hair
that looked just-got-out-of-bed after an hour with a hairdresser tweaking the ends with wax. A look that screamed
money.

Meredith hadn't grown up with money but she could
certainly recognize it, even if the people she'd grown up with
wouldn't recognize *her* these days. Gone was the mousey
hair and the shy smile. In their place was a sleek curtain of
blonde hair, perfect teeth thanks to a fortune spent getting
titanium screws drilled into her jaw, the right clothes and
an accent that a gifted linguist would have been pushed to
place.

Meredith might not have grown up with money, but these
days, nobody would ever guess.

She gave an almost invisible nod to Charlie, the gallery's urbane young male staff member.

Pippa was given an equally almost invisible look that said 'hide'. Meredith was well used to running the gallery and if the staff she hired didn't do as she said, she fired them.

Pippa, clad in the sleek grey skirt-suit that allowed rich male buyers to admire her long legs, slipped obediently upstairs, while Charlie, wearing a sleek grey suit with an open-necked shirt that allowed rich female buyers to admire his strong physique and the tanned column of his neck, went over and murmured words which Meredith couldn't hear but which she had taught him to say.

'I'm sure you're perfectly happy to peruse on your own but if you need any help, I'm here.'

Charlie really had been a find. Like Pippa, he had a fine art degree and also like Pippa, he'd gone to one of the *right* schools, so his social background was impeccable. But his special talent was looking at a woman and making her feel as if she was the only woman in the world.

He'd thought of acting, he'd told Meredith when she hired him. 'But the money's crap for nearly everyone except about five per cent of them.'

The commission on selling a painting was miles better.

Or it had been.

Few people were buying anything these days. Most were selling in desperation, hoping to get back even a quarter of their initial investment. The Alexander Byrne Gallery was handling the recession rather well, though, partly because of Sally-Anne Alexander's incredible contacts around the world.

There were always people with money and there always would be, Sally-Anne said, green eyes shining. The trick was hunting them down and befriending them. This month alone, she'd sold four huge paintings to a billionaire from the United Arab Emirates whom she'd met on a buying trip to Switzerland.

The money hadn't come in yet, according to the bank, and

Meredith was watching the gallery's account online with a hint of unease.

The artist in question was going mad and Meredith had been consoling him all week.

'Have I ever ripped you off, Mike?' Meredith had said on the phone, behaving as if she wasn't in the slightest bit worried.

'No, you haven't ripped me off before, but I still want the money,' Mike said. 'The work's sold. I need my share now instead of waiting until Sally-Anne feels like it. What's going on there, that's what I'd like to know? I'm broke, Meredith. Haven't sold a thing for months – you know that. If it wasn't for the money I make teaching, I'd be on the streets.'

Mike's paintings weren't the sort that sold in the current climate: giant canvasses that only worked on the walls of huge office buildings or hotels, neither of which were spending on art.

He hadn't rung since Thursday and Meredith decided she'd stop staring at the gallery's account, which was distinctly in the red, and give Sally-Anne the benefit of the doubt. She'd always come through in the past.

Sally-Anne, who was still away, kept saying on the phone, 'Calm down, Meredith, the guy's good for the money. Honestly, he has two planes and owns a bank in Abu Dhabi. He's rolling in cash.'

'Why hasn't he rolled some this way?' Meredith asked. 'We need an injection of cash, I told you about the two cheques that bounced, Sally-Anne. Get the money out of this guy . . .'

But Sally-Anne was in a rush as usual. 'Must fly, sweetie. I've a delightful old French aristocrat with some bits and bobs she wants to sell. I'm taking her to tea so we can talk. Apparently, she struck up a friendship with Dalí years ago. Yes, yes, everyone struck up a friendship with Dalí. He had more friends than Facebook, but I think this one might actually be true. Talk when I'm back, byee.'

It was frustrating, but that was the way Sally-Anne operated.

Great when it came to chasing deals, but details like overdrawn accounts bored her rigid. Which was a pain for Meredith, trying to handle the everyday running of the company. The previous day she'd had an awkward conversation with the caterers she'd planned to use for a forthcoming exhibition.

Carlos, the owner, had refused point-blank to take the booking: 'Your cheque for the last opening bounced,' he told her. 'I'm giving you two days to pay us with a non-kangarooing cheque, or I'm getting our lawyers on to it.'

'Be reasonable,' Meredith had replied, 'you know us, would we do this to—'

'I didn't think so – till now,' Carlos said. 'But there's a five and a half grand hole in my bank account with the Alexander Byrne name on it. You'd better settle that before you even think of phoning me for another booking.'

Something was wrong, she thought instinctively but then buried the thought. Sally-Anne had never let her down yet.

Meredith decided she'd have to talk to Keith, Sally-Anne's husband, when they got back from their trip. Keith was the money end of the partnership and he might know why several of the accounts were in the red. Meredith had paid the Friday wages out of her own bank account, and was wondering whether transfers on a Saturday came in or not. It would be such a relief if they could start the week with money in the bank.

'Do you want a coffee, Meredith?' asked Pippa as she joined Meredith behind the glass wall of the mezzanine.

'Yeah, why not,' sighed Meredith, even though she'd had four already. No wonder sleep was harder and harder to come by these days.

She wished Sally-Anne would sort things out. Meredith had an eye for art and was great with the artists themselves. Despite her expensive clothes, however, she still hadn't entirely cracked dealing with clients. The rich were different. Pippa and Charlie, who'd always been a part of that world, could chat happily about skiing in Meribel, that summer in someone's house on Long Island, or the polo in Sotogrande, where everyone went down to the tiny port afterwards to hang out in the bars. Though Meredith had been to all those places with Sally-Anne and Keith, she hadn't been born into it. Try as she might to forget her origins, she could never shake off the memory of St Brigid's Terrace.

Plenty of people in the art world had started from much humbler beginnings, but they'd been honest about it. Meredith had simply reinvented herself. Redstone didn't exist as far as her new world was concerned. Yet the bedrock of Redstone was still inside her.

Leaving Charlie to charm the woman, she followed Pippa into the office section of the mezzanine. When buyers went upstairs, they could view paintings on a false wall behind which a glass cube of offices stood.

Meredith used to love the gallery but lately the enjoyment had gone out of it. It was hard to say why, exactly. The economy and worries about money had played their part, but it went deeper than that. The older she got, the more alone she felt. She was thirty-two; everyone her own vintage was already engaged or married. Even the younger ones seemed to have hooked up: Pippa, a mere child of twenty-four, had a boyfriend she spent weekends with in his mother's horse yard. Even Mike the painter, who was a gifted man but a stranger to soap and toothpaste, had a partner. Only Meredith was still alone. Soon thirty-three would be knocking on the door and yet there was no sign of a man on the horizon.

She did her very best not to think about it, but sometimes the thought slipped sneakily into her head: this wasn't what she'd had in mind when she left Redstone all those years ago.

Meredith had always had a passion for art. She'd been good enough to secure a place in a prestigious art college, but it hadn't taken her long to realize that she wasn't original enough to make money from her paintings. Laura, her best friend

167

from college, was the opposite: a gifted painter but hopeless at business.

'You're good at that stuff,' Laura said. 'I can't say nice things to galleries, I don't want to. I just want to paint.'

So it came about that Meredith dragged Laura's canvasses round the galleries, and then other people's too, and suddenly, she became the go-to girl for anyone interested in investing in new and interesting art. Which led her to Sally-Anne and Keith, and eventually, the opening of their gallery: theirs, because they had the capital, but they'd made her a part of it too.

'You know so much about art, you're an asset to us,' Sally-Anne had said to her six months ago. 'We'll call you partner, put your name on the gallery, and I'll get my lawyer to sort it all out. Of course, we'd need some investment. Twenty thousand ought to do it.'

Meredith had borrowed the money using her apartment as collateral. Once she was made partner, Meredith got used to people phoning up and begging Sally-Anne to get them in on her deals.

Meredith hated to ask outright questions, *hated* it. People in the know never needed to ask which were the right clubs or the right hotels. If you had to ask, it was a dead giveaway that you were an interloper, an outsider. Meredith had made it her mission in life to look as though she was one of those people in the know.

But eventually, curiosity got the better of her. She asked Sally-Anne outright what sort of property deals she did.

Sally-Anne, slim and tanned from always being in some hotspot or other, and dressed as usual in the season's most expensive clothes, fixed her entirely unwrinkled eyes on Meredith, giving the matter some thought. And then Sally-Anne explained:

'People invest money with me and I invest it for them. Usually short-term property deals with a twenty per cent profit margin. I deal with people I've known for years; mostly, people from school.'

She'd gone to a posh international school in Switzerland, the mention of which made Meredith feel entirely working class.

The deals, Sally-Anne explained, were in investment schemes quite apart from the gallery's business. With so many of her rich friends involved in complex property and trading schemes that required only a few extra million to get them off the ground, it was the most natural thing in the world for Sally-Anne to introduce them to prospective investors eager to sink their money in short-term schemes that would yield a twenty per cent return on their capital.

'Try getting that from a bank,' she used to say happily.

She'd been running her schemes for years and people were clamouring to get in on the lucrative deals.

Which explained why Meredith was getting calls from people begging her for introductions to Keith and Sally-Anne.

'I heard everyone involved in that London City thing made a quarter of a million profit,' they'd wail. 'Please tell Sally-Anne we've got money to invest and would love to get involved. Please.'

Eventually, Meredith borrowed another twenty thousand euros to invest herself. Six months later, twenty-eight thousand was deposited into her bank account.

And when Sally-Anne blithely mentioned another deal, Meredith had eagerly transferred her precious twenty-eight thousand into the Alexanders' bank accounts.

With each deal, more and more money found its way into her account. And she began to steer other people to Sally-Anne's investment fund; people like her friend Laura.

Through Sally-Anne, Meredith now owned shares in an American golf hotel, a Turkish apartment complex and a Russian shopping centre – as did Laura.

'We are so lucky,' Laura had said to her the last time Meredith had visited Laura's studio in the wild and windy Kerry mountains. 'We have a safety net, thanks to you.'

Laura was now married to Con, a bear of a Kerryman who sculpted giant figures out of reclaimed metals. They had a small daughter, Iona, who toddled happily between her parents' studios, covering the walls with small painted finger-prints, which neither Con nor Laura appeared to notice. Their home nestled at the foot of a mountain and was full of strange hand-made wooden furniture, Con's mad bronze pieces, and Laura's vast canvasses filled with moody Kerry skies and swooping ocean waves. They had two rescue dogs, a pot-bellied pig who snoozed in the kitchen in front of the fire, and a clutch of guinea pigs for Iona. The latter lived in a pen in the dining room so that the dogs couldn't stare hungrily at them and induce guinea-pig heart attacks. When you sat down in Laura and Con's house, you invariably sat on a dog chew or a cushion covered with pet hair.

When Meredith had visited in the past, she'd always wondered how the heck Laura could live in such a remote spot without a coffee shop in sight and with no restaurants, theatres or galleries within miles. But on her last trip the previous Christmas, she had been shocked to find herself envying Laura's life with little Iona and the bearded Con, who filled doorways when he stood in them.

Meredith was supposed to be the one who had it all, but as she sat at her friend's crumb-covered kitchen table warming herself in front of the Swedish wood-burning stove with that damn pig snuffling round her feet, she realized how much she envied Laura.

What Meredith had were the things money could buy. Somehow she'd failed to capture the one thing it couldn't. Why hadn't anyone ever told her that money and prestige weren't everything?

Con had persuaded her to stay over that night.

'Why drive down the hill to find a hotel in this weather when we've a spare room here? We can open a decent bottle of wine and talk about how the world is going to hell in a handcart – what do you think?' he said cheerfully, one big arm round her. 'I've got local lamb in the fridge and Herself's herb garden was doing well enough in the summer for us to make our own mint sauce. She freezes the herbs.'

'Himself's potato patch isn't going too well because Himself hates going near it. He's allergic to the spade,' Laura teased, coming into the kitchen with Iona balanced on one hip. 'They got eaten by blight, therefore the mashed potatoes will be locally grown but not from *our* garden.'

'Go away with yourself, woman,' growled Con in mock-hurt. 'Vegetables are women's work. Come here, lovey,' he added, scooping Iona into his arms and nuzzling her cheek. 'Protect me from your mother – she wants to work me to death.'

Iona, dressed in a red velour sleep-suit with a Santa motif, was quite happy to mind her daddy from all comers, even her beloved mummy.

'Dada's good, Mama,' she said gravely. 'No hitting.'

The three grownups all laughed.

'See – proof that she beats me,' said Con, with his sad face on. 'I'm just a helpless artist stuck out here with this madwoman. You need to sell more of my pieces so I have my running-away fund.'

They ate the lamb, drank the good wine, and finished up with local cheese on oat cakes, talking till Iona fell asleep in her father's arms.

'I'll put her down and you two can chat,' whispered Con, carrying the child off to bed.

'You're very lucky, Laura,' Meredith said quietly when they were alone with the dogs, the snoring pig and the flickering candles from the table.

'You'd go nuts if you lived here,' laughed Laura, leaning

171

back in her chair and stretching. 'Where's the woman who once told me she'd die if she had to live in either the countryside or the suburbs?'

Meredith shuddered, both at the memory of such a ridiculous statement and the notion that the suburbs would kill her. Wasn't that where she'd come from, after all?

'Did I really say that?'

'You always wanted different things: you wanted what the gallery has given you.' Laura shrugged, helping herself to more cheese and giving a bit to the two dogs. 'You'd hate this life.'

'I think that what I wanted then and what I want now are two different things,' Meredith said slowly, staring into the fire.

'You're not happy? Then leave.'

It was all very straightforward to Laura. You did what you wanted. Doing just that had given her a career, Con and Iona.

'It's not that simple,' Meredith protested.

'Of course it is. People make it hard for themselves. You only get one chance at life, so why stay doing what you don't want?'

'But . . .' Meredith was confused. 'You were the one who got me into working in a gallery. You started me on this road by saying I was made for it.'

Laura shoved the greedy dogs away and gave Meredith her full attention.

'That was years ago. You're in charge of your own life, Meredith. You did want the money and the prestige, don't deny it. You chose that. But if you want something different now, then leave the gallery and do something else.'

Meredith shook her head. Laura was being so childlike. Nothing was ever that simple. Meredith's whole life was tied up with Alexander Byrne. Her work and her social life were all part of it. If she thought about it, she didn't have one single friend who wasn't linked to the gallery. Even Con was

172

represented by them. And what about the money? She couldn't give that up. Would Sally-Anne let her in on the schemes if they weren't partners?

It appeared as if Laura had reached the same conclusion.

'You've got investments with Sally-Anne – so have we, since you told us about them all. They're our pension. But you don't need to work any more, Meredith,' she said, 'so leave. Get a life.'

With that, Laura rose and began to tidy the table, murmuring that she had to get up early with Iona and she couldn't handle late nights any more. 'Half ten's my limit for going to bed these days. Iona's up at six every morning, come rain or shine.'

As she talked and tidied, Meredith sat there in silence, stunned by Laura's comment: *Get a life.*

She had a life, thank you very much.

With nothing more than a curt good night, she marched off to bed, wishing she hadn't drunk any wine so she could drive off to a hotel. But she was stuck now, stuck with people who clearly thought she was a sad spinster with no life whatsoever.

In the sweet guest bedroom with the wooden bed and a wardrobe accessorized by the weirdest ever metal knobs, courtesy of Con, Meredith got ready for bed, muttering to herself all the while. How dare Laura say what she'd said. It was so rude now that she thought about it. Almost the sort of thing Molly, who lived next-door to her parents, might say. Molly had been behind the door when tact was being handed out and could put both feet in her mouth at the same time.

The last time Meredith had seen her, at her father's awful sixtieth birthday party, she'd said something along the lines of: 'Have you no man with you for us all to admire, Meredith? I was sure you'd have caught yourself a fine fella in Dublin, what with your fancy clothes and the new teeth and all.'

Suddenly, the memory of the tactless Molly faded as

Meredith thought of that party and how badly she'd felt afterwards. She'd bought all that stupid champagne because she'd wanted the Byrne party to be cool, even though nobody else in the family cared in the least about being cool or what the waiters or the hotel management thought of them.

The Byrnes only cared that Ned enjoyed his birthday. Ned and Opal had tried to dissuade her. They didn't care a hoot about champagne.

How stupid that *she'd* cared so much.

Meredith had lain on the bed without removing her make-up with her expensive cleanser and without putting her special moisturizer on. She wriggled out of her clothes, pulled the bedclothes over her and then sobbed herself to sleep.

Nobody else crossed the gallery's doors that Saturday afternoon. The only thing of any importance that happened was that Keith phoned to say he'd be transferring money into the gallery's account first thing Monday morning.

There was something very reassuring about Keith. The careful, thoughtful opposite to Sally-Anne's butterfly ways, he even spoke slowly so that people trusted him implicitly.

'Keith, I'm worried about money, full stop,' Meredith told him, glad of the chance to speak to him instead of Sally-Anne. 'I don't know if Sally-Anne has told you, but a couple of cheques bounced and . . .'

Right, let me sort it out,' Keith said and Meredith felt some of the weight lift. 'Oh, and can you get that big Robinson painting shipped out this evening. I'll give you an address.'

'On a Saturday?' said Meredith. 'OK, I'll do it. Email me the address. It's the most expensive piece in the gallery, we'll need insurance.'

'I'll sort it out,' said Keith smoothly.

At six, they were all getting ready to leave when Pippa came up to Meredith, who was packing away papers into the leather tote she used as a briefcase.

'Hey, you probably aren't interested,' Pippa said, 'but a few of my friends are going out tonight. You're probably doing something . . .'

Meredith thought of what she normally did on nights when she wasn't attending work events or at dinners with people Sally-Anne was courting: telly and a stir-fry. She thought of Laura telling her to get a life.

'I'd love to,' she said.

The official opening was at five and Peggy and Fifi worked hard clearing the space in the shop and putting out canapés and wine. Sue at the bakery had promised Peggy that she'd drop in when she got a chance. Sure enough, she was there at five.

'Just me I'm afraid,' she said. 'Millie, who works with us, isn't well today, possibly a hangover. That girl has to go – breathing alcopop fumes over the customers is not good business practice. So, what with the little difficulty of having hungover staff, poor Zeke can't come. But I'm here.'

'Thank you,' said Peggy, hugging Sue. It was both strange and yet felt madly right that there was this camaraderie between the two shop owners on the crossroads.

Sue had explained it to her one of the first times they'd met.

'We're all trying make a living, none of us are in competition and, to be totally honest, even if we were, we'd have to find a way of working together. That's how it is, running a business in a small community. We each believe that there's enough pie for us all, so to speak. So Bobbi in the beauty salon has a special menu with coffees from the Java Bean and scones and buns from us. And if a customer wants one of our spelt muffins, Bobbi sends one of the girls over. We have her signs up in the shop and recommend her to our customers. I wish I could make more use of her services – my roots are dreadful,' Sue said ruefully.

Peggy laughed. 'Your roots are fine,' she said.

175

'That's only because you don't know what you're talking about, Peggy,' Sue said with a smile. 'You have lovely long hair that has never seen dye in its life. You want to be a bottle-blonde like me; keeping the roots up is tough. My sister's pregnant –'

Peggy wondered, was she imagining the sudden catch in Sue's voice?

'– and she isn't getting her hair dyed at all. Says she doesn't want to risk anything going wrong because she's had a miscarriage already.'

Peggy realized she wasn't imagining it: Sue's eyes were suspiciously wet. Peggy put a hand on hers.

'No,' said Sue fiercely, 'don't be kind. Don't ask me about it now. I'd cry, I'm sorry. Another time, I'll tell you . . .'

Peggy nodded and went off, feeling terribly inadequate. She needed to know how to fit into this community properly. It was all very well being friends on the surface, which was what she and her mother had done all their lives, but this – living with decent people who opened up to you – this was both important and difficult. Promising herself that she'd ask Sue out for a cup of tea one day to see if she'd open up about what was bothering her, Peggy mingled with her guests.

Paul and Mark from the delicatessen turned up too, bearing plates of prosciutto wrapped around tiny figs, as well as crackers covered with a delicate cream cheese with snipped chives on top.

'Oh, you're so sweet,' said Peggy. 'I didn't want you to bring anything but yourselves, but that is so lovely.'

'Stuff and nonsense,' said Paul, swatting the notion away. 'You'll pay it back in kind, trust me. My sister-in-law's expecting twins, I shall be expecting advice on exquisite hand-knitted things in – what's that word?' He looked to Mark to supply the word he was missing. Peggy had noticed that they finished each other's sentences, something that made her feel unexpectedly emotional.

176

Again, the community that was Redstone was pulling at her heart. These people had somehow become her friends: she, who had never really known what it was to have friends before.

'Cashmere, that's the word. But I don't know if you can buy cashmere wool,' said Mark. 'Can you?'

'You can,' Peggy said. 'We do stock a teeny-weeny bit, but it's expensive – too expensive for the majority of people – and not easy to wash. However, tell me what you want and I will knit you the most adorable things, little cardigans and the softest hats, because babies' heads get cold. I've knitted loads of baby clothes in my time.'

'Really?' said Paul with an engaging smile, 'tell me more. You see, Mark and I have been discussing you, and we've decided you don't look like a knitter.'

Peggy laughed. 'What does a knitter look like? Someone in an Aran sweater with big, jam-jar glasses, strange hair and flat Mary-Jane shoes?'

'Well . . .'

Peggy smiled at them both. 'I got rid of the bad hair and the Mary-Jane shoes before I moved here. This is a new look I'm trying out. I've knitted since I was very young . . .'

She was about to explain, but suddenly she thought the story would be too revealing. Most twelve-year-old girls didn't sit in the corner quietly knitting in order to stay safe.

'It's a boring story, honestly. Teenage girls!' she said vaguely, shrugging. 'Always doing mad things like getting into knitting instead of spending hours on the phone with their boyfriends. Anyway, I have to circulate, boys.'

There were about thirty people there, a good number, according to Sue, who had seen quite a few places open with much fanfare and no customers.

'Craft people are very interested in new places,' Peggy had pointed out. 'Where I lived before . . .' her voice trailed off. She didn't want to go into her peripatetic lifestyle now. 'There was no wool shop in some of the places I lived as a child and we had to travel miles to buy wool, so you notice when there's somewhere new.'

Bobbi popped along for five minutes.

The week before when Peggy had gone, as per Sue's instructions, and introduced herself to all the other shop owners, she'd been slightly in awe of Bobbi. Small and yet very stately, Bobbi looked as if she took no prisoners in the game of life. Peggy half expected to be sent out of the elegant beautician's with a flea in her ear after being told that their establishment had no interest in attending the grand opening of a wool shop. But to the contrary: Bobbi had been charm itself.

'Great,' she said. 'A bit of new blood is always good. Where are you from, Peggy? That's an unusual accent: a mix of lots of places, it sounds to me? Tell me all about yourself. Will you come in for a cup of tea in the back?'

'No,' said Peggy, startled.

She didn't like cups of tea and telling people like Bobbi things. She'd a feeling that Bobbi could extract information with great skill.

'Thank you, but I'm in a bit of a rush. Please do come along to the opening,' she'd said, thrusting a load of fliers into Bobbi's hands. 'Do you knit yourself?'

Bobbi grinned. 'No, child, after a day in here my hands are bone weary. I sit in front of the box and watch other people's lives on the soaps. Great fun.'

'OK,' said Peggy, 'but you never know, I might get you knitting or crocheting yet.'

'You never know,' said Bobbi, in such a way as to imply that hell would freeze over before she'd take a pair of knitting needles in her hands.

'You've done an amazing job, pet,' she said to Peggy now, looking around the shop admiringly. 'I love the colours you've used for the paintwork, very clever. It almost makes me want to start knitting or something.'

The small fair-haired woman who'd accompanied her laughed: 'Bobbi, *you*, knitting? Get out of here!'

'Oh, all right,' Bobbi said good-naturedly. 'Peggy, this is Opal Byrne, my dear friend. Now *she*'s a knitter.'

'Are you?' said Peggy eagerly, keen to meet a potential customer.

Opal nodded. 'I love to knit,' she said.

'She's fabulous, has knitted things for my two granddaughters. She's just waiting for a load of her own to really get into it,' Bobbi added and laughed.

'My son's getting married soon,' Opal went on. 'Brian. I have two lovely unmarried sons, though. David and Steve. You must meet them.'

'You're turning into a matchmaker, Opal!' said Bobbi cheerfully.

Peggy felt herself go weak at the knees. Opal was David's mother. It would be too much of a coincidence for it to be otherwise. As usual, the very thought of him made her feel shaky.

'And yourself?' Bobbi asked.

'I'm a spinster of this parish,' said Peggy lightly, hoping she was hiding her nerves. 'I have to get this shop up and running. I've no time for men, I'm afraid.'

Bobbi nodded. 'You're probably right, love,' she said sagely. 'Men tend to complicate things.'

Peggy agreed wholeheartedly. Let Bobbi and Opal leave, please. She couldn't bear to talk to this lovely woman who was the mother of the only man who'd ever touched her heart. It was too much to take.

Elysium Garden had a mall beneath with a gym, a convenience store and several restaurants, but the walls of the luxury apartments were sliver-thin. Meredith awoke with a groan the following morning and pulled a pillow over her aching head to block out the noise of the vacuum cleaner next door as it whacked into the walls with abandon. Yes, size matters in apartments, she wanted to roar retrospectively at the sleek and eager estate agent who'd sold her the place, but insulation matters most of all!

Meredith couldn't remember the last time she'd had a hangover. She didn't drink much usually. Though the champagne inevitably flowed whenever the gallery opened a new exhibition, there was never enough time to drink more than half a glass as she whirled around with Sally-Anne, smiling, placating, chatting, talking up, all the things gallery owners did at shows.

Her father's sixtieth: that was probably the last time Meredith could recall having had even vaguely too much to drink. Her mother loved a toast, though it would have been sparkling wine if Meredith hadn't stepped in at the last moment, feeling it was wrong to celebrate this important birthday for her dad without, well, the proper stuff.

The Byrnes didn't spend money on extravagances like champagne and her mother had been scandalized when Meredith had got one of her brothers to bring in the crate of Premier Cru, far more than was needed for the party.

'Oh goodness, Meredith, that must have cost a fortune,' Opal had said.

'Don't be silly, Mum,' Meredith had said lightly. 'We can't have Dad's special day without making a fuss, can we?'

Watching the pennies had long been a fact of life for Opal Byrne and to spend money on such a frivolity as alcohol was a terrible crime. In St Brigid's Terrace, the only drink on the premises was a bottle of sweet sherry kept in a cupboard for special occasions.

Meredith, however, felt it important that they turn up at the hotel that had been booked for the occasion with something decent to drink so nobody would look down their nose at the Byrnes. No one had looked down on Meredith for a very long time and she didn't want it ever to happen again.

Meredith could always feel it on her skin, a slow burn that started somewhere on her cheeks and spread all over her. The burning embarrassment of not fitting in, of not being good enough.

She didn't want her mother to know she'd felt this way. That would have hurt Opal desperately, which was the last thing Meredith wanted. No, it was easier to smile and pretend that every daughter bought 600 euros worth of champagne for their father on his birthday, that this was entirely normal.

'If you're sure, Meredith,' said Opal doubtfully, 'but love, I like to think of you putting your money aside for yourself you know . . .'

For when you're married and have children, if that ever happens, Meredith mentally supplied the words that were left unsaid.

'. . . for when you're older,' her mother went on. 'You need a nest egg. Rainy-day money.'

'I like spending it on you and Dad,' was all Meredith had said. But it had upset her all the same, and she'd had too many glasses of the champagne at the party to make up for it.

Not enough, though, to escape the looks the waiters gave her father when he had a sip of the champagne and said, 'It's lovely stuff honestly, Meredith, but it isn't as sweet as that nice Asti whatchamacallit stuff we used to get at Christmas. Do they have any of that? Just a little bit?'

Meredith had felt the burn then.

Lying in bed in her tenth-floor apartment, she fought the headache from hell. Why couldn't that stupid cow next door do her housekeeping at normal hours, she thought, shoving the duvet off and making it into the bathroom. She thought she might be sick. It was the combination of that nagging feeling that something was wrong at the gallery – plus the awareness that she was at least ten years older than everyone else in the club – that had made her drink too much last night.

181

She'd hated the music and while the others went off to dance she had remained at their table watching them having a good time and feeling lonely and old.

She perched on the edge of the corner bath with its Jacuzzi jets, which had been a major selling point in the apartments at the time, although in truth, Meredith was usually too busy to have a bath. Instead she opted for a power shower early in the morning and sometimes late at night to combat the exhaustion of the day. She didn't bother with that today. It was going to take more than a shower to fix her.

It was still six thirty in the morning but it felt as if she'd been awake for hours. She rummaged through the bathroom cabinet for headache tablets and an antacid for her stomach, then made it into the kitchen where she thought some nice sweet tea might help. Tea and toast in bed with the papers, that ought to make her feel human again. She made the tea and toast, had a few sips of the tea and a bite of toast to sustain her for the trip downstairs, then threw on the sweat-shirt and sweatpants she usually wore to the gym, grabbed her purse and took the lift down to the ground floor. There was nothing open yet, but a man was hefting bundles of newspapers under the half-opened security shutter of the newsagent's.

'Five more minutes,' the guy said.

'Oh, please, please.'

'Go on then.' He allowed her into the shop and she picked up two newspapers. Rooting around in her purse, she found the exact change.

'Thank you,' she said as she left the shop. She didn't read in the lift going back up to the apartment, afraid she'd be sick all over the sheeny marble floor.

Inside, she kicked off her shoes, sat at the kitchen table, took another bite of toast and checked that her tea was still warm. Perfect. She flicked through the headlines: politics, politics, a sports victory . . .

A reality TV star was marrying for the fourth time. Meredith, who loved that stuff, settled down to read. Other people's disasters made her own life choices seem sensible in comparison. OK, so she wasn't married and didn't have a boyfriend, but she had a great job, a career, a luxury apartment: things were good. She wasn't splashed all over the newspapers wearing dark glasses with the most lurid details of her private life revealed. She flicked the page, broadsheet wavering in the air, and read another headline:

INJUNCTION TO FREEZE ASSETS

OF DUBLIN GALLERY

Late on Saturday, an ex-parte injunction was sought in the High Court by a painter and sculptor represented by the Alexander Byrne Gallery to freeze the gallery's assets. Mick Devereux and Tony Sanchez, whose works sell for in excess of fifty thousand apiece, are owed several hundred thousand euros by the gallery's owners, Keith and Sally-Anne Alexander, and their partner, Meredith Byrne.

The *Sunday News* has learned that the fraud squad are currently investigating the Alexanders in relation to a separate pyramid investment scheme in which both artists had invested. The scheme is alleged to be similar to that run by convicted New Yorker Bernie Madoff, who scammed thousands of investors of millions of dollars in a vast Ponzi scheme.

It is estimated that the Alexanders have accumulated losses in the region of five million euros. Fraud squad officers have as yet been unable to question the couple, who are believed to have fled the country. A case is being prepared for the Director of Public Prosecutions . . .

Have YOU been a victim of this scam? If so, phone the newsdesk on . . .

Meredith scanned the rest of the article, holding her breath. This couldn't be true. How could the gallery's assets be frozen? What was going on? If they were likening Sally-Anne's investment schemes to the one run by the infamous Bernie Madoff, then all those property deals were fictional, a ruse to keep transferring money around so that investors would think they were getting huge returns when in reality it was simply someone else's money. Lured by the prospect of a twenty or thirty per cent profit to be made, people would immediately reinvest without demanding to see any paperwork.

Meredith began to shake. Not only had she borrowed money in order to invest it with Sally-Anne, she'd encouraged friends to invest. Friends like Laura and Con.

It had to be a mistake. The newspaper had got it wrong. There was no way Sally-Anne and Keith would do this to her. They were her friends. How *could* they do this? The sense of betrayal was overwhelming.

She'd had an intuition that something was wrong, but she'd ignored it. Instead of trusting her instincts, she'd trusted Sally-Anne. If this was a Ponzi scheme, as the paper said, she'd sunk everything she had into it. What chance did she have of getting any of it back?

Meredith ran to the bathroom and threw up.

She needed a lawyer, she decided when she emerged pale and still shaking from the bathroom. She had been named as a partner in the gallery. She would be interviewed by the police and she needed to prove that she had been a victim of the fraud and not part of it.

They *had* to believe her: she'd lost everything – the money she'd borrowed to become a partner, the money she'd invested in Sally-Anne's schemes. But would anybody believe that a grown woman could be so stupid? That she'd been so desperate to fit in, it never occurred to her to question *anything*?

Even to Meredith, that didn't sound the most credible defence.

Meredith knew one lawyer. There had been a girl called Serena something at the law firm who'd acted for her when she bought her apartment. A total professional, Serena had made the whole transaction so painless and simple. But there were different sorts of lawyers. Serena was a house-buying one. What was the word . . .? Meredith's brain was barely functioning this morning. Conveyancing, that was it.

If the gallery's assets were frozen, and she was the only partner still in the country, it wouldn't be long before the police showed up, wanting to talk to her. What she needed was a criminal lawyer.

Serena's mobile number was stored on her phone. She sent a text and followed it up with a phone call a few minutes later, which was answered on the second ring, and she launched into an explanation.

'Oh my Lord,' said Serena, sounding very unlawyer-like and shocked. 'You're involved in that thing with the Alexanders?'

'Yes, I mean, no,' said Meredith, wondering if this was the way all conversations were going to go from now on. 'I'm Sally-Anne's business partner, a partner in the gallery, and—' Suddenly another thought hit Meredith.

Keith had asked her to send the gallery's most valuable painting out of the country. How would *that* look?

'I may have done something very stupid which will look incriminating,' Meredith said wearily. She sounded like a character in a television cop series. 'I had nothing to do with any of it. If it's true that they were operating a Bernie Madoff scam, then I have lost literally everything. But I will need a lawyer to help me, because I am a partner in—'

'Don't say anything else,' interrupted Serena, firmer now. 'You need to talk to one of the firm's criminal lawyers. I think it's James Hegarty on duty. I'll ring him this instant and give him your number.'

James turned up at noon, after Meredith had spent frantic hours phoning every single number she could find for Sally-Anne and Keith. Part of her was still clinging to the hope that it was all a big mistake and that the Alexanders would roll into town with a plausible explanation that would make everything right.

The first thing James did was sit her down and ask her about her involvement in the gallery.

'I took care of things at home while Sally-Anne was abroad. She travelled a lot because of her investments,' Meredith said.

'Yes,' said James with portent. 'And you invested your own money?'

'Yes.'

'Do you have any paperwork?'

'Well, no,' said Meredith, feeling stupid. 'I trusted Sally-Anne.'

'I'd say that everyone else who trusted her is phoning the police as we speak.'

'But they're not partners in the gallery!' wailed Meredith. 'It'll look as though I was part of it.' She thought of the painting Keith had asked her to send off – the most valuable piece in the gallery. One more thing for Sally-Anne and Keith to steal. And she'd delivered it right into their hands.

She told James all about it.

'I see,' he said, writing everything down.

'I'm the innocent one in all of this,' Meredith protested. 'I borrowed the money that I invested and now I'll have to pay that back. Everything I own will have to be sold. How can we get the money back and how long will it take?'

James took his time answering.

'These cases drag on for years while the police gather evidence and take statements to make a case for the DPP. As for getting your money back . . .' He looked at her solemnly. 'It doesn't look good.'

Meredith got up and rushed to the bathroom again to be sick. Then she sat on the tiled floor with the expensive under-floor heating and cried.

She thought of all the gallery parties where people had talked to her about the mythical Alexander investment funds and their fabulous returns. Meredith had loved being an insider, part of the charmed circle. She'd boasted about the money she'd made, endorsing their schemes in the process. With her luxury apartment and her designer clothes, she was a living advertisement for the Alexanders.

She'd even brought her friends in on it – Laura and Con. And now they'd lost everything too. All thanks to her.

On Sunday night, Freya, Opal and Ned sat in the cosy sitting room drinking mugs of tea, eating Hobnobs and doing their best to answer some of the questions on *Who Wants to Be a Millionaire?* Uncle Ned was addicted to the programme and watched endless reruns on the cable channels. Even Freya had to admit it was madly compulsive. After spending Friday and Saturday with her mother, she felt gloriously happy to be back with Opal and Ned.

'Greenland, definitely Greenland,' said Ned with determina-tion, and Freya smiled over at him. She loved it when he didn't know the answer but tried to convince himself that he did. This time he was sure Greenland had the highest popula-tion in the world of some species of rare duck, so Greenland was the correct answer, absolutely no doubt about it. He got quite worked up about it.

'No, Ned, you're wrong,' Opal said. 'Canada – it's bigger, it's got to be right. Freya, what do you think? More room for ducks.'

Freya didn't know for sure and was therefore wary of putting her money on one or the other. When you didn't know the answer for something factual, you didn't know the answer. Life, now that was different. Life's answers were often a matter of instinct, so things could go either way. But when it came to ducks, Greenland and Canada, it was all down to facts and she simply hadn't a clue.

Foxglove let out an outraged miaow. They all turned to look. Her favourite perch was on the radiator, where she liked to curl up next to the tank of Steve, the bearded dragon. Steve belonged to Freya's cousin Steve, but once the first flush of love was over, the human Steve had not been up to the day-to-day minding of his namesake. So the reptilian Steve had ended up a permanent resident at 21 St Brigid's Terrace, where Ned dutifully fed him live cockroaches every day. Freya and Opal, though they both loved animals, could only cope with holding Steve for a millisecond and had drawn the line at handling live cockroaches. Which was why Ned had ended up the designated zookeeper. The cockroaches lived in the shed. Freya and Opal had been firm on that point.

The human Steve loved the fact that his pet had somewhere nice to live.

'Do you think he recognizes me?' he'd said to Freya one day, crouching down so he was eye-level with Steve the bearded dragon, who gazed at him with unblinking, mysterious eyes.

'To tell you the truth, Steve,' said Freya, 'I don't think he knows or cares where he is as long as the cockroaches keep coming. He's not a very touchy-feely pet.'

'Ah, it was stupid getting him,' Steve sighed. 'I saw him in the window of the pet shop. Couldn't resist going in. You know the way. Some guys get warm-water fish, I got Steve.'

Freya grinned. 'If you ever feel the need to get any

warm-water fish,' she said, 'call me and I'll talk you out of it. I'd say they'd be even worse than Steve here for looking after, feeding and cleaning. Besides which, Foxglove could stick her little paw in and have lunch every day for a week and we wouldn't notice.'

Steve the bearded dragon didn't move much and when he did it was so stealthily that nobody noticed. But once in a while something would come over him and he'd give a quick tail-swishing wriggle and it must have been this, during the great Canada Versus Greenland Duck Argument, that had made poor Foxglove screech out loud.

On the television, they'd moved on to another question.

'No, no!' gasped Ned. 'We missed it! Oh my God, how could we have missed it? I can't bear it. How can we see that episode again?'

'There's bound to be a website or something,' said Freya. 'I'll look it up, Uncle Ned, promise.'

Ned was still in anguish when the doorbell rang. The three of them looked at each other in puzzlement. Who would be calling at this hour on a Sunday night?

It was half past nine. Opal liked a house that ran along particular lines. Nobody turned up at the house or rang after nine o'clock at night.

'Otherwise,' she'd explained to Freya years ago, 'I think somebody's died. That's what you think when the phone rings late at night. Sorry Freya, I didn't mean . . .'

Too late, Opal had remembered the late-night phone call when Freya's father had died.

'I'll go,' said Freya, getting up.

It couldn't be the boys, she thought, they all had keys. And Molly next door never turned up this late, being a complete slave to Sunday night costume dramas.

Freya opened the door. There hadn't been many occasions in her life when Freya was lost for words, but this was one of them. Standing at the door were two suitcases. Coming up the small path dragging two more was her cousin Meredith. But she didn't look like the Meredith that Freya knew.

That Meredith was sheeny and glossy, all salon-dried hair, perfect nails, discreet make-up and the cool, slightly edgy clothes that people wore in the art world. Stuff you could only buy in fashionable designer shops.

This Meredith was wearing old jeans and a scruffy sweat-shirt. Her hair was lank and tied back and if she'd put on any make-up that morning, it was long gone. Her face was pale and almost haggard. Opal came up behind Freya to see who was at the door.

'Meredith, what happened?' she gasped.

Meredith stopped in her progress with the third and fourth suitcases. Her face crumpled and tears flowed from her eyes.

'Oh, Mum,' she said, 'Mum, I've nowhere else to go.' She threw herself at her mother and Freya watched as her aunt stroked Meredith's hair, the way she'd so often stroked Freya's.

Freya watched Meredith in absolute astonishment. Why on earth was she here and what had happened to the glossy cousin she knew?

Chapter Ten

Freya went down for breakfast the next morning earlier than usual for a Monday. She'd been wakened during the night by Opal and Meredith's voices on the floor below. At one point it sounded, Freya thought, as if somebody was being sick, but she couldn't be sure.

She knew *she* was shattered from lack of sleep, but when she walked into the kitchen and saw Meredith, hollow-eyed, sitting at the kitchen table, staring listlessly at a cup of tea and a plate of scrambled egg on toast, Freya decided that she was supermodel fresh compared to her cousin.

Opal didn't look much better than her daughter. Probably nobody in the house had slept last night – aside from Foxglove, who was sitting on a chair at the table cleaning her paws contentedly.

'Morning,' said Freya, determined to bring a little bit of normality to the house.

'Breakfast?' said Opal, cheering up at the sight of her niece.

'Em, yes,' said Freya unexpectedly, and she hugged her aunt. 'Meredith's scrambled eggs look amazing, I might manage some—'

'Of course, pet, I'm always saying you need filling up,' said Opal.

Freya didn't really want eggs, but she knew it would cheer her aunt up to make them, especially given that Meredith clearly hadn't touched any of hers.

'Morning, all,' said Uncle Ned, coming into the kitchen with the morning paper tucked under his arm. 'Beautiful day out,' he said, eyes staring anxiously at his daughter all the while.

'Morning, Ned,' said Freya cheerily.

Meredith sat mute.

You could have cut the tension with a knife, Freya thought. She had to fix it somehow. This was ridiculous. Making herself some black coffee, she switched on the radio, but instead of the morning news programme that everyone normally listened to, she tuned it to something suitably bright and sparky with songs from the fifties and sixties that she knew Opal and Ned loved. Then she turned it a shade higher than normal.

'I love that station,' said Opal, a smile in her voice.

'I know,' said Freya.

That would cheer up her aunt and uncle. Freya wasn't sure what could be done with Meredith.

Her cousin had seemed incapable of speech the night before and had just wanted to be allowed to go to bed. 'She didn't even get undressed,' Opal said later. 'I made up the bed, then she just took off her shoes, got under the duvet and pulled it over her head. Oh good Lord, what are we going to do? I've never seen her so upset, I don't even know what it is. Something to do with the job, she said, and money missing from investments and the gallery's involved.'

'Dear God,' Ned blessed himself. 'Well, it will be nothing to do with Meredith,' he said, as if this was the most obvious fact in the world. 'Not our Meredith. She wouldn't steal a ha'penny off anybody.'

Freya reckoned he was probably right. Meredith didn't look as if she'd steal so much as a nail varnish from the euro shop.

Opal slid some eggs on to a plate for Freya and put them on the table. Freya sat down and started to eat, managing to stroke Foxglove's head at the same time. The cat purred, luxuriating in the tenderness of Freya's touch.

'Must be nice to be a cat,' Freya said to no one in particular. 'No worries. Just letting people stroke you. Catching the odd mouse as a token of affection. Did she do that when you lived here, Meredith?' she asked.

Meredith looked up at Freya as if seeing her for the first time. Without the lip-gloss, the eyeliner and the carefully styled hair, Meredith was pretty in a natural sort of way. She'd always looked as if she was trying too hard, that was it, Freya decided. She must have changed in the night, for now she was wearing an old pair of pyjamas that she must have pulled out of a cupboard, and she looked like a normal person. Someone who suited St Brigid's Terrace.

It transpired that even the music station wasn't free of news. At eight o'clock, a solemn-voiced newscaster came on. He kicked off with the usual stuff about tensions within the government, business as usual. Then an item about new jobs being created in Naas.

Next up was a fraud case involving millions of euros, similar to the New York Madoff scandal. 'The fraud squad are investigating gallery owners Keith and Sal—'

Meredith's face went white.

'I don't think we want to hear any more,' said Freya, leaping up and turning the sound down. Whatever had happened to Meredith was clearly very big if it was the third item on the news. Freya decided she couldn't leave poor Opal and Ned here all day with Meredith in this state. Somebody needed to sort this out. It was going to have to be her. She took a slurp of her coffee.

'Meredith, love,' she said, turning sideways on her chair to face her, 'tell us, what happened?'

'I can't,' said Meredith, not looking up. 'It's so awful . . .

it's all over the papers and I'm going to have to give the police a statement because they think I'm involved. I am a partner in the gallery, you see, and it looks so bad.'

'Jesus, Mary and Joseph,' Ned said – a man who never cursed. Out of the corner of her eye, Freya could see Opal blanch and bless herself.

Meredith's face went even paler, if such a thing was possible.

'Everyone's going to be so shocked and ashamed. I can't tell you. I can't. I'm sorry,' she whispered.

With that, she shoved back her chair and ran to the door, which she wrenched open and banged behind her, startling poor Foxglove, who leapt off her chair in alarm and whizzed out the cat flap.

'Oh no,' said Opal, tears in her eyes, watching Meredith through the window as she stood just outside the door, shaking. 'I don't understand what it's all about, but she's in trouble, terrible trouble.'

'I'll stay here today,' Freya said, going over to her aunt and enveloping her in as big a hug as a small skinny person possibly could.

'No, love,' said Opal, hugging her back. 'You go off to school. Meredith will be here when you get home and maybe she'll have been able to tell us all about it by then.'

'If you're sure,' said Freya. She privately thought that by the look of things, Meredith wouldn't be up to talking about anything – or facing anything, either.

Thanks to her mother, Freya had lots of experience of people who didn't like facing reality. Trips to the doctor for tablets and the odd litre or two of wine with a pizza on a Friday night helped too, apparently. Freya glared at the hunched shape outside the back door. 'I'll be home later,' she sighed.

She gave her aunt's cheek one last kiss, hugged Uncle Ned, grabbed her bag and left. What sort of an idiot was Meredith and what sort of trouble had she got herself into? Anyone who upset Opal and Ned deserved to be shot, Freya thought furiously as she marched down the road.

In the kitchen, Opal kept herself busy cleaning and tidying.

Meredith came back in from the garden, threw away the milky coffee her mother had given her and made a fresh cup, this time black. She sat down at the table and stared into it without drinking.

When had she started taking coffee black? Opal wondered, and had to stop herself crying because it seemed there was so much she didn't know about her daughter. She'd longed so much to see Meredith and now she was here, it was all hideously wrong. The radio was on in the background, nice and low to avoid anyone hearing the news. Apart from that and the sound of Opal's dishcloth, there was almost silence. Ned kept himself busy eating his breakfast and making the odd comment about what he meant to do that day in the allotment. He had a small notebook where he wrote tasks and the odd little note to himself. This morning, he seemed deeply engrossed in it. Finally he could bear the tension no longer. He got to his feet, picked up his dishes and slotted them in the dishwasher.

He exchanged a brief look with Opal and then kissed her soft cheek. 'I'm just going down the street to see if Michael's off up to the allotment yet,' he said a little too loudly.

'Great,' said Opal, again a little too loudly and cheerfully.

When he was gone, she went over and cleaned the space where he'd sat, rubbing the kitchen table where the family had eaten for so many years as though she could somehow rub away the pain. Finally, she could bear it no more. She sat down opposite her daughter.

'Meredith, love, I need to know exactly what's happened,' she said. 'Then we can try to help you.'

Meredith said nothing for a moment, then she raised her

red-rimmed eyes to meet her mother's gaze. 'I can't talk about it, Mum,' she said.

'You must,' said Opal fiercely. 'We have to hear it from you, not the news. What happened? Why would the police need to interview you? Tell me the truth.'

Meredith wanted to cry. There'd never been any criminal activity in this house, no taint of shame. None of the boys had been in trouble for one single thing their whole lives. No, Ned and Opal's sons had been good lads, all of them, and it was she who had brought this down on the family.

'I've sort of lost my job, Mum,' Meredith said. It killed her to explain but she had to. 'The gallery has been finding things tough lately, but I thought it was all right. Sally-Anne was doing her best . . .' She knew she was rambling.

Opal nodded. She'd only met Sally-Anne once or twice and each time she'd been a little overwhelmed by her daughter's business partner. That their Meredith could be working with this glamorous, exotic woman and her husband, high fliers, always in the newspaper, was hard to believe. 'And . . .?' prompted Opal.

'It's all gone,' Meredith whispered.

'What do you mean? The business is gone, is that it?' said Opal hopefully. That was nothing. That they could cope with. 'We'll manage, it'll be fine. If you lose the flat – sorry, apart-ment,' she corrected herself quickly. 'If you lose the apartment, we'll figure something out. Your father and I have a nest egg. You won't go hungry. Don't worry. You'll find another job anyway. Aren't you as bright as anything?'

'That's not all, Mum,' said Meredith. If only it were that simple. 'You heard them mention it on the news. Sally-Anne and Keith have been running some sort of scam where they took money from people and invested it. We all thought they were proper investments. I invested in it and I told other people to invest too, even Laura and Con.' She couldn't bear to think about that. 'Except it turns out Sally-Anne didn't invest any money. She kept paying us off on a loop, getting more and more money out of us until, finally, something must have gone wrong. So they took all the gallery money and did a runner. Now it looks as though nobody will be able to get their money back – including me.'

She looked down as she spoke, staring at the kitchen table. It was so old. The kitchen had been redone maybe five or six years ago, but the table was the same big wooden one that had been in the house since Meredith was a child. She and the boys had had their tea there, done their homework on it, played games on it, got crayon marks on it. How safe life had been then.

'You weren't involved though?' said Opal, and Meredith looked up, shocked at the catch in her mother's voice. She had to tell the truth. She needed to feel the absolute shame of looking into her mother's bewildered eyes and soft confused face and tell her everything. *That* was her punishment.

'I haven't done anything criminal, Mum, no, I promise. But I am involved because I invested, and some of the investors came to them via me. I recommended the scheme. I thought it was sound . . . And then on Friday, I did something really stupid. Keith got me to deliver the gallery's most valuable painting to him. So now it will look like I'm an accessory to their crime, even though I knew nothing.'

Opal said nothing but her hand flew to her mouth and Meredith could hear her breathing harder. Her mother had always had high blood pressure. What if she killed her with this terrible story? Meredith couldn't bear to think what other people would think, when they heard, but it must be twice as bad for her mother. Imagine raising your daughter to be a decent person and then having her turn out like this, someone who consorted with criminals and got investigated by the police.'

'I was a business partner in the gallery,' she went on once she saw that her mother had her breathing under control. She had to do this, had to. 'So it looks as if I could have been part of their activities, but I wasn't. I've hired a lawyer, a criminal lawyer,' she added – might as well get it all out, all the badness. 'He said that these cases are very serious and of course they're more common these days. The fact that it's clear I haven't benefitted in any way should show that I didn't know what was going on,' Meredith went on. 'But I ought to have seen that they were doing something wrong. I was so stupid not to have realized!'

Unable to look her mother in the eye, she got up and began pacing around the room. 'The worst thing is that Sally-Anne and Keith invested money from the artists, from my friends. Nobody is selling anything these days and we all should have smelled a rat because Sally-Anne supposedly was. The thing is, my friends are all broke now. Those investments were their pensions.' Meredith's voice wobbled. 'I don't have a job or a nest egg or a pension and I won't have my apartment much longer. I'll have nothing but debts and I'll be tied up in a horrible court case that will be all over the newspapers for years because that's how long these things take to come to court,' she finished shakily.

She found herself at the sink and automatically reached for the bar of soap and began to wash her hands. Was this how people got Obsessive Compulsive Disorder? she wondered.

Her mother hadn't said a word the whole time. Meredith waited, her back turned, willing her to speak. In this house, Ned worried if he missed seeing the milkman when he came around to be paid once a month. Nobody in the family had to be reminded to buy a television licence or to pay a bill on time. Nobody had ever borrowed more than they could afford. Borrowing hadn't been something Opal and Ned had gone in for. Her mother must be shocked to the core.

'Oh love,' said Opal tremulously, and her tone was Meredith's undoing. She could have coped with anything, her mother shouting at her, accusing her: *We didn't raise you to be this sort of person*. Anything but those tremulous words that told her Opal still loved her despite everything.

'I'm really sorry,' Meredith sobbed.

She banged into a chair in her haste to leave the kitchen, then she ran up the stairs two at a time until she reached her bedroom. Racing in, she slammed the door shut, threw herself on the bed and cried until she didn't think there were any tears left.

After some time she heard her father come in with the paper. Heard their murmured conversation in the kitchen. She ought to go downstairs. What if something happened to Dad? What if he had a heart attack? What if Mum did? Her blood pressure had always been high.

But she couldn't make herself get off the bed. She wanted to stay here in the safety of her childhood bedroom. After a while she turned over and looked round the room. The bed was in the same position it had always been in. Opal kept everyone's rooms the way they were, merely removing some of the detritus so other family members could stay occasionally.

'We don't need empty spare rooms,' Opal had told her. 'This is your home, you're always welcome back here.' She'd told all her children the same thing when they left home.

Her bedroom was a pale grey, quite out of keeping with the rest of the house with its magnolias and creams. Meredith had been very specific about the colour she wanted it painted when she was fourteen.

It was the same sort of grey that her friend Clara's room was painted – the difference being that Clara's room was a big high-ceilinged room in a lovely old house two miles away with genuine antiques and a marvellous mahoghany bed that had been in her family for decades. It was a far cry from Meredith's cramped room overlooking St Brigid's Terrace with its cheap single bed.

Meredith had done her best, stapling flowery fabric on to an old headboard to lend a touch of glamour. It hadn't been enough, though. It had still looked like a room in an ex-council house with clip frames hanging on the walls and a DIY wardrobe her father and brothers had put together one weekend with a certain amount of teasing and cursing as they tried to read the instructions. No matter what she did, Meredith's bedroom would never be like Clara's.

It was meeting Clara that had changed everything in the first place.

It all came about because she was in the wrong school.

Ned and Opal had worried about her when she'd been younger because she was such a quiet, shy child. Meredith could remember the whispered conversations between her parents about how they thought of sending her to St Loretta's, a small fee-paying school several miles away from Redstone.

The boys would all go to the local, free secondary school but a plan was made to save up so that Meredith could go to Loretta's.

'I don't want to go!' Meredith had cried when she'd heard the plan. 'I'll be different, I won't have gone to their private little junior school.'

'You won't be different, lovey. It will be a great chance for you, Meredith,' her father had said. The local school would be a bit rough for a girl as sensitive as her but nobody wanted to say it out loud.

'We can't afford it,' she'd said, her last attempt at escaping.

'We can afford anything we need when it's best for our children,' said her father sternly. She'd been right about Loretta's. Meredith hadn't fitted in. Too shy to make friends easily, and too in awe of the posher girls who all knew each other because they'd been together in school since they were four, she was always on the outside looking in.

She hid her pain from her parents and they really believed that she loved it.

'I told you that you'd fit in,' Ned would say, delighted.

In truth, Meredith had no friends because she was too embarrassed to invite her wealthier classmates back to her ex-council-house home. Other girls didn't see this as shyness, they saw only standoffishness.

So school became a kind of hell until the day she met Clara.

Meredith could remember exactly where she was the day Clara had first spoken to her. Sitting at the back of the school at the top of the steps leading down to the basketball courts. It was a sunny day in late September. Most of the girls had finished lunch and were either playing sports or lounging in the playground at the front of the school, which was a suntrap. Meredith didn't mind sitting in the shade even though everyone else was obsessed with getting a tan. It didn't bother her because her pale skin never went brown. It just went from lobster back to white again.

The new girl, Clara, sat down beside her.

'Do you ever feel,' Clara said in the very upper-class tones that had caused the girls in Meredith's class to snigger at her, more out of envy than out of anything else, 'that you just don't fit in?'

Meredith had looked at Clara in fascination and saw the strain in her fine features.

'And there's no point fitting in or trying to, because you never will?' Clara went on.

For all the teasing and bullying Clara had endured since she'd arrived at the school three weeks ago, it hadn't appeared to have hurt her. She wasn't crying. She was just stating the way things were in a matter-of-fact manner.

'I've been here two years and I don't feel as though I fit in either,' Meredith said shyly.

'Maybe we can hang out together,' said Clara, beaming at her. 'Show the rest of the world that their opinions don't matter.'

Until that moment, Meredith had desperately longed to fit in. Suddenly, *not* fitting in seemed the most thrilling thing ever. If not fitting in meant being like Clara, then it suited her just fine.

From that moment on Meredith was Clara's slave. Clara had rescued her from being on her own and Meredith had been on her own for what felt like all her life. Her brothers had each other, her mother had her father, but Meredith had always felt like the odd one out – and since the day she started at Loretta's, Meredith had had no one. Her old best friend Grainne had made new friends at the secondary school and spent all her time with them. The other girls on St Brigid's Terrace all thought Meredith was a snob because she went to a posh school. A posh school where everyone looked down on her and she hadn't made a single friend. Until now. Gorgeous, glamorous Clara, who was teased by the other girls as much for her looks as for her accent, was saying they were alike.

Before Loretta's, Clara had attended a very expensive girls' school on the other side of the city. But something had happened, something Clara never spoke about, and the family had relocated. Clara and her older brother had been sent to state schools and Clara's parents had picked Loretta's as a suitable replacement for Clara. It hadn't gone well and Loretta's girls had turned on Clara. She'd once had money, and had gone to a far more expensive school than theirs – even if the money was gone now, she was surely looking down on them. So they'd look down on her first. Clara had beautiful clothes. Been on glamorous holidays. How dare she come there with her posh voice and look down on everyone.

But Meredith knew – as the others would too, if they'd only taken the time to get to know her instead of being so hostile – Clara didn't look down on anyone. She liked people whether they had money and had been on exotic foreign holidays or not. Those weren't the standards by which she judged people, otherwise she wouldn't have been Meredith's friend, would she? Shy, quiet Meredith who was good at art but who came from St Brigid's Terrace.

Clara didn't give a fig where her new friend came from, but Meredith found that she cared very much where Clara came from. Clara's new house was a gracious period property for all that it represented a decline in the family fortunes. Her father drove off to work every morning in a big shiny black car. Her mother wasn't like other mothers Meredith had known. She wandered around the house, sometimes cutting flowers for indoors, looking perpetually elegant and glamorous with her short mop of blonde hair, her elegant blouses, her neat pedal-pusher trousers that revealed slender ankles in dainty pumps. The first time Meredith had been in Clara's house, she'd peeped shyly at Mrs Hughes in fascination.

'Would you girls prefer to go up to Clara's room and talk, or sit in the garden? It's such a lovely day,' Mrs Hughes said. 'Your aunt sent over some of her homemade elderflower cordial,' she told Clara, who grinned. 'It's probably dreadful but we could give it a go. Do you want to stay for supper?' Mrs Hughes enquired. 'I could telephone your mother and speak to her if you like?'

'No, it's fine, Mrs Hughes, I won't, thank you – maybe another time,' stammered Meredith, thinking that in the Byrne household they had tea in the evening and her mother might faint if someone like Mrs Hughes phoned and inquired if Meredith would like to stay for supper. What *was* supper, Meredith wondered. Why was it so different from tea?

'Clara, don't forget your piano practice,' her mother reminded her. 'Just because you're not taking lessons any more, darling, doesn't mean you shouldn't keep it up.'

It was like something out of a film, Meredith thought. She longed to be part of that world. Longed to have supper instead of tea. Longed to have a bedroom like Clara's, carelessly decorated with old bits of family furniture. Not that Clara looked down on what Meredith had for a second.

'Oh, I love your house!' she said after Meredith had found the courage to invite her. 'It's fabulous, so beautiful and unique. I'd love to have three storeys. Our house is so boring.'

'But your house is so big,' Meredith said, astonished.

'I know, but it's dull. Our old house was nicer, more like your house, more character,' she said but Meredith was sure she must be lying.

Clara's father recovered from whatever financial setback had sent them to Redstone in the first place and after a couple of years, the family left. Clara and Meredith promised to keep in touch, but distance meant that the friendship petered out.

However, Meredith had learned an important lesson from Clara. She'd observed what it was that set her friend apart from everyone else in school: class, breeding, *knowing things*. Meredith, who had never felt that she belonged anywhere, had found something to believe in.

Lying on her bed in Redstone, Meredith stared around her at the grey bedroom walls and thought of her beautiful apartment in Elysium Gardens. If she knew Clara now, would Clara still want to be her friend? She doubted it.

Freya's best friend Kaz wanted to come around to meet Meredith. Well, to look at Meredith.

'She's not some creature in a zoo,' Freya pointed out as they ambled across the playing field.

'Yeah, but I've never seen her before, remember. I only saw those pictures of your dad's birthday where she looked like something out of *Hello!* magazine.'

'She doesn't look like something out of *Hello!* magazine now,' Freya said with feeling. 'I wish I could get to the bottom of it. Opal's probably going to talk to her, but Opal is so easily hurt. I wish I was there. I'd ask her straight out. "What the heck is going on? Why are you here and why do you have to go off and meet your criminal lawyer in the middle of the morning?"'

'You don't suppose it's drugs, do you?' said Kaz.

'You never know,' Freya said. 'I don't think she's the type. I mean, if she was on something she'd probably be more laid back. I'm telling you, Kaz, she's wound so tightly, she's like a coiled spring.'

'Wow, coiled spring, huh?' said Kaz, thinking this over. 'Will we bunk off lessons, go and have a coffee and fag break?'

'No, I'm giving up the fags,' Freya said. 'Opal caught a whiff off me the other night and she got so upset. I cannot tell you how upset she was. And I hate to upset her or let her down. Besides, she's right: smoking kills. We all know it.'

'Getting in a car can kill. Having a drink can kill. Getting on an airplane can kill,' Kaz grumbled, 'but they don't all have pictures of corpses and a skull and crossbones on the side of every car, do they? Why is it us poor smokers who take the rap?'

'Yeah, well, I don't really need them,' Freya said. 'Plus I can't afford them.'

'You could,' said Kaz, 'if you keep doing people's art and maths homework, you could have a very good habit going there.'

'I don't need a very good habit going there,' said Freya.

'Is that why you don't drink?' Kaz asked.

'I do drink,' said Freya, 'just not much. Listen, if you had spent much time with my mother and watched her "coping" with life on a Saturday night thanks to a litre bottle of wine, then you wouldn't be so keen on booze. I don't want to turn out like her.'

They were both silent for a while. Freya rarely spoke about her mother.

Freya was so low-key about it all that Kaz tended to forget her mother was a bit of a madzer. She patted her friend's arm awkwardly.

'Your mother will come round in the end. She'll be fine, I bet ya.'

'No,' said Freya, 'she won't. But I'm doing OK. I've got Opal and Ned to look after.'

'I thought they were supposed to be looking after you,' said Kaz.

'You know me,' Freya pointed out, 'I like to do the looking after, which is why there is a problem with this whole Meredith coming home thing. The boys, Steve, David and Brian, they're great, they love their parents. They're typical guys apart from the fact that only David has the vaguest clue how to work the washing machine so poor Opal still does the other pair's washing no matter how much I tell her she shouldn't. But they're normal, wonderful – not that I tell them that, obviously. They appreciate Ned and Opal. But Meredith, I don't think she appreciates anything. *That's* what's wrong with her. I've never been able to figure out what her problem was, but that's it. And now she turns up on the doorstep looking all miserable and sobbing but not able to tell anyone what's wrong.'

'And she doesn't look all glossy and fabulous any more?' asked Kaz excitedly.

'No,' said Freya. 'She looks pretty wrecked – dragged through a bush backwards sort of stuff.'

'Please can I come home with you?'

'No, you can't. It'll only make it worse. She's like one of those feral kittens. You can't introduce too many people to it at once or else it'll go and hide. You can come home with me tomorrow and see her. I'll have figured her out by tomorrow.'

''Kay,' said Kaz despondently. 'Phone me if there are any developments. I live a boring life you know.'

'I'll send out bulletins every hour, OK?'

Chapter Eleven

Seth was taking things so slowly that Lillie wondered how she'd ever energize him enough to do anything with the house.

Lillie felt she'd been taking things slowly for what seemed like a lifetime. She'd been at Sorrento Villa over a week before she managed to persuade him to venture upstairs and show her around the rest of the house.

'I'm almost ashamed to let you see it, Lillie.'

He looked forlorn, almost like one of her own children rather than her brother, Lillie thought. His facial expression said 'it's my fault it's a mess and I'm full of shame at that fact'.

'Don't be silly,' she'd announced cheerfully, using the voice she'd used on her sons when they were little and needed encouragement. 'I know how it is with old houses: they need a lot of work and a lot of money. If you don't have the funds, it can be a struggle to get started.'

Seth looked relieved to have a bit of sympathy.

'I think,' he said, as if he was revealing some great secret, 'that Frankie would like me to get started myself but I'm no good with my hands. I'm more of an ideas man.'

'Of course you are,' agreed Lillie. 'Architects don't do the actual building work. I expect what Frankie really wants is for you to be doing something that would make you happy and content,' she went on, venturing a bit into unknown territory here. 'But you and I could have a look and see what we could do . . .'

Lillie knew how to paint and garden, but that was her limit. Sam had taken care of everything practical around the house, and now that he was gone, Martin and Evan were there. She could understand Frankie's irritation at Seth's inability to do anything with their home. Especially when Frankie was clearly such a practical person that she'd probably start on pulling down dividing walls herself, given the time and a sledge hammer.

The basement where Seth and Frankie, and now Lillie, lived was the best part of the whole place, a self-contained apartment that had been kept in reasonable condition, but when Lillie stepped through the door that led into the ground floor she saw that the rest of the house was a very different state of affairs. Each of the lovely, high-ceilinged rooms had been divided into a series of bedsits, all cobbled together with ugly wood and with old-fashioned sinks stuck in all over the place. There were horrible little two-bar electric fires in the beautiful old fireplaces and Lillie thought it was a miracle the whole place hadn't burned to the ground years ago.

The first floor was the same, if not worse. It was as if the previous landlord had had a competition with himself to see how many single rooms he could make out of four large elegant ones. Some of the bedsits only had half a window, the original rooms having been ruthlessly cut in two with cheap boarding dividing up the room. In those cases, the window itself was nailed down lest the two occupants argued over having it open. 'I suppose they were able to exchange notes between bedsits,' Lillie laughed. 'Although they could have just talked through the partitions. But it's a beautiful house,' she added hastily, as she saw her brother take it all

208

in with a gloomy face. 'And such an exciting project for an architect like yourself.'

Seth ran his finger along the peeling paint on a lovely and original heavy door.

'We had so many plans for it,' he said sadly.

Lillie peered out of the half-window onto the jungle below. Seth joined her and looked down. He said: 'I had this wonderful design for extending the kitchen and creating a conservatory which would link with an open-plan living room. Then I'd drawn up plans for hard landscaping in the garden. I know I'm not a landscaper but I've worked with enough of them . . .' His voice trailed off.

Standing at the window, hands in his pockets and shoulders slumped, he had been the picture of dejection. For all of a millisecond, Lillie wondered what she'd got herself into. At home, the person in need of rescuing had been her. Here she felt as if she needed to rescue Seth and Frankie and possibly even their marriage. She wasn't a meddler, not by any standards. Never had been, even with Martin and Evan when they left home. She'd always let them make their own mistakes and been there in the background to lend support and guidance.

That was how she'd been raised: by a wonderful mother and father who loved her enough to let her go.

In bed each night, she'd wondered if she would have been a different person if her birth mother hadn't given her up to the nuns for adoption.

People had to learn by their own mistakes. And yet this was different. This wasn't a mistake, this was a crisis, a disaster. Seth needed her. Frankie needed her. They were circling each other like the walking wounded, each locked in their own prison of pain: Frankie wondering where her vibrant husband had gone and Seth hating himself for what he'd become but feeling helpless to change it.

No, there was nothing else for it: Lillie had to step in.

Silently she looked up. Her husband Sam was definitely up wherever he was. *Is this what you sent me here for?* she whispered. Behind the house she could see the neat lines of the allotments and beyond that the wasteland that was being turned into a park. There was great industry going on in the allotments. People moving about, wheelbarrows being shifted along, digging, weeding, whatever.

'Did you ever grow things?' Lillie asked Seth. 'Did our mother grow things? Was that something you did?' There were so many things she didn't know. Her own tomato plants used to groan with the weight of beautiful tomatoes and she made her own chutney in the autumn, and as for the fig tree, beautiful, old, curving and just outside her own kitchen window, she used to love to sit under it and reach up for a giant juicy fig.

'Not me,' Seth replied. 'There was farming in Mam's background – as with most people in the country – but she only grew flowers. She loved roses.'

'Oh, me too,' said Lillie, touched at this link with her mother. 'You could grow a lot in that garden down there,' she said. 'That's something we could certainly make a start on.'

She'd given up trying to persuade him to make a start on the house – at least for the time being. Each time she'd suggested that they do a bit of wallpaper stripping, or knocking down a partition, or hiring a builder's skip to chuck some of the rotten carpets in, his face would take on a rabbit-in-the-headlights look of sheer terror.

'Let's at least try,' Lillie said, determined to breathe some enthusiasm into her brother. 'Come on, it's such a nice day, why don't we take a walk round the garden and start making a list of what we need and what we have to do?'

The garden cheered Seth up somewhat, partly because it was a balmy March day and the sun was shining, but also because Lillie kept unearthing real plants underneath the weeds.

'What a lovely hydrangea!' she'd exclaim. 'Totally hidden here – we'll have to move that.' And then a little further on: 'Oooh, this looks interesting . . .'

Lillie was quite enjoying herself, poking back the briars with Emer's hockey stick – the only piece of equipment she could find in the house suitable for jungle exploration, given that there was no machete. 'Just look at those beautiful fuchsias against the wall. They'll give you lots of colour, we might free a bit of space for them to breathe.'

Halfway down the garden she turned to him and said, 'We should draw up a bit of a garden plan, just something rough but enough to give you and Frankie something to start with.'

Lillie was careful with her words because she wanted Seth to see this as his and Frankie's project: not hers. She would be going home eventually, and they needed to be able to look after this garden themselves, to *own* it.

The garden contained a frothing mound of red-hot pokers and a few laurel bushes, not to mention enough nettles to sting the entire population of Redstone. Lillie had come prepared this time and was wearing jeans and thick socks.

'You can keep your stinging bits to yourselves,' she told the nettles, whacking them back with Emer's hockey stick. 'The soil looks good, you know,' she told Seth, digging a bit with the tip of the stick. 'Emer doesn't use this any more, does she?' she added suddenly.

'No,' Seth laughed, and Lillie smiled at the sound. 'She dropped out of hockey during the exam years and never went back.'

'Good. I'd hate to wreck it.'

Lillie poked the earth some more. 'It's not stony topsoil or anything but proper, decent earth, Seth.'

'Maybe we can forget about the house and live in the garden,' he said, with added irony this time.

'Too chilly,' said Lillie, determined not to let him sink into introspection. 'Though the copper beeches would make a lovely shelter.'

At the end of the garden was an arch leading to a small walled-off garden. Seth and Frankie hadn't ventured into it since the day they came to view the property with the estate agent.

'It was nearly dark, so we only poked our heads in,' he said now. 'Basically, it's more brambles with a few trees in one corner.'

Lillie led the way over to it now, bashing nettles and briars out of her way with the hockey stick. The arch had a rusted gate, which was stuck in a half-open position.

As she passed through, Lillie felt a little shiver of anticipation, as if this place was somehow important and she should pay attention.

Sam's mother, a second-generation Irishwoman named Maeve, had once talked to Lillie about instinct. Lillie had been a young mother then and worried over Martin's spiking temperature, but she didn't want to take him to old Dr Howard without good reason. The doctor was notorious for sending people home with a flea in their ear if he felt they'd wasted his time.

Maeve lived only a few doors away, and she'd taken in Martin's fevered face and bright eyes, and seen how distressed Lillie was.

'What's this telling you – in here?' she said to Lillie, pointing to her stomach. 'What's it telling you? And here?' She pointed at her heart.

'That Martin's sick and he needs the doctor,' said Lillie instantly.

'Right then, off you go,' said Maeve. 'And find another doctor when this is over. Old Howard's been doing it too long, he's jaundiced and bitter at the world. He's no good for looking after young kids – or their mothers, for that matter.

He won't trust you, although he should. A mother knows when something's wrong with her child, and a smart doctor realizes that. So trust your gut and your heart, Lillie. They won't steer you wrong.'

Trust the wise woman inside, Lillie thought now. The wise woman who helped her see the truth. Lillie had stopped listening for a while, but the wise woman was definitely telling her something now. There was something special about this little walled garden.

Lillie took Seth's hand and they went in together.

The stones that made up the walls were very old, Lillie could see, and clearly pre-dated the house itself. In one corner stood a magnolia and a few apple trees, one of which looked diseased. But the other trees were magnificent. Comparatively recently, there must have been a small kitchen garden in the middle, although now only wild garlic grew. But it was so silent, utterly insulated from the noise of traffic, a little magical spot hidden from outside view.

It would, Lillie realized with excitement, make a perfect place for a couple of hives. They could be set away from the trees, which would suit the bees, yet still be beautifully sheltered. If she closed her eyes, she could imagine the pagoda-styled hives that Sam had used. WBCs, he used to call them.

Lillie had helped him choose those because they were the sort she could recall seeing with her mother Charlotte, in a garden many years ago.

I see that you're in cahoots with the wise woman, Sam, she said to him in her head.

'Seth,' she said aloud, 'have you ever thought of becoming a beekeeper?'

Chapter Twelve

Peggy knew it in her bones long before her brain allowed itself to accept the possibility. She was pregnant. *You're pregnant, you know you are*, the little voice in her head said to her reflection in the old-fashioned bathroom cabinet in her green tiled bathroom. The face in the mirror did not turn around and say, *Don't be ridiculous! You're imagining it. You're imagining that your breasts are larger and feel tender, and you're imagining that it has been almost exactly six weeks since your last period.*

She'd worked it out many times in her head: her night with David had occurred mid-cycle, the most fertile time for a woman. Four weeks ago.

The face in the mirror looked the same as usual, except for the fear in her eyes.

It's stress, she told herself. Periods are often late if the person is stressed. And starting a new business is stressful.

She sat with her calendar and worked out the dates. No matter which way she worked it out, she'd made love with David in precisely the most fertile segment of her fertility cycle. And her cycle was as reliable as the Angelus bell tolling before the television news at six every evening.

No matter how often she had silent conversations with

herself, mind racing over every *other* possibility, she always came to the same conclusion. She was pregnant.

If the breast tenderness and the two-weeks late period hadn't been enough to tell her, waking early every morning needing to throw up was the final giveaway. She'd hoped that this sickness might be a long-running bug, because surely nobody got morning sickness this early? But a few hours on the Internet told her that morning sickness and its arrival or otherwise was as varied as babies themselves.

When the nausea and the dry retching were finally over, she'd step glumly into the shower and try to wash away the way she felt. This never worked no matter how much grapefruit Body Shop shower gel she used. It was one of her few treats and now she couldn't even enjoy that. Pregnancy did that to people, she knew: made scents they loved suddenly smell dreadful.

She didn't have many indulgences, she thought tearfully. Nice shower gel and plants to brighten up the cottage. Ferns in the bathroom and kitchen, pansies in the living room and a small, grocery-store orchid in her bedroom. They helped, but they couldn't make the house beautiful. Her little rented cottage was stuck defiantly in the 1950s. From the aqua-coloured fittings in the bathroom – complete with black-and-white flooring, naturally – to the gingham curtains – red – in the kitchen, it was like living in some crazy offshoot of *Mad Men*. The kitchen and the bathroom were cute and her bedroom was absolutely adorable with a tiny balcony that looked out over a handkerchief of a garden, helpfully covered in gravel. But the rest of the house could be a little depressing, especially the living room with the orange tweed couches and the strange wallpaper that looked as if a few random children had scrawled along it with orange and brown crayons. It had probably been wildly hip sixty-odd years ago, Peggy knew, and it was a complete miracle that the whole place had stayed so clean. The letting agent had explained that a little old lady had lived there for a long time and had never changed a thing.

'Immaculate condition,' she'd said, looking around, trying not to touch anything. 'But you know . . . dated.'

Flowers and plants helped dress it up a bit. Peggy bought flowers whenever she could afford them. But today the scent of the single Tiger Lily in her bedroom was making her sick.

The vain hope of it being stress delaying her period or a bug making her ill every morning this week could not be clung to any more. She had to face the truth and buy a pregnancy test.

On Saturdays, she opened the shop at half past nine instead of nine. Most people were up a bit later on Saturdays and she allowed herself a smidge of a lie-in. A concept which was of no benefit at all when she was awake and nauseous at six. By half past eight this particular Saturday, she was on her way to the pharmacy at the far end of Redstone, a twenty-four-hour one she'd passed before but had never been in.

It was small, gloriously unmodern and unlike any of the glossy chain-store chemists where rows of intimate products were laid out for all to see. After ten minutes wandering around peering at shelves looking for something with a predictor or 'Are you or aren't you?' on the box, Peggy realized that if you wanted condoms, pregnancy-testing kits or anything of that nature in here, you had to ask.

'Can I help you, love?' said a middle-aged woman at the cosmetics racks sticking prices on lipsticks.

A young male pharmacist sat on a chair reading a car magazine and didn't even glance up, while another middle-aged lady with long purple fingernails that matched her chunky necklace and floaty lilac T-shirt was doing paperwork behind the counter. There were no other customers in the shop but even so, Peggy felt weirdly embarrassed to be asking for a pregnancy test.

There was so much fear and anxiety churning around inside her that it took her a moment to find the courage to reply.

'I'm . . . I'm looking for a pregnancy-testing kit,' she said, realizing how loud her voice sounded in the silence.

'Una, pregnancy-testing kits,' said the woman loudly to her colleague behind the counter. 'Get them out there, will you?'

'Right you are, Marjorie,' said the other woman in return.

The man reading the magazine took no notice as Una rifled through drawers, pulling out a variety of boxes, which she put on the counter. Una and Marjorie displayed them all for Peggy and began discussing the pros and cons of each of them.

'Now this one,' said Una, pointing with her purple nails, 'this one is super because you have two packets in case you don't believe the first one entirely. Very reliable – you'd like that one. Sells well, but it is a bit dearer.'

'It is a bit dearer,' agreed Marjorie, who was in tasteful pearls and a floral blouse like somebody's granny. 'But then you have a double test so it's *double* the reliability. Although sometimes,' Marjorie added, 'they can be wrong, even so. False positives or false negatives or whatever, I can't remember.'

'How long do you think you're pregnant?' Una said, peering over her spectacles at Peggy. 'I mean, are we talking a few weeks . . .'

Peggy shifted uncomfortably.

'Mmm,' said Marjorie, scanning Peggy's figure, 'you're very slim, love. No sign of a bump. How are your boobs? That always does it for me. Do they feel bigger? Or, you know, tender, like you couldn't bear anything to bang into you?'

Both of them looked expectantly at Peggy, who wasn't sure whether to laugh or cry.

'That's always a sign. That was always a sign for me,' Una said, patting her own considerable bosom, which was more of a bolster than a pair of breasts. 'Lord, how many times did I fall? Seven! Lord have mercy on dear Stanley! Even his

217

old mother used to say she didn't know he had it in him. 'Course, we didn't have pregnancy tests in those days. You had to go to the doctor and do a wee and they sent it off to a laboratory with a rabbit. If the rabbit died, you were pregnant – or was it the other way round? You didn't see the rabbit or anything,' Una went on, keen to point out that whatever rabbit cruelty was involved, the patient wasn't privy to it.

'A rabbit?' said Peggy.

'That's the way they used to do it,' Marjorie said. 'You did your specimen in the doctor's and then he sent it off and they did something with the rabbit. I think the rabbit died if you were pregnant. Or perhaps if the rabbit died, you weren't pregnant,' she added, turning to Una. 'Very cruel really. I don't hold with that type of carry on. No rabbits any more, you just pee on the stick. Do you think you're pregnant though? Do the boobs feel . . . you know . . .?' She looked enquiringly at Peggy.

'Well, yes,' Peggy said, wondering whether to get into the spirit of things or burst into tears. After all, this chattiness was what she loved about Redstone. The fact that there was a real sense of community. And there could be no more sense of community than standing in the pharmacy discussing whether you were pregnant or not with two middle-aged women. It was just a pity that neither of the women was the one woman with whom she really wanted to be having this conversation: her mother.

For a brief moment, Peggy wanted to lie her head down on the counter and cry. She felt so terribly alone. Instead, she said, 'I'll take this one,' gesturing at the double-test kit.

'Come back if you are pregnant and we'll fill you up with all the right stuff,' said Marjorie. 'You know, folic acid and the like and iron. The iron is great. Now me, I couldn't take the iron, went right through me.'

She gestured from her mouth down to her middle and out

218

on to the floor. Peggy got the picture. 'But if you can take it, it's great. Very good for the baby.'

The baby. Peggy swallowed. If she didn't want to go ahead with this, she mustn't think of what was inside her as a baby. She felt as if she might possibly faint. The blood drained from her face. Una and Marjorie looked at each other, went round the other side of the counter, grabbed hold of Peggy and sat her on a chair.

'It does come over some people like that,' said Una, or was it Marjorie?

Peggy was getting confused at this point.

'Never mind, love, I'll make you a cup of tea. The double test is the best one and you can head off and do that. You're the girl running that nice wool shop, aren't you?'

'Yes,' said Peggy faintly. So much for discretion.

'You shouldn't be going into work today, I mean people will understand.'

'Oh no, I have to,' said Peggy. 'I mean, it's my business, my shop, I have to be there.'

'What about your assistant?' Una turned to Marjorie. 'You remember Fifi: sweet girl, dark hair. Used to come in with her mother. Such a nice family. The father died a few years ago, decent man he was.' She turned back to Peggy: 'Let Fifi take over, tell her.'

'I don't want anyone to know,' Peggy said awkwardly.

'Ah,' said Una.

'Right,' said Marjorie. 'We get it totally. Our lips are sealed.'

Fifteen minutes later with a cup of hot sweet tea inside her, a big chemist's bag and a list as long as her arm of the things that would help the morning sickness – including apparently crystallized ginger, ginger biscuits and dry crackers – Peggy was back on the street again. This time there was a smile hovering on her lips. It hadn't been what she'd expected when she'd gone in to buy a pregnancy test, but somehow the whole visit had made her feel better. She wasn't the only one who knew. Marjorie and Una knew too.

It helped, having someone else in on the secret. But she wasn't about to go telling anyone else. Certainly not David Byrne. Not now, not ever. Because he'd want to make a family of them, and Peggy just couldn't. There were too many family scars inside her to ever dream of recreating any sort of family.

As she crossed the road to the shop, she realized that it was indeed a glorious morning. March was bursting out and the trees lining both sides of the street were shooting fabulous green buds towards the sky. Primroses had replaced the daffodils around the base of the trees and Peggy wondered, not for the first time, who did all the careful tidying of the streets. It wasn't normal council work, it had to be a group of local people who wanted to make their home as fabulous as possible. This was an idea she *loved*.

The thought of people sitting down and making plans: *Right, in January we'll do a tidy-up and make sure the bulbs have some hope of coming through. Keep an eye on the trees, too, mind. Aye, and don't forget we'll need to have the primroses ready to go down as soon as the daffodils die.* She could imagine someone saying that.

Peggy thought of her bungalow at home – not that it had ever felt like home to her. Her mother didn't have time for gardening and the ground was useless in any case. Terrible top soil. It wasn't as if there wasn't plenty of manure from the neighbouring farms that could be brought in to help make the soil vibrant, but her father had never been bothered so her mother's plants had been limited to a few little supermarket pots placed here and there. But they would invariably be dead within a week or two. The sad thing was that her mother loved flowers. Loved the few times Peggy had bought her peonies.

There was something about peonies; all those delicate petals like ladies' crinoline skirts. Her father wasn't impressed though.

'You shouldn't be spending your money on flowers – it's a waste, a total waste,' he'd say when he saw them.

Peggy knew better than to respond. She had an all-purpose smile she'd perfected for such occasions. It said, *Of course I agree with you, you're completely right*, without her ever having to open her mouth.

Because if she opened her mouth, she might be tempted to tell him he was a mean bastard and that it was bad enough he never bought Kathleen flowers himself, but did he have to begrudge the bit of pleasure she got when someone else bought them for her?

Why was she thinking about him now? That was then. The past. Although the past was still with her because she would have to visit soon for her mother's birthday.

She stopped, the key to the metal shutter in her hand. If only her family were different, she'd have been on the phone to her mother first thing.

Mum, I'm pregnant! I'm not with the guy any more, but I want this baby.

But her family were what they were, she was the way she was, and there was no place in that world for a baby.

She knelt down and unlocked the steel shutters, letting the world know that Peggy's Busy Bee Knitting and Stitching Shop was open for business.

'Hiya, Peggy, beautiful morning, isn't it?'

It was Sue from across the road, waving energetically at her.

'Lovely,' she said, waving back automatically.

She thought of the night Sue had come to the shop opening and how upset she'd seemed at the thought of her sister being pregnant. Something to do with miscarriage . . . Peggy had never got round to having that quiet chat with her. How could she do that now, if she was pregnant? Seeing other

221

people get pregnant must hurt like a knife to the guts if you wanted desperately to get pregnant yourself and couldn't, she thought.

Inside the shop, she went through her morning routine, switching on lights, checking the shop, getting the till ready, and all the while her mind was working away quietly. Una and Marjorie from the pharmacy had hit the nail on the head: tender breasts, ready to burst into tears at any moment, nausea . . .

Peggy pictured Marjorie and Una at her age: settled and content, husbands that loved them, wanting to share it all with a child. Not like her: twenty-seven and single, with a new business to run in a dubious financial climate, an unasked-for baby inside her and an ache in her heart.

It was still only ten past nine so she locked the front door behind her and went through to the back. The kitchen and toilet were spotless. Fifi had cleaned it all yesterday. 'Better to keep on top of the dirt,' she'd said, a jaunty red apron protecting her jeans and hand-knitted pink mohair sweater.

They'd take it in turns to clean the place, Peggy had said: her carefully worked out business plan didn't include money for anyone else to clean up. One member of staff apart from herself was as much as the budget allowed. Running the place on her own would be a mistake, as one of her night courses in entrepreneurship had explained. Fifi was glad of four days' work a week: she was a single mother. How did she cope? Lots of people coped, Peggy reminded herself. It was perfectly possible.

And just because single motherhood hadn't featured in her must-do-before-I'm-thirty plan, that didn't rule it out, did it?

She set the kettle to boil, found a herbal teabag instead of her normal instant coffee and went into the bathroom.

Ten minutes later, what she knew instinctively had been confirmed by the appliance of science. There were two blue lines on the tester. Peggy rubbed a finger gently over the window of the tester, as if the spirit of the baby had rippled through it, making her mark.

Her. It should be two pink lines, she decided. Because she was having a girl, she was sure of it.

She sat heavily down behind the counter and looked out on Main Street. The place was already busy with Saturday-morning activity. There were people walking dogs, people strolling along with the Saturday newspapers swinging in bags and people rushing in and out of the deli and Sue and Zeke's place, buying breads and olives for lazy Saturday lunches. She could see Bobbi's Beauty Salon from her seat, the door was opening and shutting, people whizzing in and out. Wouldn't that be nice now, to have time on a Saturday morning to go in and have all your things done: hair done, toenails painted coral, nails painted . . . Coral! Suddenly she wanted coral toes desperately, and fingernails too. Yes, that was it, that's what she wanted. That and an almond croissant. Coral toes and fingers, an almond croissant with a squelch of frangipane in the centre, and time to think.

Normally, the notion of leaving the shop for something as self-indulgent and expensive as a manicure would have shocked Peggy, but Fifi would be in at ten. Surely it wouldn't matter to open half an hour late?

She didn't do little luxuries for herself. That was how she'd built up her savings: from doing her own nails, toes, every-thing. But nothing about today was normal.

She locked up the shop and ran across the road to the salon.

Bobbi herself was behind the reception desk, majestic today with ruby lipstick and nails to match. Peggy didn't feel as scared of her as she had initially. It was Opal who had worked that magic. Anyone who could be friends with such a tenta-tive, gentle, sweet woman could not possibly be the tough cookie she presented to the rest of the world. No, the

223

toughness might be the outer shell to help her get on in business. Peggy suspected that Bobbi had a soft centre.

'Good morning, Peggy,' said Bobbi, 'I'm delighted you are gracing our establishment at last. Two of our girls are already crocheting in their breaks with stuff they got from you. Since you showed them how to do it, they haven't stopped. Even Shari, my daughter, is making a hat for one of my little granddaughters.'

'I love showing people how to crochet, and it's so simple,' Peggy said. 'Honestly, you should try it. I have some easy patterns to get you started, nice fat needles, lovely threads, lovely wools. You'd love it.'

'Ah no,' said Bobbi, 'I wouldn't love it, thank you. Not for me, thanks. I'd probably end up stabbing someone with a crochet hook but still, they're all delighted with themselves and when my girls are happy, I'm happy.

'You see, love, to me the crochet hook is still that wicked little steel thing we used years ago to do highlights. You're too young to remember, but we used to stick a plastic bag on someone's head and poke the scalp off them with the hook, making holes out of which you pulled the hair. It was so sore, you wouldn't be able to brush your hair for a week! No, Peggy, I'll never be able to see beyond that, so crochet's not for me. But I'm delighted the girls are busying themselves. One of them says she's making a handbag for her holidays. It's good to see you here today, giving a little return business, my dear.'

'I'm probably being very cheeky and crazy and there isn't a hope in hell of it happening . . .' Peggy started, suddenly thinking how reckless this whole venture was. What salon like Bobbi's would be able to squeeze her in on a Saturday morning?

'Tell me,' said Bobbi, 'I'll be able to tell you if it's wild and reckless.'

'Well,' Peggy began, 'I had this sudden mad desire to have my toenails and my nails painted coral?' She looked

224

quizzically at Bobbi and said, 'I know it's ridiculous and I don't really get those sorts of things done, I can't afford them, but it just came over me all of a sudden.'

'These things do,' Bobbi said soothingly. 'Hold on here till I look up the book.'

She ran a glossy red-nailed finger down the day's appointment list.

'Veronica, one of the younger but very talented members of staff, is not doing anything for the next hour. If you can stay now, we could do you a mani-pedi. After that, there isn't a hope in hell. There's weddings and hen parties coming in all day. The place is going to be wall-to-wall insanity and hissy fits until six o'clock tonight.'

Peggy thought of the shop. She didn't think that Fifi would mind. Suddenly she thought of all the years she'd told her mother that a little joy in her life was allowed. Kathleen Barry had known no joy no matter how much her daughter tried to make her see it. Well, Peggy and her baby daughter would know joy, that was for sure.

'Give me five minutes to run back and put a note on the door saying we won't be open until ten. I'll ring Fifi and tell her she has to open up, then I'll be straight over. Is that all right?'

'Perfect,' said Bobbi, smiling. 'By the time we've finished with you, you'll be walking on air, darling.'

Peggy grinned. Her world had been officially turned upside down but she didn't care: she felt an excited thrill rippling up through her from her feet to the top of her head.

Five minutes later, a sweet young girl named Veronica, who couldn't be more than nineteen, was examining Peggy's nails critically. Peggy had a cup of tea at her side and her feet in a footbath of bubbles.

The salon was buzzing but it wasn't hectic. Low, gentle music filled the background and Peggy realized why Bobbi's was always so popular: it was an infinitely soothing place.

'Do you use cuticle oil?' Veronica asked.

'No,' said Peggy cheerfully. 'Should I?'

'Yes,' breathed Veronica. 'Without it, your cuticles dry up and . . .'

Bobbi sailed past and leaned down to the low stool where Veronica was perched.

'I think Peggy wants a bit of peace before her day, Veronica, dear,' she whispered.

Peggy shot a grateful look at Bobbi, who smiled back. Peggy had the strangest feeling that Bobbi could see into her head. But that was ridiculous.

She sat back in the pedicure chair and closed her eyes, but her mind went back to her parents.

She would tell her mother about the baby soon, when she drove there for her mother's birthday. As for her father – she didn't really care if he never knew.

She could imagine what he'd say: 'You're pregnant with no man beside you? Didn't I say you'd come home to us with your tail between your legs, didn't I say that?'

She didn't care what *he* said, though. Her mother's opinion was what mattered and if it made Peggy happy, her poor mother would be pleased.

And David – what would David say?

Nothing, because she could never tell him. Men messed things up, that was the way of the world. Peggy would bring her child up on her own with no help from him. He would never know. On that, her mind was made up.

'The colour's lovely, really suits you,' said Veronica, admiring her own handiwork on Peggy's long, slender fingers.

'I've never had them this colour before,' said Peggy. 'I normally paint them with clear varnish myself, but it's time for a change, I think.'

From the appointments desk, Bobbi looked across and saw that Peggy, who'd come in looking a bit stunned and unlike herself, was now smiling in delight over her nails. She was a nice girl, that one. Tried to project a tougher image of herself than was entirely truthful. She was tender really – wounded, in fact, Bobbi would guess – and today, well, there was definitely something strange going on today.

Still, it would come out. Everything did. Look at poor Opal and that daft Meredith, come home in disgrace. Everything came out in the end.

Chapter Thirteen

*M*iranda was simmering. She was organizing this wedding almost single-handedly, nobody seemed to appreciate her hard work, and to add insult to injury, her daughter's future mother-in-law hadn't seen fit to even phone to discuss the agenda for the final wedding planning dinner party – to be held in the Byrnes' poky little house – that they were having in a few days. If Miranda hadn't insisted on another meeting, everyone would have been happy to let her carry on doing everything. She'd planned an elegant party in her home until Brian had stuck his oar in and said it was time one of these planning things was held at his mum's. Liz had agreed, to Miranda's fury.

Opal seemed to have no interest whatsoever in the wedding. Oh, she'd sent the 'we would be delighted to attend' cards back and hadn't even bothered to phone to say how beautiful the actual invitations were. No, not even a message had been left on Miranda's mobile to say that Opal had received and loved the beautiful gold envelopes and the glittering gilt-edged invitations inside. Miranda was cross. No, cross wasn't the word for it. She was furious. Raging.

She'd said as much to Elizabeth.

* * *

228

'Your future mother-in-law hasn't had the manners to phone me up to say what she thought of the invitations,' Miranda had snapped to her daughter only the night before.

'Oh Mum,' said Elizabeth tiredly, putting the shopping basket on the supermarket floor because it was so heavy. 'That was weeks ago. You were the one who loved them more than anyone else. I wanted the red ones, if you remember and does it really matter at this stage?'

It had been an exhausting day for Liz. She had fifth class now and they were a lot harder to manage than third. Third class still looked up to the teacher. Those little eight- and nine-year-olds thought Miss was a wonderful human being. By the time they got to fifth class, they had revised their opinion – thanks to Mrs Brock, who taught fourth class and treated her pupils as if they were juvenile delinquents sent to her for harsh treatment. Consequently, with a few exceptions, fifth class thought that all teachers were demons and their main aim was to do as little work as possible and to glare at her fiercely as if daring her to transform into Mrs Brock. Sometimes, Elizabeth felt like telling the kids that everyone avoided Mrs Brock in the staffroom too, but she knew this would be a mistake on so many levels.

Having an Easter wedding had originally seemed like a super plan so that she and Brian could have a short honeymoon over the school holiday, and then she'd be around for the school summer camps in order to add to her and Brian's fund for their own house.

But now everything to do with the wedding stressed her because as with anything where her mother was involved, there was trouble. Liz was a fabulous organizer and had planned the whole thing with Brian until her mother had insisted that Liz was busy and she'd love to help. That help had turned into a taking over of so many things and then making a big fuss over whatever she'd done, as if she'd been the one who'd discovered the God particle instead of those scientists in CERN.

Liz knew it was easier to let her mother carry on with her fussing but it still annoyed her: this was their wedding and they'd wanted no fuss. Except Miranda liked fuss.

Brian didn't appear to have noticed anything amiss with his future mother-in-law and he'd been relaxed about it all. Probably because his mother was normal and didn't feel the need to claim things for 'their side', Liz thought darkly.

'It'll be a great day,' Brian said. 'Something simple, just all the people we love in the world, coming together to celebrate our marriage.'

Liz had stared at him. Brian was so clever with computers but often so blindingly innocent when it came to people.

'Are you nuts?' she said one night, finally losing it after her mother had gone on a bender buying ludicrously over-the-top table decorations and making enquiries with a string quartet who'd had their own album in the classical charts. 'Weddings are battlegrounds,' Liz said. 'Archetypal events where the two families feud and everything goes wrong and . . .'

'Hang on there a second,' said Brian, startled. 'Weddings are lovely. Our wedding will be lovely. I'm sure everyone will have a great time.'

Liz thought of the frenzy her mother was in over her only child's wedding. She thought of her mother's cutting comments about the Byrne family in general – Brian was lovely and David was obviously cut from the same cloth as his brother and was on the way to making a few bob with his new business.

But as for the rest of them . . . Miranda didn't appear to have words to explain precisely how lower class the rest of the Byrne family were. More and more, Liz wished that they could just elope – slip away to Vegas and get married in one of those dinky little chapels where you could buy a dress and a wedding suit in one room, and tie the knot in another, with a free glass of champagne thrown in.

'It'll be a wonderful wedding,' said Brian, thinking of how happy his parents were about it all because they could see how much in love he and Liz were.

'Look you're right,' Liz had sighed, determined to think positively. 'It'll be lovely. An expression of our love, yes.'

This was supposed to be the best day of her life and she didn't want to remember it as an occasion of tension.

If only her mother would stop treating the wedding as a military campaign where she was at war with just about everyone. She'd gone to battle with the florist, the caterers, Opal.

What was deeply annoying to Miranda was the fact that Opal wasn't the sort of woman you could have a proper battle with. Even Miranda had to admit that there was nothing malicious or spiteful about her. Worst of all, and this really enraged her, Opal seemed oblivious to Miranda's disdain.

Miranda's attempts to show superiority all failed because Opal never entered the game. There was no reason, for example, for Miranda to get in a fit of jealousy over Opal's fabulous hat or outfit because Opal never seemed to dress up at all. Still, Miranda continued to judge the Byrnes by her own standards because that was the only point of view she understood.

'You'd think she'd have the manners to phone about the arrangements, wouldn't you?' said Miranda again.

It was a habit of hers. Repeating the question in different ways until eventually she got the answer she required.

'I expect she's busy,' Liz said.

'Busy? Doing what?' hissed Miranda. 'I am the mother of the bride. I am shouldering all of the work. What has she done? Absolutely nothing. Those two brothers are going to be ushers and I can't imagine what that young girl who lives with them is going to turn up like. I'm very glad she's not a bridesmaid.'

'I'll have to talk to you about that, Mum,' Liz said. 'I've

been thinking it over and perhaps we should ask Freya and Meredith after all. I know it's late in the day, but I feel guilty about it. Chloe's dress won't be that hard to match. Or we could have Chloe in her pale pink, and Meredith in coral and Freya in a warm blue. You know, not matching dresses, just pretty colours. It's very common these days to have brides-maids in totally diff—'

'But Chloe's your best friend since you were four,' shrieked her mother. 'You said you only wanted one bridesmaid! What changed your mind? Was it something Brian said?'

'Brian has said absolutely nothing,' Liz went on, determined to have her way in this. 'No, I've been thinking that it would be better to be *inclusive*,' she said, 'and to have Freya and Meredith as bridesmaids. I feel mean, not having asked them.'

'It's too late,' squawked Miranda. 'Chloe has a dress and everything. It's all sorted. I can't stand the thought of all the dresses not being the same.'

'It can be unsorted, Mum,' said Liz crossly. She might as well stick to her guns. 'It's not too late. Meredith and Freya can get something off the peg. If they're in different colours, it'll look as though we made them all different on purpose. I'm going to tell Brian tonight. We can finalize arrangements when we have dinner at the Byrnes on Thursday.'

Liz was conscious that this would be only the second time that her parents had dined at the Byrnes'. Their first visit, when the engagement had been announced, had not been a wild success. Their second looked set to be even worse. Thus far, Miranda had been so preoccupied with the wedding arrangements that she hadn't made the connection between Brian's sister and the Dublin Ponzi scheme that was splashed all over the papers. There was no telling what she might come out with when she realized one of her daughter's prospective bridesmaids was under investigation by the fraud squad.

'And, Mum, about Thursday . . .' said Liz. 'Please be nice

to Opal. She's always been so good to me, and she has a lot on her mind at the moment.'

Liz prayed that her mother would for once do this. The Meredith saga had been discussed at length between her and Brian and they both knew how upset Opal and Ned were about it all.

'How could Meredith not have known what they were up to?' Liz had wanted to know.

Brian had shrugged. 'I don't know. I think she looked up to the Alexanders so much that she would have believed any old rubbish they told her.'

'My mother still hasn't put two and two together and realized the stuff in the papers is about your sister. She'll go into orbit,' Liz said gloomily.

'I hope she doesn't blast off before Thursday night,' Brian had joked.

'Of course I'll be nice to Opal,' announced Miranda loftily now. 'I'm nice to everyone.'

'Sure, Mum,' said Liz, finally plonking her basket of groceries on the conveyor belt. 'I'm at the checkout, I have to go.'

'Fine,' said Miranda smartly.

The following morning Miranda looked at her lists with distaste. She had lots of lists in coloured folders. There was one for the flowers. Flowers were proving to be remarkably difficult. The florist Elizabeth had chosen didn't seem to understand her place at all, spoke to Miranda as if she were some sort of artist, when she was nothing of the sort. Just a girl who got up early enough to buy flowers in the market. Anyone could do that.

So far the only bit of the wedding that was going to plan were the invitations, and nobody apart from her close friends from bridge had commented on how wonderful they were. Nobody had a clue how much they cost, certainly not Noel.

They'd been many times more expensive than she'd let on to her husband, but they were one of those important details that you daren't overlook if you wanted the thing to be a success. This was setting up your stall, showing people what class of wedding it was going to be and she was determined that Elizabeth's was going to be the most classy wedding Redstone had seen in years.

In fact, it was about time she had a word with Opal Byrne and put her right on a few things. Better to get the whole thing out into the open before they went to dinner there, in that poky little council house.

People like Opal simply didn't know the correct way to behave.

Miranda marched down the parquet hall in The Borough, the imposing mock Georgian mansion where she and Noel had lived for the last ten years.

Manuela, the cleaner, had the front door open and was trying to scrub the granite step. The granite had been a wonderful idea, but it was proving very difficult to keep it clean. Miranda had given Manuela several different products to try, but so far none of them had worked. Finally, she had decided that a scrubbing brush and old-fashioned elbow grease would do the trick.

'Is it working, Manuela?' Miranda enquired.

Manuela did not look up at her employer. 'I cannot see,' she said. 'It is wet so it still looks dirty. We will see when it dries.'

'Hmmm.' Not entirely satisfied with this answer, Miranda picked up the cordless phone from the hall and stalked into the living room. She loved this room, which was a symphony in creams and pale blues, two of her favourite colours. One of the two outfits she'd bought for the wedding was this exact pale blue. The existence of a second outfit was another of those details she'd neglected to mention to Noel. Only Elizabeth knew, because they'd gone to London together to shop for dresses. She needed to find out what Opal was wearing first. Nobody knew. Opal hadn't even phoned her to discuss that. She probably didn't understand that part of the wedding etiquette either. It really made Miranda seethe.

Opal herself answered on the fifth ring.

'Hello,' she said. She sounded so distracted that Miranda, who rarely picked up on other people's moods, noticed.

'Opal, it's Miranda, Elizabeth's mother.'

'Oh,' said Opal, the lack of excitement in her tone even more apparent. 'How are you, Miranda?' she said. 'Is it about Thursday? You can still come, can't you?'

'I'm fine and of course we'll be there,' said Miranda sharply. 'I'm telephoning about a few things. What did you think of the invitations? Did you like the gold envelopes? Most of my friends phoned as soon as they arrived to tell me how beautiful they are. They came from New York, you know.'

'They're lovely,' said Opal, wondering how it was that she'd been so upset to find them on the mat a month or so ago. It was hard to imagine a time when something so silly mattered. What really mattered was Meredith, who was currently upstairs in her bedroom with the door shut. She spent much of her time up there. Not coming out. Today, there had been no noise, no music, no telephone calls. Nothing. Occasionally, Opal went up and listened closely at the door just to hear some movement so she'd know Meredith was OK. She'd knocked once or twice to ask, 'Would you like some tea, darling?' But each time Meredith had muttered, 'No thanks.'

'The envelopes were lovely, really pretty,' she told Miranda.

It was a struggle to summon the energy to say that much, but from Miranda's impatient sigh she detected that it wasn't enough. 'Well done,' she tried. 'You're doing it all so marvellously and I know I'm doing nothing, but you're very good at organizing; Liz always says so.'

This must have been the right thing to say, for she could almost hear Miranda preen.

'Well, it is one of my strengths,' she began, then she stopped. She didn't want Opal to think the Byrnes could sit back whilst the bride's mother did everything. Well, she did – but she wanted them to appreciate her cultured approach. *That's* what she wanted. 'We need an agenda for tomorrow night, Opal. There's such a lot to discuss, as I'm sure you're aware. There's the rehearsal dinner and someone needs to check if people have booked their hotels and if they need any help this end. We've people coming from the States and the UK, you know. And Bahrain. Places Noel and I have visited on our travels, people we—'

'Right,' said Opal. 'We can talk about all that on Thursday.' Opal could hear a stirring upstairs, the sound of Meredith's door opening and footsteps on the landing. Maybe she was going to the bathroom. Opal should race up and grab her, make sure she was all right. She hardly noticed what Miranda was saying. Something or other about dresses and colour-coordination and how it would be a mistake to add any more bridesmaids: 'Chloe's dress is so divine, there would be no point in having anyone else being a bridesmaid if their dress was different, would it?'

'No,' said Opal, not listening at all. All she could think about was Meredith wandering around the house like a wraith, barely eating, never going out.

Opal would do anything, *anything* to take away the pain from Meredith's face. To make it all go away. But she couldn't.

Miranda was still talking and Opal had had enough.

'Listen, Miranda, I have to go. The invitations were very nice and everything. See you on Thursday,' and she put the phone down quickly.

At the other end of the line, Miranda glared at the dead phone. The cheek! How dare Opal Byrne cut her off in the middle of a sentence! Wait until she told Elizabeth. It was plain rude.

* * *

236

On Thursday, in the house next door to Opal's, Molly was having a bad day. It was the radio news. She'd heard different versions of the news and it had all been about death. People were dropping like flies: a Hollywood star she'd swooned over when she was a girl had died at the age of eighty-four after a brief illness. Molly had been shocked and heartbroken. Shocked at the discovery that he was eighty-four. Old, for goodness' sake. She'd thought he was still swaggering round film sets setting hearts aflame when in fact, he'd been in a nursing home.

The next news bulletin solemnly announced the death of a local politician she'd once liked because he'd called at the door during an election and had been so nice.

'They're all nice at election time,' her dear departed husband, Joe, had pointed out.

'No.' Molly had been adamant. 'He cared about the problem with the drains, I'm telling you.'

Finally, a newspaper columnist she'd adored because he wrote just the way Molly thought had died unexpectedly.

Molly was wary of expressing particularly wild views on certain topics because people tended not to appreciate them, but this man had said the maddest things and got away with it. In fact, he'd been paid for it and was always on the television driving people demented and making the phone lines hop. It was one of life's great mysteries that some people got paid for something that another person might be reprimanded for saying.

Molly turned off the radio and decided she'd drop in and see Opal, who would surely be grateful of a visit, what with things being so difficult now that Meredith had come home on account of *the money scandal*. Ned and Opal got all white-faced and sad at the slightest mention of that.

She looked out of her kitchen window and saw that Ned was in the garden cutting flowers. He kept the place spick and span, Molly thought fondly. But the Byrnes' garden wasn't all formal with a bit of lawn and straight lines of blooms like a lot of them round here. Ned had an eye for clusters of things. He waved hello as Molly swung herself over the wall and went to his back door.

Molly liked the old ways: she'd go to the kitchen door during the day but never in the evening. Evenings were for family. No, she rang the bell at the front, then.

Opal was standing at the cooker, browning onions and floury bits of chicken in her big old frying pan.

'Hello, Opal, that smells delicious. I should keep out of here when you're cooking – my Weight Watchers diet hasn't a hope. What are you making?'

Molly sat down at the table without waiting to be asked.

'Chicken casserole. Good afternoon, Molly,' said Opal, with a worn smile. 'Will I put on the kettle? Are you staying for tea?'

'Ah no, you're busy cooking the dinner and I've just had a cup, but, oh, perhaps I might have a drop of tea while I'm here,' said Molly, all in the one breath.

'Actually, will you fill the kettle then,' Opal asked. 'If I leave this, it'll be sure to burn and this is the last batch. I hate browning things.'

Then she felt guilty because Molly had lived on her own since Joe died and when Molly cooked it was only to reheat one of those microwaveable low-calorie meals. Molly never needed to brown great batches of anything any more.

'Liz's parents are coming again tonight,' she sighed. 'They go to all the fancy restaurants, Brian tells me. If it has a Michelin star or any sort of recommendation, they're off like a shot. Miranda has some experience in the restaurant trade, apparently and she likes to keep up with the fashion.'

Opal looked harassed, which was unlike her. She had already spent hours ironing napkins, and laying the dining-room table. Ned was providing flowers for the table and had promised to polish the glasses.

238

Molly had met Liz's mother when the Flanagans came for the engagement announcement, and had been silenced by Miranda's sheer rudeness.

Now, she decided that Opal needed a bit of moral support.

'You're a fabulous cook, Opal Byrne, and don't worry for a moment,' Molly said.

It was no lie: Opal was an inspirational cook, all home taught and with a bit of the magic of the instinctive chef who could add a pinch of this and a spoon of that to bring the whole dish together.

'Besides, if she prefers fancy restaurants to dinner at her future son-in-law's family home, then she ought to have her head examined,' joked Molly.

'I don't want to be disloyal to Brian or to Liz, whom we love,' said Opal slowly, 'but I don't think Miranda entirely approves of us as a family. And now with all this problem over Meredith – I just can't take any more hassle. She rang yesterday, demanding to know why I hadn't phoned about her gold invitations. I know it's uncharitable of me, Molly,' said Opal crossly, 'but I cannot bring myself to like that woman.'

After that, there was no way Molly was leaving.

'I'll stay and keep you company,' she said, and Opal hadn't the heart to send her away.

It was nice to have someone to talk to as she cooked, even if Molly did most of the talking.

Molly was still there at seven o'clock when Brian and Liz arrived with the Flanagans. Noel, Liz's father, was fine, Molly decided. He was a big man who liked his pint, judging from the belly on him, and who smiled at everyone because he liked a quiet life.

As for Miranda, it was easy to see where Liz had got her looks. Miranda had the same sheeny coppery hair and almond-shaped eyes. But while her daughter was a smaller, curvier version with a face permanently crinkled up with a big smile,

239

Mrs Flanagan was tall and bony, with deep frown lines in her forehead. She glared at Molly as if to say, What on earth is someone like you doing here? When Miranda was seated in the sitting room, an act which required her to sweep imaginary crumbs off the chair, and had graciously said she might drink a small gin and tonic, Opal escaped to the kitchen to check on dinner.

Molly followed her, saying loudly to the guests, 'I must be off, enjoy your dinner.'

As soon as the two of them were alone in the kitchen, she said to Opal, 'I've just had a thought, isn't she the image of your woman from the corner house on the avenue? Lots of lipstick, nose in the air and a face as hard as a brick.'

Opal clamped her hand over her mouth to stop herself laughing out loud.

'Molly, you're dreadful. She might hear.'

'Let the old bat hear me. I don't envy you tonight – or,' Molly added thoughtfully, 'sharing a wedding with her. She'll be all set to outshine you, no matter what you wear, you mark my words.'

Opal hugged her friend goodbye. Molly had cheered her up, but she felt that what she wore to Brian's wedding was the least of her problems.

Miranda waited until they were all in the middle of Opal's chicken casserole before she brought up the matter of bridesmaids and how it would be a mistake to upset the symmetry of having just the one.

'You wanted me to have four,' said Liz angrily, knowing exactly where this was heading.

Briefly, Miranda looked discomfited. 'Those were girls from school,' she said quickly.

'I think it would be nice to have Meredith and Freya,' said Liz defiantly, and was rewarded by a smile from Opal.

'Thank you, love,' said Opal, 'but I don't think Meredith would be up to it. And Freya's not a frock person, really.'

'Thanks, Liz,' said Freya, poking her nose round the dining-room door. She'd been keeping out of harm's way in the kitchen in case she felt the need to take the electric carving knife to Miranda, but had been listening in. 'I'm more of a biker boot sort of person.'

She grinned as she saw Miranda's mouth purse. 'Although I'll wear a bridesmaid's dress if I can wear my biker boots?'

'Now, I really can't—' spluttered Miranda.

'She's pulling your leg, love,' said Ned calmly. 'It's all right, we won't ruin your plans. As long as Brian and Liz are happy, that's all we care about.'

He stared at Miranda with such intensity that she slowly closed her mouth and lowered her head to her dinner.

'I couldn't have put it better myself, Dad,' said Brian, wishing his future mother-in-law wasn't such a bitch.

'Exactly, thank you, Ned,' said Liz in a shaky voice. She was trying to ward off the tears, but it wasn't easy. She wanted her wedding to be beautiful and, unsurprisingly, her mother was doing her best to ruin it. Well, she wouldn't: Liz was determined about that. It would be a marvellous day, no matter what Miranda wanted.

Chapter Fourteen

Frankie hadn't seen Seth this excited in months. Every day, he was up before she was, and out in the garden come rain or shine, helping the young gardener that Lillie had recruited via an ad in the newsagent. Dessie had abandoned his course in landscape gardening, he'd told them, because he couldn't afford to finish. Instead, he did heavy lifting work in gardens, cut lawns in summer and hired himself out for all sorts of labouring work in winter.

Working in the garden at Sorrento Villa was sheer joy. 'Now, I don't want to be the interfering sister,' Lillie had said to both Frankie and Seth before Dessie came on board, 'but since you won't take a dollar of rent from me and I've been here for so long, I'd like to pay Dessie and help him work on the garden. You have no idea how different the place will look with a strong lad to help us.'

'Does he have a JCB?' Frankie had asked with a grin, and only Lillie had seen Seth's face fall at his wife's joke.

'No,' Lillie said evenly, 'but he can get a loan of one of those compact diggers, and that's what we do need. And who knows, if he's good enough, he might be the man to help us work on the inside of the house too – room by room.'

She felt angry with Frankie for being so pessimistic, particularly when the prospect of taming the wilderness had cheered Seth up so much. But there was no way Lillie could tell Frankie that. Not just yet, anyway.

'Fire away,' Frankie said. 'But don't feel that you have to spend your money, Lillie. We don't want you to pay your keep. It's lovely having you around, particularly with Emer and Alexei gone.'

She might as well have come out and said that Lillie was welcome to stay for ever because Frankie and Seth were no good together any more, that they were only held together with the glue of another person.

Lillie pretended not to understand.

'Give us three weeks,' she said cheerfully, putting an arm around Seth, 'and you'll see what we can do.'

In fact, Frankie had been astonished at what the three of them had accomplished in just one week. Dessie and his mini-digger had ripped up dead shrubs, a broken patio and an apple tree that had died long ago. Thanks to him, Seth was able to clear away the brambles and toss them into the big skip they'd hired. By the end of the week, they needed another skip.

'I love this garden,' Dessie said excitedly on Friday morning as he, Lillie and Seth stood outside with their mid-morning coffee warming their hands. 'I can see it in my mind – just the plan to make it beautiful.'

'Can you draw it up for us?' said Lillie. 'You are a landscape gardener, after all.'

'Only half-qualified,' Dessie said.

'Nonsense,' said Seth. 'It's obvious that you know what you're talking about. Maybe we can do some drawings together. I'll tell you what I had in mind before and we can see what we can make of it now.'

Lillie busied herself collecting the cups and went indoors. Out of their sight, she gave a whoop of joy.

See, Sam, she said: *he's taken the bait. If that's not the old Seth Green, then I'm a monkey's uncle.*

Frankie was getting better at clever shopping. Clever shopping meant good food for bargain prices. Once, she'd have gone to a big supermarket and bought everything. She'd have loved to have had the time to meander in and out of the greengrocer's, the delicatessen, the butcher's, to get the perfect things, but she was time-poor. Now, however, she was just poor because they were living on one salary, so she worked very hard at getting the best value for her grocery shop. Seth had done bits and pieces in the beginning, but he'd never been a careful shopper and Frankie had found it irritating when he bought the wrong food.

'We don't need more chopped tomatoes,' she said one day when he came home with a dozen tins and nothing suitable for dinner.

'They were on special offer,' Seth said. 'I thought we were saving money.'

'Yes, love,' she said, trying to rein her temper in, 'but there's saving money and there's buying things you don't need. Buying that many tomatoes is like buying cat food when you don't have a cat.'

'Fine. You can do it in future,' Seth said, clearly stung.

'I didn't mean . . .' Frankie began, feeling bad for letting her irritation show. It was counter-productive. He was doing his best. She started to apologize, but he was gone, marching out of the kitchen.

So these days, although Lillie sometimes helped, Frankie mostly did it herself. It turned out that having less money meant you spent an awful lot of time when you were shopping. She bought much less meat and they had vegetarian meals a couple of nights a week. When she did buy meat, she bought it from Morton's butcher's at the crossroads, which turned out to be a saving compared to the days when she'd recklessly thrown more meat than she needed into the trolley in the supermarket. Sometimes, she'd buy a few slices of the delicious ham they sold in the delicatessen to serve with the pecorino cheese she bought in the cheap super-market. The men in the deli were lovely and chatty though Frankie knew she was being unsociable when she refused to rise to their conversational gambits. Once she would have, but at the moment, she didn't have the energy. Everyone else seemed to treat the delicatessen as an unofficial meeting place. People stood around chatting in the queue, discussing the merits of buffalo mozzarella compared to goats' cheese mozzarella.

'There's a certain tang from the goats' cheese,' one of the men behind the counter was arguing, and Frankie wanted to yell, 'Get a move on, some of us don't have the time for this.'

One Saturday morning, exhausted after trailing around the ordinary supermarket, the low-cost supermarket at the cross-roads and the butcher's, Frankie finished by visiting the green-grocer's shop because she'd forgotten to buy enough vegetables for tonight. She'd never ventured in there before. They sold organic vegetables as well as ordinary ones and the very word *organic* had put her off. Organic meant more expensive. Frankie didn't have the money for more expensive. Seth was lucky he wasn't living on white bread and chips.

Inside the fruit-and-veg shop, there was an air of absolute relaxation as if everyone in there had all the time in the world. People browsed among the vegetables with baskets over their arms, squeezing things to see if they were ripe, the way nobody ever did in the supermarket. Frankie scanned the shelves, trying to work out what she could get to make the special-offer salmon steaks for that night more exciting than the cucumber and a bit of lettuce she'd already bought. She found some avocadoes and reached over, giving them an exploratory squeeze, when somebody said her name.

'Frankie, it is you! I thought it was when I saw you cross the road.'

She turned, recognizing the voice, but for a moment she couldn't place the woman who stood there. And then she did. She had worked in Dutton Insurance but had left several years ago. Amy, that was it. Frankie never forgot a name, a useful asset in her business. The woman had a small child with her.

'Hello, Amy. Goodness, I didn't recognize you for a moment,' she said, then added hastily, 'Sorry, I don't mean to sound rude.'

'You don't.' Amy smiled and gave Frankie a kiss on each cheek.

'This is Minnie,' she said, introducing the small cherub at her side. The little girl was wearing denim dungarees, a purple T-shirt and a mutinous look on her face. 'Minnie, say hello.'

'No,' said Minnie grimly, burrowing her face in her mother's leg.

'Is she shy?' said Frankie.

'No,' Amy said, grinning, 'just cross because I won't bring her into the café and get her a hot chocolate.'

Frankie took a moment to get used to this new Amy. The woman she'd known at Dutton had been the ultimate corporate mummy, with dark circles under her eyes, perfect hair, manicured nails, and an air of permanent rush. Amy had worked under Frankie in HR.

One day she'd complained to Frankie how *hard* it was being a working mother.

'It's impossible, I don't know how you did it, Frankie. I've only got one child and I am run ragged from the moment I go to the crèche in the morning to the moment I get into bed in the evening. It's like being on a speeded-up hamster wheel.'

'You'll get used to it,' Frankie said comfortingly, remembering her own experience when the kids had been young. 'You're wonderful at it all, Amy, and you're doing so well in the company.'

Amy had responded with the slightly deranged stare of the working mother who doesn't get enough sleep and was clocking up marathons on the guilt treadmill.

'Do you know what, Frankie? I don't want to get used to it. I've had it.'

Frankie had been quite shocked.

'Jack and I are going to downsize,' Amy said. 'I don't care about the job. What use is a great career if I go mad trying to combine it all?'

She and her husband were going to move out of their city-centre apartment and find a house in the suburbs. Hopefully, the money they'd make on the sale would enable Amy to give up work and have more children.

Frankie did her best to get her a decent deal from the company.

'I only hope you won't regret it,' she'd said anxiously.

'Don't worry, I won't,' Amy said firmly. And here she was, four or five years later, looking as though she hadn't regretted it for a moment.

Her once coiffed hair was now a soft-streaked blonde that hung in waves down to her shoulder blades. She didn't wear make-up and instead of the chic suits Frankie had been used to seeing her in, she wore a comfortable cream sweater and worn jeans, with her feet shoved into soft suede clogs.

'You're looking fantastic,' Frankie said, genuinely believing it.

'Oh thank you,' said Amy, looking down at herself. 'Once I stick something on in the morning, I never really look at it again. Jack's at home with the baby.'

'A baby as well?' said Frankie.

'We've three children now. Minnie is three.' Amy reached down and ruffled her daughter's hair. 'Jules, who I had when I worked in Dutton, is nearly seven, and the baby is Raphael.'

'Wow.'

'Wow indeed,' said Amy, and there was joy in her face. 'It's crazy, I never get a moment to myself but I love it. I'm happy, Frankie. No more rushing around being consumed with guilt. My friends and I say that we'll go back to work when the kids are older. We don't have as much money to buy them stuff, but that's all it is, isn't it, Frankie – stuff?'

'Yeah, stuff,' said Frankie.

She had stuff. The desperate dilapidated old house was stuff, and she didn't have any of the peace that glowed from Amy's face.

'We moved here last year,' she told Amy, 'bought a house to do it up, but Seth lost his job, so it's been very difficult.'

Saying it out loud felt like a big thing to Frankie, but it was true, why should she hide it?

'I'm sorry,' said Amy. 'You should come around for dinner some evening. I grow a lot of my own vegetables now, and Jack is in the process of getting hives.'

'Hives,' said Frankie. 'You mean bees?' She remembered Lillie and Seth talking about putting a couple of hives in the garden. Seth had seemed quite enthusiastic, but Frankie wasn't sure. Why add to their burdens?

'Yes, Jack's done a beekeeping course and he's going to get two hives. Two is apparently a good number to start up.'

'And . . . for what?' said Frankie. 'To sell honey?'

'Oh no. Just for ourselves. It seems such a nice idea.'

'What if someone gets stung? Are you sure it's safe with small children?' Frankie said.

'Perfectly safe,' said Amy. 'Bees don't randomly sting. Here,' she said, reaching in her bag for a scrap of paper. 'I'll write down my number. When you get a chance, give me a call and we'll catch up and set a dinner date, OK? The great thing is, these days I don't go to Marks & Spencer's and buy ready meals, I cook. Imagine, me cooking!' She laughed as she scribbled her number on the paper. 'Today we're making roast pepper and sweet potato soup. Aren't we, munchkin?'

Minnie glared up at her ferociously.

'Chocolate,' she hissed.

'We'll see,' said her mother, passing the paper to Frankie. 'I better get my shopping. You know how kids are. They get bored.'

'Yes,' said Frankie faintly, stowing Amy's number carefully in her bag.

'See you.' And Amy set off with Minnie in the direction of the peppers.

Frankie continued on her own way round the shop, but found she couldn't resist glancing over at Amy every few minutes. She looked so good. All glowing and happy, whereas Frankie felt terribly uptight. Amy joined the queue to pay, then turned and waved at Frankie as she and Minnie left the shop.

Sweet potato and roast pepper soup. It sounded delicious. Frankie decided that she was going to make it too. It couldn't be that hard. There were recipe books. Sweet potatoes, where were the sweet potatoes?

Amy was right. Things needed to be calmer in Frankie's life. Tomorrow she'd make some lovely soup and then she, Seth and Lillie might sit out on a weed-free bit of patio and eat it with the organic bread Lillie got from the bakery.

It was nice having Lillie around. She was very calming. She might even know how to make soup. Frankie paid for her purchases, buying probably more than she needed, determined that she was going to be part of the lovely golden-soup-world too. But as she carried her haul back to the car she couldn't suppress a faint sense of unease. Something wasn't right in her life. And soup wasn't going to fix it.

Chapter Fifteen

It was a journey Peggy didn't want to make but she knew she had to. Her mother's birthday was at the weekend, but Peggy couldn't afford to be away then as Fifi was off that Saturday and there would be nobody to mind the shop.

So she'd do it tomorrow. One day to drive up and see her mother. And her father. Stay the night, and then go back home in the morning.

Fifi was going to take over the shop for two days and even though Peggy trusted her implicitly, it still broke her heart to leave. 'You'll call me, won't you, if there're any problems?' Peggy had said the evening before as they'd closed up and she'd carried out her nightly ritual of checking windows, cupboards, the back door, locks, everything.

'Yes,' said Fifi, with the endless patience she showed to first-time knitters who couldn't quite get the hang of plain and purl. 'It's going to be fine, I promise you.'

'But you might have an emergency,' Peggy said. 'What if Coco gets sick?' Coco was Fifi's six-year-old daughter, an adorable imp perfectly suited to her name, with the dancing dark eyes of her mother and the milky-coffee-coloured skin of her long-gone father.

'Coco doesn't get sick. She's got the constitution of an ox,'

Fifi said. 'Listen, all eventualities will be covered. If needs be, my mum can look after her.'

'Yes, of course,' said Peggy reminding herself that Fifi had her mum as back-up.

That was important: back-up. She felt the wash of fear every time she thought of the baby inside her and the lack of back-up in her life. She felt so alone. She hadn't even dared tell Fifi about the baby yet.

'Fine, yes, I'm just being silly, aren't I?' said Peggy.

'You're not.' Fifi's endless patience turned itself to Peggy again. 'You're not being crazy at all. The shop is your baby, same as Coco will always be mine.'

'Yeah,' Peggy managed to say. She wanted to talk to Fifi about her *actual* baby, because if anybody knew what it was like to be pregnant and single it was Fifi.

But Peggy wasn't ready to talk. She still didn't know what she was going to do, what would happen and how she could go through with having this child. How on earth was she going to manage?

'Why don't you come over for dinner?' Fifi said impulsively.

'I can't, really, I'm busy,' said Peggy, which was pretty much what she always said. She'd only gone to Fifi's once for dinner and it had been so gorgeously comforting and lovely, she'd felt miserable going back to her own ugly cottage.

'I insist,' said Fifi. 'C'mon. Follow me in your car and we'll go to my mum's first and pick up Coco.'

There didn't seem to be any option, so Peggy obediently hopped into her car.

Fifi's mum lived a ten-minute drive away at the end of a rambling terrace of houses. Peggy pulled up behind her, outside a house that looked as if wisteria from space had come in and colonized the entire downstairs floor. Wisteria hung off the overhanging porch and crept along above the windows.

'It's a bit mad, isn't it?' Fifi said when they met outside the house. 'Mum loves it. One day it'll make its way into the roof and we'll probably get branches creeping down into the bedrooms. I think it wants to take over the whole house, but she's letting it. It comes in peace.'

Fifi's mum Geraldine had barely opened the door before Coco rushed out yelling, 'Mum!' and threw herself into her mother's arms. Peggy was used to seeing her in uniform on days when Fifi dropped into the shop after picking Coco up from school. But today Coco had changed out of her school uniform at her grandmother's and was dressed in a riot of colours as if one wasn't quite enough. Little turquoise jeans, orange socks, pink shoes and a T-shirt with sparkles on it in the shape of a butterfly.

'You need a cardigan, it's chilly,' Fifi scolded fondly.

'I've been telling her that all day,' Geraldine said, giving Fifi a hug and then one to Peggy.

'Is Peggy coming home to our house?' Coco asked.

'She's coming to dinner,' said Fifi.

'Oh, how nice,' said Geraldine. 'Can I come too? I was going to go to bingo, but to be honest I've a bit of a headache and I think the noise would kill me.'

'Sure, the more the merrier,' said Fifi.

Geraldine fetched her coat and a cake tin and elected to go in Peggy's car. She chatted happily as they drove to Fifi's house, another five minutes up the road.

Normally Peggy listened to music in the car but now she turned the radio off and enjoyed the comforting sound of Geraldine's voice.

'She's such a pet of a child,' said Geraldine, who seemed to have an endless store of anecdotes about her granddaughter. 'We did a bit of baking today after school. She said she had no homework – I don't believe her, the minx. So we baked muffins. Coco wanted to be in charge of the weighing. They haven't turned out too bad, a bit damp in the middle. I brought some anyway.'

Geraldine was probably the same age as Peggy's own mum, Peggy thought. But she was so different. She was happy, there was no fear in her.

Fifi lived in a ground-floor apartment in a big three-storey house overlooking some waste ground that Geraldine informed her was being turned into a park. Behind that and the allotments, was Maple Avenue, a street of large houses with one huge run-down Victorian redbrick on the corner.

In Fifi's light, bright home there were two bedrooms and a roomy open-plan kitchen/dining-room/sitting-room area. Gordon the guinea pig sat in his cage near the patio doors and looked delighted to see everyone while Shadow, an elegant, sleek, black cat, stalked past and ran out as soon as the door was opened.

'Your cat flap was there for you, sir,' Fifi said to his departing elevated tail. 'He just likes to stay home and stare at poor Gordon to frighten the life out of him. Go on, Coco, we'll let Gordon out for a bit of a play.'

'Just a minute!' Coco dumped her school bag and ran off into the bedroom. Geraldine headed straight for the kitchen area.

'Is Coco changing again?' Fifi asked.

'Yes,' said her mother, opening the fridge. 'She likes to change clothes four times a day. The washing machine will break soon. What are we having?' Geraldine peered up at her from the fridge.

'I don't know,' said Fifi. 'What have we got in there?'

'There's a little lasagne.'

'That's for Coco.'

Coco's meals were painstakingly cooked and frozen on Sundays, Fifi had told Peggy. An assortment of child nutrition and recipe books were lined up on one wall of the gleaming yellow kitchen.

There was a warm atmosphere at Fifi's that had nothing to do with heating or yellow walls. Peggy didn't have much

253

experience of other family homes – going to other girls' homes when she'd been a kid had been a no-no because then, they might want to come back to hers. This was a home that was easy, light, friendly. There was no need to be afraid she was upsetting the balance, the way she would have been in her childhood home. Here there was no anxiety about visitors. Everyone was welcome.

'You've loads of eggs,' said Geraldine, poking around in the fridge. 'Open a few cupboards there, Peggy, and see what else she has. The vegetables are in that hanging rack. We have to keep them high up or when Gordon gets out, he heads straight for them.'

Coco was now dressed in comfy sweatpants. Gordon was on the couch with her, being stroked and adored.

'Look, Gordon can do a trick,' called Coco as she put Gordon on one end of the back of the couch. 'Go, Gordon,' she said, and clicked her fingers. Gordon immediately scurried right down to the other end, turned around and came back. Everyone clapped.

'Well done, Gordon,' said Fifi, going to kiss her daughter on the top of her head. She gave Gordon a snuggle too. 'Very clever guinea pig.'

Peggy, who was searching for vegetables, could have sworn Gordon smiled up at Fifi.

'Is he house trained?' she asked Coco.

'Oh, he's very good,' said Coco. 'Guinea pigs are clever, you know. People think they're stupid and they're rats or something, but they're not. Gordon has genius IQ.'

'Really?'

'I don't know for sure,' Coco said, staring deeply into her pet's twitching furry face, 'but he's clever, I can tell. Look into his eyes.'

Peggy obediently went to look into Gordon's eyes. He gazed at her beadily. She failed to see any glint of Einstein-ness in there, but if Coco said he was a genius, that was good enough for her. She was a remarkably clever, funny little girl, full of delicious scampiness and yet kind and gentle too.

'Peggy, you sit there with Coco,' said Geraldine, watching them from the kitchen area. 'You look pale. You're probably working too hard. I'll do a bit of fluthering around here and rustle up something.'

'We'll do it together,' said Fifi companionably to her mother.

'Oooh, sit beside me, Peggy,' Coco said happily. She curled on the couch like a sprite with Gordon on her lap. 'Tell me a story about fairies and goblins and elves and a mean queen,' Coco went on, 'who built a castle and put the princess inside it and er – what else, what else, Mum?' she roared.

'How about the prince who was supposed to come but his car broke down and he couldn't fix it, so the princess had to figure a way of getting out all by herself?' said Fifi, who was chopping vegetables.

Coco giggled.

'I love your feminist fairy stories, Fifi,' said Geraldine from the stove.

'There's too much pink fairyness in girls' stories,' Fifi said cheerfully. 'I don't want her thinking that the prince is always going to rescue her.'

'I don't think we want anyone to rescue her,' Geraldine said loudly. 'We want her with us forever, don't we, Cocs? We want you with us forever, my bunny rabbit.'

Coco grinned.

Peggy felt as if she was watching everything from a slight distance, and yet she wasn't. She was here in the middle. There was so much love and happiness in this home, no strain, no tension, no anxiety over what to cook for dinner. Suddenly two more people had been added to the catering and Fifi was calmly trying to accommodate them.

'Can I have some television?' Coco wheedled.

'No television until after dinner, and then we can have perhaps half an hour of something on the animal channel. I know you'll have watched telly at your granny's and you can't sit in front of the box all day.'

'As if you'd let me,' grumbled Coco. 'Was your mummy like that?' she demanded of Peggy. 'Everyone in my class watches television all the time and I'm not allowed.'

'You'll get square eyes,' her mother cried.

'Won't.'

'Will.'

If she had a baby she'd have to have rules about television and learn how to cook nutritious meals and do things like that, Peggy thought in alarm. How was she going to do it? It wasn't that she was incapable – she was capable of so much – but taking care of a child, the welfare of a child . . . How did you learn to do all that stuff?

It couldn't just come naturally, and if it was supposed to be in you from your own childhood, well then, there was no hope for her.

The next morning the sky was dark and thunderous. Heavy clouds swollen with rain loomed ahead of her on the road as she set off for her parents' home. Peggy had gone to bed late, having sat up at the little kitchen table with Geraldine and Fifi until half past ten, talking, laughing at their funny stories. Geraldine was having great fun recounting tales of all Fifi's unsuitable boyfriends over the years, starting with Laurie, the one with the long hair who had gone off with her best friend.

'She can't have been much of a best friend,' said Peggy.

'He was very good looking,' admitted Fifi. 'I forgave her. He just had this power about him, this charisma, and you couldn't say no.'

Eventually, talk turned to Fifi's father, who'd died a few years before.

'Dad was hilarious,' Fifi said fondly. 'Whenever any of my boyfriends came into the house to collect me, Dad would stand with them in the living room and they'd have this sort of man chat. Dad would say, "Now you look after my little girl, won't you?" and try to look a bit menacing.'

'Which he couldn't really do,' said Geraldine.

'No,' agreed Fifi. 'He couldn't do menacing at all. It always ended up looking as if he had a bad case of acid reflux. He was too much of a sweetie to be menacing. But anyway, I'd be mortified and whoever it was would go puce in the face, because they didn't expect that really. Nobody else's dad did it.'

'Your dad just wanted to mind you,' Geraldine pointed out.

'I know, and he did,' said Fifi, reaching over to squeeze her mum's hand affectionately.

There were tears in both their eyes. 'It's nearly three years,' said Geraldine sadly. 'Massive heart attack. Instant. Better for him, he was such a vital man, so energetic.'

Peggy felt she ought to say something comforting. She was at a loss though. She'd never known that sort of love with her father. Still, she couldn't remain silent.

'You had someone you loved greatly in your life, in both your lives,' she said to Fifi and Geraldine solemnly. 'That's priceless.' She paused, feeling her own eyes brim. 'Not everyone has that, you know.'

'I know, I know,' said Geraldine, dabbing her eyes with a tissue she'd found tucked in her sleeve.

'Yes,' said Fifi, with a calm, thoughtful look at Peggy. 'Not everyone has that. Now, since that little minx has gone to bed and I think she is actually asleep, I've got some Häagen-Dazs ice cream in the freezer: strawberry cheesecake.'

'Oh no,' said her mother, 'my Weight Watchers diet is going out the window. Just because you're like a whippet and can eat what you want doesn't mean the rest of us can.'

'I'd love some ice cream,' Peggy said suddenly, feeling as if the only thing in the world she wanted was Häagen-Dazs – preferably the whole tub.

* * *

Peggy had been extra sick the next morning. She wondered if it was the Häagen-Dazs. She had some crackers beside her in the car and she nibbled them gently, sipping water too. She hadn't been able to face breakfast. Not after all the throwing up. She had a plastic bag in the passenger well, too. Just in case. She was planning to go on the main road for a bit of the way and then get off and try some of the back roads because – and it was very strange – she just didn't feel up to driving on the big scary motorways with the baby inside her. Cars zooming past made her feel anxious and exposed and she wanted to go slowly and carefully now that it wasn't just her.

After an hour's driving, she turned off on to one of the more country routes. It would get her home all the same, but it would take a while longer. She still hadn't stopped for a cup of tea or some toast, even though she was hungry. She wasn't sure if she'd be able to keep anything down except the crackers and water. She sighed, knowing her mother would have been cooking all day in readiness for the visit. It would taste like ashes in Peggy's mouth.

Sixty-five miles away in an ugly bungalow, Kathleen Barry emptied the kitchen bin again. She'd done it the night before but there was still a strange smell lingering and she had to get rid of that. She had her gloves on because Tommy had made some comment about her nails the other day. Just one of his acidic throw-away remarks, but she knew what he was saying. The nails were a bit of a mess, hence *she* was a mess. She'd love one day when she was older, maybe, or if Peggy came with her, to go and have a manicure.

She'd always wanted a manicure, but she'd be too ashamed of her hands. Imagine showing them to one of the beautiful young girls in the beauty salons in town. You needed to start with the whole manicure thing when you were much younger, didn't you, and Kathleen had never started at all. She'd never had a facial either. Peggy used to be quite into all that stuff and used to beg her to come with her, beg her.

'We could go away, Mam, overnight somewhere. We could save up and go to one of those spas and have a few treatments done.'

It was hard to resist Peggy when she said things like that. She was tall and beautiful with gleaming skin. So much energy and vitality, and Kathleen had wanted to say, *Yes, let's do that*, but she knew there'd be a price to pay because Tommy wouldn't want her going off.

He might *say* it was all right, but then he'd change his mind and it wouldn't be. He'd be angry and his anger would infect the house and Kathleen's very bones with fear.

So she never said yes to Peggy when she asked her to go on the girl–mother trips.

She knew she was letting Peggy down, and she couldn't bear to see Peggy looking at her sadly, betrayed. There had been too much of that over the years.

Kathleen would do whatever would make Tommy happy. He had to be happy at all costs. She couldn't bear it otherwise, couldn't bear it.

He hadn't been happy the night before, even though he'd had great plans for the next few days when he was going off to the races with his pals.

The main problem was that his evening had been disrupted – which meant hers had been too.

He'd said he was going to stay out and have a few pints in the pub with the lads from work.

'I'll eat when I'm out with the lads,' he'd announced that morning at breakfast as Kathleen served him the three rashers, two fried eggs and four sausages he had every day. The doctor had advised him against fried breakfasts, but doctors knew nothing, Tommy said. It was all a money-making scam to get people on to tablets for the rest of their lives.

'Cholesterol problem my backside,' he muttered grimly.

Tommy's going out meant that Kathleen would have a lovely free evening where she could watch what she wanted on the television and please herself.

She'd been sitting on the couch watching an old *Miss Marple* episode she'd recorded. She loved *Miss Marple*, loved the gentleness of it, despite the murder bit. People were polite to each other in Miss Marple's world.

And then, just at an exciting bit when a friend of Miss Marple was telling her a vital fact, Kathleen had heard Tommy's car pulling into the driveway. She'd felt instantly guilty: guilty for sitting down, guilty because any time her husband was near her, guilt automatically began coursing like poison through her veins. Whatever Kathleen was doing would turn out to be the wrong thing when Tommy saw it.

The wrong thing varied from day to day. Sometimes, he said watching the soaps was a sin.

Other times, he told her it was ridiculous to be knitting with the television off when she could be watching the news and informing herself. What did she want – to be stupid all her life?

Then, on those very rare occasions when he brought someone home from the garage where he worked, the only thing that would please him was to see her in the kitchen.

'She's a great cook, my wife,' he'd say, patting his own belly. It wouldn't occur to him that an outsider might think it strange that this great cook was so thin she'd obviously never eaten her own food, or if she did, never sat long enough to let it settle on her bones.

At the sound of Tommy's car, she switched off *Miss Marple* and ran to open the door. He stormed inside and Kathleen made herself small against the wall as if disappearing might help.

Then she followed him through to the kitchen and sat nervously on one of the chairs.

Tommy was ranting. He was the senior electrician in the

260

garage, he had years of experience, but nobody ever thought about him, did they? No, it was all about themselves. That's why he'd never prospered in work, never got any advancement. Everyone was out for what they could get themselves, weren't they?

Eventually he got to the point. That Richie at work had done it again, taken the overtime that was Tommy's due.

'The bastard,' Tommy hissed, 'the bastard.'

On her seat, Kathleen fingered the frayed edge of the cushion and tried to imagine herself somewhere else. There were cushions on sale in town for four euros, nice flowery ones. But she couldn't spend the money. Tommy might not like them. It was easier not to buy anything unless he was with her because if he didn't like something, he'd tell her so endlessly and all the good would be taken out of the purchase.

He was at the fridge now, wrenching open the door and looking in it as if a feast might appear miraculously instead of the few bits of sliced ham and the hard-boiled eggs Kathleen had prepared earlier.

'I didn't make you dinner because you said you were going for a couple of pints after work and you'd grab a bite in the pub,' she ventured.

She'd had a little salad herself without any of the ham and now she was glad, glad it was there so he could have it. His rage about the overtime might go into overdrive if there was no decent dinner.

'I'm not hungry for that stuff,' he said, slamming the fridge shut. 'Tea. Make me a pot of tea and I'll have some scones.'

Kathleen rose quickly, flicked on the oven with one hand and the kettle switch with the other. There were no scones but she could make them in an instant. Better if he didn't *know* she hadn't any, though. She'd meant to make some, but it had been busy at the tea shop today and she'd been too tired when she'd got home to think of baking.

'Why don't you sit in the living room and watch the news

to take your mind off work, Tom,' she soothed now, 'and I'll get you some nice tea and scones.'

She needed him out of the kitchen so she could bake the scones. Five minutes and she'd have them in the oven. He'd have his tea and scones in a quarter of an hour.

'No, I'll sit here,' he said, settling in the big carver chair and pulling a newspaper out of his pocket. 'I'll have that jam too, the one you got from work.'

'Right.' While he read the paper, Kathleen darted from cupboard to cupboard, taking out cups and the teapot, somehow managing to measure out flour, margarine and baking powder on the section of counter beyond her husband's field of vision. Years of practice meant it took hardly any time to get the mixture ready. The kettle gave one final hiss and went silent, but Kathleen was carefully adding a drop of milk and an egg to her big cream Delft bowl, then mixing it with a knife.

'The kettle's boiled,' said Tommy truculently. 'Are you deaf?'

'Just a moment, love,' trilled Kathleen, and rushed to the kettle at speed, throwing teabags into the pot and putting it on the stove to heat. Tommy liked his tea stewed, thank the Lord.

He'd only need a few scones, so she cut out six, and had them in the oven in a flash.

In order to delay things, she switched on the radio where the evening news programme was still on, and then made a great effort with laying a nice cloth on the bare kitchen table and setting out a plate, knife, mug, butter and the jar of blackberry jam somebody had given her in the café.

All the while, he sat there reading, not helping or saying a word, waiting like the lord and master for the feast to be put in front of him.

Just a few minutes more, she thought with relief, and the scones would be cooked. Piping hot, she'd say.

At that moment, he turned and caught her tidying up the flour and the bowl.

'You had to make scones?' he demanded.

'I thought hot ones would be nicer,' she whispered.

'Too lazy to bake when you got home from that daft job,' he said angrily. 'It's not as if you do anything but talk to your pals all day in that café.' He was always dismissive of the place where his wife worked eight-hour shifts, cleaning tables, mopping up spills, hauling great trays of dishes over to the dishwashing machines. 'The least you could do would be to bake a few buns. But no, that would be too much trouble.'

He got to his feet, folding up his paper.

'I'm going out to the pub. I don't want your bloody scones now. I don't like them hot, as well you know.'

He marched off and Kathleen heard the front door slamming, and his car heading off.

She was shaking, but then, she was always shaking. She jumped at loud noises at work. If anyone dropped a plate, Kathleen would get such a fright that she'd need to sit down for a moment. And if anyone shouted – she hated shouting – she'd flatten herself against the wall, as though trying to disappear.

Occasionally, she recognized that it wasn't right, the way he treated her. Peggy had said it for years, but then Peggy had never got on with her father, even though Kathleen had done her best to make it better between them. Tommy had lashed out with his tongue often enough at his daughter too, but Peggy had learned to cope with him and he didn't reduce her to a bag of quivering nerves.

Not everyone lives like this, Peggy used to say. *Leave him before he destroys you. He tells you it's all your fault, that you make him angry, that you cause all the problems. But you don't – he does. And he'll never see this.*

I love him, was all Kathleen could say in return. *Where would he go if I threw him out? Who'd look after him?*

She had married Tommy Barry and marriage was a sacred thing, not to be thrown away lightly. Her mother had stayed

263

with her father, and he'd been a devil, truth be told. All marriages had their problems and it wasn't as if Tommy hit her. He'd never so much as raised a hand to her, had he? That was something.

Outside Mullingar, Peggy decided to take a break to settle her nerves. There was a pub she knew and she parked and walked in. She'd done this in the past. It allowed her to catch her breath before she actually went home. She ordered tea and buttered toast, then went into the bathroom. In the mirror she looked the same. But inside she felt so very different. Precious. Feeling precious wasn't something Peggy was familiar with. Her mother was precious to her, but really, there'd never been anyone else who'd made Peggy feel an incredible warmth inside. Until David, she thought, then shoved that thought from her mind. And now the baby.

The pregnancy book she couldn't seem to put down in the evenings had said her baby was bigger than a kidney bean by this stage. Moving up to the size of an apricot. Little apricot, she muttered to herself as she locked the toilet door. My little apricot. There was always a moment of fear when she went to the toilet in case she found blood on the toilet tissue, but there was none. Little apricot was safe.

Peggy hadn't seen children in her destiny. She'd met lots of wonderful families, people like Fifi, Geraldine and Coco, who lived together in harmony. But Peggy had always felt that this particular path wasn't for her. You had to come from happiness to make it. It was that simple. Worse, people chose what they were used to, that was what it said in the self-help books. The same books tried to say that you could do it differently if you really worked at it, but Peggy knew they were wrong. What was in you was in you.

What was in her was what had been put there as a child and as a teenager, and there was no getting away from it. She wanted little apricot so badly and yet . . . a tiny, frightened

264

part of her wanted the choice to be taken away from her, for there to be blood in the toilet bowl. For little apricot to slip away so that Peggy wouldn't have to choose.

The 1970s bungalow on the other side of Mullingar had never felt as if it had been Peggy's home, any more than the many other houses she'd lived in over the years while her father dragged them all over the country in the endless search for a job in a garage where he'd be appreciated for his full worth. As she grew older, Peggy knew such a job did not exist, for in her father's warped mind, nobody ever appreciated him. And in reality, he was too volatile and too self-obsessed to ever achieve anything in any job. Tommy Barry was a tinderbox of rage and there was no telling when he'd ignite.

As she drove in the bungalow's gate past a vast hedge that had clearly never been cut in its life, she realized that she felt absolutely no sense of attachment to this house. The houses on each side of her parents' were beautifully maintained and she imagined how much they must hate this run-down premises between them. But there would be nothing they could do, any more than there was anything Peggy could have done. Her father had no interest in painting the outside of the house, clearing the garden and cutting the grass, trimming the hedge. Those were jobs for 'fools'.

Many people were fools in her father's eyes. If not fools they were people who had got ahead in life because they already had a chance. They were related to someone in power. They knew someone in the system. Or they'd been born with money. What could a poor man like him hope for, from a big family, denied his rightful inheritance? Nothing, that's what. He wouldn't play by their rules. No not he, not Tommy Barry. He'd do it his own way, thank you very much, and to hell with them all.

Peggy parked in front of the house and saw her mother's attempts at a little garden on the scrubby ground. There were

265

two little conifers in pots outside the front door and clearly her mother had taken great care of them, for their silvery-blue pine needles grew healthily. The lawn was full of weeds and overgrown. She could see the old push lawnmower leaning up against the side of the house, as though her father had had the mind to cut the grass one day and then suddenly changed his mind. She could imagine him speaking: 'What's the point?' And he'd be off. Off with his mates, off where he'd be appreciated.

His car wasn't there and Peggy felt a surge of pleasure that she was going to see her mother on her own. It happened so rarely. She took her overnight bag out of the boot, and the bag of gifts she'd brought for her mother, glad that with her father out she wouldn't have to sneak them in by the kitchen door later. She rang the doorbell and listened for her mother's quiet, tentative footsteps.

Opening the door, Kathleen's heart almost stopped for joy. There on the doorstep, as welcome as a warm sunny morning after rain, was Peggy. Even though Peggy had never missed her birthday, there was always the fear that this year she might not bother. And now, because Tommy had decided to go away overnight to the races, for a glorious twenty-four hours she would have her daughter all to herself.

'My sweet child,' she said, reaching forward bony hands through which blue veins were visible. She drew Peggy into her embrace and held her as tightly as she possibly could. Kathleen would have cried if she knew how, but she no longer did.

Instead she leaned against the strength of her daughter, the way she had for many years. 'I knew you'd come for my birthday,' she said. 'I knew you'd come.'

'I always come, you know that,' Peggy said.

'But with the shop and everything I thought you'd have moved on and wouldn't want to come back here,' Kathleen

266

said, and Peggy wanted to kill her father for making her mother feel so worthless that she'd think her daughter would miss her birthday.

'Where's the man of the house?' said Peggy, unable to disguise the scorn in her voice.

'Away at the racing overnight,' said Kathleen in delight. 'I have you all to myself.'

Peggy picked up the two bags she'd brought from the car and carried them inside. Her mother tried to take her overnight bag, but Peggy wouldn't let her. Kathleen was so thin, so frighteningly thin. Peggy tried to remember if she'd ever looked like this before. All the bones on her face seemed too close to the surface, the pale skin stretched too tightly.

'Look at you!' said Kathleen delightedly, when they were in the kitchen with the kettle on. Peggy sat down on the old fireside chair and memories came flooding back.

The chair's cover was now threadbare in places, but the odd hint of velvet gleamed on it still. It was heaped with worn cushions and once upon a time, in a previous house, Peggy's dog, Clover, used to curl up on it, her tiny little whippet-cum-sheepdog body quivering with delight.

Of course, she never was allowed to sit there for very long. Tommy would give a fierce yell that would frighten anyone.

'Is that dog on the seat again?' Tommy would roar. 'Off! Off with you!' And if Clover couldn't move fast enough, she'd get a kick.

Eventually, Clover became too afraid to curl up on the soft velvet any more. Now Peggy could never sit there without thinking about Clover and how much she'd cried when the little dog had run away for good. Peggy had been eleven at the time and she'd wished she could run away too.

'You really do look lovely, Peggy,' Kathleen said, as the kettle boiled and she got down the nice biscuits for her visitor. 'Looks as though you're eating properly at last,' she went on, not noticing the irony of a woman as thin as she was remonstrating with her daughter for slenderness.

Now was her moment, Peggy thought. Her father being away meant it was the perfect time to break the news to Kathleen. It wasn't as if her mother would come to Redstone to stay with her, to talk to her, to tell her all the things a mother told her only child when that child was expecting her first baby.

'I have put on some weight,' Peggy admitted.

Almost unconsciously her hands slid down to caress the faintest hint of curve in her abdomen. It was tiny, so tiny nobody else could possibly notice it except Peggy, who looked at herself sideways in the mirror every chance she got, feeling the strange fullness of her breasts, breasts that had always been rather nonexistent. She got up to help Kathleen make the tea.

'No, don't move, Peggy, I'm doing it all. You're so busy with that shop of yours.'

So Peggy sat and watched her mother race around, opening cupboards, looking for plates and cups. Everything in the cupboards was lined up as perfectly as if a ruler had been used. Every cup handle was at exactly the same angle. Every tin faced exactly the same way. Because that was the way Tommy Barry liked it.

He'd never picked up a sock or put a wash on in all the years she'd known him – his wife did everything.

It was still an ugly kitchen, Peggy thought. Bright yellow cupboards, an ugly black-and-white chequered linoleum floor and the cheapest wallpaper going: off-white wallpaper with bits of wood stuck into it, giving it its name, woodchip. The idea was that you painted over the wallpaper to give it some identity. Naturally, it was the same off-white as when the Barrys had moved in. Paint was a waste of money, according to her father, and her mother didn't dare argue.

Peggy thought of how much she'd loved painting the shop. The joy she'd felt opening those wonderful tins of lavender emulsion. Watching it go up with slow steady strokes, thinking of the future it meant, the pleasure it gave her to recreate the room exactly to her liking. Her mother had never known that pleasure. Instead her mother lived in a house that hadn't changed one iota in the eleven years since she'd moved in.

It was a warm sunny day and Peggy would have loved for them to eat lunch outside, but there was nowhere suitable. The patio was a wreck, with broken paving slabs and no seating. Unless they hauled the kitchen table and chairs outside, they'd have to sit on the grass.

'Let's get a blanket, Mam,' she suggested, 'and have our lunch out here, near the roses.'

After they'd put the blanket down, she asked her mother to show her the roses. There was only one tiny rose bed, but Kathleen had planted several varieties and even attached a trellis to the wall so they could scramble up it. It was obvious to Peggy that the trellis was her mother's handiwork because of the inexpert way nails had been bent into the painted brickwork. Her father couldn't even be bothered to do that for her.

'I got these from a catalogue,' her mother said enthusiastically, pointing at a couple of very young roses in front. 'The David Austin catalogue – oh, Peggy, I must show it to you.'

Peggy heard the joy in her mother's voice and felt the sadness again. Her mother needed so little to keep her happy but even that had to be in stolen time.

'And this one I think of as yours,' Kathleen went on, pointing out a bush with slender stems waving gently in the breeze, topped with tiny mother-of-pearl white rosebuds. 'Isn't it beautiful? I got that last year with some of the money you gave me for my birthday. I call it Peggy's Rose.'

'Oh, Mam,' said Peggy, putting her arm around her mother's waist. 'I wish you had the sort of garden you deserve. I wish – I wish so many things.'

She stopped because there was no point trying: she'd said everything over the years and still her mother refused to listen. It appeared to hurt Kathleen so much when Peggy said anything about leaving her father that Peggy had vowed on her last visit not to do it any more. Kathleen was like a person kidnapped who'd convinced themselves that the kidnappers, despite their bad treatment, were really looking after her. Stockholm Syndrome, they called it in kidnappings. Peggy wondered what it was called in emotionally abusive marriages.

They ate ham sandwiches and drank cool water as they sat beside Kathleen's beloved roses and Peggy filled her in on all the details of her life. She rarely wrote letters because her father would intercept them and read them first. Phoning home was a hazard as her father might answer, and Kathleen didn't own a mobile and was nervous of using the café's phone at work.

'And is there – is there a man on the horizon?' Kathleen said wistfully.

'That's complicated,' said Peggy slowly. 'Very complicated, in fact. I've news, Mam,' she said. 'I'm pregnant.'

Her mother was the first person she'd actually told. Saying the words made it all seem so much more real. Suddenly, little apricot inside her wasn't just a little apricot.

'Oh, darling!' said Kathleen breathlessly, and she reached over the remains of the sandwiches to hug her daughter. Peggy could feel the thin ribs like xylophone keys.

'And what about the father?' said Kathleen excitedly.

Peggy knew she had to proceed delicately. She didn't want to hurt her mother, but there was no kind way of saying that her childhood had put her right off having the father around. 'It didn't work out,' she lied.

'Peggy! I'm so sorry,' her mother said, distraught. 'But you can come and live here, with us, we'll take care of you . . .'

'No,' Peggy interrupted fiercely. 'No,' she said again, in more gentle tones. 'I've got it all figured out, Mam. I can

270

manage now that I have the shop and Fifi, my sales assistant. Things are going so well. But . . .'

She thought about what she'd wanted to ask her mother. This visit was about more than bringing her mother a birthday present. 'I wonder if you'd come and live with me and help me with the baby?' she asked quietly. She knew it was so unlikely the answer would be yes, but she had to ask.

The blood rushed to Kathleen's pale cheeks. Anxiety flared in her eyes. 'No, Peggy, no,' she said. 'I couldn't leave your father. You know that. He needs me. I'm sorry, I—'

'It's fine,' said Peggy, as if it really was. 'Fine, honestly. I'll manage.'

She got up off the blanket and went back into the house, calling over her shoulder: 'I've got something for you, Mam.' She returned with a small cake with *Happy Birthday to the best mother in the world* written in delicate icing. Sue from the shop across the road had spent ages working on it.

In the other bag was a bottle of perfume, scented with grapefruit and lime blossom. Something so beautiful and expensive that her mother would never own such a thing unless Peggy had given it to her.

'We have to celebrate with cake and then you have to cover yourself in perfume,' said Peggy, determined to make this a happy event. She wouldn't let the shadow of her father ruin it, no way.

They talked all day, with Peggy carefully staying away from the vast range of subjects that might upset her mother, and when they went to bed that night, Peggy wanted to cry at how worried she felt. It was worse than ever now: her mother was like a prisoner, in thrall to the rage and temper of her father, always trying to convince herself and Peggy that things were fine, really.

Peggy thought about the baby growing inside her, and how that baby had a father too. A father who had no idea of her

271

existence. Over the last couple of weeks Peggy had begun to feel that this wasn't right. A couple of times she had gone so far as to drive past the townhouse where David lived, but she had fought off the crazy desire to go in and tell him. She knew it was crazy. What was the point?

Peggy had been so sure she knew what was right that it had come as quite a shock to find something inside her asserting that her actions were all wrong. She didn't like it. It skewed everything. Despite all her carefully laid plans to run her life precisely the opposite way her mother had run hers, everything was coming unravelled.

The next morning, Peggy had planned to leave by noon, so she'd have some time with her mother and then be on the road before there was even a hope of her father returning.

But fate wasn't on her side. At eleven, she and Kathleen were in the front room looking through the hand-knitted baby clothes Peggy had worn as a baby, when they heard the front door slam.

'Hide it all, quick,' hissed Kathleen, but they weren't quick enough.

Tommy Barry burst into the room, the smell of smoke and cheap beer all around him.

He'd aged in the year since Peggy had seen him. He looked angrier and more bitter than ever now, his mouth a permanent sneer.

'So you're back,' he said. 'After something, are you?'

Then he looked down on the bed where all the baby garments were laid out. His eyes swept over his daughter's figure and the sneer turned into a snarl.

'Got yourself pregnant, did you?' he said. 'That turned out well for you, didn't it, Miss Peggy, with all your fine notions of what you'd do and what you wouldn't do. Carrying some-one's bastard, I suppose. No sign of a ring on that finger, is there?'

'Stop it!' hissed Peggy, her fury startling even herself. 'Don't you dare talk to me that way. You're the bastard, and don't you forget it.'

He took an angry step towards her, but she raised her mobile phone in his face. 'If you lay a hand on me or my mother, I'll phone the police in an instant and I swear I'll have you locked up for so long that you'll rot in jail, do you understand? Now get out of this room and leave us in peace.'

She'd never spoken to him like that before. But then, she'd never had a precious life inside her before either. Her baby made her strong. No way was she going to allow her child to witness her mother being treated the way she'd seen Kathleen treated.

She turned to see her mother sitting on the couch, almost catatonic, tears on her face but no expression there.

Peggy knelt beside her. 'Mum, you've got to leave. Please! Please come with me. He's destroying you. He might not use his fists, but he's battering you into the ground just the same.'

'No,' her mother said, rocking to and fro now. 'I can't, we're married.'

'Screw marriage!' yelled Peggy. 'He's a bastard and he's ruined both of us. Please get out. You could live with me in Cork, mind the baby, do whatever you want to, just leave.'

'You don't understand,' Kathleen said. 'I'm all he has. Without me, he'd kill himself. I understand him, you see.'

Peggy leaned her head down on the couch and rested. She didn't have the heart for such fights or such fierce loathing any more. She had done everything in her power over the years to get her mother to leave him. And there was nothing more she could do.

'I'm going now,' she said. 'But I'm sending you a mobile phone. I'll send it to Carola in the craft shop. You can pick it up off her and I'll program in my number. Please, please phone me if you need me. I'll call you when the baby's due.'

'Not Carola!' begged Kathleen. 'I told her he's been getting better—'

Peggy looked with pity at her mother. 'Men like my father never get better, Mam. Carola knows that damn well. Talk to her. You need someone on your side, because I'm too far away in an emergency and he's getting worse. He'll never change and he'll destroy you. Promise me that you'll talk to Carola. Promise me?'

Her mother nodded mutely.

They hugged silently, clinging tightly to each other. Then Peggy gathered up the precious baby things and took them out of the room. Her last sight of her mother was of Kathleen rocking back and forth on the couch.

Chapter Sixteen

The exhaustion was killing Frankie. It had come out of nowhere, like a hurricane, and now she woke up exhausted, spent parts of every day exhausted, and fell into bed at night after struggling to stay awake through dinner. Most evenings she barely felt able to join in the dinner-table conversation. Seth didn't appear to notice, so delighted was he to chat endlessly with his sister about the work they were doing on the garden. Positive proof that couples married forever had nothing to say to each other, Frankie thought with unaccustomed sourness.

Frankie suspected that Lillie had noticed. In fact, over the past month, Frankie had come to the conclusion that there wasn't much Lillie *didn't* notice.

Her new-found sister-in-law was a very clever woman, but her predominant characteristic was kindness. And it was a kindness that extended to everyone she met. In the time she'd been staying with them, she appeared to have made friends with the whole of Redstone, from the people running the bakery to the young woman who'd set up the new wool shop, and she'd apparently struck up firm friendships with both Bobbi the beautician and Freya, a strangely adult fifteen-year-old who lived with her aunt and uncle in the row of houses that ran directly behind Maple Avenue.

'Freya's a marvellous girl,' she told Seth and Frankie. 'She's very grown up, an old soul.'

Lillie had begun dropping in daily on an old lady she'd met one day, wheezing for breath as she tried to carry a bag of groceries home from the shops. Now, Lillie was doing the old lady's shopping and tending her window-boxes.

'I thought it was us Irish who were supposed to befriend every Tom, Dick and Harry,' said Frankie one Friday evening, when she was leaning back against the window seat in the basement kitchen with a glass of wine, savouring the aromas of Lillie and Seth's cooking.

'My husband used to say that,' said Lillie cheerfully, putting a dish of honey-roasted parsnips and carrots on the table. 'His mother said he had the Irish charm.'

She looked sad suddenly, and Frankie felt like an absolute cow. There she'd been, feeling sorry for herself because Lillie had gotten to know all the locals while she never had the time to chat to anyone, forgetting that the poor woman had lost her husband only a few months ago. Frankie, who normally was very empathetic, had found herself so locked up in her own miseries that she hadn't taken the trouble to ask about Sam.

'Tell me about Sam,' Frankie said now.

Lillie bowed her head.

'I'm sorry,' Frankie said quickly. 'I didn't mean to upset you.'

'No, you haven't, not at all.' Lillie poked the parsnips with a serving spoon. 'Freya gave me these from her uncle's allotment,' she said absently, 'and the honey's from the delicatessen. It's local. They say honey's very good if you suffer from hay fever. When you get the hives, Seth, you'll see what I mean. Now that we've cleared away everything from the walled garden, we've got the perfect spot for them.'

'Here, I'll do that, Lillie,' said Seth, gently taking the spoon from his sister.

She seemed unaware that tears had begun streaming down her face.

Frankie jumped up from her seat and went to her sister-in-law. 'I am so sorry,' she began.

'No, I was the one brought up the subject,' said Lillie. 'Sometimes I can talk about him. Only today, I told Sue in the bakery that Sam could never resist fresh bread, and we laughed, because she says Zeke eats almost more bread than he cooks, and he's so skinny!' Lillie's face fell. 'But other times, it hurts so much thinking that Sam's gone and I'll never see him again. Never.'

She turned anguished eyes to Frankie and Seth. 'I've loved being here, loved it, and I feel happy and needed, but today it's hit me again that he's gone. That I'm trying to find things to do to occupy myself so I don't think too much about him.'

The way Lillie spoke made Frankie want to burst into tears.

'But there are times when I get so wrapped up in here, in Redstone, that I can't feel him. It's as if he's moving further and further away from me.'

Nobody spoke. There was nothing to say.

In bed later, Seth and Frankie instinctively moved together and settled into a comfortable hugging position, the way they used to every night, once upon a time.

'Poor Lillie,' said Seth, arms around his wife. 'I can't imagine what I'd do without you.'

Frankie lay there in silence, enjoying the unaccustomed feeling of her husband holding her.

Lillie's anguish had upset her so much and yet even now she couldn't sweep aside the anger she harboured towards Seth. It might have been irrational, but it was still there.

'Love you,' she muttered finally. Then, with a swift kiss on his cheek, she rolled over and turned off her bedside light.

It was a long time before she could sleep and she lay there, trying to be still, sensing her husband lying awake beside her.

Lillie would give her right arm to be this close to her husband, Frankie thought wearily, and all she could do was lie there letting the resentment flood through her. Seth hadn't wanted her at all recently – she didn't want to be rejected again. Far better to turn away before he got the chance to do it first.

She felt sure of only one thing: her marriage was falling apart.

Frankie had never doubted Seth's love. From the very first time they'd met all those years ago in college they knew they'd been made for each other. They laughed at the same jokes. Read the same books. And Frankie could look at him across a crowded room and see that Seth was thinking exactly the same thing as she was just by the flicker of his eyes in her direction.

And now . . . now it was all different. Seth was different. It wasn't that he was no longer the man she'd married; people changed, she knew that. Neither of them were the people they'd been all those years ago. But something fundamental in Seth had shifted since the loss of his job. Was it the lack of status? she wondered. Working in HR she knew that men and women approached work very differently. For a lot of women, work was a means to earn money and take care of their children. They were ambitious, yes, but the ambition ran side by side with the practical. For men the ambition was more important. She'd have thought that Seth was never the type of man whose job defined him; family had always come before career with him. He could have risen much higher, gone much further, if he hadn't put Frankie and the children first. Yet somehow, when his job was taken away from him, it was as if his identity had been removed. And for all her theoretical and professional understanding of the effects of redundancy, Frankie hadn't been able to help.

The renewed spring in Seth's step was entirely thanks to Lillie. Together with Dessie, they'd transformed the bramble-filled wilderness into a soft landscaped haven, planted with cuttings supplied by Lillie's new friends. *That* hurt like hell – Seth's recovery had nothing to do with her. She knew Lillie was trying to help but Seth and Frankie had been so distant before Lillie arrived that perhaps her work now was just pushing them further and further apart.

Once upon a time, Frankie reflected, she and the children were the answer to every one of Seth's problems, but now the children were gone and she was the answer to nothing. Sometimes she felt incredibly angry about it, all this rubbish about forty being the new twenty-five – it was complete cobblers. With a few dermatological tweaks and a bit of Botox here and there, forty might *look* like twenty-five. But these were just cosmetic things. The inner changes, the realization that life was not infinite, that you were no longer everything to the man you loved: *those* were the effects of ageing that mattered.

Frankie wondered if she should consult Dr Felix about Seth. Maybe say: 'Seth is down and I can't deal with that. What's your advice? I need help because I'm struggling enough with my own things.'

She was now on hormone replacement pills, but none of it seemed to be making her feel any better. She was still as tearful and grumpy as ever. And sad, so very sad.

Frankie Green wasn't ready to turn into an old lady just yet, but where did she fit in the world? Where did she fit in Seth's world? For years she'd watched friends getting separated and divorced and thought how crazy it was, how perhaps they just hadn't tried. And then Seth had retreated into his own world and left her behind. He'd practically slammed the door in her face and pinned a notice on it saying *Don't enter, don't come after me. I don't need you. I don't want you.* How could she explain all that to Felix? She couldn't, because she didn't understand it herself. All she knew was that it hurt.

* * *

Rather than consult Felix, she rang her sister.

'I need to say something to him, Gaby, but what?'

Gabrielle had more than a hint of their mother in her.

'Tell him he's going round like a wet rag unless he's talking about that bloody garden and you'll have no marriage left if you don't both make an effort soon.'

'Thank you, Dr Phil,' said Frankie wryly. 'I'll say it tonight, then. Just the facts – stop being a rag or pack your bags.'

'Oh, I didn't mean you should say it *that* baldly,' Gaby protested. 'But this is Seth you're talking about. You can talk to Seth about anything. Just explain that things have gone wrong and you want to fix them. Is that so hard?'

Yes, it is, Frankie thought sadly.

As if in some telepathic act of helpfulness, Lillie said she was tired that evening and wanted to go to bed early, leaving Seth and Frankie alone in the kitchen with football on the TV.

Now is the perfect time to say something, Frankie told herself. But for once, she was at a loss for words. Normally she could find the words for anything: going-away speeches, mediating disputes, counselling someone who'd been sexually harassed . . . Telling the children when they were small that they were wonderful and they were capable of everything and really it didn't matter if they didn't win a medal on sports day. She'd had all those words, but now her supply of words had dried up.

Seth sat at the kitchen table, a glass of wine to one side, the newspaper crossword in front of him, vaguely watching the football. The sports channel always seemed to be on in the background these days. Did Seth like having the television on because it meant there could be no talking? Did he think that if they actually *talked*, everything would fall apart?

Frankie toyed with the idea of turning the television off, then thought: At least it's noise. What if I tell him what's in

280

my heart and he doesn't answer me? What if he says, 'It's over, I don't want to be with you any more.' What then?

There was something else. Frankie was worried that Lillie had become the glue holding their marriage together. When Lillie went home, maybe that glue would shatter and they'd be left with nothing.

'Seth, I love you,' she blurted out. 'I love you so much and . . .'

Oh, what could she say? He was peering at her in puzzlement over his bifocals. He, too, was looking old, she realized with a shock.

Why did nobody tell you about this stage in a marriage? Why did no one ever speak about *this*?

'I just feel we've drifted so far apart and I don't know what to do, it frightens me,' she said, astonished to find that her voice was tremulous.

'Do we have to talk about this now?' he said. He looked weary, as if he'd just come back from a marathon and simply needed to lie down and not utter a single word.

'No, no,' Frankie said, suddenly taking the easy way out. She didn't want to hear what he had to say. Maybe it *was* over. She couldn't cope with that knowledge right now.

'I'm tired,' she said quickly. 'I'll go to bed.'

'I might stay up to see the end of the match,' said Seth.

'Fine.'

Frankie climbed the stairs wearily to bed, feeling she might cry her heart out. But she wasn't going to let herself start. Not now.

Chapter Seventeen

The night before the wedding, Opal considered all the wonderful people and things in her life and thought how blessed she was.

There was Ned, and she loved him as much as she had on their wedding day, even though his mother would have liked him to marry Concepta, who had a farm to inherit from her uncle when she was older. Land meant money and some security in those days.

'What's your philosophy, Opal?' Freya asked dreamily, sitting at the table, stirring her hot chocolate. Freya hadn't a yen for sweets but when it came to hot chocolate, she was addicted.

'Philosophy?' said Opal, startled.

Freya was a great one for questions out of the blue, questions you had to think about. The lads hadn't been like that and although Opal suspected Meredith was, she'd never *asked* the questions but kept them inside her head. Opal had tried to gently lever them out, like she'd once seen someone open an oyster shell on a television cooking show, but Meredith hadn't been that type of kid. She kept her feelings locked in her heart and Opal had never been allowed close, a thought that still made her sad. But Freya – now there was a girl who could release her thoughts into the air like butterflies . . .

'Bobbi's philosophy is to be a warrior woman on the outside – but she's melted caramel on the inside. Like when there's a dark chocolate coating that's a bit bitter and then you bite into it, and it's all melting and soft. Don't you agree?'

Freya stared up at her aunt with those big Bambi eyes.

'And David's like an oak or something, a tree that looks strong but can be hurt too. I wish I knew what was eating away at him, but he won't talk. Now, you, Opal, I think your philosophy is to shine golden light on us all and make us better people. Lillie's the same.'

'Lillie?'

'The Australian woman I meet in Redstone sometimes. She talks to Seanie and Ronnie at the bus stop too. Most people don't,' Freya said. 'Which is mad, because they're very wise.'

Opal stared back, thinking. 'You're right,' she agreed. 'They are wise. And you're right about Bobbi, she is soft despite everything that louser of a husband put her through. And David . . . I wish I knew who'd hurt him. How could anyone hurt him?' She sighed sadly. 'Having children is heartbreaking, love, that's all I'll say. You never stop worrying about them.'

She paused and looked at Freya. 'Did you do this kind of thing with your mother?' she asked curiously.

Gemma was a mystery to Opal. For a mother to be so unmotherly was almost unnatural in Opal's eyes. And yet everyone's path was different and poor Gemma had her own pain. It wasn't for Opal to criticize her. And Gemma not being able to care for her daughter had meant that Freya had come like a blessing to live in their home.

'Mum doesn't care for this game,' Freya said simply.

There was no recrimination in her voice: plain fact instead.

'She begins to fret about what people think about her and then she gets upset . . . Dad and I were forever trying to make her see that it didn't matter what other people thought. What she thought mattered. But she's fragile; she can't take pain, even imagined pain from someone else looking at her in the street. What other people think are their ideas floating around in their head. It's bad to colour them with what's in your head.'

Opal stared at her niece, a fifteen-year-old girl on the outside and the Dalai Lama on the inside.

'Freya, has anyone ever told you that you're very deep and wise?' she said proudly, reaching over to stroke Freya's face.

Freya grinned and the dimple on her left cheek sprang into action. 'Only you, Opal. Only you.'

Meredith woke early on her brother's wedding day. Early enough to register the presence of the sun sneaking in through a slit in her bedroom curtains. Briefly, she wondered where she was. This still happened, even though she'd been living with her parents for almost a month now. St Brigid's Terrace was home and yet it wasn't home. Despite everything, the apartment in Elysium Gardens had felt like home to her for five years and she missed the airy spaciousness of it, her aloneness. Back here in the bedroom where she'd grown up, she felt again like a confused teenager, trying to find her way out into the world.

Meredith shoved back the duvet quickly. She was fed up thinking about her teenage self. Teenage stupidity had been responsible for so much. It had made her search for a far-flung dream she'd had no hope of ever achieving – or perhaps she *had* had a hope of achieving it, except she'd believed in the wrong people. Sally-Anne and Keith were definitely the wrong people and she'd been too blind to see it. She'd been taken in by money, glamour, the fact that they knew the *right* people. But the right people had turned out to be the wrong people.

It was still only half past seven and Brian was getting married at one o'clock. It was the Saturday before Easter, and Meredith thought it was a ludicrous time for a wedding. But Brian had explained that he and Liz were taking advantage of the school holiday to fly off for a week's honeymoon in Ibiza. Lucky them, Meredith thought. She wished she could escape to Ibiza.

Before a wedding where she'd take a day off in her old life, Meredith would just be waking up, stretching luxuriously in her king-size bed with the Frette sheets. Not that the king-size bed with the Frette sheets had done her much good. She'd been too uptight to have anyone else in them. And now the thought of paying thousands of euros for bedclothes struck her as ludicrous. Her mother would be horrified at the thought of such waste. Meredith could imagine her voice in her head.

'Thousands of euros for sheets?' Her mother would stare at her uncomprehendingly.

In Mum's world, sheets were things you prized more when they were so worn they became soft to the touch. Her mother's mother, Granny Cordy, had come up from the country to live in inner-city Cork and she was forever telling her children that when she was a girl they'd lain on sheets made out of flour bags, three to a bed. 'Well, Granny Cordelia,' Meredith whispered. 'If you're looking down now, you're probably shocked – and you'd be right to be shocked. I spent more on my sheets than you spent on a year of groceries. More fool me, as you'd have said yourself. But I've learned my lesson, Granny Cordelia. I've learned my lesson.'

Still in the camisole top and shorts she'd worn to bed, Meredith went down to the kitchen to get herself some coffee. It was already abuzz. Despite the fact that he should, theoretically, have been lying in bed with the hangover from hell after his stag night, Brian was sitting at the kitchen table with his phone pressed to one ear and a set of table plans in front of him.

'Oh God, Liz,' he groaned. 'I can't work this out. There is no answer to this problem. Your aunt Phil will just have to sit at table thirteen and like it. There's nowhere else to put her.'

Meredith tuned out. She felt spectacularly uninvolved in the wedding but also guilty for feeling that way. Brian was the first of the family to get married, but that sort of irked her too. She was the oldest. She was the only girl and by rights she should have legions of boyfriends running after her now. These days the only legions running after her were tabloid journalists wanting the latest on the Sally-Anne and Keith Alexander story.

Where have they gone with the money? How can you claim you knew absolutely nothing? How much money did you lose? Is it true that you smuggled a valuable picture out of the country on the day the gallery's assets were frozen? Meredith shuddered. Things had died down a little in the past week. Some new scandal had hit the papers and interest in the glamorous Alexanders and their wealthy investors had waned. Meredith felt she was able to turn her mobile phone on again. The blissful relief of no longer being the one pursued was like the relief of having a tooth filled at the dentist after a week of nerve pain.

The back door was open and she looked outside. Her mother and Freya were sitting on the kitchen step into the garden, sunning themselves in the early morning sun and drinking tea out of big mugs.

'Meredith, love,' said her mother warmly. 'Come and join us. Freya and I are taking a bit of a rest before the madness begins.'

'There's tea in the pot,' said Freya kindly.

Meredith instantly felt her hackles rise. She didn't know why, but her cousin annoyed her. There was Freya, sitting companionably with her mother as if *she* were Opal's daughter. It didn't matter to Meredith that she hadn't been about for years, that Freya was the one who'd helped Opal get her hair highlighted and had gone with her to the doctor when her knees were bad. No, Meredith felt the full wave of resentment

286

wash over her as she looked down at the pair sitting cosily together. She wanted to burst into tears like a child.

'I think I'll have coffee, actually,' she snapped before turning and going back inside.

Freya and Opal looked at each other and Freya could see the glitter of tears in her aunt's eyes. She put her arm around Opal's shoulders.

'There now, Opal,' she murmured kindly. Rather than say what she really thought and risk hurting her aunt, she had to improvise. 'I expect it's hard for Meredith on her brother's wedding day. You know how it is with us girls, we love to think of getting married and it's a bit tough when it's not your own wedding. And after all Meredith's been through too. When things are bad and there's no sign of a romance for you on the horizon, it can be terribly upsetting. It's obviously getting poor Meredith down.'

'Do you think so?' Opal gazed at Freya hopefully. 'I could understand if she felt that way, Freya. I was just afraid,' she added with great effort, 'that she was jealous of you and me.' She hated saying it, but she'd begun to wonder. After all, Freya fitted into the household so much better than poor Meredith ever had. Oh, that was an awful thing to think.

Freya watched Opal shrewdly, with a pretty good sense of what was going on in her mind. There were times when she could cheerfully kill Meredith. If she ruined this day for Opal, Freya would not be responsible for her actions.

'Gosh no, Opal,' Freya said gently. 'I'm sure it's just single-person-at-the-wedding misery. Today's going to be hard for her. And Brian is her baby brother. It's difficult seeing him go off to Liz.'

'Yes, of course,' agreed Opal, delighted to be given this new explanation to cling to. She really was a terrible woman for imagining things. Of course Freya was right: Meredith must be upset about her little brother getting married because he was the first of them to really go. And even though Meredith had gone for a while, she'd come back, hadn't she?

Lillie popped into Bobbi's on Saturday morning with some roses for the reception counter. Even at ten past nine, the salon was buzzing, with every seat full, and two women waiting patiently on the chocolate-brown sofas, flicking through glossy magazines.

'Mrs O'Brien is so thrilled with her new "do" that she begged me to bring you these,' said Lillie. 'They're from her garden.'

Bobbi took the tinfoil-wrapped lemon-yellow narcissi and breathed in their heady scent.

'Isn't she an absolute pet?' Bobbi said to Lillie, as pleased as if she'd been given a huge, shop-bought bouquet. 'And so are you, for dropping in on her all the time.'

'She's lonely,' said Lillie, 'and she's great fun to talk to. I enjoy visiting her and she has nobody else. Let's hope someone does it for us when we're ninety.'

Bobbi grinned. 'I'll probably be in one of those maximum-security nursing homes where strapping twenty-year-old nurses who think they'll never be old talk to me in baby talk and assume I'm delusional when I tell them that I was once their age with a string of admirers.'

Lillie shuddered. 'Sounds dreadful.'

'I look at the young girls working here and I know they think I'm past it,' Bobbi pointed out. 'They can't imagine you and I romping with a man, and we're hardly ninety yet.'

Lillie roared with laughter. 'I'm not in the market for romps, right now. I'd prefer a night in with a fire in the grate and something good on the telly.'

'You can't still be feeling the cold after Australia?'

'It's the house,' Lillie revealed, shivering from memory. 'It might be called Sorrento Villa, but that's wishful thinking. Siberian Villa might be more apt. The basement is cold, no

288

doubt about it. The upstairs rooms aren't so bad, but downstairs needs some extra insulation or a damp course or something done, anyway.'

'How's Seth getting on with it all?'

'Oh, we've made a start on the garden. I think he's quite enjoying it.'

Bobbi had met Seth a few times with Lillie on their morning trips out for coffee and had quickly sized him up: a sweet, gentle man, and clever with it. He was also handsome too, she thought, not without a hint of envy for the unknown Frankie. Bobbi hadn't been able to get much information from the ever-loyal Lillie about what had got Seth looking like a puppy who'd been thrown out of the house, but reading between the lines, Bobbi had worked it out.

One income, a new house that needed pots of money piled into it and a man who couldn't work a screwdriver would drive a saner woman than she into a fit of rage.

She really had to get a look at this Frankie to continue the analysis. Bobbi loved watching other people and finding out what made them tick. A hair and beauty salon was the perfect calling for her in that so many people treated their hairdresser as a mother confessor once they were in the chair.

'It's like the mirror frees them to talk to you,' she'd explained to Opal years ago. 'They're not looking you in the eye. Plus, you're gently touching their head, and that makes the quietest of people blab. That's why women love beauty and hair salons. They might have to pay for it, but for a couple of hours, they have someone being kind to them, making coffee, giving them magazines and generally treating them as if they mattered.'

'You make them look good too,' pointed out Opal.

'That's almost a by-product,' said Bobbi. 'The transformations we do on the inside are just as important as the outside ones.'

Lillie and Bobbi looked up as the door swung open and in came Opal (tremulous smile), followed by Freya (determined smile) and Meredith (no smile at all).

'My most important bridal party have arrived!' Bobbi announced.

Meredith was going to be trouble, by the looks of things. She'd bet the day's takings that there had been a row chez Byrne that morning. Well, what sort of wedding would it be without a few rows?

'Freya, hello,' said Lillie delightedly.

'Hiya, Lillie,' said Freya, giving her a hug.

Bobbi laughed. 'I should have known that you pair would know each other. I've never seen two people who know more about what's going on around here.' Seeing that introductions were in order for the other members of the party, she went on: 'Lillie, this is Opal Byrne, Freya's aunt. The pair of you live back to back, as it were – Lillie's staying with her brother and his wife in the big house on the corner of Maple Avenue.'

The two women shook hands with a hint of recognition.

'This is Meredith, Opal's daughter,' Bobbi added, giving Meredith a prod to make her smile. 'Of course, you know Freya.'

'Freya's mentioned you,' said Opal.

'I told her how you like to have a chat with Ronnie and Seanie the same way I do,' Freya explained.

'I was planning on passing by the bus stop on my way home,' said Lillie. 'It always cheers me up to see them sitting there.'

'Me too,' agreed Freya. 'If they ever got on a bus and went somewhere that would ruin it all entirely.'

'What's the point of sitting at a bus stop if you don't get on the damn bus?' snapped Meredith, bored with this conversation.

The look Freya shot her cousin reminded Bobbi of the intensity of the pulsed light machine she was thinking of getting to remove bikini-line hair permanently. Laser-like and painful.

Seeing Opal's face begin to fall, Bobbi sprang into action.

Grabbing Lillie and Opal, she sat them on the vacant couch, handed them a pile of magazines and ordered one of the juniors to bring them coffee.

'I'm not staying,' Lillie protested, trying to get up.

'You are now,' muttered Bobbi fiercely into the ear furthest away from Opal. 'There's trouble brewing and I need you to take poor Opal's mind off it. Her son is getting married today and she's got enough ahead of her without a row this early in the proceedings. The bride's mother is a prize bitch whose main aim in life is to make other people upset. She behaves as if she's the Queen's second cousin and she's going to have a lovely day making poor Opal feel like an illiterate, dragged-up eejit from the former council houses in Redstone.'

Lillie nodded. 'Enough said,' she murmured. 'What's up with the daughter?'

'The blonde with a face like a bulldog chewing a wasp?' said Bobbi. 'It'd take too long to tell you. I'll soon sort her out. You take Opal and make her see what a lovely day she's going to have and that all weddings involve some difficult people, though.'

As she stalked off to deal with Meredith, Bobbi called over her shoulder: 'Freya, grab a seat at the basins.'

'I just need to talk to Meredith outside,' cooed Freya, who wasn't sure if she could still remember any of the karate she'd done when she was twelve, but felt that she'd manage an old-fashioned punch in the nose to make Meredith have to stay the day in bed.

'Freya,' said Bobbi in the voice that made grown men quail. 'You go to the basins. I need to talk to your cousin.'

Meredith, who'd already been taken aside for a word once this morning by that little bitch Freya – 'I don't know what your problem is, Meredith, but don't take it out on your mother!' – was in no mood for another lecture.

'I don't want—' she began, but got no further because she found herself being marched into the staffroom.

'Scram, girls,' Bobbi ordered the two members of staff chatting by the coffee machine. 'You can come back in two minutes.' They scrammed.

'Now, madam, listen to me,' growled Bobbi. 'You have put your poor parents through enough.'

'It's not my fault—' Meredith said furiously.

'It never is with people like you!' hissed Bobbi, dark eyes flashing. 'You abandoned the whole family years ago, only came home once in a blue moon, flashing your money like you were better than the rest of them. Remember your father's sixtieth? Turning up with all that stupid champagne and making your poor mother feel she hadn't done it all properly because you had to swan in and fix it. Which, if we're going to be entirely truthful, was for nobody's benefit but your own!'

Meredith was about to protest, but thought better of it.

'Then you land on their laps with a trailer load of trouble, and behave like a spoilt brat. Your cousin Freya has gone through far worse, but she's a trouper. You won't hear her complaining, and she looks after your mother in a way you never did. So stop the grandstanding and behave. Opal's going to have quite enough to contend with, thanks to Liz's snooty mother, so she doesn't need you throwing tantrums. Got it?'

Meredith felt the tears coming. She knew she'd been horrible but she felt so low and to see Freya and her mother together like that had shaken her. Her mother was the one unchanging person in a rapidly shifting world. Now it looked as if Freya had taken her place in Opal's affections . . .

'Enough with the tears,' said Bobbi brutally. 'I'm sorry for everything you've gone through, Meredith, but I'm sorrier for the way you've treated your mother all these years. How often did you phone home? How often did you invite anyone from St Brigid's Terrace to the fine events in the gallery? Tell me that?'

In full fury, Bobbi was truly terrifying. And she was livid.

She'd seen Opal over the years, trying to pretend that she knew how Meredith's posh business was getting along, when in fact all she knew was the odd detail she'd managed to pick up from the newspapers.

'How about *not* thinking of yourself for one day?' Bobbi said.

With that, she marched out of the staffroom, telling the two hovering juniors outside the door: 'You can go in and make the coffee now.'

Meredith was too proud to let the tears flow as the girls, wearing Bobbi's trademark chocolate uniform with the little pink silk scarf, shuffled in and stared at her. Like teenage birds of paradise with their beautiful eye make-up and perfect hair, they kept staring until Meredith got up and stormed out.

'Who's that?' asked Magda curiously.

'The one who was in the papers over that fancy art gallery thing. The owners robbed everyone blind and all the money's gone. She's Opal's daughter.'

'*Her*? I didn't know Opal had a daughter.'

Veronica began to make coffee. 'That's the problem, according to Bobbi. Thinks she's too good for Redstone. Got too big for her boots.'

She put a little malted biscuit in a packet on the saucer for her client. 'Although that won't last if she's got Bobbi on her case. Nobody like Bobbi for knocking someone down to size.'

Over on the soft chocolate-brown couch, Lillie had managed to calm Opal down by asking about her wedding outfit. She was now telling the story of a wedding she'd been to where an old school friend who'd come into money kept boasting about her fabulous homes, her staff and her designer clothes.

'Then she asked me if Sam and I were still in our little house out in Beaumaris. She'd moved away, to a huge property on the beach. She was so rude, it really got to me,'

293

Lillie admitted. 'I was going to tell her so – which isn't like me at all – but Sam, my husband, stepped in. "As long as you're happy, Denise, that's all that matters, isn't it? No amount of dollars can make up for not being happy . . ."' Lillie realized that this had to be the first time since Sam's death that she'd managed to say *my husband* without wanting to cry. 'This look came over Denise's face, and I felt sorry for her,' Lillie went on, collecting herself. 'After that, Denise didn't look happy, despite the houses and all the rest. And I felt bad because I'd let her stupid boasting upset me. From what Bobbi tells me, your son's future mother-in-law sounds a bit like Denise. Would you say she's happy?'

Opal giggled nervously as she thought of Miranda's cold, hard face permanently set into an expression of distaste. 'I've never thought about it,' she said.

'Think about it now,' said Lillie with a comforting smile. 'People who aren't happy waste far too much time trying to make other people unhappy so they're not alone in their miserableness. I simply leave them to it, myself. Now, what are you getting done to your hair?'

By twelve forty-five, the Byrne family were sitting in the front pew of the church on the groom's side, with Opal looking exceptionally pretty in her lilac lace jacket and matching dress. She, Bobbi, Shari and Freya had gone on an all-day trip into the city and had come home with this beautiful creation which perfectly suited Opal's soft colouring.

Opal had then dutifully phoned Miranda to tell her she was wearing lilac and had got off the phone quickly before Miranda had time to tell her that lilac was ageing or something else hurtful.

A crack team of Bobbi's hair and make-up people had spent two hours on her in the salon that morning, blending and shading her make-up, curling her silvery blonde hair and attaching the violet silk roses that Opal was wearing instead of a hat.

'Hats don't suit you,' Bobbi had stated firmly, and Freya agreed.

'The roses will frame your face,' she added.

Meredith, desperate to be forgiven, nodded. 'You look beautiful, Mum,' she said, then had to leave the salon in case she burst into tears. She might as well go back and get into her dress for the wedding. She'd been back to the apartment the previous week to work out what she could sell to salvage some money out of the whole mess, and she'd brought all her clothes back with her. The small bedroom in St Brigid's Terrace wasn't big enough for them all, and most lay, untouched, in black plastic sacks. With no enthusiasm for the task, she'd settled on a pink silk sheath. After running an iron over it, she slipped it on and then unearthed a pair of antique gold sandals that probably cost more than her mother and father's electricity bill for a month. Then she'd set off for the church feeling that, no matter how much money she was wearing on the outside, on the inside it was as if she was dressed in the cheapest rags ever.

Over on the other side of the church, Miranda looked magnificent enough for Buckingham Palace in a royal-blue suit with startlingly purple spike-heel shoes and a purple hat that resembled a vast taffeta flying saucer perched at an angle on her head. The hot pink lipstick was a mistake, Freya thought with a grin. Only people like Kaz – fifteen, with naturally pouting lips – could get away with a slash of hot pink.

She wished Kaz was beside her, so they could nudge each other and have a giggle at Miranda's rig-out. But Kaz, who'd come as her plus-one, was further down the church, while Freya was stuck beside Meredith at the end of the family pew. Whatever Bobbi had said to her must have worked: Meredith had been making more of an effort to be considerate towards her mother, but you couldn't exactly say she was caught up in the joy of the wedding day. She had the look of someone who was waiting for their chance to make a run for it. To the pub, no doubt. Just before they'd set off for the church, Freya had caught Meredith having a sneaky glass of the champagne that Steve had brought over that morning.

'That,' said Freya, 'is not the answer to anything.'

'What do you know?' said Meredith, guilty to be caught but convinced that a bit of champagne-induced numbness would help her through the day.

'Opal and Ned have enough to put up with without having to send you into rehab, you stupid mare.'

Meredith wasn't about to let some interfering kid tell her what to do. So she polished off a second glass. Stupid brat. Who the hell did she think she was?

Unfortunately, the champagne wasn't working. It didn't numb the pain of seeing the way all the arriving guests looked at her and muttered into the ears of their companions as they filed into the church.

She could imagine the conversations: *That's the woman from the Alexander fraud case, the business partner who claims she didn't have a clue what was going on. How could you not know?*

Everyone felt that way – even her old friend Laura.

When Meredith had seen Laura's name come up on her smartphone a few days before, she'd answered it without hesitation. Even though she'd given up answering calls after days of being besieged by investors and artists who'd fallen victim to Sally-Anne and Keith's scheme. And journalists, of course. There had been hundreds of calls from the media. She didn't know how they'd managed to get hold of her mobile number. James had warned her against speaking to them:

'There's absolutely no point,' he said, 'and I would strongly advise against it.'

'But I want people to know that it wasn't me, that I wasn't involved in it,' Meredith had protested.

'At this stage, let's keep it simple. You say nothing, I'll deal with the police. Later, when we know exactly where we stand, if you wish to engage a PR firm, you can. But don't go off talking to the media yet.'

Meredith had felt so chastened, so stupid. She thought of the days when she'd been an avid reader of the scandals plastered across the front pages of the Sunday papers, never dreaming she'd be caught up in one herself. She'd always rather looked down on these people, not being able to understand how they couldn't deal with it privately. Now she understood all too well. When everyone was publicly denouncing her she wanted to tell her side of the story desperately. And if that meant discussing it with newspapers who wanted to ask her the most personal of questions, then she understood it very well. But Laura was different, though. Seeing Laura's phone number on caller ID had felt like a blessed relief. Laura would understand.

Eagerly, she answered.

'Oh, Laura, it's so good to talk to you. You've no idea what I've been going through—'

'We've been going through something as well,' Laura said, in a tone the like of which Meredith had never heard her use. 'Have you any idea what you've done to us, Meredith?' Laura went on. 'You've bankrupted us. I didn't want to say anything, we didn't want to say anything to you until we knew, but our lawyer has been on to the police and all they'll tell us is that the money is gone. The investments were fake. We have no money in a shopping centre in Bulgaria or a hotel complex in Dubai. We have no pension. We have nothing. Sally-Anne and Keith have run off with every last penny. And I find it quite impossible to believe, Meredith, that you could not have known about this.'

Meredith was silent. The silence of utter shock.

297

'Laura,' she said finally, 'how can you think that? You know me so well, I would never have told you to invest your money if I thought they were swindling us. I've lost everything too. My lawyer says I might lose my flat, my car, everything. I'll have nothing.'

'You worked with them every day for what? Six years, seven years? And you say you knew *nothing*. How could you get your close friends to invest with these people, how could you not have seen what they were? I never liked Sally-Anne, never, but I trusted you, Meredith. I *trusted* you, and that's why Con and I invested our money with her. Because of you.'

'Oh, Laura,' said Meredith, and she began to weep. 'I'll do everything I can to sort it out.'

'There's absolutely nothing you can do to sort it out. All the money from the good years, the money that we invested for our future, for Iona's future, it's all gone. We're going to have to sell the house. We'll have to buy something smaller, and Con and I will have to get regular jobs because artists like us are luxury items in a recession. People don't have money for art. Until now we were just about getting by, but we knew we had the investments, they were our nest egg, our safety blanket. Thanks to you, now we have nothing.'

'But you can't blame me,' said Meredith. 'I didn't know it was all a con.'

'I do blame you,' Laura said. 'I blame you because I believed in you and you clearly didn't have the judgement to see what sort of woman she was. Oh, I blame you all right.' Then she hung up.

Meredith had sat numbly looking out the bedroom window, the phone still resting in her hand. She'd never felt so lonely or so stupid in her whole life. She hadn't thought that Laura and Con would turn against her. But why shouldn't they? They had lost everything because they'd put their faith in her. And she had been too naive, too blinkered to see Sally-Anne for what she really was. She'd been blinded by Sally-Anne's accent and her access to all the coolest places and all her rich, posh friends.

Opal sat in the church with her hand held firmly in Ned's big one. His fingers were calloused from working both in the garden and on the allotment, but to Opal, their touch was as comforting as if they were curled up together on the couch, watching telly. After meeting that lovely Lillie in Bobbi's salon, Opal had decided that Miranda's insults were not going to get to her today.

Miranda was an unhappy person – Lillie had been right. Today, Miranda should be joyful that her dear daughter was marrying the man of her dreams. Instead, she faced the world like a high-speed Jekyll and Hyde, smiling at people she liked one minute and glaring ferociously at those she didn't approve of the next.

She'd already attempted one put-down, the minute she set eyes on Opal in her wedding outfit. Hissing, 'No hat, Opal!' in scandalized tones, as if Opal had arrived dressed in black studded leather on the back of a Harley Davidson.

Knowing that Freya was beside her, poised like a Rottweiler ready to leap into action, Opal merely smiled, patted her roses and said: 'Flowers are so feminine, I think. I love roses and I'm so happy today, Miranda.'

And with both Freya and Miranda gaping at her in aston-ishment, for entirely different reasons, Opal had taken her niece's arm and walked happily into the church, stopping to admire all the blush pink and cream roses at the end of every second pew.

Now she looked at Brian and David standing at the front, with Liz coming down the aisle, a vision in cream lace and tulle. The back of the dress was so pretty, lots of tiny buttons. Wedding dresses needed lovely backs because most people saw the back of the bride first in the church.

Ned squeezed her hand and Opal squeezed back. It was

going to be a perfect day. No matter what Miranda said or did, it would be just perfect.

At the reception, Miranda looked around her with pleasure. It was all going so wonderfully. The golf club was a prestigious venue and showed people – well, people like her new son-in-law's family – how things should be done. At the Rathlin Golf Club, it was full silver service all the way. Crisp white linen napkins perfectly set off the glorious towers of tumbling white flowers on each of the tables. Elizabeth had been worried that people wouldn't be able to see each other across the round tables, but Miranda had won the day on that point.

'Darling, since your father and I are paying for it, at least let us have some say in what happens on the day,' Miranda had sniffed.

She was sure that Elizabeth hadn't been so wilful or determined to have her way before getting involved with Brian Byrne. The Byrnes were the main fly in the ointment, no doubt about it. Opal, Brian's dreadful mother, wasn't even wearing a hat. All Miranda's friends had mentioned it, generally when they were complimenting her on her spectacular Stephen Jones creation. 'I got it in London, obviously,' Miranda had told them. 'There's nothing in Ireland really. One has to go to London.'

But Opal . . . Honestly, what sort of a name was Opal? So common, so nineteen fifties lower class, as were all those silly names like Pearl and Daisy. Opal had made do with some violet flowers in her hair – far too simple for a society wedding.

At that moment Miranda spotted Noel coming back from the bar with a pint of Guinness. Her lips tightened. She'd told him not to drink Guinness tonight. Let the Byrnes and their lower-class relations drink stuff out of pint glasses; nobody from *their* side should be seen dead doing it.

Gloria Devine glided past, head to toe in Louise Kennedy.

Miranda loved Louise Kennedy and had toyed with the idea of wearing something from her crystal beaded line to the wedding, but then one of the other guests might have turned up in the same thing, which was why she'd gone to London. Miranda had wanted her dress to be totally different.

'You've outdone yourself, Miranda,' Gloria said. She was a dear friend from tennis. They hadn't seen each other much over the last two years, but still, Miranda had insisted that she be invited.

'Mum, you never see the Devines any more, you know that,' Elizabeth had said crossly when they were doing the lists. 'Besides, we've got way too many guests as it is from our side of the family. Brian hasn't invited half so many people.'

'It's not my fault if the Byrnes have no friends,' Miranda had snapped. She'd regretted it immediately; there was no point in falling out with her daughter over the wedding plans. It was enough that she had managed to get the wedding and the reception where she'd wanted and not somewhere like that horrible low-class hotel near Redstone.

Never mind, Miranda comforted herself, if Elizabeth ever married again, then they'd really do it in style. She knew that her mother, long dead, would have been horrified at such sentiments, but her mother had been a good Catholic in an era when it made sense to be doctrinaire. These days, everyone could get a divorce. And if Elizabeth divorced Brian, she might marry up the next time.

A woman in a blue suit with an alarming tan waved at her. She looked vaguely familiar. Who on earth was she? Ah, that's it, one of Opal's awful friends.

'Lovely wedding, Miranda,' said Molly loudly, 'although I'm not sure about the hat, love. I think you can take it off inside. Unless you're trying to get Sky Television on it?'

For once Miranda couldn't think of a thing to say.

* * *

'I love you,' said Brian on the dance floor that evening as he stared down into his new wife's hazel eyes.

'I love you more,' she replied, beaming up at him.

It had all gone so marvellously and somehow her mother hadn't been outrageously rude to the Byrne family, which had been Liz's main fear. She thought back to the many wonderful moments: the soloist's haunting rendition of *Pie Jesu*; the sun coming out from behind a cloud as they'd left the church, dusting every tree and leaf and Liz herself with golden light; the perfectly judged speeches, particularly David's best man speech, which was positively the nicest she'd ever heard.

'I can't believe my mother behaved herself,' Liz murmured, leaning against Brian's shoulder and thinking how nice it was to be dancing finally as husband and wife. When people said marriage didn't matter and it was only a piece of paper, they were *wrong*.

Liz felt entirely different from the way she had that morning. She'd gone into the church a girl, and had come out a woman. Totally different.

'Your mum's great,' lied Brian, who treated Miranda with the careful attention of a zookeeper feeding a new and highly dangerous rhino. 'I think everyone's enjoying themselves too.'

'Yes,' said Liz happily. 'Weird to think that it's nearly over, isn't it?'

Brian held her closer. 'It's only beginning, love,' he said, and they began to try waltzing, because they'd had all those lessons and it seemed a shame to waste them.

A few yards away, Miranda was dancing with Brian's father. Ned was a remarkably good dancer, she thought in surprise, as he whirled her expertly round the floor.

It reminded her of dancing with an early boyfriend, someone who'd dumped her because he said she was a 'stuck-up cow'. Miranda had never forgotten it. Even after forty years, it still stung.

'This is lovely,' she said happily to Ned, who held her further away from him and looked at her coolly.

'Really?' he said. 'I thought you couldn't wait to be rid of all us annoying Byrnes so you and your friends could celebrate in style.'

Miranda flushed.

She *had* said that to a few of her pals, suggesting they should get a couple of bottles of champers to themselves later when the rough dancing was over and the Byrnes and their people were propping up the bar.

'Oh, I didn't mean it like that—' she began.

'I know exactly how you meant it, Miranda,' said Ned, in that firm tone, a tone she wouldn't have thought him capable of. 'I didn't appreciate hearing it at our son's wedding. For a start, your Liz is part of the Byrne family now. Secondly, if Opal had heard you, she'd have been devastated. I've seen the way you've tried to put my wife down over this wedding and I've had enough. I'm only dancing with you now because it's protocol and I don't want to upset Brian or Liz, but you better change your tune, Miranda, or I won't have you in my house. I'll tell Liz what you said too, and see what she thinks about it all.'

'Please don't,' begged Miranda, blushing now.

'You think you've got lovely manners, don't you, Miranda? Well, you don't have any decency in you.'

With that, Ned simply dropped his arms from hers and walked away, leaving Miranda standing on the dance floor.

He was angry he'd had to say such things because it went against his nature, but Miranda had done her damnedest to ruin Opal's day out and his wife had been through enough lately. She wouldn't suffer Miranda's rudeness if he could help it.

Flustered, Miranda looked around for her husband, Noel, but he wasn't dancing with Opal, as he was supposed to be doing. Instead, he was at the bar with a couple of Ned's

303

cronies, with whom he seemed to be getting along famously, judging by their raucous laughter.

Brian whirled past, dancing with his mother. 'Noel wasn't up for a dance with my mother, Miranda,' he called, loudly enough for everyone to hear, 'but I'll take care of it. I love dancing with my mother,' he added, smiling fondly down at Opal.

'What did you say to Ned?' demanded Elizabeth, dancing past with David. 'He looked very upset. If you said—'

Miranda couldn't bear it any more. She rushed off to her hotel room. None of it had worked out the way she'd planned. Even Elizabeth was turning on her and Noel had let her down by not doing his duty and dancing with Opal. Plus, everyone had noticed, including all the friends she'd wanted to impress. The Byrnes were the ones acting with dignity while Noel was getting plastered at the bar and she was in danger of her daughter hearing the awful things she'd said about her new family. Miranda began to cry as she went to the lifts. She'd done her best, hadn't she? Or had she?

Half an hour later, she had repaired her make-up and was about to leave the room when there was a knock at the door.

She opened it to find Elizabeth standing there, beautiful in her wedding gown.

'What happened?' she demanded in a hard voice. 'I saw you speaking to Ned and I saw the way he just left you in the middle of the dance floor. You said something horrible to him, didn't you?'

Miranda considered a lie but then Elizabeth might find out about it.

'He was upset because he overheard me saying something—'

'What did you say?'

Miranda sank on to the bed. 'That we'd get some champers later when the Byrnes were all propping up the bar,' she said weakly.

Elizabeth's face was rigid with rage as she stared at her mother. 'How could you?' she said. 'I am now a Byrne and they're good, decent people who've welcomed me into their family with such kindness. The only welcome you've given Brian was to say he didn't have a bad accent and that he was better than the rest of them. You're spiteful and nasty, and I don't know if I can forgive you for behaving this way on my wedding day.'

'Oh, sweetie, now don't be like that. I was only saying what people are thinking, after all. You and Brian *do* come from very different backgrounds. Redstone might be a bit more upmarket than it used to be, but still, it's got that council house taint to it, and our people—'

She never got to finish the sentence.

'Mother,' said Liz in a deathly cool voice, 'the only person here who thinks like that is *you*. Everyone else is enjoying a wedding of two people who love each other. I love Brian and I love his family and the way they've welcomed me. I told Brian that I was worried you'd try to ruin today and he kept saying I was being silly. But I'm not. He just doesn't know you the way I do. You are cold and heartless. All you care about is the way things *look*. There's more to life than that. I'm ashamed of you, Mother. Ashamed.'

With that, she turned and left the room.

Brian was waiting for her outside.

'Is she OK?' he asked anxiously.

Liz buried her face in his shoulder. 'She's not OK, and I doubt she ever will be. You won't believe what she said, and what your poor dad overheard her saying . . .'

'Hush.' Brian silenced her with a soft kiss. 'Your mother is not ruining our day, right? Let's go down and dance our hearts out. Whatever's wrong with her is her problem.'

He produced a hanky and mopped up his new wife's tears.

'Come on – Dad wants a dance with you.'

'But what she said was horrible.'

'It doesn't matter,' Brian said simply. 'If she ruins the atmosphere, then she wins. That's not going to happen.'

Liz nodded, sniffling now.

'She said mean things about Redstone too. I love it. I want
us to buy a house there.'

Brian grinned. 'Let's tell that to Mum and Dad – that will
finish off their day beautifully.'

Inside the bedroom, Miranda could hear their voices but
couldn't make out what they were saying. She looked down
at her hands and saw that she was shaking. All she'd done
was say the truth.

She remembered years ago going out with a lovely guy,
handsome, looked like that George Clooney, and she'd dumped
him because he came from the wrong side of town.

Some of her friends had teased her about him.

'Are you teaching him to talk posh, Miranda?' they'd joked.

And embarrassed, she'd finished with him.

'I thought you were different, Miranda,' he'd said to her
bitterly. 'I thought class and where you came from didn't
matter to you.'

'It doesn't,' she begged, suddenly sorry, suddenly seeing
that her so-called friends had been jealous.

But it was too late.

He was gone.

She'd regretted that for years and now she'd gone and made
the same mistake again: judged people for the wrong things.
If only Elizabeth would forgive her. She hadn't meant to ruin
the day. But sitting in the bedroom on her own, with the
sounds of merriment all around her, Miranda began to think
that it might be a long time before her daughter forgot
Miranda's cruelty today.

'You look miserable,' Freya said to David an hour later, as
they whirled to a slow song. It wasn't like her cousin to be

306

so down. He was instinctively a merry person, saw the best in everyone and brought humour into every room. Freya marvelled that Meredith could be his sister.

She wanted to broach the subject of Meredith but wasn't sure if tonight was the occasion for it, especially now that she could see the misery in her cousin's eyes.

'What's up?'

'Nothing,' he said.

Freya stood on his toes on purpose.

'Don't lie,' she said. 'I am a human lie-detector, you know.'

'All I know is that you've got a very painful stamp for a shrimp of a girl,' he grumbled.

'It's a woman, isn't it?'

'OK, it's a woman,' David said. 'But it doesn't matter because it's long over and she made it pretty clear that it was over for good.'

Even talking about Peggy hurt. She'd felt so right to him in every way. He'd been crazy about her, and it hadn't been a one-night, several-beers-induced craziness, either. How could one woman turn your whole life upside down in just a week?

After all this time, it was still as if he could think of nothing else but Peggy. He'd even driven slowly past the shop a few times. He wondered if she'd seen him, if she thought he was some weird stalker. He wasn't. He simply had the strangest feeling that there was something Peggy wasn't telling him. Some reason why she'd broken up with him, something entirely unconnected to him. But she'd clearly been frightened of him that morning in the shop and that, David felt, was part of the mystery. He didn't want to scare her but he wanted to see her again to find out what was troubling her.

Freya said nothing. From a personality point of view, she couldn't imagine anyone not falling in love with David. Physically, she couldn't judge. He was her cousin and you never looked at a cousin that way.

Kaz reckoned he was a fine thing and she wouldn't mind,

307

thank you very much. At this point, Freya had feigned throwing up.

'He's my *family*! Stop.'

'He's not mine, though, is he? You just see Mr Nice Guy, but I see a great body, hot face and someone who doesn't have spots.'

Kaz was down in the dumps because the last three people who'd asked her out had acne, while the guy she wanted to ask her out – and was blemish-free – was currently dating the part-time model from the fifth year in their school.

'He's too old for you,' Freya had pointed out. 'You're jail-bait for someone his age – a one-way ticket to prison.'

'He might be waiting till I'm old enough to declare his love for me,' sighed Kaz in a most uncharacteristic way.

'You've been reading Mills and Boon again, haven't you?' Freya said.

Still shuffling around the dance floor with David, Freya decided she needed to know who this woman was. Anyone who hurt the Byrne family hurt Freya too.

'What's her name?' she asked idly.

'No, my little killer cousin,' David chuckled in her ear. 'I am not telling you who she is in case you abseil down the side of her house and tell her she is dead meat if she doesn't go out with me instantly.'

Freya laughed. 'What makes you think I'd do something like that?' she demanded, all injured innocence.

'Because I have you figured out,' David said. 'You're the best, you know that? But I am big enough to look after myself.'

And with that, Freya had to be content.

Six miles away, Peggy sat on the hideous orange couch that she'd threatened to cover with a throw millions of time and still hadn't, and read another of the pregnancy books she'd bought.

She'd gone to a shop in town to buy them because Redstone was so small that if she went to the tiny independent bookshop down near the mini-mart, somebody was bound to tell somebody else. The local secret-distribution system made James Bond look like an amateur. Five minutes in the mother-and-baby section of Redstone Books, and she might as well walk around with a sign inscribed: *Yes, I'm pregnant.*

She felt lonely and yet not lonely at the same time. She loved the feeling of her baby growing inside her. But there was no getting away from it: she wasn't doing the right thing. David deserved to know about it.

She didn't want money from him or anything, but he was a nice guy. Her baby deserved a father.

But how could she possibly tell him now?

Part Three

Royal Jelly is the name given to the nutritional substance that queen bee larvae feed on. This wonderful food helps the queen develop, but the entire colony receive a little at some time. Early beekeepers called it family food, because it enhances the lives of all the bees. Royal Jelly is used in Chinese traditional medicine and for a whole range of healing products and balms.

The Gentle Beekeeper, Iseult Cloud

Chapter Eighteen

*O*vernight it seemed to Meredith that she'd become afraid of big glossy buildings, the sort of places she had once felt entirely at home. She used to accompany Sally-Anne on trips to corporations to discuss where they might hang the latest giant oils they'd just bought from the Alexander Byrne Gallery. Now, gazing up at the sheeny monolith that housed her lawyer's practice, she felt like a mouse who'd strayed into the territory of a gang of cats by mistake.

Even her clothes felt wrong. She'd finally unpacked all her bin-bags of clothes so that she could decide which items to sell off, but even so, she couldn't find anything to wear. What exactly did you wear for a meeting with your criminal lawyer? She'd sold her car to write the cheque for the first tranche of James's fees. She'd borrowed David's car today to come into town to meet James and his team to discuss what was happening with the case against Alexander Byrne.

To get to James's office she had to walk past the waiting area of the conveyancing department, which was full of happy-looking clients clutching house details. Some were sharing cups of coffee with lawyers or celebrating the conclusion of the deal. She wished she was one of them and not herself. What a sad mess she'd made of everything.

James was all business. Time is money, Meredith thought grimly.

'They're still looking for Sally-Anne, but the pace of the investigation seems to have slowed down a little. She's no longer public enemy number one.' He gave her a cynical smile. 'There's always somebody else to catch, another crook who's making bigger headlines.'

'OK,' said Meredith, 'but where does that leave me?'

'Waiting,' said James. 'Waiting. These cases are all about waiting.' James hadn't asked her very much about her involvement. He'd just wanted all the documentation that Meredith said she had which proved her absolute innocence in all of this.

'The fact that they've freed up your bank accounts and allowed you to sell your car is a good sign,' he told her. 'It proves they don't think you're involved. But that could change. There are a lot of people out there with no money, and they want a scapegoat.'

Meredith left the offices feeling sadder and lower than ever. No one had offered her a cup of coffee or smiled warmly at her. She was in a different part of the legal system now.

When she'd had money, Meredith had occasionally shopped for vintage clothes. Not often – she didn't really care for the idea of wearing someone else's cast-offs – but enough that she knew the right place to go to sell her things. *The* place to buy vintage was not so much a shop but an emporium, where rich people discreetly got rid of bits and bobs they no longer wanted or purchased new bits and bobs. The owner, an exquisitely beautiful former model called Angelique, ran it almost as a hobby and Meredith had been in there a couple of time with Sally-Anne, who had seemed totally at home among shelves filled with crocodile Hermès handbags and furs with little fox faces staring up at you. Meredith had shuddered when she'd seen these. She'd never understood wearing fur. It seemed to her a bit like wearing your pet around your neck, your dead pet.

Today though, she didn't care what was on sale in Angelique's: she just needed to get rid of her own stuff. She'd deliberately tried to go at a quiet time, mid-afternoon, when the wealthier women might be picking up children from school or getting ready for dinner, when there'd be nobody there to see her shame. There was no point pretending otherwise, it did feel like shame, particularly since the clothes were packed in three large black plastic sacks.

Angelique opened the door herself, a slender woman in her sixties with rippling silver-white hair tied up in a knot. She wore almost no make-up apart from carmine lipstick on her full lips and looked effortlessly glamorous in a long 1930s tea-gown.

'Hello,' she said warmly, smiling at Meredith and glancing at the bin-bags. 'It looks as though you've got a marvellous haul for me, sweetie. Do come in.'

She picked up one of the bags and half-carried, half-dragged it along the marble floor while Meredith struggled in with the other two.

'Now,' said Angelique, beaming kindly, as if her beautiful antique-laden house hadn't been invaded by three bin-bags, 'you look absolutely shattered. Would you like a cup of tea in the kitchen? I have shortbread biscuits.'

It was the kindness that was Meredith's undoing. She'd been so careful to keep away from the people she knew from the past, despite all their desperate phone calls. Everyone seemed to think she was either in on Sally-Anne and Keith's scheme or that she was a complete idiot not to have known about it.

And now here was Angelique, doyenne of vintage shops, someone reputedly with blue blood and ancestry she could trace back hundreds of years, and she was being kind. Meredith burst into tears.

315

'Oh, you poor love,' said Angelique, putting an arm around her shoulders. She led Meredith down some small stairs into a large, airy kitchen with a conservatory attached. 'You have been through the mill, haven't you?'

'Yes,' sobbed Meredith.

It was quite plain that Angelique knew exactly who she was – something that would have once thrilled Meredith, seeming to suggest that she had *arrived*. Now it was merely a sign that her face was familiar from the newspapers.

'You're being so kind and I'm . . . I'm so sorry, I don't mean to cry but . . .'

'It's absolutely fine.' Angelique showed her to a big fat armchair covered in an old floral throw with a selection of well-worn tapestry cushions on it. 'Make yourself comfortable there,' she said. 'The cats will come and sit on you in a minute – they're very comforting.'

'I thought you had a dog,' said Meredith, remembering an article in a glossy magazine about Angelique's wonderful life. Angelique's smile dimmed.

'Yes,' she sighed. 'Pumpkin, love of my life. The dogs were always more loyal than the men, I found.'

Meredith hiccupped and half laughed at the same time.

'I shouldn't be giving you my warped view on life,' Angelique continued, with a certain merriness in her voice. 'Pumpkin was my familiar, old and wise and very beautiful, but he had to go. Petit mal seizures, the vet said. It's the hardest thing, isn't it, to hurt the thing you love, but some-times we have to do it.'

'Yes,' sobbed Meredith even harder.

She didn't know why, but all of a sudden she thought of her father and mother and how *she'd* hurt them so much and they so were loving and loyal, not that she was comparing them to Pumpkin . . .

'You cry if you want to, pet,' Angelique said.

She walked into the conservatory part of the kitchen, picked

316

up a large marmalade cat from his spot on the window seat where the sun was gilding his fur, carried him over and deposited him on Meredith's lap. 'This is Marmaduke, obviously,' Angelique said.

'Obviously,' said Meredith, astonished that she could joke.

She stroked Marmaduke gently, letting the calmness of the house soothe her, until Angelique put a cup and saucer of tea and a plate of shortbread biscuits, along with milk and sugar in front of her.

'Take lots of sugar,' said Angelique briskly.

She settled herself in a chair nearby.

'Now, I'm going to spend five minutes telling you a story I haven't told anyone for a very long time, and then you're going to go away and wait till I phone to say if I've sold your clothes or not, right?'

'Right,' said Meredith, startled.

'Years ago, before you were born I'd say, I was married and myself and my husband were in all the gossip columns. He was handsome, charming –'

Meredith smiled at this vision.

'– and a cheat in every respect,' finished Angelique. 'When my daughter was three, he stole money from his father's firm and ran off with his father's secretary. He left me with no money, a huge mortgage and no hope of getting a penny out of him.'

Meredith stared at her.

'I got by,' Angelique continued, 'by concentrating on my daughter and holding my head up. Yes, I felt hideously foolish to have fallen for him in the first place. And yes, it was all over the papers because people love reading about other people's misfortunes. Nothing makes us feel more secure in our lives than knowing someone is worse off, apparently. I didn't think it would ever end, but it did. Now, you need to do exactly what I did, Meredith. Concentrate on something you love and hold your head up. It will end one day and

317

nobody will remember much about it except you and the other people who were conned.'

'But it's all gone—' began Meredith.

'The money?' said Angelique. 'You can earn more. Find what you love doing and do it. That heals the soul – it's what I did.' She gestured at her surroundings. 'I would have lost this house, but by turning it into a second-hand clothes shop I found a way to hold on to it. Be inventive. You'll think of something. And you're only down when you think you are. Stop feeling sorry for yourself. Now, that's my advice.'

She produced a notebook and a silver pencil from a pocket. 'Tell me your telephone number and I'll phone you.'

Meredith obediently recited it.

'Let yourself out when you're ready, darling,' Angelique added. 'I'm going up to look at the clothes.'

Meredith drank her tea and ate two biscuits, all the while looking around at this beautiful home. She'd never heard a word of a scandal involving Angelique and yet, it had clearly been the cause célèbre of the day. Maybe there was some hope for her after all.

Chapter Nineteen

*J*t turned out that having a weekend by herself wasn't as much fun as she'd imagined, though Frankie had been full of enthusiasm when Seth and Lillie announced the time had come to visit their mother's people in Kerry.

'What a wonderful idea,' she said. 'You need to see everything, Lillie, understand what Ireland was like then.'

But Frankie wondered how Lillie would cope with seeing her mother's grave. Perhaps it would add to her grief for her husband, Sam. Or maybe, Frankie reasoned, it would bring home to her the greatness of the loss of the mother she'd never known.

People handled things very differently, although from what she knew of Lillie, Frankie wasn't sure if either scenario fitted the circumstances. Still, she wasn't going to expect too much. Seth's mother had been a wonderful person but perhaps Lillie didn't appreciate that just yet.

Frankie was looking forward to having the house to herself – or the basement to herself, she thought grimly.

Lillie and Seth headed off on Friday morning and weren't due back till Monday afternoon. Once they were gone, Frankie resolved to make the most of having the house to herself. She decided she would start by taking a walk around the whole property to look at exactly what needed doing and consider how it could be done on the cheap. It was the only option. She couldn't bear to live in this squalor forever.

When she thought of the beautiful, albeit much smaller, house she and Seth had sold to move into this dump . . . Well, no point thinking about the old house now. They'd been mad to sell it. Mad and caught up in a dream of gracious living in a big old house and a big old garden, the two of them happily gardening side by side on sunny afternoons. It had been a stupid dream.

On Saturday morning, she'd woken early, thrown on some old clothes and, armed with a pen and her trusty notebook, she'd marched upstairs to inspect the disaster area she and Seth now called home.

If anything, walking through the house made her more miserable than ever. The previous owner had certainly had an eye for ugly wallpaper. Either that or there'd been a job lot of disgusting mustard paint on offer the day he called in the paint shop. All the rooms' woodwork were painted the same horrible, cat-diarrhoea colour.

How had they been so oblivious to the horror of it all? She remembered those early days when Seth had showed the building plans to anyone who'd even vaguely expressed an interest. And they'd been such beautiful plans, too. Seth really was a marvellous architect. Never sacrificing function to form and never overspending, understanding that people did not want to be bankrupted by the wild dreams of their architects.

She knew of one man in his office, a horrible man who'd actually been kept on, who was the master of making people spend at least twice what they'd planned to in the beginning. That was probably why he hadn't been let go. He'd winkle money out of anyone.

She went back downstairs and sighed as she looked at the basement anew. Seth's plans for this part of the renovation had been particularly clever: an unashamedly modern extension leading into a kitchen/dining area with huge glass walls. It had been fabulous and now they were far too broke to even think about it. But maybe, just maybe, she thought, looking round with new eyes, there were things they could do that wouldn't cost too much.

Lillie had insisted that Dessie, their garden miracle worker, could do the heavy work, knocking down partition walls and ripping out sinks and things. Apart from some replastering and new plumbing, the place really just needed to have every wall stripped and everything painted. It was do-able, Frankie thought with mounting excitement. Seeing the way the garden had turned out had made her feel more cheerful about the prospect. Yes, the work would be painfully slow if they did it themselves, but they could do it. The fine furniture they'd need for such a house was off limits for cost reasons, but they'd get there eventually, furnishing rooms one by one as they got the money. It could be a labour of love.

But by Sunday the exhaustion was back, and with it the doubts. When Gabrielle rang to see if they might be free to come over for lunch, she leapt at the chance to get away from Sorrento Villa for a few hours.

'Would you mind awfully if I came on my own?' pleaded Frankie, longing to see Gabrielle. 'The others are down the country looking up old relatives and I need you to myself so I can talk all this stuff off my chest. I'm more cheerful about the house, though, if that's anything. I'm beginning to think that we could do it ourselves. Seth and Lillie have done such good work in the garden, you wouldn't believe it. The house would take forever, but still.'

'You sound so much happier,' said Gabrielle. 'Of course, come on your own, darling. We can have a proper sis to sis talk,' said Gabrielle. 'One o'clock, then. I'll tell Victor he can go fishing.'

Parking her car in the driveway of Gabrielle and Victor's

wisteria-covered cottage with Georgia, the spaniel, barking madly at the car, Frankie realized with sudden clarity that *this* was what she'd wanted all along. This small but pretty house with its lovely gardens front and back and the sense that once inside the gates, you were in a different place of calm beauty.

If only Sorrento Villa looked like this, she'd be able to cope with anything, even this bloody menopausal darkness.

The hall contained the usual mess of coats draped over the banister. Frankie's niece, Cameron, now twenty-one, was sitting on the stairs and talking volubly on the phone, pausing only to blow Frankie a kiss. She was a lanky, equally blonde version of her mother, dressed in the same sort of trailing T-shirt and tight jeans combo as Emer, and Frankie felt at once desperately lonely for her daughter.

Despite Skype, both her children were gone from her and it was so hard to deal with. The empty nest was the wrong description for how their leaving had made her feel. The ripped-apart nest might suit it better.

'I've just made soup and salad,' said Gaby once they were in the kitchen, but all thoughts of lunch were abandoned when Frankie suddenly burst into tears.

'Sorry, I did say I was happier. Don't know why I'm crying. I don't know what's wrong with me,' she sobbed to her sister.

'Is it difficult having Lillie there, do you think?' Gabrielle asked, wisely.

Frankie shook her head. 'It's actually proof of the old adage about another woman keeping a couple together. Not,' she said hastily, seeing Gabrielle's eyebrows lift, 'that Lillie is the *other woman*. It's simply that having her around creates a buffer between Seth and me. She's fitting into the whole place so much better than I am,' Frankie sobbed. 'I love Redstone and could see myself swanning down to the village with a basket on my arm, buying organic vegetables and waving hello to the butcher. Now, it's Lillie who's doing it. Everyone loves her.

'She's palled up with the woman who owns the hair salon,' Frankie went on, 'and the people at the bakery. She helps this old lady who can't get out much, and she's in cahoots with just about everyone, from the fellas at the bus stop to some fifteen-year-old girl whom she keeps telling me is "an old soul" because she's so wise.'

Her sister listened sympathetically as Frankie poured out all her troubles.

'She says she's started work on the garden because she doesn't want to take advantage of us – and you have to come to see what they've accomplished, because you wouldn't believe the transformation. We have a lawn and shrubs, and Seth is booked in to do a beekeeping course. Lillie's like this angel coming in and fixing all the problems.

'She offered to move out for the rest of the time she's here, but Seth won't hear of it. "You're my sister and you're staying," he told her. He wouldn't mind in the slightest if I pushed off,' Frankie finished miserably.

Gabrielle looked at her sister, stunned by the outburst. She'd never seen Frankie so sad or so unsure of herself.

'Don't assume it's all over just because you're in the middle of a difficult period,' she said. 'All marriages need work.'

'Yours doesn't!' said Frankie.

Gabrielle rolled her eyes up to heaven. ''Course it does,' she said. 'You're shocked because this has never happened to you before, but we all go through difficult times. You've just been too busy up to now to have things lose their shine. Marriage takes work.'

'That's just it,' said Frankie. 'I don't think Seth wants to be married to me any more. I'm so bad-tempered, and I was hopeless when he was made redundant. He wants out, I can tell.' Then she burst into tears again.

Away from the lovely elegance of Maple Avenue, Lillie found the wild landscape of rural Kerry very different. As a true

Australian, she'd travelled far around her beautiful homeland. When the boys were teenagers, she and Sam had taken them on a never-to-be-forgotten trip to the Outback. The photographs, a couple of which she carried with her, still made her smile. There, land stretched out an infinite distance, broken up by nothing but gum trees, with a vast horizon reaching into the pale, pale blue sky.

Seth had kept to the main road to begin with, with glimpses of houses and side roads that were not unlike Redstone and Maple Avenue. But then they had turned off into a series of winding narrow roads lined with hedges made of briars, brambles and trees.

'What happens if you meet another car?' she asked curiously. 'There's no way to get past.'

Seth grinned at her. He seemed at home, more relaxed, in this rugged, mountainous landscape.

'When that happens,' he said, 'one of you has to decide to go backwards. The people around here are used to it. The roads get narrower than this, believe me.'

Today was only the first part of the journey. Their mother had been brought up on a remote farm on the Beara Peninsula, a beautiful rocky place where the Atlantic lashed against the coast. Here the roads were even narrower and they were as likely to meet a tractor as another car. To Lillie, used to the concept of vast open farming, where sheep and cattle roamed over thousands of acres, the tiny, rocky fields with their rusty five-bar gates were very strange.

'It must be hard to make a living as a farmer here,' she said, looking around.

Seth agreed. 'I wouldn't want to do it myself. Even the cows don't have a lie-in on Christmas Day and Saturdays.'

Lillie laughed. 'Tell me, what was it like when you visited here as a child?' she asked. 'It must have been so different from your life in Cork, so . . .'

'Alien?' he offered. 'Yes, it felt strange. But my mother, *our* mother, was so at home here, and that was enough. I fitted in because she fitted in and she made it all work so easily.'

Lillie was silent for a while as they drove. The hedges were growing sparser, and soon they were replaced by stone walls that didn't appear to be held together by cement or mortar. The land seemed perilous, inhospitable, dotted with the same grey rocks that made up the walls. Like the trip to Seth's old home in Cork, all this was helping her think of her mother as a real person now. Before she'd come to Ireland, Lillie's mother had been a distant, far away person. Like a phantom or a fairy in a children's story.

Now Lillie thought of her as real, a flesh-and-blood woman who had such strength of character she was able to make her shy and sensitive son fit in when they visited from the city. The image Lillie had carried around all her life of a frightened, scared young girl who'd been forced to give her baby up receded a little. What had her mother really been like? How had someone raised in this desolate landscape been both frightened enough to give up her child and strong enough to go through with it?

'We're nearly there now.' Tonight they were going to stop at the small farm where his uncle still lived. There wasn't much of the family left, and no surviving relatives on the peninsula. Some had settled in Wales, others in America. All had scattered. Seth had emailed them and was waiting for replies.

'They'll want to see you or talk to you,' he said. 'Searching for long-lost relatives is all the rage here, you know!'

'How far is the sea?' she asked.

Seth considered. 'Maybe seven miles,' he said. 'I learned to swim here. You won't believe it when you actually see the sea because our "swimming pool" was a rocky basin. It was easier to swim than to walk on the sharp stones.' He laughed, clearly thinking of days spent with his cousins on the small farm.

'Your uncle won't mind me coming to see him?' Lillie asked

tentatively. She knew not everyone welcomed the emergence of relatives they never knew they had. She'd read enough about it to understand that adopted children were often rejected. Some families couldn't forgive the lie that one member had lived with all their lives. Others didn't want their lives cluttered up with another person, thank you very much.

She turned in her seat and smiled at Seth, who seemed so happy now that he was driving along these treacherous narrow little roads. He'd not been like that. He'd welcomed her with open arms, into his life and into his heart. She was so lucky. *Thank you, Sam*, she prayed silently. *Thank you for sending me here and making Seth and Frankie open their arms to me.*

Of course, she knew that the universe liked balance. If her heart was swelling from the love she'd received from her long-lost brother and his wife, then she was certainly giving something back. She could see the huge cracks in Frankie and Seth's marriage and she was determined to do everything she could to help mend them. Not in an interfering way – no. But they were like two swimmers in a lake in a fog. Calling each other, needing each other and yet just not able to touch. Frankie and Seth loved each other, of that Lillie hadn't the slightest doubt. But they were at that dangerous moment where everything could go horribly wrong and if she could help prevent that, then she would.

'We're here,' said Seth, without warning.

'Already?' she said, but he was driving in a narrow gateway and up a muddy track.

In front of her was a stone cottage set on the hillside, looking like something from a child's drawing. A low roof, two small windows at the front and a wide door, painted red. A water barrel sat under the front gutter and a stack of turf was neatly to one side. The house had held her mother's seven brothers and sisters and it was tiny. Lillie just stared when Seth stopped the car.

It was neat and tidy, but so poor, like, like . . . like nothing she'd seen before. And this was the place her mother had called home?

An old man with a stoop wearing a very old dark suit peered out of the door.

'Uncle Liam!' said Seth, and got out of the car.

He and the old man embraced as Lillie slowly unfolded herself from the front seat and walked over to them. More pieces of the puzzle were falling into place.

'Lillie, *a stór*,' said the old man, and he held out his arms to her.

'It means darling in Irish,' said Seth helpfully.

'Aren't you the cut of your mother, Lillie!' Liam added, and then she was in his arms and she smelled the scent of pipe tobacco and salty skin and old clothes that were probably not aired enough. He had to be at least ninety, the last of her mother's siblings alive, and he was welcoming her home.

'Liam, how lovely to meet you,' she said, holding on tight.

'That's a great accent you have there,' he said, a smile in his voice.

'Right back at you,' said Lillie tearfully.

They sat in the dark kitchen of the house, which was clean but so very old and apparently had no comfortable seats at all. Liam poked at the stove and put a big, dull tin kettle on to boil so he could make tea.

From the cream sideboard, he produced a box of photographs and set them on the table in front of Lillie.

'Have a poke around in those, now, and you'll find some of your mother.'

There were not that many photographs in the box, but among the very small, white-rimmed sepia-toned ones, she found her mother as a young woman, wearing a 1940s dress with the era's big shoulders and a scoop neck. Her hair was in a Betty Grable roll and she wore bright lipstick, probably the red of the day, Lillie thought tremulously.

327

She'd seen photos of her mother in Seth's albums, but they'd been from after her marriage. These were pure gold, the pictures taken before.

'Was she pregnant then?' Lillie wondered.

Liam cast a look at the photo as he passed with the teapot.

'She was a fine woman, no doubt about it, the best-looking of us all.'

'Did you know about me?' asked Lillie.

She wasn't sure if it was the right thing to say, but she needed to know. Liam was the youngest but even so he might have heard the stories, might have some light to shed on the old mystery.

'Arra, I did,' he said softly. 'Jennifer was like yourself, Lillie, always a beauty, and she was doing a line with young Michael Doherty for a few months when he upped and went off to join the war. His poor mother never got over it, to be honest.' Liam took a sip of tea slowly. He did everything slowly, Lillie realized. 'He was killed in the basic training. An accident, they said. Didn't even get on to a boat to see the action. We all knew that Jennifer had a baby to come and we knew no good could come of it.'

His ancient eyes, of a blue not unlike Lillie's own, sought hers.

'A stór, you might be thinking it was cruel because of the way it happens today, but then, sure, she'd have been ostracized. Mother Vincent in the convent in the town was a good woman, she said she'd help, seeing as how Michael had been killed and that. She came up with the plan and that was that. Jennifer went off to the convent in Cork and she didn't come back to us until she was a married woman, five years later. I think,' he said sorrowfully, 'that she couldn't cope with seeing the land and the people because she'd grieve too much for the baby. For you.'

'Did my father know, do you think?' asked Seth.

Liam took another sip of tea and considered it. 'I can't say

328

as he did and I can't say as he didn't,' he announced finally. 'But he loved Jennifer better than any man, and that was the end of it. She was a good woman, you know.'

'I know,' said Lillie.

Liam smiled, his face creasing into a multitude of wrinkles. 'As long as you do,' he said. 'Come on and we'll walk along the road and I'll tell you about your mother. Seth here thinks he knows it all, but he doesn't,' teased Liam. 'I have plenty of tales in my head about her.'

He led them out of the house into the bright, almost white light of the sea and the sky combined. 'Now, Michael's people lived over there on yonder hill, but they had weak chests, you know, and when Michael went, his brother only lasted another year and he was gone too. It was a cruel life then. Walk with me and we'll see their house. It's only a ruin now, but you need to stand in it and get a feel for him.'

He held on to Lillie's hand as they walked, and he talked to her in his gentle accent. As they drew closer to the ruin of her father's house, Lillie felt that she'd finally completed her journey in Ireland. This was what she'd come to see.

That her young mother had done the very best for her baby was clear to Lillie now. She was in awe of this woman who had gone on to build a life for herself after an early unmarried pregnancy.

In this wild landscape, with the wind whipping around them, she felt closer to Jennifer than ever.

Half-listening to Liam, she closed her eyes and prayed: *I hope you're with Sam, Jennifer, and with your husband, Daniel, and Ruth, and everyone you ever loved, plus my mother and father too. And poor Michael. You're all a part of me.*

'I like to pray when I walk too,' remarked Liam. 'It must be a family thing. You can take the girl out of Kerry, but you can't take Kerry out of the girl, can you?'

Seth and Lillie joined him in his laughter.

'Will you come and have dinner with us tonight in the town?' Seth asked.

Liam considered this carefully.

'If I can hear all about your life, Lillie, I will,' he said. 'If I'm going off on my travels to visit you now, I'll need to know.'

Lillie hugged him. 'That you will,' she said fondly, 'that you will.'

Chapter Twenty

On Monday morning, Frankie drove to work, happy to think that Seth and Lillie would be back by the time she got home and she wouldn't be alone any more. She might cook something special for supper. Her mind whirred with possibilities. Lillie and Seth had been doing most of the cooking and Frankie thought how nice it would be if she did it for a change. The night before, she'd finally rung her old colleague, Amy, and they'd arranged a dinner in the next week. Amy had insisted they come and meet her husband, and see the garden, complete with the two hives. Just talking to Amy – who clearly loved cooking – had made Frankie feel in one of her Domestic Goddess moods.

She'd go out at lunchtime and see if she could get ingredients for something nice.

Frankie had an early morning appointment with Dr Felix to talk about how she was getting on with her HRT. She sat in the waiting room making notes about things she had to do that day and scanning through emails on her BlackBerry. There was one from Anita, sent via her mobile, with a link to a news item.

Everyone in Dutton was het up about rumours of an

impending merger with the giant US insurance corporation, Uncle Sam. Despite many of the staff worrying about it, Frankie was convinced it would never come true.

'Look, guys, the Monopolies Commission would go berserk,' she reasoned. 'Uncle Sam already own Unite Insurance, which has been cleaning up the market here. They'll never be allowed to swallow us up.'

'But if they do,' persisted Lydia, the office junior and proud possessor of a mortgage the size of a Saudi prince's Ferrari repair bill, 'it would mean job losses, wouldn't it?'

'If it happened,' said Frankie patiently, 'then yes, there would be redundancies. There always are in these situations. But it's not going to happen.'

She hugged Lydia in a way definitely not encouraged in most Human Resources manuals. There was something about Lydia's small, oval face and wild curls which reminded Frankie of her own darling Emer. She had the same sweet smile but Lydia didn't have Emer's fiery spark of independence, inherited from Frankie herself.

Had Frankie taken the rumours seriously, she'd have marched into the CEO's office and demanded an answer. But she knew that in the current economic climate, the business sector was a hotbed of wild rumours about receivership, mergers and massive pay-offs for hopeless executives. Frankie had always been too shrewd to buy into any of it.

Besides, she had enough to worry about without adding the latest conspiracy theories to the list.

When she got in to see Dr Felix, he checked her blood pressure and asked how she was getting on with the HRT.

'I don't know if it's working,' she said bluntly. 'I'm still permanently exhausted, and I'm being an absolute bitch to Seth,' she added guiltily, because she felt that she had to tell someone other than her sister.

'Come back in three months for another check-up. You'll be fine,' Dr Felix had said in that comforting way of his.

I hope so, Frankie thought as she left the surgery and returned to her car.

If she hadn't been so absorbed in her own problems, Frankie might have thought a little more about Anita's email. Her work antennae might have been up and if it had been, it would have been shivering with the signals it was picking up. But Frankie was mentally off her game because she felt so tired. She hated the fatigue days. They came out of the blue: a sweeping sense of utter fatigue that could drain her whole body of energy and make her feel up to doing absolutely nothing but lying down. Of course, this was not a possibility in Dutton Insurance. So when Frankie got to the office she took two effervescent vitamin C energy tablets in water instead of one with her morning coffee and made the coffee stronger than usual.

'Any messages?' she called to her assistant.

Ursula, who was hurriedly painting her nails under her desk, called back, 'No.'

'Are you doing your nails again?' Frankie asked.

'Yes,' admitted Ursula.

'Darling, just because you work for me and I understand the effort it takes to look good,' Frankie said, 'doesn't mean that all bosses will feel the same. So as a general rule, do not paint your nails in the office. Run to the ladies' loo and do it if absolutely necessary. Otherwise just take the polish off.'

'I can't,' said Ursula. 'They were blue and there's still some on and I have to paint another bit on or they'll look terrible.'

'I have nail-varnish remover in my drawer,' said Frankie. 'Every working woman needs a kit.'

Her mentor, Marguerite, had drummed this into her:

'You need spare tights, spare knickers, tampons, headache tablets, deodorant, and a fresh top in case something gets spilled on yours. Possibly even a spare suit hidden away in a cupboard somewhere, and definitely a nice pair of high heels.'

Frankie walked out to Ursula with the nail-varnish remover and some cotton wool. 'Quick,' she hissed. 'Get into the bathroom and take it off now.'

'Frankie, you're brilliant,' sighed Ursula. 'You're the best boss ever.'

'Oh, stop that,' chided Frankie, walking back to her desk, but there was a smile on her lips anyway.

By midday the effervescent vitamin C and the extra-strong coffee had started to do their stuff. Frankie had managed to get through an enormous amount of work and was feeling pretty pleased with herself, answering with a cheery, 'Hello, Frankie Green,' when her phone rang.

Immediately the slightly adenoidal tones of the Deputy CEO's PA came on the line. 'He wants to see you in the boardroom at two,' said Maire sharply.

'Do you know what it's about?' said Frankie, marking the meeting in her diary. 'Should I bring anything?'

There was a slight hesitation on the phone. 'No,' said Maire firmly, 'goodbye,' and she hung up.

Frankie sighed. She hated meetings with no agenda. She was a busy woman and had things to do.

After lunch she marched upstairs to the boardroom, having checked first that there were no ladders in her tights, no lipstick on her teeth and she'd reapplied a fresh coat. She looked perfect: elegant and in charge. She was slightly taken aback to see a stranger sitting at the table with the Deputy CEO, but put on her game face, held out her hand and introduced herself. 'Hello,' she said coolly. 'Francesca Green, HR Director.'

'Mike Walters from Unite Insurance,' he said.

All of a sudden, Frankie got it. Oh boy, she got it. Managing not to shake or to show either of the men how jolted she was, she pulled out a chair and sat down, grateful to get her shaking legs under the table where they couldn't see them.

'So,' she said, facing Giles, the Deputy CEO, 'what are we here to talk about?'

Giles did what he always did: passed the buck.

'You're here, Mrs Green,' said Mike formally, 'to discuss the forthcoming merger.'

His demeanour and the choice of wording removed all doubt. Frankie knew absolutely that she was in trouble.

'Right,' she said, her voice even. 'It's going ahead then, is it?'

'Yes,' squeaked the Deputy CEO, without looking at Frankie.

'Human Resources is going to be one of the most important departments during the takeover,' went on the smooth man from Unite. Under other circumstances, Frankie might have thought him handsome, because he was. A full head of dark hair, all his own – unlike the Deputy CEO, who was balding and desperately trying to hide the fact.

Frankie knew there were two ways this conversation could go, she'd been in business long enough to understand that. Either she was part of the solution – or she was part of the problem. She thought of Marguerite and how hard she'd worked for the company for years, only to be let go when moods had changed. Marguerite had given her life to Dutton Insurance but when she was surplus to requirements she had been cut off. Just like that. Fleetingly, Frankie thought of how Seth must have felt the day he was told he was being made redundant. Despite twenty years in HR, she hadn't understood. It was different in a small firm like his, he'd argued. Different because he'd been there in the beginning, he was part of its success, he was friends with the men who'd set up the company. Unfortunately, he wasn't a partner.

Frankie had spent many hours raging against Seth's blind acceptance of his fate. Why hadn't he done something? Why hadn't he got up and shouted, convinced them to keep him?

Now, staring across a boardroom table at two men, one of whom was doing everything on the planet not to look at her while the other calmly returned her gaze, Frankie knew

335

that this was one of those times when there was nothing you could do.

'Have you decided whether I am part of the solution or the problem?' she asked Mike. There was no point talking to Giles.

'You're not part of any problem, Mrs Green,' said Mike coolly. 'But we are bringing in our own HR executives. If you were to stay, you would have to work under them, which would essentially be a demotion. I don't believe this would work.'

'No,' agreed Frankie, thinking quickly, 'it wouldn't work. So what are you offering me to leave? Let me talk to my lawyer, OK? I've been here a long time and I've got a great deal.'

There was a certain satisfaction in seeing the flicker of anxiety on Mike's face. Plainly he hadn't checked her employment file that thoroughly.

Half an hour later, walking back through the HR department, Frankie was struck by how much she'd miss it all. It wasn't a big area. Low-ceilinged with grey partitions on which people stuck family pictures and up against which they shoved plant pots, hoping to keep something alive under the glow of the fluorescent lighting overhead. On Tracy's desk, a spider plant had flourished, spawning several spider plant babies which other people took and then tried to make grow on their own desks, but none of them did. Only Tracy's. Frankie smiled at the thought.

'None of you have my green thumbs,' Tracy would say in false pride. 'I am the queen of the spider plant.' Frankie passed Jon, one of the juniors, who was on the phone again to the IT department where a newly hired employee wasn't working out and where office supplies like pens and A4 pads were disappearing at an alarming rate.

Frankie walked straight into her office without even

acknowledging Ursula sitting outside. Strange, thought Ursula. One of the reasons Frankie was such a pleasure to work for was because she always acknowledged you and never asked you to do anything she wouldn't do herself. Plus, Ursula thought darkly, she was nothing like her last boss, a letch by the name of Paul who'd taken every opportunity to stand close to Ursula and peer down her top. Frankie must be very busy, that was all. Or distracted. Ursula went back to work again, tapping away on her computer keyboard for a few minutes, then paused. In retrospect, Frankie had looked tired. Maybe a coffee would be just the thing.

Frankie stood looking around her office as if she'd never seen it before. She had one of the few big corner offices in Dutton Insurance and over the years, she'd made it totally hers, with family photos on her desk and pictures she liked on the walls.

But everything in the office looked different now, at a slight angle almost, because Frankie herself felt at an angle. The world wasn't in its right place. Was she imagining this? It must be shock, she thought in some vague faraway corner of her brain. Shock made things seem different and she'd had a big shock. She was being *let go*. Let go. How could that happen to her, to Frankie Green, when she'd been the mainstay of Dutton Insurance for so long? She thought of all those years when she'd juggled – gosh, she hated that word – the job, the children, Seth, the house, meals, groceries, laundry . . . she'd juggled like some crazed magician to keep it all in the air, never letting her work suffer because she was being pulled in so many other directions.

Marguerite used to say that women were the most ethical employees because they wanted to give their employers what they were supposed to give them. Most working mothers tried so very hard to do their best. The only people they short-changed were themselves. And now *this*. There was a knock on the door and Ursula peeped around.

'Frankie,' she said in her cheery, light voice. 'Everything OK? I thought perhaps a cup of coffee might help?'

Frankie felt the sting of tears in her eyes but she kept looking out the window. She tried to keep her voice as neutral as possible, tried to look as if she was staring out the window thinking up some deep bit of business she needed to do.

'No, Ursula, thank you. I'm fine.'

'OK,' said Ursula, and the door closed gently behind her.

Frankie continued to stare out the window but nothing became plainer, nothing.

Chapter Twenty-One

*I*n May, Peggy decided that at three months she finally had an actual baby bump. It was tiny but it was there. What was also still there was the morning sickness.

She came out of the bathroom in the shop looking a bit green about the gills. Fifi handed her some kitchen roll so she could wipe her face properly. 'Will I run out and get some ginger tea?' she asked kindly.

'Ginger tea?' said Peggy, feeling bewildered *and* nauseated.

Fifi stuck her head to one side. Ever the eccentric where fashion was concerned, today she'd outdone herself with wild pigtails holding up her curly black hair and a full-skirted fifties-style dress in yellow-and-pink striped linen. 'A lot of pregnant women swear by ginger tea. It's supposed to be great for morning sickness. Didn't work for me, but it might help you.'

'Morning sickness?' said Peggy, shocked. She'd thought she was hiding it so well and now here was Fifi coming out and saying she knew.

'Yeah, morning sickness,' said Fifi, sounding irritated now. 'I don't know why you didn't tell me, Peggy,' she said. 'It's not a state secret, is it?'

'Well, no . . .' muttered Peggy. 'But I didn't want to tell anyone.'

'That's the problem with having babies,' Fifi said. 'People tend to notice when you're pregnant. There are a whole host of things that give you away, and morning sickness is certainly on the list.'

'I . . .' began Peggy. She sighed. 'You've got me bang to rights,' she admitted. 'Stupid of me to think nobody had noticed. I've wanted to talk to you about it for so long because, well, the father's not going to be involved and I thought you could talk to me about that.'

Fifi looked at her sadly. 'I'm really sorry, Peggy,' she said. 'That's a tough one for sure. Coco's father didn't want to know, and part of me,' Fifi grinned ironically, 'a part of me didn't want anything to do with someone who didn't love Coco as much as I do.'

'I understand,' said Peggy. 'It's a bit different because I haven't told the father. And I'm not going to tell him,' she added hastily. 'It wasn't that sort of relationship and it's not fair to land this on him.'

She'd expected Fifi to nod and agree with her. Fifi knew what it was like to bring a child up on her own. If anyone would understand, it had to be her. But instead of understanding, something else was spreading across Fifi's little face, something like anger.

'You're not telling him? You've got to tell him. Whatever he does or however he reacts after that is up to him, but you have to tell him you're pregnant with his child. It is his child too.' Fifi enunciated each word separately. She did it again, just to make sure Peggy had got the point. 'It is his baby too.'

'It's not!' said Peggy furiously.

'What,' demanded Fifi, 'have you got against men?'

'Too much to have a baby with one,' raged back Peggy.

Fifi was silent, and Peggy began to cry.

'Blinking hormones,' she said, reaching for her ever-present tissues. She was used to the jags of crying now, when all the emotions she'd suppressed so successfully for so many years flooded out of her: rage, pain, fear and sheer grief.

'I used to cry when I was pregnant with Coco,' said Fifi, going over to the shop door, locking it and turning the sign to closed. 'But it was nothing like that. I'm sorry I said what I did. I was out of line. I thought you were arrogant, not letting the father in on it when it was his right to know.'

She gave a wry laugh. 'I know, it's hard to get your head around me saying that sort of thing when Coco's father has been no use at all, but in theory, I'd love him to be present in her life. Kids need both parents if they can, split up or not, because it's harder on your own and two people who care about a child are better than one. I've had to be both parents to Coco, but I worry still.'

Fifi touched Peggy's shaking shoulder and began to lead her into the back room where the small kitchen was.

'You've no idea of the worries I have in the middle of the night: what if she can't have normal relationships with men because she's never seen me go out with anyone? I don't, you see. I'm afraid if I get close to anyone and introduce them to Coco, and then it all goes wrong, I'll have given her a father figure and then taken him away. People say that motherhood makes you think you're doing everything wrong, but for single motherhood, you can quadruple that feeling.'

Peggy listened silently. If only she could tell Fifi everything. She wanted to unload all the feelings and have someone comfort her.

As if she was reading Peggy's mind, Fifi said: 'Why don't you tell me the whole story.'

So Peggy did.

Frankie wasn't sure quite how she drove to Gabrielle's. She wasn't even sure how she'd got out of the building. She could recall grabbing her handbag and leaving everything else behind, telling Ursula that she wasn't feeling well and that she'd be back in the next day. She knew she should have said something to Ursula about what had happened, but Mike, the hatchet man, had laboured the point that it was all top secret and in her shocked state in the boardroom, she'd agreed not to tell a soul.

Under other circumstances, Frankie might have told him exactly where he could shove his 'top secret', but instead she'd stared at him blankly and nodded. That had seemed the most sensible thing she could do. No – the *only* thing she could do.

She'd rung ahead to check that Gaby was at home and been told, 'Yes, of course, drop over.' And then she'd asked the question Frankie had been dreading. 'What's wrong, Frankie?'

'I'll tell you when I get there,' Frankie had said, unable to say another word. It was hardly surprising, then, that Gaby was standing with the front door open, watching for her arrival.

She was at the car door as soon as Frankie had pulled up.

'What happened, what's wrong?' Gaby said, and for once her beautiful calm face looked anxious.

With Georgia the dog happily snuffling at her and Gaby standing there looking at her, Frankie allowed herself to burst into tears.

'Frankie! What is it?'

'I've been let go,' Frankie said.

For the first time since hearing those words nearly an hour ago they began to sink in. Let go. She had another month at Dutton Insurance and then she'd be redundant, let go, on the scrap heap. She must have said 'on the scrap heap' out loud, because Gaby repeated the words back to her.

'On the scrap heap?' Gaby said. 'Don't be ridiculous, you'll never be on the scrap heap. What's happened? How . . .?'

'Dutton has merged with another company and I'm now surplus to requirements,' Frankie said.

Georgia had decided that she'd had enough of this snuffling around at the edges of the car and that if any serious progress was to be made on finding food she was going to have to clamber over Frankie to get into the car. She began to attempt this, putting her two paws up on Frankie's lap and giving her a lick as a way of saying 'I'm hungry, can I get in?' Somehow, this stemmed the tide of tears.

'Oh, you daft dog,' said Frankie, half laughing, half sobbing.

'Georgia,' remonstrated Gaby, pulling at her collar. 'Get down, there's a time and a place for everything. I'm sorry,' she apologized. 'It's always food. She thinks you might have something edible in the car.'

Frankie laughed. 'Perhaps I should let her in, it does need a valet.' She petted the dog. 'Georgia, love, would you be able to get rid of all the crumbs?'

Gaby started to laugh too. 'She only eats the things she likes,' she said. 'She's absolutely no good at hoovering up things like dried fruit or seeds. Thinks they're evil things. But if you have a bit of a sausage or a few chips or best of all crisps in there, she'll hoover marvellously.'

Frankie dragged herself out of the car. Her muscles ached, her joints ached. She felt her age – no, she felt more than her age. She felt a hundred. She dragged her bag from the passenger seat.

'It's a company car, you know,' she said to Gaby. 'It'll have to go.'

It was a pale-blue middle-of-the-road, middle-range sedan. Frankie had had a company car for years, it was one of the perks of the job and she'd known she was lucky, even though she was taxed for it. But still, it had been part of her, part of the job. Gaby called Georgia out of the car, shut the door, then put her arm through Frankie's and walked her towards the house.

'I know this is probably the worst time to have a drink,' Gaby said, 'but sometimes a glass of wine helps. I know, I know,' she said holding up one hand, 'that's not the correct attitude and we don't want to turn into raving alcoholics, but I don't think either of us has that problem so maybe some cheese, crackers, a few grapes and a nice glass of red might make you feel a little bit better?'

Frankie grinned. 'Bring it on,' she said. 'I might even have two glasses.'

They sat in Gaby's back garden and let the sun toast their limbs. The garden was much like the rest of the house: pretty and with a hodge-podge of things. Gaby's method of gardening was to plant things and then let them get on with it. The house was the same: lots of paintings and shelves with books on them and odd curios that Gaby and Victor had bought on holiday. There were things upon things. It was all very charming and lived in. It suddenly felt very peaceful to be sitting out here on the terrace where honeysuckle, an old climbing rose and what was possibly a clematis were having a battle to see who could take over most of a trellis first.

Gaby never had two dishes the same and she'd set out an eclectic collection of pottery plates and bowls, with bits of cheese, crackers, olives and relish, along with a bunch of grapes, all higgledy piggledy on the old mosaic-topped cast-iron table. Georgia sat between the two of them, eyeing each of them in turn and hoping for a giant lump of cheese to fall at her feet.

'Georgia, go away,' said Gaby, in exasperation. 'You're dreadful! You get two big meals a day.'

'She's fine,' said Frankie calmly. It felt good to be sitting out here, away from the cares of the world. As long as she didn't move from this spot, she could almost pretend that today hadn't happened.

'What does Seth say?' said Gaby, and Frankie looked at her in surprise.

'That's why I came here, Gaby,' she said. 'I don't know

how to tell Seth. He texted me to say he and Lillie are home, but I didn't have the courage to ring him back.'

'Oh, Frankie,' sighed Gaby, 'you poor darling. They're total bastards – *bastards* to let you go. I hope the place falls apart around their feet without you.'

'It won't,' said Frankie in a resigned voice, 'it never does. We're all replaceable – even me, maybe especially me. I don't know. I don't think I'm past it, I think I'm very good at my job, but politically speaking I'm just in the wrong place at the wrong time. The head of HR from Unite is clearly the one who's getting the big job, not me. And I know exactly how hard it is out there at the moment and how nobody is going to want to employ me. I'm too old, I've been too highly paid and had too big a job for too long.'

She took another sip of wine. She was on her second glass. She'd have to leave the car at Gaby's. She couldn't possibly drive it home now, and the last thing she wanted was to turn into some lush who got trolleyed in the afternoon. 'I suppose I should phone Seth and get him to pick me up,' she said slowly. 'I keep thinking about him, how I'm going to tell him.'

'If anyone knows how it feels,' said Gaby, 'it's Seth.'

There was silence and Frankie reached over and petted Georgia's shaggy head. 'That's the thing,' she said, 'I feel so incredibly sorry for Seth because he went through all this and I didn't really understand. I gave him hell because I had no idea what it felt like. I thought I did, because I worked in HR, but I didn't. I wasn't there for him,' she said. 'I wasn't there at all. He had no one until Lillie came – *she's* been there for him.'

And then she knew what had upset her most all afternoon. Not being let go, but the knowledge that she'd been so unhelpful to Seth. She was the one who'd created the chasm between them.

'You've been under enormous pressure, Frankie,' consoled Gaby. 'You can't be superwoman and—'

'No,' said Frankie. 'I messed up. I blamed Seth for things he had no power over. I should have supported him and I didn't, but that stops now.'

'Really?' Gaby's eyes were wide.

Frankie nodded. 'Really. I have two calls to make. One, to the best employment lawyer in the business, and the other to Seth. If I leave Dutton, I'm going to leave with enough money to make us comfortable for the rest of our lives. What Mr Let's Fire You doesn't seem to realize is that I've been with the company for so long, it'll cost him the GNP of some small nation to pay me off! And when we've got that, well, I'm not saying our money worries will be over, but we'll be doing fine. We'll even be able to do up the house. I can get some part-time work to build up the pension . . . You know me, Gaby, I'll do anything!'

Gaby laughed. 'I know you hate the idea of being told you take after Mum,' she said, 'but you do remind me of her sometimes. You've both got some of the warrior queen going on there.'

Frankie held out her glass. 'More wine for the warrior queen,' she said, and once Gaby had filled it up, Frankie searched her phone's contacts list quickly and made the first call.

When she dialled the second number, Seth answered. She launched straight into it.

'I'm at Gaby's and I've had three glasses of wine so I really can't drive home.'

There was a stunned silence at the other end of the phone, then:

'What's happened? Is everything all right?' Seth asked with an urgency that made him sound like the old Seth.

'I've been made redundant,' she said slowly. 'The best thing to do seemed to be to come to Gaby's house. I thought that you and Lillie weren't going to be home for a while and I wanted some company.' This was a lie. She hadn't wanted to face Seth and tell him this awful news, knowing how clumsily and unhelpfully she had reacted when it happened to him.

'Oh my darling,' said Seth, and this time he really did sound like his old self. 'My baby. Those idiots. Wait till a few weeks go by and they find out what they've lost,' he said with venom.

Frankie felt herself begin to cry. How could she have doubted him? He had been there all along and she hadn't realized it. 'Thank you, darling,' she muttered.

'I'll be there quick as I can,' he said. 'Don't worry, love, it's going to be fine. We're going to be fine. I love you, bye.'

'Don't go,' she yelled into the phone.

'Why?'

'Because I want to tell you that I love you, you wonderful man, that I'm sorry for not understanding, but that I'm going to make it right.'

Again, there was silence.

'I am sorry,' Frankie repeated. 'And the good news is that I've talked to a brilliant employment lawyer. With my experience, my years with the firm and the deal I signed all those years ago, I think things could work out OK.'

Beside her, Gaby whooped.

'You're sure?' Seth's voice was almost a whisper.

'I'm sure, darling,' said Frankie. 'Sure about both things.'

Chapter Twenty-Two

There was a party going on on Friday night, Kaz informed Freya.

'In Decco and Louise's house. Their parents are away and the next-door neighbour's deaf. We've been invited. D'you want to go?'

Freya gave a knowing smile. Kaz was conducting a love affair from a distance with Decco, who was one of their friends' older brothers. It was very one-sided, with Kaz staring at Decco whenever their paths crossed and blushing puce whenever he looked in her direction.

There were only two impediments to the love affair: one, Decco hadn't ever spoken to Kaz, and two, he already had a girlfriend, an impossibly gorgeous-looking Polish-born girl with cheekbones like the Steppes, glossy long dark hair down to her bum and a look in her eyes that said she would take on all comers.

'Bad idea?' Kaz went on, misinterpreting Freya's silence for a negative response. 'You're thinking I'd be his little sister's drippy friend and everyone would *know* I fancied him?'

'No,' said Freya. 'Faint heart never won fair hot guy and all that. I was wondering what we'd wear.'

* * *

Since Decco and Louise lived closer to Freya's house, and since Kaz said getting ready in her place would be hampered by her four older sisters instantly running off with the new metallic cotton T-shirt she'd bought to go with her tight skinny jeans, the getting ready marathon took place at Freya's.

Opal was delighted Freya was going to a party, although when she heard it was going to be composed of mainly eighteen-year-olds, she said she wanted her home by ten.

'Do you good to get out for an hour, pet,' she said, as she made the two girls tea and tried to fill them up with freshly baked cinnamon buns. 'But do be careful. Phone at any time and Ned will be round to pick you up.'

'You're so understanding, Opal,' sighed Kaz, already on her second cinnamon bun, despite an earlier plan to eat nothing after lunch so she could zip up her jeans. 'My mother growls at me when I say I'm going out and wants me to phone in every hour with an update on my whereabouts.'

'Freya texts me to tell me how she's doing,' Opal said fondly. 'She knows I worry. After rearing three sons and a daughter and hearing the high-jinks their pals got up to, I know all about what goes on out there.'

She paused mashing potatoes for that evening's shepherd's pie.

'Your mother worries, Kaz. That's all. You can only see the fun out there tonight, but when you're a bit older, you see all the pitfalls. You might be too young to drink, but the older lads won't be.'

Kaz bit her lip. She had every intention of having a beer or two. Louise had said that Decco was getting kegs in – all legally bought, since he was over eighteen.

Opal sat at the table with them and poured herself tea from the pot.

'Look at yourself, pet. You might be sixteen, but you look at least nineteen or twenty when you're all made up with your finery on. Fellows only see how you look on the outside

349

and not the vulnerability on the inside. I'd hate to see you getting hurt from having sex with some drunk lad who won't remember your name the next moment. You'd be the one who'd feel devastated and violated the next day, not him. That sort of thing stays with a woman, is all I'm saying.'

Kaz stared in awe at Opal, marvelling that this silvery-haired woman who could easily be somebody's granny was talking so calmly about under-age sex and under-age drinking. Not doing the head-in-the-sand thing of not mentioning it, but actually discussing it.

Kaz's mother, Grace – a woman with five daughters – had a different approach.

'Don't you dare have a drink until you're old enough, missy. I don't want you coming home some night with a baby on the way,' Grace had snapped at her.

There had been no talk of how fumbled, drunken sex might upset Kaz. Just a straightforward lecture on how the family would not be able to afford a baby and how they'd been lucky that time with Leesa, when her being a week late with her period had turned out to be stress-related rather than embryonic baby-related.

'If any of you put me through that again,' Grace had told them all grimly, 'I'll kill you.'

In the calm of her yellow-painted kitchen, Opal added milk to her tea from a jug decorated with fat peonies.

'There's pressure on young girls today to grow up before their time. I know there will be drink at that party and I know Freya won't touch it because . . .' Opal paused and then, realizing Kaz knew all about Freya's mother and then some, went on: '. . . because she's seen what it's done to her poor mother, Lord help her. But you might get tempted, Kaz. You're too young, that's all I'm saying. Drink has done enough damage to this country. Have fun for an hour, and then come home.'

* * *

350

Kaz sat on Freya's bed and stared out of the window at the allotments behind the garden, neatly laid out in formal lines, some wildly verdant with growth, others scattered with what looked like weeds.

'I feel dead guilty now,' she said. 'I meant to have a drink or two, but Opal makes me feel . . .'

'. . . like you'd be letting her down if you did?' Freya finished.

'Exactly.' Kaz sighed, then took out her make-up and began the transformation.

She was halfway into applying a layer of foundation when she put her sponge down.

'What if Decco offers me a drink? What then? I can't say no and let him think I'm just a kid, can I?'

Freya, who could line her own brown eyes with smoky kohl in two minutes flat, was blending in dark ochre shadows around the kohl. She never wore make-up to school and liked the effect now, thinking that she was looking more grown up these days.

'If he likes you, he likes you,' she said. 'Doesn't mean you have to do whatever he thinks is cool.'

'That's easy for you to say,' grumbled Kaz. 'Just 'cos you do what you want and don't listen to anybody, doesn't mean the rest of us are like you.'

'Hey, it's not easy for me,' protested Freya.

Make-up finished, she looked at herself in the mirror. If Kaz looked nineteen done up, then Freya looked much the same as she always did: small, thin, entirely flat-chested and her head a cloud of dark curls.

Her mother never discussed boys or sex with her, or even told her whether she'd been a mere 32AA like Freya before blossoming into the 36C she was now. Gemma never told her anything useful like that.

Instead, Gemma talked about life *Before*.

Before Your Father Died and *Before I Was Married*.

351

Before fascinated her to the extent that she never wanted to talk to Freya about *now*.

There was no bitterness in Freya but occasionally she wanted to shake Kaz and remind her that she had her original family, a mother and father. That she hadn't landed on someone's doorstep like a cuckoo with her mother's problems weighing her down like a millstone.

'You need to wear your push-up bra,' advised Kaz, looking up from her mirror. 'I have some chicken fillets with me. If we're going to a party with eighteen-year-olds, we may as well look the part.'

At a quarter to ten the party was in full swing. Outside, the barbecue was busily burning cocktail sausages because the chef had wandered off. Various people came along and poked the grill, letting sausages fall through to the charcoal below, which was deemed to be fabulous fun.

The barbecue was smoking now, what with the charcoal and the sausages mingled.

Very loud music was coming from huge speakers in the house and Freya wondered who was being DJ, because so far, she hadn't recognized one single song.

'Not one,' she said to Kaz. 'It's all mad, experimental stuff. How are we supposed to dance to it?'

'It's meant to be a cool party, so no dancing,' explained Kaz, who was wearing the skinny jeans that no longer really fit her about the belly but which she'd squeezed into painfully because they made her long legs look even longer. Her middle sister's platform heels finished off the ensemble, although they were half a size too small.

When Freya had mildly remarked that killer heels a person couldn't stand up in was taking the whole fashion thing too far, Kaz had pointed out that she didn't intend to be standing up in them for long.

'The general plan is that he sees me, drags me off to a

352

couch to wrap himself around me and ask where have I been all his life, and then I can get the shoes off.'

'They can't be any tighter than your jeans,' pointed out Freya.

'Don't worry – they're not coming off tonight. He has to know I'm not cheap,' Kaz said.

'We definitely do not want him thinking you're cheap,' said Freya kindly, doing up two more buttons on Kaz's shirt, which was already showing off a vast amount of cleavage boosted with the aid of a push-up pink leopard bra from Victoria's Secret.

Kaz had then ventured into the mass of people necking beer bottles or drinking wine from paper cups. Freya decided that her first really serious older teenage party was a lot like the younger teenage ones, just with older people and more drink. A table was covered with bottles of wine, vodka, beer and strange-shaped bottles with acid-coloured liquids inside.

'Some sticky liqueur from Ibiza or Mexico or somewhere,' explained the guy making cocktails behind the table, as Freya picked up a round bottle with a giant pineapple on the side.

'It smells like paint stripper with a hint of pineapple, but nobody will notice in my cocktails. Do you want one? This is the Purple Passion-ihto.'

He passed her a paper cup filled with purple liquid, a tiny onion and a straw.

'We're out of olives. Declan only bought one tin and nobody thought to bring fresh fruit, but who cares, right?'

'Thanks, but no,' said Freya, putting the cup down after a sniff. 'I came on the bike and don't want to get breathalyzed or anything.'

'What sort of bike?' He was interested now.

'Norton, a classic. Hid it next door or it'll be robbed,' Freya whispered. 'You can really pull girls when you've got a bike like that.'

Mr Cocktail Man took a step back.

353

'Well, absolutely, whatever you're having yourself,' he said, flustered at this notion of Freya being interested in girls.

'That's just between you and me,' she added, with a hint of a growl in her voice. '*Mano a mano*.'

'Yeah,' he said nervously.

'We need more lesbians in Redstone,' Freya said as she and Louise went out to the garden later to escape the heart-thumping beat of the music. 'I implied I might be gay to the cocktail bloke and he nearly fell over. It's sexism. Men can be gay now and it's fine, but women being gay – not so acceptable.'

'What's got you into gay rights?' Louise demanded.

'I was just thinking.'

Louise and Freya had been sitting outside in the garden – a large pretty garden with a patio, a central lawn and lots of rocks for the alpine plants to climb over – and talking. It seemed as if Decco, or rather Declan, had invited his entire school year along to the party and the semi-detached house was full of tall eighteen- and nineteen-year-olds, out of school and delirious with the free house.

'I told him he was mad to invite everyone,' Louise said to Freya, as they watched a girl from their own sixth form throwing up into the rose bushes. 'Dad will kill him, for a start. Mum said he could only have a party if it was a small one and he promised: only a few friends.'

'It's probably going to get worse,' said Freya thoughtfully as the DJ cranked up the sound once more.

'Of course it's going to get worse,' said Louise mournfully. 'The thing is, if I ring Mum and Dad, they'll go ballistic and there's nothing they can do to stop it because they're away in Bruges for the weekend. He shouldn't have got the kegs of beer, I told him that was a big mistake.'

'Won't the neighbours complain?' asked Freya, thinking that if anyone had such a party in the winding terrace where she lived with Opal and Ned, the neighbours would have been around in an instant.

'We're the end house on the row,' pointed out Louise, 'and on the other side, he's deaf.'

'Well, if he wasn't deaf in the beginning he's sure to be deaf now,' Freya said with a grin. 'I better go and look for Kaz. She's been gone for half an hour and it doesn't take that long to go to the loo.'

'She's probably trying to find Declan,' said Louise. 'She's crazy about him. That's the only reason I invited you guys, otherwise I think I'd have gone to stay with my aunt. At least that way, I wouldn't be to blame for any of the mayhem.'

'You can come home with us,' offered Freya.

'No,' sighed Louise, 'I better stay. Somebody has to be able to ring the police if it all gets out of hand and somebody puts it up on Facebook and four hundred more people turn up.'

Freya shuddered. 'What a complete nightmare. OK,' she said, hauling herself to her feet, 'I'm going to find Kaz. We'll come and say goodbye before we go.'

She went in through the French windows, which were wide open. Inside, some people were dancing but most were sitting on couches or on the floor, snogging, drinking, chatting and giggling. Freya could smell the unmistakable tang of grass being smoked and thought that things would go horribly wrong if the police did have to be called. She decided she'd better tell Louise so that Declan could throw out anyone using drugs at least. Freya didn't know Louise's older brother very well but she thought he was a reasonably straight sort of guy.

There was no sign of Kaz in any of the rooms but she did find Declan, sitting on a long, dark, red couch, engrossed in a heavy kissing session with his beautiful girlfriend. Freya didn't know her name but she looked even more stunning tonight than normal. Poor Kaz, she didn't have a chance. At that moment, Freya wondered if Kaz's earlier vow not to have a single beer had been revised. Seeing the love of your life – well, the longed for from a distance love of your life – with his exquisite girlfriend could drive any woman over the edge.

Kaz wasn't in the kitchen or the hall or even sitting out in the front garden sharing a cigarette with some people who were playing a game of Cluedo and apparently acting out the scenes.

'Miss Scarlet with the axe in the library,' shrieked a guy holding up the tiny plastic axe from the box and pretend-whacking someone else over the head to squeals of laughter. Freya went inside again and upstairs. The bedrooms all appeared to be occupied with heaving bodies. Oh hell, she better tell that to Louise too. Things were really getting out of hand and it wasn't even eleven o'clock. There was a queue for the bathroom and Kaz wasn't in it. Unless she'd gone home, which was unlikely, it was her in the bathroom.

'Kaz,' Freya knocked hard on the door, 'are you in there? It's me, Freya. Let me in.' She banged a few more times and the toilet line grew restless.

'She's been in there for ages. I'm bursting to go.'

'Yeah,' said someone else, 'bursting.'

'There's a loo downstairs,' Freya pointed out crossly.

'Someone got sick in it. It's gross.'

'If you're that bursting, you'll ignore the sick,' snapped Freya. Finally there was a noise from the bathroom and Kaz opened the door. It only took one look for Freya to realize that Kaz was very, very drunk and looked as if she'd been crying and throwing up in equal measure. She was lying on the floor and she looked barely conscious.

Seeing her best friend in that position made something inside Freya crack. She relied on Kaz and now Kaz was behaving badly, just the way her mother did – not caring about Freya and doing whatever stupid thing she felt like.

Instead of hauling Kaz out of the bathroom, she ran downstairs. Louise was talking to a tall, slim boy who was every bit as good looking as Declan, but a leaner, much shyer version.

'Louise,' she cried. 'Kaz is stuck in the bathroom and she's dead drunk. You've got to help me, something awful could happen, she could choke on her own vomit. Please help.'

'Come on, Harry,' said Louise, getting to her feet. 'Harry's my cousin. He'll help.'

Between them, they got Kaz to the door and tried to wake her up, but Kaz only moaned and slumped her head in a different direction.

Louise and Freya stared at each other in horror.

'What's her mother's number?' demanded Harry. 'My mother's a nurse,' he said, 'and she told me what to do if this ever happens. Your friend needs to go to hospital to have her stomach pumped. You call her mum and I'll call an ambulance.'

'What?' said Louise aghast. 'But the party and what's going on—'

'People die when they drink too much,' Harry said, more softly now. He reached over and patted Freya's shoulder. She was crying openly now, upset by what was happening. It felt as if the world was rocketing towards the same sort of chaos she'd experienced when her father had died.

'Sorry,' she said brokenly. 'I just can't stop.'

'It'll be OK,' Harry said firmly and got out his mobile phone. 'You phone her mum and I'll do the ambulance.'

It took just ten minutes for the ambulance to arrive, during which time Freya and Louise held on to Kaz and tried to stop her slumping down on to the ground.

'If she gets sick, she'll choke and die,' Freya kept saying in distress.

'You've done great,' said one of the paramedics when they came. 'Leave it to us, and it's good you called. Which of you is her friend?'

'Me,' said Freya and looked at Harry.

'I'm coming too,' he said. 'Freya's my sister and she's had a shock. She needs me.'

When Opal phoned Freya's mobile at eleven, worried sick, she and Harry were sitting in the emergency room eating some chocolate Harry had got from the machine. Kaz's mother had raced in without even noticing them and had been whisked off into the emergency room itself.

After about half an hour, she came out and found them.

'Thank you,' she said to Freya and Harry. 'The doctor told me that somebody had been very wise to phone the ambulance. Thank you.'

Then she went back inside.

Freya was calmer now and could explain to Opal what had happened. She was leaning against Harry and he had his arm around her, which seemed entirely normal and very comforting. She'd never felt like this with a guy before, so close and so comfortable.

'Ned and I will be there in half an hour,' Opal said. 'Sit tight.'

'They're coming to pick me up. We can drop you home too,' Freya said. 'You were brilliant, you knew just what to do.'

'Anybody would have done the same,' he said.

'No.' Freya looked at him properly. It seemed inappropriate at such a time, but Freya felt a sudden ripple of attraction towards him. 'Anybody wouldn't have. But you did. You saved her life.'

'All in a night's work,' said Harry, grinning, and Freya grinned back.

She wondered how she'd tell people she'd fallen for Harry in the emergency waiting room.

Chapter Twenty-Three

On Saturday morning, Frankie woke up early to see the sun streaming in through the ill-fitting curtains. Normally, this might have annoyed her. But not any more. Don't sweat the small stuff was her new mantra.

She got out of bed quietly and went into the kitchen to make coffee. Then she opened the French windows and went out into the garden to breathe in the scent of fresh earth and newly planted flowers and to let the sun warm her face. Drinking her coffee, she walked around the garden in her slippers, looking at the different plants and vowing to get Lillie to write the names of them all down in a notebook before she went away, because Frankie hadn't a clue what any of them were.

She was tired. It had been a very strange and exhausting week. First, she'd met with the employment lawyer and they'd discussed the most she could get out of Dutton.

'You've given them twenty-four years of service,' the lawyer said. 'I'll negotiate on your behalf, but I think you'll get a size-able sum. I don't think they'll have a problem with that, either. In takeovers, one set of executives always have to go and they won't want the bad publicity of making people redundant and giving them terrible deals after years of loyal service.'

Going into work the next day felt so strange.

Overnight, Dutton had ceased to be the place where her life was a busy, satisfying blur and had become somewhere she was leaving. She was reminded of when Emer was twelve and about to finish junior school. It had felt like the end of an era, realizing how many of those teachers, parents and kids she'd known for years would no longer be in her life.

Ursula had been in tears when Frankie told her the news.

'But what will we do without you?' she'd sobbed.

'You'll get on just fine and you'll remember to have nail-varnish remover and a whole kit of useful things in your desk drawer,' Frankie had said.

Her friend Anita from the legal department had been shocked. 'I can't believe they'd let *you* go, Frankie,' she said. 'I mean, you're brilliant at what you do, everyone says you're the best HR director ever. It's so unfair, you must be devastated.'

'Funny thing is,' said Frankie, 'I'm not. It's not personal. It's a commercial decision. If I took over a company, I'd want to move my team in. I understand that.'

'But what will you do?' said Anita. 'You love your work!'

'I do and I did,' said Frankie, wondering how she was going to explain this. 'But if it was up to me, I'd probably never retire. I'd carry on working like a mad woman, getting more stressed and stressed with age. Look at these age lines,' she said, gesturing to the lines around her face. 'Stress makes you age! I wish I'd known *that* years ago. This way, I can stop work and do up my house, spend time with my family, that sort of thing.'

Anita was silenced. 'Seth didn't feel that way, though, did he?'

'No,' said Frankie, feeling guilty. 'He didn't.'

During the week, Seth had been much more like his old self, telling her it was a great time for her to retire and discussing all the things they might do with Sorrento Villa once they got her settlement.

Frankie had been aware of Lillie watching from the side-lines, because after her tipsy phone call to Seth from her sister's house, Frankie hadn't been able to broach the subject of their relationship again.

The guilt was crucifying her. That last week in Dutton, where everyone had been so kind and thrown her a party on Friday night to say goodbye, Frankie had realized that she hadn't really defined herself through her work. She'd thought of her old mentor, Marguerite, and how she'd had nothing to go home to once she'd retired. Marguerite really had lived her life through the office. But Frankie had so much in her life: Seth, the children, even the damn house with its ugly wallpaper. Nobody would feel she was less of a woman because she'd stopped working: they'd probably commend her for avoiding work-related stress. She knew Dr Felix would, for a start.

But it was different for men. Work did define them and she'd ignored that entirely when it had come to Seth's redundancy.

So each night, she, Seth and Lillie had chatted happily about the plans for the house, and then Frankie would plead exhaustion and head to bed early, so she could be asleep – or pretend to be – when Seth came to bed.

She didn't know how she could possibly say sorry to him. Blaming empty-nest syndrome and the menopause wasn't enough.

Frankie thought of all this now as she looked at the garden and smiled at the herb garden Lillie had planted in a sunny corner.

'It's lovely isn't it?' said Seth, making her jump.

He put his arms around her from behind and pulled her so that she was leaning into him.

The time was right, Frankie thought.

'Seth, darling, I am so sorry,' she began. 'Sorry for not realizing how hard it was to be dumped from work, sorry

361

for being so bad-tempered with the menopause, sorry for letting all my stress land on your shoulders – just sorry. I love you so much and I'm afraid of losing you.'

With it all said, she let out a deep breath and waited. This could be the moment when Seth said, 'Actually, I don't love you any more, Frankie' and what would she do then?

He gently turned her round to face him and Frankie realized that it was like looking at the old, contented Seth, not the man she'd been living with these past months.

She wanted to cry but stopped herself. Please, please let it be OK.

'I'm sorry too,' he said. 'I pushed you away but Frankie, how could you even think I don't love you. I adore you, even when you're peri-whatchamacallit. I. Love. You. Is that enough?'

Frankie had never thought she was much of a crier, but tears began rushing down her face now as the strains of the past few months flooded out of her.

'I'm sorry,' she sobbed, 'I really thought you didn't love me, that I wasn't what you wanted any more. And I felt so old, so ugly. Ageing is horrible for women. Men just get grizzly and handsome, women fall apart and the whole world cringes if they're not all smooth-skinned and young.'

Seth took her half-empty coffee cup and set it on the path.

'I love you so much I want to drag you into our room and ravish you,' he said gently. 'I might ravish you here, now, but it would shock the neighbours. Have we met the neighbours yet? Lillie must have. She knows everyone else within a fifty-mile radius. You're not old, you're gorgeous and I love you. Sex isn't exactly on a man's mind when he loses his job, Frankie. I'm sorry I rejected you. I felt so bloody awful, such a leech. You were earning money and what could I do? What woman would want to make love to that man?'

'I would,' said Frankie tearfully. 'This menopause thing is

362

awful too because your hormones are all over the place and it's terrible. You feel old, Seth. When you can't have babies any more, you do feel all dried up and old. So when—'

'—when I didn't want you, you felt worse,' he finished for her.

She nodded.

'But that was a phase, love,' he reassured her. 'I love you and I want you. We just went through some difficult times and every marriage goes through that.' He smiled at her and said: 'What would we have done without Lillie, our own guardian angel putting balm on every hurt?'

Frankie shook her head. 'I don't know. I think we were heading for splitting up, which is crazy.'

'Insane.'

'Mad.'

'Deranged.'

Suddenly, Seth was picking her up and whirling her around, so that she felt as if she were flying.

'I love you, Frankie Green. Never forget that.'

Holding on to him tightly, Frankie nodded, then said, 'I won't, darling. Never again.'

Lillie watched Ned weeding his turnips in the allotment and her fingers itched to get into the ground. Freya had brought her up here to talk to Ned and get some seedlings for Frankie and Seth's garden.

'There's nothing like gardening for taking your problems away,' Ned explained as, clad in his old brown gardening trousers, he diligently weeded.

'I agree,' said Lillie, lifting her head and breathing in the scents of earth and plants. The leaves were all dusted with a hint of manure and compost.

'Is Mr Green any good at growing things?' Ned went on, still bent to his task.

'Not yet,' said Lillie frankly, 'but he will be before I leave, and it would be great if you could come round and give us your advice on where to put things.'

She would be flying home next week and she wanted to get a lot of things ironed out. Introducing Ned to Seth was one of her plans so that when he was gardening, Seth would have someone to ask about things.

'Sure, even if he started with a grow-bag full of tomatoes, he'd love it,' Ned said. 'You get a lot of satisfaction from growing your own crop. And he could grow greens too, lettuce does really well around here. Now, Jimmy over there –' Ned straightened up and pointed to another allotment that looked like a salad department in the local greengrocer '– Jimmy has all manner of fancy vegetable things growing, lettuces of every variety, you never heard the like. I don't think he eats them himself, but his wife is into that sort of thing.'

'I'm not sure if Seth is a lettuce sort of person,' said Freya, thoughtfully, on the strength of three brief meetings in Redstone. 'But his wife might be,' she added. 'Is Frankie a lettuce sort of person? You know, Caesar salad without the dressing, without the croutons, without the everything nice?' She looked quizzically at Lillie, who shook her head.

'No,' Lillie said, 'I must have given you the wrong idea about Frankie. She's not one of those sort of people at all. But I think Seth would like to grow lettuce, just to see if he could, before he moves on to more difficult things.'

'True,' agreed Ned, wiping his hands on his trousers. 'Even the most experienced gardener can have things go wrong.'

As Lillie and Freya walked back down to Sorrento Villa, their arms full of early sweet carrots and some rocket, they chatted away about what was going on. 'I wanted to ask your advice,' said Freya, when they reached the gate. Automatically they both looked up at the house, which had become more beloved and less decrepit to Lillie the longer she spent there. Now that she was due to go home, it had somehow become cherished for its air of dishevelment, rather like an old lady who'd had nobody looking after her for so long.

Now, finally, Seth and Frankie had the money to do it up. Frankie's employment lawyer had come up trumps and Frankie said they were happily pensioned. They'd changed their mind about Seth's grand extension though.

'Let's not run away with the money,' Frankie had said shrewdly.

'Come on in for tea,' Lillie said to Freya.

Lillie boiled the kettle and made two cups of tea to take into the garden.

'We'll sit outside. So tell me, what's up?' She often thought that if Doris and Viletta knew that one of her fondest friends in Ireland was a fifteen-year-old girl, they might have looked at her with astonishment. But then, Freya was more like a ninety-year-old being who had somehow been magicked into the body of a girl.

Freya got into it straight away. 'It's Opal's sixtieth birthday next Saturday and I want to do something special, but the thing is, the last big birthday was Uncle Ned's and we don't have the money for a hotel this time, not right now. Plus, I know Opal feels it would be upsetting for Meredith to have another big party because at the last one she was Lady Muck coming in with all the champagne but at this one she'll be sitting in the corner looking depressed and miserable. She's started work at the supermarket, you know. She says it's the only job she can get with this cloud hanging over her.'

The look on Freya's face said exactly what she thought about Meredith's looking sad. But Lillie had a certain sympathy for Meredith.

'You'd be miserable if the same thing happened to you, you know that, Freya,' she said gently.

'I'm sure I would be,' said Freya prosaically, 'but I wouldn't make everyone else's life a misery into the bargain, would I?'

Lillie laughed, 'No you wouldn't. Anyway, what were you considering doing for Opal's sixtieth?'

'Well,' Freya went on, 'as her birthday's on a Saturday, I was thinking of having a big party in St Brigid's Terrace. The problem is, people would have to go outdoors because the house is too small to have a big party indoors, and then we'd be relying on the weather – which isn't necessarily a good thing to do in this country. I had this idea about fairy lights in the trees and lanterns and seats for people to sit on, cushions spread on the grass, all sorts of wonderful things. Maybe a barbecue and a table groaning with fabulous things to eat but . . .' she broke off. 'I can't cook and I don't have lots of fairy lights or lanterns, and what if the weather is absolutely horrendous?'

Lillie was thinking. 'We need a plan A and a plan B,' she said. 'Plan A if it's a nice evening and we can go outside and plan B if we can't. I'll get some paper, you look around for a pen. I can never find a pen in this house when I need one.'

'You'll help me?' said Freya, delighted. 'I wanted to ask Bobbi, but she's so busy with the salon she hasn't a moment.'

'Oh, we'll ask Bobbi to pitch in as well,' said Lillie. 'Now there's a woman who can organize a party, I imagine. Between the three of us, we can think up something brilliant. Let's go talk to Bobbi.'

Bobbi thought Meredith needed to be involved.

'Freya, honey,' Bobbi said, 'I know you're not her biggest fan, but I think things have been pretty tough for your cousin for quite some time. Everyone in the country now knows she was nothing short of an idiot for believing everything those people said for so long. She was the respectable face of the place and it was because of her they managed to dupe so many people. Imagine what that would feel like.'

'I don't want to imagine,' Freya said crossly. 'She's had it tough for a few months – big deal. That doesn't give her carte blanche to treat the world as if it was her own melodrama

366

with her in the starring role and us as the villains. She never does anything for Opal, yet her poor mum runs around trying to make Meredith things that will tempt her appetite, worrying if it was all her fault . . .'

Lillie interrupted her. 'That's what parents do, darling,' she said gently. 'Worry it's their fault somehow and ask themselves whether, if they'd done things differently, it would all have turned out another way entirely.'

'You've never met my mother then,' said Freya bitterly, and got up and left.

Bobbi and Lillie exchanged a look.

'I can see you don't really know much about Freya's mother, do you?'

'Only what Freya's told me,' Lillie said. 'Have I put my foot in it?'

Bobbi grimaced. 'You could say that. This is definitely a mug-of-tea story. Right, let's come up with a plan to get Opal out of the house so we can transform it into party central next Saturday. She loves that new knitting shop. Peggy has classes on a Saturday now, so maybe we could book Opal in for something? That would keep her occupied for a while.'

Freya marched down the road towards the supermarket where Meredith had been working for the past week. She'd said she wanted to earn some money to contribute towards the housekeeping.

Some chance of that, Freya thought angrily. She didn't trust Meredith in the slightest and it made her furious, watching her beloved Opal doing everything she could to try and make things better. She was sure Meredith didn't care in the slightest about her poor mother. If she had, she'd have been there for Opal. Freya knew how much she owed to her Aunt Opal and Uncle Ned, but she supposed she hadn't real-ized how angry she was with her own mother until she watched Meredith appearing not to care about how much Ned and Opal loved her.

Meredith had no idea what it was like not to have family support, no idea whatsoever. All she did was mope around the house, looking sad and droopy, until everybody was afraid to say anything in case Meredith started to cry. Freya was sick of it. She stormed in the door of the supermarket and looked around for her cousin.

Meredith had got the hang of the scanning pretty quickly. It wasn't difficult. You learned where the barcodes were on most products, although sometimes they put them in completely ridiculous places, so that some pizzas in boxes had the barcodes on the lid and the only way to scan them was to turn the whole thing upside down, thereby dropping all the toppings on to the inside of the lid. But those sort of errors aside, it wasn't a difficult job. Just utterly exhausting.

A few of the staff had figured out who she was, but they were OK about it. Glenny, a tall girl of about Meredith's own age who looked ten years older, and had a husband and five children, thought it was great gas to tease Meredith about it. She didn't mean any harm. There was no malice in Glenny.

'Meredith, don't run off with the till money, now! We're watching you!' she'd roar happily from her own till.

Amazingly, Meredith had got used to all the jokes.

'No,' she'd roar cheerfully back. 'It's the coupons. I have a ton of them in my pockets. I'm going to go off and get a load of free toilet rolls at the supermarket down the road. Nobody'll ever catch me,' and Glenny would hoot with laughter.

The people in the store were nice to her generally, but the young manager had an air about him that said he slightly objected to having someone with Meredith's educational abilities working on the checkouts. She often caught him staring at her grimly, as though he imagined she was dreaming up great plots to take over his job any minute and the only way to stop such a coup would be to watch her. As if, Meredith thought. She barely had the energy to get dressed in the morning, never mind stage a coup over the assistant manager's job in Super Savers.

The unsocial hours were the problem, that and the fact that you could spend three hours sitting at your till until your back ached and you had a crick in your neck from turning your head all the time and from the wind rushing in from the electric doors every time someone came in or out. And then there were the people. Some customers were nice and chatty, like the older people who needed someone to talk to and might not have said hello to a single soul that day until they came down to buy a bit of milk and cat food. Then there were the women with young babies and screaming toddlers; they nearly always said a few words, something along the lines of *Oh heck, I'm sorry I'm just throwing it all down and I know she's screaming but there's nothing I can do because she wants her bottle and we were too long going around because Taylor wanted sweets and I said no he couldn't have any and now I think she's got a dirty nappy as well. I should have had it delivered, I know, I should have had it delivered.*

Meredith felt very sorry for all these people. Once there was a girl she recognized from school, a tall girl with bright eyes who'd been one of the sheeny, glamorous basketball captains, her sleek brown hair always tied in a glossy ponytail. She'd always done well academically, and was expected to go off and become a rocket scientist or something. She hadn't recognized Meredith. Mind you, if Meredith hadn't been imprisoned in the cashier's chair she didn't think she'd have recognized the former basketball captain either. Gone was the pupil-most-likely-to-succeed look and the glossy hair. Instead she had straggly greying hair tied back in an untidy ponytail and was wearing a shabby tracksuit that had clearly had breakfast thrown at it earlier.

Meredith hadn't said hello; not because she was embarrassed on account of her own circumstances, but simply because the woman was clearly having such a bad day and Meredith hadn't liked to intrude.

Another day, she'd met Grainne. Embarrassingly, she struggled to remember her name at first. Grainne was with a small girl whom she introduced as Teagan.

'Freya must have told you all about her,' Grainne said cheerfully. 'She always tells me that you send your love when I meet her on the street.'

Meredith had felt both embarrassed and like a bad excuse for a human being. Freya had been nice to Grainne, once one of her friends, when in reality, Meredith had barely given Grainne a thought since she'd left Redstone.

'We must meet up for a coffee one day,' she said now to Grainne. 'I'm back for a while.'

'I'd love that,' said Grainne, smiling.

This morning it was nearly break time and she was counting the minutes until she could close the till. Two more customers put their baskets down, brilliant, and then suddenly behind them was Freya, looking murderous. Meredith felt her heart sink. Freya hated her, there were no other words for it. They usually managed to avoid each other quite successfully in the house, with Freya spending time with Mum and Dad in the sitting room watching TV and Meredith either up in her bedroom or sneaking down the stairs to make a quick cup of tea in the kitchen.

'I wanted to talk to you about your mother's sixtieth,' Freya hissed.

Meredith stuck up the *Till Closed* sign. 'Pull that little gate closed, will you?'

Freya slammed it.

'Meredith,' roared a voice from the distance, 'it's not time for your break yet. Open that gate.' Meredith flushed, an ugly dark purple.

'Open it again,' she said to Freya, and she removed the sign. A woman with a heavily laden trolley and what looked like an inadequate supply of bags lumbered towards her.

'Oh God,' said Meredith, 'I'm exhausted.'

She looked at her cousin, who appeared to be almost smirking.

'Why do you hate me?' Meredith asked wearily.

'I don't hate you,' said Freya, wondering if that was entirely the truth. 'I just hate the way you treat your parents after all they've done for you. I know how good they are, and I know how devastated they've been by this whole thing, yet they never mention it to you, they never ask you when you're going to start paying them proper money for your keep. They never do anything. You don't volunteer information and you let them simmer with worry. *That's* what I hate,' Freya said.

She looked Meredith up and down, noting that her nails weren't varnished and the beautiful blonde hair needed new highlights.

'Anyway, I came down to talk to you about organizing your mother's sixtieth. You might have thought of it yourself, but no, you were too busy thinking about person number one: Meredith. Well, maybe when you come back to planet Earth as opposed to planet Meredith, you might talk to me, Bobbi and Lillie about it. And by the way, it's a secret – if you can keep it.'

With that, Freya turned on her heel and marched out. Meredith stared stonily after her. She wouldn't cry, not here, not with mister smarty pants assistant manager watching her, but she wanted to.

Freya ran home. She didn't know what had come over her, attacking Meredith that way. Harry, whom she saw all the

371

time now, had once asked her why she seemed to hate Meredith so much when she loved all the rest of her cousins and she hadn't been able to explain it fully.

'She's just fake,' was all she could say.

'She doesn't seem fake,' Harry said mildly. 'I guess if she was, what happened to her would knock the fakeness out of her, don't you think?'

But Freya didn't know what to think.

Chapter Twenty-Four

'You can't call her Apricot for ever,' said Fifi, as they sat in the shop's tiny kitchenette and sipped tea. Peggy, despite being a coffee addict, had found it no trouble at all to give up, because even the scent of a macchiato made her want to retch.

'I know. I'm scared of going through baby-name books, though, in case something happens.'

Peggy found she had a wildly superstitious fear of doing anything that implied certainty of Apricot's birth. So she hadn't given in to her desire to buy so much as a single pair of baby socks and refused to think of her baby as anything other than her beloved Apricot.

'I'm waiting till the twenty-week scan before I get confident enough to think of names or anything,' she admitted.

The bell above the door in the shop tinkled to show that a customer had entered.

'My turn,' said Peggy, getting up. 'You're on your lunch-break.' She went through to the shop.

'Hello,' said Bobbi.

'You're going to start knitting!' said Peggy in delight.

'No,' said Bobbi. 'I need to ask you a favour. I need to get my friend Opal out of her house this Saturday so we can do up the house for a surprise sixtieth birthday party. What do you think? Could she come on one of your courses or something?'

Fifi had come out at this point.

'A surprise party,' she said, 'wonderful! Who's it for?'

'Opal,' said Bobbi.

Fifi shot a glance at Peggy, who was quite pale. 'We could do a felting course. She told me once she'd love to give it a try. I could email our customers and say we've places for ten people for this Saturday.'

'Great,' said Bobbi. 'You tell me what time and I'll tell Opal it's a present from me.'

When Bobbi was gone, Fifi looked at her employer.

'What are you going to do?' she asked.

'Give a felting course,' replied Peggy shakily.

'That's not what I meant.'

Peggy sat down on the stool behind the counter. 'I know,' she said.

'Peggy, you have to tell David. It's the right thing to do.'

'I know,' said Peggy, feeling wretched, 'but he'll hate me for keeping it from him.'

'Why *are* you keeping it from him?' said Fifi. 'I don't understand you, Peggy. He's a great guy and he was clearly crazy about you. You don't have to marry him, but morally, you really do need to tell him you're having his baby.'

Peggy burst into tears. 'I can't,' she said.

'Why?'

Peggy looked at her through wet lashes and began to explain.

On Saturday, Bobbi dropped Opal at the knitting shop and casually asked Peggy to drive Opal home after the felting class.

'We need to know exactly when she's getting home so we can all jump out and say "Surprise!"' Bobbi said. 'You should say something along the lines that you're going up past St Brigid's Terrace if anyone wants a lift, imply that you know somehow that Opal lives up there. She'll be sure to say yes. Then her family can tell her about the party and she can get into her glad rags and my girls will come up and beautify her. Shari's going to do her make-up and Lizette, my senior stylist, will do her hair . . .'

It was a plan that had all seemed very simple and straightforward, except when you factored in that Opal was David's mother. The grandmother of little Apricot.

Peggy wished there was a way she could get out of doing this. She didn't want to go anywhere near Opal's house in case she bumped into David. No, it was more than that, it was because it would hurt too much to even be near their home. She remembered the way David had described his childhood: idyllic and loving, for all the lack of funds and having to make do. But there was no way out – she had to drive Opal home.

All through the class, she felt on edge. It would be terrible if David saw her. She wasn't hugely pregnant by any means, but her baby bump was obvious now.

But there was no getting away from it. After the course, Opal settled herself comfortably into Peggy's Beetle.

'This is a nice little car,' she said. 'I never learned to drive, myself. We didn't have a car when I was young,' Opal went on, oblivious to the strain on Peggy's face.

'Really?' said Peggy, to keep the conversation going.

'When is the baby due, love?' asked Opal cosily. 'You're really hardly showing at all,' she said, 'but then you're tall and I think tall women always carry pregnancy off so much better. Now me, I looked like a football when I was pregnant. Is it your first?'

'Yes, actually,' Peggy said in a strained voice.

'And—'

Peggy knew that Opal was going to ask her about the

father. Not out of nosiness, but simply because Opal was a kind woman who would ask all the right questions.

'—the daddy, is he thrilled? People often think men aren't interested in babies, but they are, trust me. I've had four and I've never seen Ned so thrilled as each time we found out I was pregnant.'

'I'm on my own,' Peggy said, feeling her hands shake on the steering wheel.

'Oh, pet, I am sorry,' said Opal, with such heartfelt sorrow that Peggy thought she might blurt out the truth.

'So what are you up to tonight, Opal?' Peggy asked wildly, anything to divert Opal's attention. She didn't think she'd be able to hold it together if Opal asked anything else about the baby's father.

'Oh, the girls are cooking dinner, I think,' said Opal. 'On Saturday nights, to be honest I like to sit at home and watch a bit of telly. It's a very relaxing night, isn't it? I know young people like to get out and go dancing and whatnot on a Saturday night, but when you get to my age, sitting in front of the fire with family is just beautiful. Now, Freya – she's my niece that lives with us – she occasionally goes out on a Saturday night, now that she's got a boyfriend: Harry. Nice boy, he is. They go to the cinema and have a pizza, but she has to be home early. She's still very young, fifteen going on forty-four, as Ned says. Ned's my husband and he loves her to bits. His favourite thing is when we all sit in and watch *Who Wants to Be a Millionaire?* He loves that show,' Opal said happily. 'I think at this stage we've seen all the episodes about four times over, but still, you'd be amazed at how you don't remember the answers to some of the questions. They're very tricky, aren't they?'

'Yes,' said Peggy faintly, 'very tricky.'

'Just take the next left,' said Opal. 'It's so kind of you to be driving me home, Peggy, love. I really appreciate it.'

'Not at all,' said Peggy. They were nearly there. Soon Opal

would be out of the car and Peggy would have to make sure she was never left alone with her again. Opal was such a lovely woman, so into her family, and she'd love grandchildren, Peggy was sure of it. And Peggy wasn't giving her the chance to know her grandchild. She knew it was wrong. The bigger little Apricot grew inside her, the more she knew how wrong it was to deny David the chance to know his baby. But Peggy didn't dare tell him, because she knew the sort of man David was. He'd want them to move in together. To be a family. To get married, even. The whole family package.

Peggy didn't know how her parents had been before they got married, but she saw how they were now. Saw the way her mother was shrivelling up under her father's bullying. She couldn't inflict that blueprint upon her child, no matter how wrong it was to deny David a chance to know his baby. Lots of women had babies and the father was not involved. She'd just have to be another one.

'There we are, the turquoise door on the right, just up there, see.' Peggy pulled in where Opal was pointing: a pretty house with a garden full of pink flowers. There was a man walking out of the front door. He'd obviously been waiting for a car to arrive. Then more people were streaming outside. Shari was there, Bobbi's daughter, whom Peggy recognized from the beautician's. An older man, two more men, a woman in her thirties, Bobbi, and a young slim dark-haired girl who must be Freya. But Peggy could hardly concentrate on any of them because the first man, opening the gate and standing by the road, waiting for his mother, was David. Peggy parked the car and stared straight ahead.

'Bye, Opal,' she said in a strained voice.

'Thank you so much, love,' said Opal, getting out. 'I don't know what's going on here, I hope there's nothing wrong.'

'No idea,' squeaked Peggy. Opal shut the door and Peggy drove off at high speed.

* * *

377

Opal could barely speak.

She just stared around the house, beautifully decorated by Freya, Meredith, Ned, Steve, Brian, David, Liz, Lillie and Molly. Bobbi, Shari and Lizette were there too.

'Happy Birthday,' said Shari delightedly. The whole place gleamed from top to bottom.

There were gold and silver balloons hung over the curtains and picture frames, and a garland saying 'Happy Birthday Opal' over the fireplace.

Hundreds of tiny white fairy lights were festooned around the room and entwined around the banisters in the hall. On the stairs were tiny tealights at the edge of each step, waiting to be lit. Walking through the house, admiring vases of Ned's roses and Molly's fat blossomed hydrangeas, she had to bite her lip so as not to cry.

They all followed her, beaming.

'Do you think she likes it?' Freya asked, worriedly.

'I think she loves it, pet,' said Molly, patting Freya's shoulder. 'Who wouldn't?'

From a pal at the allotment who had a greenhouse, Ned had procured gorgeous giant yellow dahlias, forced specially for the occasion and decorating the dining room, which was all laid out for a buffet. Meredith's artistic flair had been put to good work and all sorts of containers had been turned into vases with greenery tumbled in and the dahlias' smiling faces shining out at them. More twinkling fairy lights adorned the back door, where an old carpet runner had been cleaned and laid down carefully on the step from the back door down to the garden, which had been transformed.

Ned and the boys had gathered a selection of garden chairs, along with two long tables laid with colourful floral tablecloths and decorated with vases of flowers and more plates than Opal knew she possessed. More twinkly fairy lights were draped in the trees and all manner of jam jars and tiny coloured glasses were dotted around the place for lighting. Three of the big patio heaters she'd always wanted but had never thought they could afford were standing ready to be lit when it became cooler.

'They're rented, Mam,' whispered Brian, seeing a flicker of anxiety mar her face.

'How did you do it all so quickly?' she said, finally finding her voice.

'Everyone joined in to make it beautiful for you, my love,' said Ned, moving through the crowd to give his wife a hug. 'Happy Birthday!'

'It's beautiful,' she said, entirely choked. 'How did you keep it a secret?' she asked suddenly.

Freya grinned. 'Bobbi and Lillie organized that,' she said. 'We think they were secret agents in a different life.'

A thought occurred to Opal: 'But look at the state of me! When are people coming? I'm covered in wool and my hair . . .'

It was Meredith's turn to hug her mother. 'Shari and Lizette will have you beautiful in no time.' A quelling glance from Freya made her correct herself: 'Even more beautiful.'

'Well, everything's just—' said Opal, and then her hand went to her chest. They could all see her face going grey, the colour leaching out of it, before she crashed to the ground.

Only Ned was allowed into the coronary care unit with Opal. Everyone else had to sit outside. Freya was shaking as she sat beside David, who was holding her tightly, saying, 'It will be all right.'

'But will it?' said Freya in desperation. 'Will it?'

'Yes,' he said, hugging her. 'It's going to be all right.'

He could barely concentrate. All he could think of was that his beloved mother had had a heart attack, and his own heart felt rocked from seeing Peggy again.

It hurt so much. He'd thought he was over her, he'd done his best, even going out with a couple of different women on double dates with guys from work. But it was no good. Peggy was the one for him.

He'd kept away from the side of the street her shop was on so he wouldn't have to see her. But tonight, it had hurt as much as it had when she'd left him. He knew it was a ridiculous thing to think outside the Intensive Care Unit, but he felt as if his own heart was broken too. Still, he couldn't think about himself: his job was to protect his family now and make sure his mother got the best care possible. Everything else, even his broken heart, had to be put on hold.

Opal was stable, the doctor told them that night at ten: he'd allow them in one by one, but they must promise to be totally silent and just hold Opal's hand.

'She was lucky – it wasn't a massive attack,' he told a white-faced Ned. 'We'll have to scan and do tests to see how badly her heart was damaged. She'll have a raft of tests while she's in here but right now, the best thing for her is rest.'

Ned went in first. To give herself something to do, Freya said she'd get coffee from the machine if anyone wanted it.

To her dismay, only Meredith wanted anything and elected to come with her.

They walked silently to the nearest vending machine.

Freya went first and Meredith watched with irritation as she kept putting the euro coin in and it kept sinking straight to the bottom, clattering into the change tray.

'Bloody machine,' she said, trying again, though it appeared to be a futile gesture.

'Here,' said Meredith, producing another coin. 'Let me try. Sometimes, I think, you get a coin that's a milligram out weight-wise and the machine can't process it.'

'No, go away,' hissed Freya with wild ferocity.

'Why do you still hate me so much?' asked Meredith wearily.

She looked at Freya's tear-stained face, the eyeliner and

380

mascara from her party make-up now panda-ed around her eyes.

Freya's lips quivered.

'I don't hate you,' she blurted out. 'I actually like you now you're not Miss Perfect. But since you came home, you're all Opal goes on about. Opal's all I've got now and you're taking her away from me. And now she's sick . . .'

Once she'd actually spoken the thoughts that had been burning inside her for months, the flood gates finally opened. Great heaving sobs emerged and she leaned against the hot drinks machine as if she'd fall to the ground without it.

Meredith looked at this kid who'd given her such a hard time. Finally she understood.

'Oh, come here, Freya,' said Meredith, and she pulled her cousin close, stroking the sobbing teenager's hair as though she were a small child. How stupid she'd been, Meredith thought. Freya was so adult in so many ways because she'd *had* to be an adult, left with a mother who'd fallen apart after the death of her husband. And yet Freya was still so young and she deserved to be taken care of, something that she, Meredith, hadn't had the faintest notion of.

No, she'd treated Freya the same way she was treating the rest of the world: as if they were ready to pounce on her at any moment, circus lions to be kept back with a chair.

Plus, she'd been angry with Freya because Freya was the only person – apart from Bobbi – who'd taken her to task over the way she'd treated her parents. In her misguided mission to become something she wasn't, she'd left them carelessly behind. Freya had been right on all counts: Meredith *had* behaved selfishly.

All Meredith's past deeds piled up in her mind and she began to cry too.

'I'm so sorry,' Meredith managed to say.

'No, I was being horrible,' sobbed Freya.

'But you were right. I wasn't kind to Mum and Dad. I was

381

selfish. It's so stupid and I'll tell you about it some time, but right now I can't believe I ever cared about any of that rubbish – the apartment, the clothes, the *being somebody*. It's all fake and I can see that now—'

'And I knew Opal would get upset with me if I got angry with you, but I couldn't stop myself,' Freya said. 'I was so scared that you'd be back for good and Ned and Opal wouldn't care about me any more because they'd got their daughter back.'

'That's rubbish!' said Meredith fiercely. 'They love you. And not because you're some sort of fill-in daughter. Everyone loves you. And look how good you've been to Mum. That makes me feel so damn guilty.'

A pale young man with dreadlocks and giving off a distinct whiff of marijuana appeared beside them.

'I'm sorry for your trouble, girls,' he said in a slow, lazy voice, 'but could I get at the Coke machine?'

Meredith and Freya looked at each other and suddenly the desire to laugh came over them.

'Coke?' laughed Freya.

'Yeah, Coke!' Meredith laughed with her.

It wasn't until nearly eleven that night that the doctors said Opal was strong enough to see her family for longer than a few minutes at a time.

'It's supposed to be only two at a time,' said the nurse, looking at Freya along with Opal's four exhausted adult children and daughter-in-law, Liz.

Opal was lying in the bed with lots of wires attached to her. Meredith and Freya held hands and Opal started to cry when she saw this.

'Oh, my darlings,' she said, 'I'm going to be fine.'

'Yes, you are,' said Ned.

Opal gazed at Meredith and Freya, standing close to each other, and smiled at them, as if she could already work out what had happened.

Liz stepped forward and hugged her mother-in-law. 'We weren't going to tell anyone, Opal, because it's not even three months yet, but you're going to be a granny.'

Opal beamed, Brian held his wife close, and suddenly everyone in the family was hugging everyone else.

'Now, you all have to go home,' said Opal firmly. 'I'm going to be fine. I kept thinking about that lovely young Peggy and her baby,' said Opal dreamily. 'I don't know why. It's so sad. I have all of you and she doesn't.'

'What baby?' whispered David.

David finally dropped his father home at six the next morning. Everyone else had gone but David and Ned, keeping a silent vigil outside the Intensive Care Unit because hospital policy restricted people staying all night in ICU.

'She's going to be fine, you mustn't worry,' Ned said to his son.

Sitting side by side on two hard chairs in the corridor, David put an arm around his father. Ned seemed to have become thinner overnight and yet, even though his second eldest was a thirty-something man, Dad was still comforting him. 'I know,' David said. 'She's a strong woman with a strong heart. And she has you and all of us to look after her.'

Ned rubbed his tired eyes. 'That's the problem with your mother, isn't it? Always minding other people, taking care of them and not bothering about herself, not allowing people to look after her.'

'We'll change that,' David said. 'No more running round after Steve doing his washing, no more picking up the pieces when Gemma blows her money on salsa lessons.'

Ned laughed, the way David knew he would.

'Lord help her, as Opal would say, but she can't cope. And look what it gave us: Freya.'

'Who likes to think she looks after everyone,' David said, feeling his father's mood lighten. If only he could get Dad home to bed. He'd drive back to the hospital and sit vigil, but Ned needed to be in bed. He looked so tired and old, frail almost, as he sat in the chair, all bones and none of the big strong man he had been left.

'There'll be more to look after now that Brian and Liz are giving us grandchildren,' Ned said, brightening. 'Opal is going to love that.'

'Yes,' said David thoughtfully, his mind on a woman in a small Volkswagen Beetle who was pregnant and alone.

She hadn't looked pregnant from all he could see of her in the car, but he needed to know for sure. His mother had said so but then, she was on heavy medication, so who knew what things she'd say.

The need to rush from the hospital to find Peggy was overwhelming him because he needed to find out the truth. If she was pregnant, was the baby his? But family came first. He could be totally wrong about Peggy.

When he'd brought his father home, made his toast and tea, and carried them on a tray upstairs to Ned and Opal's bedroom, David had said he'd drive back and wait in the hospital so one of them would be there when Opal woke up.

'You sleep,' he told his father. 'You're going to be no good to Mum when she's back home if you're laid up with exhaustion. Or if you're sick,' David added shrewdly. 'When you're run down and stressed, you pick up bugs. Imagine if she comes home and you're ill . . .'

The ploy worked.

'I never thought of that,' said Ned anxiously.

'I'll phone around one o'clock,' said David.

Opal was awake when David returned to the hospital and there was some colour in her delicate face.

Her eyes brightened with tears when she saw him. David caught a warning glance from a nurse who came out to see him.

384

'Don't wear her out,' she said. 'The consultant will be doing his rounds at eight, so you can talk to him then.'

'Of course not,' said David. 'May I sit here beside her? I'd like to talk to the consultant.'

'Love, I'm sorry for causing so much bother,' Opal began tearfully and both David and the nurse hushed her.

'You're no bother at all,' said the nurse, small and fortyish with blonde hair tied back in a ponytail. 'You're already top of the patient of the week chart and you're only in since last night,' she added cheerfully. 'Every time you opened your eyes and we were doing something, you said *thank you*. Some of them –' the nurse looked around as if the whole ward was on tenterhooks, listening '– some of them blame us for them being in here, and by day two, they want to be moved to a private room with their own TV and running hot and cold staff.'

David and Opal laughed, Opal holding her hand up to her chest as she did so.

'I never thought it would hurt afterwards,' she said.

David sat with his mother and he agreed silently. He'd never thought it would hurt so much either.

At ten, his mother was dozing and Meredith, Freya and Steve came in to take over.

David left the hospital feeling shattered and knew he should head home to bed. But he had to know. He had to see Peggy one last time.

If she didn't want to know him, then she'd made her decision and there would be nothing he could do about it. But he had to try.

As he parked in Redstone, he tried to rehearse things to say, but everything sounded wrong.

I love you – and is that my baby?

No, that sounded stupid, confrontational even. And he remembered how frightened Peggy had become the day he'd gone to the shop and she'd been there with Fifi.

He knew that Peggy opened the shop for four hours on a Sunday and closed on Mondays, like many of the local traders. Sunday was a good shopping day and he'd driven past a few times, sometimes seeing Peggy in there and other times, seeing Fifi inside.

When he pushed open the door to Peggy's Busy Bee Knitting and Stitching Shop, Fifi was there again, this time taking coloured skeins of wool out of plastic bales and arranging them on the shelves.

'Hi, Fifi,' he said, 'it's your day, is it? Is Peggy at home?'

Fifi regarded him thoughtfully, as if trying to decide something.

'No,' she said. 'She was supposed to be in today but she's not feeling well.'

'Morning sickness?' he asked.

She nodded. 'You know she's pregnant, then?'

'My mother had a heart attack last night—'

'Oh God, is she all right?' asked Fifi, shocked.

'She's doing well – comfortable, they call it in hospital-speak. But she told me that she felt so sorry for poor Peggy who was pregnant with no father on the scene for the baby. Is it mine, Fifi? Come on, tell me. I need to know.'

'I can't tell you that,' gasped Fifi.

'Well, why won't Peggy see me?' demanded David. He leaned against the cash desk and ran his fingers through his hair. 'I'm crazy about her, I care about her, but . . . You remember that day I came here? She looked terrified of me. You've known me since I was a kid, Fifi, since when did I frighten anyone?'

Fifi stopped working.

She took a deep breath. 'It's not you that's the problem,' she said. 'It's her father.'

Peggy sat curled up on the couch watching *Sleepless in Seattle* again. She'd cried through most of it today. It seemed to sum

386

up all that was wrong with her life – a beautiful baby on the way and the love of her life not there because she'd turned him away.

Had she made the biggest mistake of her life doing so? She asked herself that endlessly and seeing David last night had plunged her into total misery. She'd have to move, she decided. She couldn't bear to live near him and face the prospect of bumping into him around Redstone.

She didn't care about the shop any more. She'd have to sell it as a going concern. She longed for him so much and it would kill her to live near him and risk bumping into him. Imagine if Apricot looked like him, with that dark hair and those amazing blue eyes? He'd know then that she was his child, and what would he do then?

She was so deep in thought that she didn't hear the bell at first. When it rang again, she set the film on pause and went to the door, only to find David himself standing on her doorstep.

Peggy gasped, and her hands instinctively cradled around her belly.

'Peggy, hello,' David said gently. 'Can I come in?'

She nodded, not sure why she was saying yes but he was here and why not.

She went into the room where Tom Hanks and Meg Ryan were staring at each other on screen, caught on pause, and he shut the door and followed her.

'My mum had a heart attack last night,' he said.

'Oh no, how is she?' said Peggy, sinking into the couch.

'She's doing OK. She's strong for all she's so gentle and that's why we all love her,' David said. 'She's the kindest woman I have ever met and my father adores her. We all do. That's why we organized a party for her sixtieth: to show her how loved she is. But the thing is, she knows.'

He looked at her meaningfully. 'She knows we all love her. Nobody in our family has ever said a bad word to my mother

387

in her life. I think we'd all go insane with rage if anyone ever did. That's the sort of family I come from, the sort of family I want: where you treat the people, the *woman*, you love with respect and kindness. Men who do anything else aren't men, they're bullies and cowards.'

Inside her belly, Peggy felt the dolphin flip of Apricot.

She beamed up at David. 'She moved!' she said.

'Really!' His face was awed. 'Can I . . . ?'

She nodded and he sat on the couch beside her and gently, as if he was touching a tiny baby, he felt the curve of her belly.

'Just there,' Peggy said, moving his hand.

Apricot flipped and David gasped. 'I can't believe that!' he said and Peggy saw tears in his eyes. His hands were so delicate as he laid them on the mound of her belly, and she watched his face all the while, watching pride and love on his face.

He looked at Peggy, his hand still warm against her belly.

'Is the baby mine?'

She nodded.

'I'm sorry,' Peggy said. 'I couldn't tell you, David. I haven't had much experience of decent fathers, I didn't know what to do. I can't explain it to you—'

'It's OK, I understand,' he said. 'Fifi told me.'

This man wasn't her father, she thought. This man was different. A man who knew how to love, a man not wracked by bitterness.

'I don't think I'll ever understand someone like your father, but I can promise you, Peggy, that I am not that man,' David told her earnestly. 'I know you believe that you will somehow choose someone like him and you're terrified to be with any man in case that happens. But I'm different. I am not like him. My father is the most gentle man in the world – that's what I come from, that's what I believe. That's what I want to do for you. Can't you give me the chance to do that?'

The fear that Peggy had carried for so much of her life was still there, but stronger still was the sense that David was a good, decent man. He would protect her and her baby, he would treat them with kindness. He loved her.

And she loved him.

'I've been calling her Apricot,' she said softly, putting one hand over his as he touched her belly.

'It's a girl?' David said, and there was no mistaking the glitter of tears in his eyes.

'It's a girl,' Peggy said. 'Our little girl.'

'Our little girl,' repeated David joyously. 'Wait till I tell Mum this – she'll be out of hospital so fast because she'll want to be here for us.'

At last, Peggy allowed herself to sink into David's embrace. There, she felt comforted, safe and loved.

'What are you watching?' he asked curiously.

'*Sleepless in Seattle*,' she replied.

'Is this the good bit? Where they meet?'

Peggy laughed. 'Men hate this movie.'

David kissed the side of her cheek as delicately as if she were china.

'Not this man, my love.'

Freya and Meredith were in the kitchen cooking a speedy dinner that evening when Gemma phoned Freya in consternation.

'I heard that Opal's had a heart attack,' she screeched down the phone, so loudly that Meredith could hear every word.

'Yes,' said Freya patiently.

'It's just like your father! Just like him! I am so upset. I need to get to the doctor to get some of my tablets,' shrieked Gemma.

Meredith stared at Freya in astonishment. She hadn't met her aunt in years and had no idea that this was what she'd turned into. Freya's face was pale with anxiety, and at that moment, Meredith made a decision. Her mother wasn't here to take care of Freya, so she would.

'Can I have the phone?' she asked her cousin gently.

Freya looked relieved and handed it over.

'Hello, Gemma, this is Meredith. You sound somewhat upset.'

There was more screeching.

Meredith held the phone away from her ear.

'Is she often like this?' she asked Freya, who shrugged.

'You never know. Sometimes. She forgets I'm coming and doesn't have food in. Or else we get pizza and she has too much to drink.'

'And you stay with her every month? Who decided that?'

'Opal said I should visit her because she was my mother—'

Meredith nodded. 'Except she doesn't behave much like a mother, does she?'

'Gemma,' she said clearly into the phone. 'Have you been drinking? Just a few glasses, OK. Well, how about you go to bed now. Tomorrow, I'll come over and talk to you. Yes, tomorrow.'

She hung up.

'Freya, your mum probably isn't the best person for you to stay with when she's like this. In future, one of us should go with you to see what state she's in. If she wants you in her life, she needs to clean up her act.'

Freya nodded eagerly. 'Opal never says anything, 'cos Ned would go mad.'

'Dad might need to go mad,' Meredith said. 'You deserve better, and I'm going to see you get it.'

Freya didn't speak but the hug she gave Meredith said it all.

Lillie was flying off the next morning. She was both excited and sad because she'd loved her time in Redstone, and had loved learning about her mother. But there was peace in her heart at the thought of going home too. There was just one more thing she had to do and that was talk to Frankie.

'Come on into the garden,' Lillie said to her sister-in-law.

They were alone in the basement. Seth was upstairs with the builder, discussing things.

Lillie let Frankie walk ahead of her. She didn't want Frankie to think that this was Lillie's garden, with Lillie leading the way and showing her the plants.

'Thank you for being so welcoming to me, Frankie,' she said.

She stopped at the buddleia she'd planted in great clumps because it was a magnet for the bees.

'It's been great having you here,' Frankie said. 'I know you've seen how . . .' She paused. 'That Seth and I weren't getting on so well for a while. Having you here made it easier.'

'Like having children around when you're having an argument,' said Lillie, and Frankie smiled.

'Exactly,' she admitted.

'Shall we try out Ned's bench?' asked Lillie.

Ned had donated many seedlings and vegetables to the garden, not to mention a lovely bit of willow that Seth had attached to one wall for the honeysuckle and clematis to cling to. The bench was his biggest gift, a heavily disguised contraption made of tea chests and painted olive green.

'He sanded it down,' Lillie pointed out, running a finger along the surface. 'Said he didn't want us to rip our legs to shreds when we were on it. Ned's such a kindly man.'

She sat on one end and Frankie sat on the other.

'You've really got the gift of making friends,' Frankie remarked.

'You've got that gift too, Frankie,' said Lillie gently. 'But ease up a little on yourself: it's hard to make lots of friends when you're racing from dawn till dusk every day, trying to work, trying to keep your own head above water and watching the man you love suffer. You have time now, time for both of you. That's what I wanted to talk about.'

Frankie searched for a tissue to wipe her nose. She felt ridiculously like crying. Lillie understood. She'd been working so hard, desperately trying to hold on to her job, because she was the person the rest of the family would have to rely on financially, and when she'd lost it, there had been no chance for her to break down and cry. She was supposed to keep going as if she were a robot and she couldn't. Because of that, she'd nearly destroyed her marriage. Lillie stroked the tea-chest bench, fingers finding a bit that Ned's careful sanding had missed. It was the same in real life – there were always bits you missed.

'I can see you're so angry with yourself for what happened, but, Frankie, it wasn't your fault,' said Lillie. 'So many things happened to you at the same time: the house, Seth's job, Alexei and Emer going away. You were shoved at high speed into the second stage of life.'

'You mean the *old* life stage,' said Frankie wryly.

'No, the second stage. The one when the kids have left home, you're with this person who used to make your heart pulse and who now makes your blood pressure zoom up when he forgets to buy bread in the supermarket.'

In spite of herself, Frankie laughed. 'Have you been watching me that carefully?' she said.

'I don't have to watch you,' Lillie said, 'I only have to remember myself.'

Frankie's eyes widened. 'But you and Sam—'

She stopped. There was no way she could say that the departed Sam sounded like a paragon, that Lillie had clearly adored him, and therefore how could Lillie have any stories about fractious moments in their marriage?

'Sam and I had our troubles too,' said Lillie, her eyes twinkling. 'I never thought I was wise,' she went on, 'but I appear to have a knack of seeing things simply and that translates to wisdom. If you take away all the surrounding problems and look at the actual issue, it's quite easy.'

'Easy with other people's problems,' said Frankie.

'No,' said Lillie. 'Easy with your own. This is a new life: enjoy it and let go of the guilt.'

'We'll miss you,' said Frankie.

'Yes, but you'll be coming to see me and we'll be emailing,' Lillie pointed out.

Frankie nodded tearfully.

'And you can get someone in to mind the bees when you're away.'

That made Frankie's face light up. Since she and Seth had gone to dinner at Amy's house, Frankie was even more keen on bees than Seth.

Amy's lovely house and garden, with its two hives and vegetable patch, had spurred Frankie on. She was wildly eager for them to get their own bees – and to start planting their own vegetables.

She'd bought several books, they were both doing a beekeeping course, and Frankie, being Frankie, had immersed herself totally in the world of bees, having found several huge tomes from the library, which she ploughed through each night.

'It's incredible,' Frankie said now. 'I never gave much thought to bees or honey before, but without them, the planet would be in such trouble. No pollination, no crops – disaster. How did I not know all this stuff?'

'You didn't have time,' said Lillie simply. 'You were doing so much, and now, you have time. The greatest gift of all.'

'The second greatest gift,' said Frankie quickly. 'Emer and Alexei are home soon. Emer's flying in on the tenth and she says she's entirely broke, and needs a job *now*! While Alexei actually managed to save some money.' Her face was soft as she talked about her beloved children. 'I can't wait for them to see what we've managed to do with the house and what you managed to do with Seth in the garden. I've told them they can take their pick of the upstairs rooms for the moment, and that once we've got round to doing all the painting – which is going to be slow – they can share the basement.'

It was a plan Seth had come up with.

'The kids might be coming home,' he told Frankie, 'but it won't ever be forever again, you know that?'

Frankie knew it.

'I thought we could give them the basement, when we've beautified everything upstairs,' he added.

They'd decided against spending Frankie's settlement on painters and decorators. They'd do as much of the work as they could themselves. It would be their project, together.

Two rooms upstairs had already been stripped, sanded down and painted. Dessie, the landscape gardener in training, had found a guy who'd spent years on building sites but was now unemployed. Between them, they'd ripped down all the jerry-built partition walls, and stripped the wallpaper in all the other rooms. The old, thin doors had been replaced, the many damaged ceiling roses had been taken down and replaced with new ones.

Everything was ready to be painted.

'Sorrento Villa is a beautiful house,' said Lillie. 'I can't wait to see it when it's finished, and I'm sorry I won't be here to meet Emer and Alexei, but I'll meet them when you all come to visit us in Melbourne. I've stayed long enough. I'm sure you thought I was never going home.'

'No.' Frankie hugged her sister-in-law. 'I'm so glad you came, Lillie. You saved us, you know.'

'You saved yourselves,' Lillie said.

Frankie shook her head. 'We couldn't have done it without you. I don't know what would have happened. You saved us, you soothed us all, Lillie.'

The two women held hands in the sunlight.

'You've done so much around here – befriending people and taking care of us. You're like a fairy godmother.'

394

'I'm glad I'm flying home on a plane,' said Lillie gently, 'those broomsticks are hard on the old hips!'

And they both laughed.

From the plane the next day, Lillie looked out of the window at the fields beneath and thought how she'd miss this island that she could now call her second home. Ireland hadn't simply allowed her to visit – like the people itself, it had grabbed her, squeezed her and then patted her back down.

She didn't need to write emails to Doris any more, but she liked writing them. Besides, she'd be writing to Seth, Frankie and everyone in Redstone now. Opal would probably have her own email account any day, and Freya would want to write giant tracts of whatever came into her head.

Lillie had made her promise to keep her informed about everything, including the goings on at the bus stop.

'Seanie and Ronnie will miss you,' Freya said. 'If they can keep off the cigarettes for a while to save money, they're toying with the idea of flying out to Melbourne to see Australia next summer. I wouldn't hold your breath, though. That's a lot of Woodbines. When you're sitting at the bus stop, you need a cigarette to give you a bit of heat – that's what they say.'

'You'll be all right, Freya?' Lillie had asked tenderly.

She wished Freya were nearer so she could be on hand to help her navigate the treacherous waters of youth. But then, knowing Freya, she could probably give classes in negotiating treacherous waters.

'I'll be fine. I've got Harry, remember?'

Harry was wonderful and every time she was with him, Freya fell a little more in love.

Opal and Ned had had a chat about her and said she was a bit young to have such a serious boyfriend, but Freya had countered it easily: 'You already know that Harry's a very responsible person,' she said. 'If he hadn't called the ambulance, Kaz could have died. And he's a good guy. He's the only person in his transition year who's interested in veterinary medicine, and he's arranged to spend the summer helping out in the local animal shelter. I might help too,' she'd added.

'Just no more pets,' Ned had begged. 'I'm sick of feeding cockroaches to that darned lizard!'

Lillie had grinned at Freya as they both thought about Harry. 'He's a good boy. He appreciates you.'

'My cousins would stab him if he didn't,' Freya said, with a smile. It was nice to be able to say that about Meredith especially. It didn't seem too long ago that the only person Meredith seemed likely to stab was Freya. But that was well behind them now. So far behind them, it seemed weird to remember it.

'Meredith's really changed,' she said thoughtfully. 'Total transformation, really, like one of those corny TV shows where people dye their hair a different colour, get their eyes lifted and they're different. 'Course, they're not. That's only surface. But Meredith is really different and I love the sound of her new plan. Before, she'd never have thought of running an artists' retreat in the middle of nowhere. She'd die if she wasn't within ten feet of a latte.'

'What happened with the gallery was the best thing that ever happened to her, in my opinion,' said Lillie.

'Funny you should say that – Opal says exactly the same thing.'

Lillie nodded. 'I once heard a businessman say that, for a business to work, first you had to survive two bankruptcies and a fire. Life's a bit like that – if you can weather the storms, you come out a lot stronger than when you went in.'

'She's certainly going to have plenty of storms where she's going,' said Freya laughing. 'The retreat is literally on the edge of a cliff in County Clare. And the nearest town is about twenty minutes away down a wild road, apparently.'

396

'How did she find out about the job?' asked Lillie.

'This lady who sells vintage clothes, Angelique something or other, she told her about it. Angelique's daughter runs it but she's going to Canada for six months to work in a similar retreat, so she needs someone to take over the Clare one temporarily.'

'Is she happy?'

Freya didn't have to think about it. 'Very. She's in the clear when it comes to the whole Ponzi scheme. People know she had nothing to do with it, which has helped a lot, she said. Plus, she told me she's going to start painting again when she's there. I didn't even know she used to paint, but she did. Says she stopped 'cos she didn't think she'd make a career out of it.'

'Creativity is a great soother,' Lillie said. 'Wish her well from me, and tell her there's always a spot for her to stay in Melbourne if she's ever in my part of the world.'

'What about me and Harry?' asked Freya cheekily.

Lillie laughed. 'Don't settle down too young, darling. You need to explore the world a bit, you know, before you settle for one man.'

Freya had hugged her then, and they'd both shed a few tears.

'I won't be gone for ever. You can email me and you can visit,' Lillie said, searching her sleeve for a tissue.

'You need to see your own family now,' Freya said, snuffling.

She was, as ever, right. Lillie did need to see her family again. The great thing about travelling was knowing that you had somewhere you were sadly missed.

It turned out that Doris liked emailing too.

Viletta is dating a gentleman from poker night. She calls him a gentleman and for once, she's not kidding. He holds doors open, stands up when she enters the room and insists on paying for dinner. He bought her a gardenia nosegay, as he calls it, for their second date. *A gardenia.* He didn't say it was his dead wife's favourite flower or his mother's favourite flower or any of the other crazy remarks some men might make second time round – no, he saw a painting of a gardenia on Viletta's kitchen wall and he thought they might be *her* favourite flowers. He's a keeper, honey, I told her and she's not talking about cougars any more. No, it's all 'the older the fiddle, the sweeter the tune'. I said: 'Don't let him hear you talk that way, Viletta, he might not like it,' but she says he likes the way she talks.

Doris even had news of Lillie's own granddaughter, Dyanne, who was apparently phoning the residence of Doris's grandson, Lloyd, who was a respectable six months older than her. Doris's daughter, Natalie, was thrilled with this because Lloyd's last girlfriend had come from a family where not too much importance was placed on constant school attendance.

Your Dyanne comes round a lot, I hear, and she's over the wanting to be famous phase, for the moment, anyhow. She and Lloyd are thinking of becoming political journalists – and no, I haven't a clue where this idea came from. But it's a step up from wanting to sing in front of a television audience and risk them voting you off the show on a whim.

We can't wait to see you. Viletta says her gentleman has a friend for you, if you want him, but I said I didn't think you would.

Lillie had laughed out loud at that one. She had Sam, she didn't need another man. And she had a new family, a very extended one, at that. There were so many people in Redstone who felt like family now. Seth and Frankie, of course, Freya, Opal, Peggy who was so thrilled about her forthcoming baby, and her new man, David, and of course Bobbi and Ned. The

398

whole place felt like a second home. She'd come to Ireland looking for her past and she'd found some of that, had understood a bit more of what would have made a young girl give up a baby many years ago.

I hope you've met Sam, Jennifer. I thought it was his idea to come on this trip, but now I think that perhaps you had a hand in it?

You were a great mother to Seth and you couldn't be a mother to me, not then. I hope you're happy now in the hereafter with the people you love. I hope it's full of light and happiness, all the cats and dogs people have ever lost, and hives for the people who kept bees on earth. I'll come one day, but not yet.

There was no answer, but then, even when she talked to Sam, there never was. Still, Lillie was sure her words were heard all right. She felt it inside.

But the most important part of her trip hadn't been about the past at all, strangely. It been about the future and what was yet to come in her life, the next stage in her life, as Bobbi wisely called it.

Lillie settled into her seat and let the stewardess give her another glass of that delicious orange juice.

Martin and Evan had insisted on flying her home in the luxurious front of the plane.

'I can't let you,' she'd begun on Skype one night, and then Frankie had stuck her head round the door and said, 'You will, you mad woman! Think of DVT. They love you, let them spoil you!'

Frankie was different these days too. She'd abandoned her glamorous work clothes for tatty old jeans and ancient shirts of Seth's, overseeing the work in the house or else heading off for her beekeeping course.

Seth was like a man who'd been given some of that royal honey Frankie had been telling them about.

'It's the most important part of the worker bees' job to

provide this for the queen bee. It helps her grow and lay new babies.'

Frankie had her head buried in that big bee book most nights.

The Gentle Beekeeper it was called, by Iseult Cloud.

'You could write your own book when you're finished,' Lillie said thoughtfully, 'all about being a beginner beekeeper and how you came into it through redundancy.'

Frankie's eyes gleamed. 'I do love that idea,' she said, 'but right now, I'm working towards getting the house sorted for us.' She shot a glance of pure love at Seth. 'And I want to enter the Honey Queen competition. It'll take me another couple of years to get to the point where my honey is ready, but I really want to do it.'

'Isn't she amazing?' Seth said proudly. 'My honey queen.'

Lillie didn't mind leaving at all. She'd be back soon enough and, besides, they were all doing fabulously on their own. She could happily fly off and leave them.

Six months later

When the phone rang one evening in the small bungalow in Portlaoise, Kathleen Barry jumped at the noise. Nobody rang the house at this hour of the day. Tommy's pals talked to him on his mobile and none of Kathleen's friends even had the number.

Women cackling on the phone annoyed him, he said.

She'd been about to pour his tea after he'd finished a feed of dinner: shepherd's pie topped with a cloud of fluffy mashed potato, which had been lumpy, he'd said irritably.

'Make decent tea, now. Not that weak slop you like.'

'I'll be back in a minute to pour the tea out,' she said, hurrying into the hall where the phone sat on the old telephone table-and-seat arrangement that nobody had any more.

Even more anxiety than usual was flooding Kathleen's shattered system because unexpected phone calls were always bad news. Peggy only rang on her mother's mobile – she knew better than to call the house. This had to be bad news.

'Yes,' she said faintly into the phone.

'Is that Kathleen Barry?' said a strangely accented voice.

Kathleen gripped the edge of the old table.

'Is it Peggy? What's happened? Has she been hurt?'

All the fears Kathleen usually kept tightly inside her tumbled out now. She had to lever herself on to the seat in case her legs gave way and she fell.

'Peggy's fine,' said the voice. 'Honestly, Mrs Barry, she's fine, I promise you. My name is Fifi and I work with her in the shop. Peggy's told me all about you.'

Unexpectedly, tears came into Kathleen's tired, unmade-up eyes. Peggy had told this strange woman all about her. There were so many people in Peggy's life and yet Kathleen knew none of them.

'I'm glad,' Kathleen whispered.

'She couldn't come to the phone herself, but she asked me to phone you when she went into labour and she has. She gave me your cell phone number and I've rung that, but you didn't answer.'

'It's on silent a lot,' Kathleen said. 'In labour? The baby's coming?'

'Yes, but everything's fine. It's a few days early, but you know babies. They come according to their own schedule.'

Fifi sounded so happy, so cheerful.

'Is she in the hospital now? Who's with her?' asked Kathleen.

'David and Opal,' Fifi went on. 'I don't know if you've met Opal,' she added tactfully. 'She's David's mother. Peggy's in good hands; Opal's a very comforting person to have around. She was the one who was with Peggy when her waters broke, so she went with her in the ambulance.'

On the other end of the phone, Kathleen was clutching the receiver very tightly.

'Peggy's going to be fine, I promise,' said Fifi, mistaking Kathleen's silence for anxiety.

But Kathleen's silence came from another place: a place of huge sorrow to think that her daughter was going to give birth with another woman by her side.

'Kathleen!' came a roar from the kitchen. 'Who is it?'

She wasn't sure where the strength came from. Certainly, she'd never had it before, not for all the years that Peggy and

402

the women at work had been telling her to leave Tommy Barry before he wore her into the grave.

'Can you give me your mobile number and tell me the name of the hospital she's gone into?' Kathleen whispered.

In the kitchen, she poured out Tommy's tea and gave him a big slice of the fruit cake he'd decided he liked more than scones these days. It took longer to bake than scones, but it was worth it if it kept him happy.

Then she left the room and went to their bedroom with her mobile phone. Stored on it she had the number of Carola Landseer.

Carola was at her book club and couldn't really hear properly because of all the talking.

'Sorry, Kathleen, what?' she roared.

'I want to know if you meant what you said about helping me leave Tommy?' hissed Kathleen, head half in the wardrobe so her husband wouldn't hear her from the kitchen.

'Dear God,' said Carola, and Kathleen knew this was a prayer of thanks. 'I said it and I meant it. Will I come now?'

'Yes, please.'

It didn't take her long to pack. She hadn't many clothes and the precious memories of Peggy's childhood were all in a box in Peggy's room. Kathleen put them in another suitcase, along with some of the ornaments she'd collected over the years.

There was so little of her in this house, really, she thought. She'd always been too scared to buy things in case Tommy got angry. She'd feared his anger so much: it was almost as if his anger was a physical presence in the house, making her fearful and afraid to live.

But what sort of mother would let her only daughter give birth and stay away, purely in case her husband got angry with her? Tommy would get angry no matter what happened or didn't happen. She would not stay around to witness any more of it. She was going to her daughter. As to what would happen afterwards . . . hadn't Peggy offered her a place to stay? There was a way out of this life and she was taking it.

When Carola drove up, Tommy, unaware of what was going on, opened the door and gave one of his polite nods. Kathleen had long suspected that he was afraid of the tall, graceful woman, who now swept past him into the house, giving no heed to his, 'What's going on here?'

Kathleen was in Peggy's room, looking around one last time.

'Only three suitcases?' said Carola in the commanding tones that made her such a successful chair of local charities.

'Not much, is it?' said Kathleen, shaking inside. Tommy had followed Carola into the room and was looking at Kathleen in amazement.

'Tommy, be a good man and put these in the back of the car,' commanded Carola.

Tommy did exactly as she'd asked. It took two trips and each time he left the room, Carola and Kathleen smiled at each other.

Then Carola took Kathleen by the arm and led her firmly from the house.

'Where are you going?' demanded Tommy.

Kathleen was shaking visibly now. He'd kill her for showing him up like this in front of the posh Mrs Landseer. But Carola had a good grip on her arm and she gave it a reassuring squeeze.

'Get into the car, Kathleen.'

She opened the passenger door and handed Kathleen and her handbag in. Then she shut the door and clicked the lock shut with her keys.

From inside, Kathleen could hear her speaking.

'Your wife is leaving you, Mr Barry, and if you attempt to contact her or frighten her in any way, I shall be in touch with the police. I took the precaution of phoning them before I came here tonight, by the way. I have also informed my brother, who runs the family law firm. He tells me that he would be delighted to take on your wife's case.'

Suddenly, Tommy became reanimated.

'What case?' he blustered. Inside the car, Kathleen winced.

Carola Landseer stared contemptuously at the man she had loathed since the first time she saw him verbally abusing his poor wife in the supermarket. That had been years ago and ever since, she'd spoken to Kathleen every week, telling her that if ever she needed to leave, to just phone.

'My brother hates bullies, Mr Barry. It will give him great pleasure to see you ripped asunder for the way you have treated Kathleen. Please go inside your house and shut the door now, or I will phone the police.'

She held up her mobile phone. 'It's a moment's work, Mr Barry.'

Tommy Barry glared at the car but his wife was looking down at her own mobile phone and was sending a text to the number Fifi had given her:

Tell my dear Peggy that I am on my way with my suitcases. She'll understand. Kathleen.

Carola went to the driver's side and stood with the car locked until Tommy lowered his eyes and went meekly into his lonely house and shut the door.

Only then did Carola unlock her car, hop into the driver's seat and drive off.

'Thank you, thank you,' whispered Kathleen.

'You've been so brave,' Carola said. 'You're braver than a hundred lions.'

'I don't feel it.' Kathleen felt something strange on her face. She reached up. She was crying. She never cried. Not any more. Crying was too dangerous because she always felt as if, once she started, she'd never stop.

'Teddy's going to drive you to Cork. He's got to hand a

paper into college by tomorrow, anyway. He'll take you wherever you need to go. He's not a bad driver for a twenty-four-year-old, I promise you.'

Kathleen reached over and put her hand on Carola's.

'I can't thank you enough for everything you've done.'

'No,' said Carola. '*You've* done it, never forget that. Now make that call.'

Kathleen picked up the phone Peggy had sent to her all those months ago and rang it.

'Hello?' said a male voice.

'Hello,' whispered Kathleen. 'This is Peggy's mum, Kathleen, could I speak to her?'

'Yes!' said the man eagerly. 'I'm David, Mrs Barry. I'll put you on to Peggy.'

There was some talking and then the noise of the phone being handed over.

In the delivery suite, just after the most horrendous contraction, Peggy Barry picked up the phone.

'Mum?' she asked tremulously.

'I'm on my way, love,' said Kathleen Barry. 'I'm with Carola now. I've left your father. Carola's son is going to drive me to Cork to be with you. I love you.'

'Oh, Mum,' said Peggy, clutching the phone in one hand and David's large hand in the other. 'I love you.'